OLD ENEMIES

OLD
ENEMIES

Janet LaPierre

CHARLES SCRIBNER'S SONS
New York

Maxwell Macmillan Canada
Toronto

Maxwell Macmillan International
New York Oxford Singapore Sydney

Copyright © 1993 by Janet LaPierre

Charles Scribner's Sons
Macmillan Publishing Company
866 Third Avenue
New York, NY 10022

Maxwell Macmillan Canada, Inc.
1200 Eglinton Avenue East
Suite 200
Don Mills, Ontario M3C 3N1

Macmillan Publishing Company is part of the Maxwell Communication Group of Companies.

Library of Congress Cataloging-in-Publication Data

Old enemies/Janet LaPierre.
    p.   cm.
    ISBN 0-684-19614-X
I. Title.
PS3562.A62404   1993
813'.54—dc20   93–13209
                        CIP

Macmillan books are available at special discounts for bulk purchases for sales promotions, premiums, fund-raising, or educational use. For details, contact:

Special Sales Director
Macmillan Publishing Company
866 Third Avenue
New York, NY 10022

10 9 8 7 6 5 4 3 2 1

Printed in the United States of America

This book is for my daughter, Jacqueline,
who came along to see the wolves.

OLD ENEMIES

· PROLOGUE ·

June, ten years ago—in the Modoc

The sky-splitting blast of the shotgun faded into the mare's panicky squeal and the thud of her hooves. But she was middle-aged, and placid by nature; she came to a halt less than fifty yards away and stood trembling and white-eyed, nostrils flared at the reek of cordite and blood.

The gelding, although spirited and much younger, was a hunter's horse. He'd stood to rifle and shotgun fire; he'd carried home many a bloody haunch of antelope or deer. Now, in the astounding silence that followed so much noise, he simply tossed his head and jittered for a moment with his front hooves. Probably human blood didn't smell much different from that of a deer.

Put the gun down now very carefully, lean it against that rock *don't* close your eyes need to focus on something, anything. And swallow. Easy now, grab your knees, flex and bend and keep them bent and let your head hang, eyes still open mouth open. Big deep breath in, slow. And blow it out, whooo. Ignore the smell.

So. Have to look at him. At *it*, no life no face. No person, just a bloody . . . thing. Need a place to put it.

Stow the gun, clean it later. Think. Where? Not near here, this is trailhead for other riders and sometimes hikers. You've got two horses, you can go in deep to . . .

Ah. That little high meadow, by the beaver pond. Bury him—it!—bury it in the mud, or find a cave, should be some in the upslope along the west edge. Rock fault, old badger den, something deep you can close off against . . . animals.

Mouth dry as *hell*, something to rinse it. Right, canteen on the mare. Easy, old girl, just take it easy, in a few minutes we'll get you moving out of here. There, you're ground-tied now, and you've got a little patch of grass to munch on. Stay easy.

Hard part will be getting it up on the gelding. Tie him to that tree first. Good boy, just stand there now. Long but skinny, heavier than anybody'd expect, dead weight. Ugh. Leave it a minute and think. Can't trail this mess along and look back at it, need something for a cover. A shroud.

The down sleeping bag in the saddle roll. God, I *can't* yes you can. Wait, the other way, the . . . head first and then just work it on and pull it down. Tight fit too bad this is a mummy bag. Don't giggle don't vomit or you'll never stop. Boots sticking out never *mind* just tie it shut.

And lean against the tree for a minute and look at . . . the sky. Oh, and clouds piling up. Forecast didn't say rain, but it's coming.

So. Steady, boy. Oops, okay, deep breath and try again. If this doesn't work, we'll toss a rope over a branch and try to haul him . . .

It is only a package, a long, awkward package. With feet. Shut up. Sit *it* on that rock, against the bigger rock. Shoulder into it, let it bend, up now. Flat rock there beside the gelding you can climb onto that, stand on it. Easy, boy. Just a package.

Whooo. Tie it on good and tight, can *not* do that again. Oh God, look at your hands and arms; the mare will go crazy. What . . . bottle of bourbon, in the truck, use it to wipe down. Another shirt there, too, get this one *off*.

Okay, think. Three and a half hours, maybe closer to four, to the meadow. Good idea to get there before the rain starts. Lock the truck, close up the horse van. So. Kick some stones and loose dirt around, like *that*. With luck rain will finish the job before anybody comes by. Now, is there anything else that might . . . ?

Oh God, how did his hat get way over there? Tuck it under the rope, fold the brim over so the conchos on the band don't shine.

Ready to go. Good old girl, here's an apple and there'll be oats later. Going for a nice walk now, nice little climb. Don't you pay any attention to the gelding behind us. He'll be peaceful back there, he's working too.

On the way back we'll be in the rain, clean us all up.

Tchk-tchk. Let's go.

◇ 1 ◇

Your mother hates me. Meg Halloran put a hand over her mouth, the words so clear inside her head that she was sure she'd spoken them. But Vince Gutierrez's weary face, the pouched eyes and furrowed brow and deep cheek-grooves that resembled tribal scars, didn't change.

She took a deep breath and tried again. "I stopped by her house after school. But she was in pain and, um, irritable. So I left as soon as the nurse came back from her errands."

Vince gripped her shoulders and leaned his forehead against hers for a moment. " 'Irritable' is a very kind way of putting it," he said, and then, taking her hand as he led the way to the kitchen, "Come on, I'm making us a drink."

He carried the pitcher, Meg the glasses, back through the living room and out the sliding glass door. Their house, Vince's house before they were married, was built into a hillside high above the coast highway. From its deck, a gaze directed straight ahead, straight west, met no road, no other buildings—only the restless, blue-green-gray Pacific and the lighter, fog-streaked blue of the sky. The early-summer afternoon was cool, but people who live on the north coast of California never expect anything else; Meg wore a windbreaker, and Vince had on a long-sleeved flannel shirt.

Meg set the glasses on the railing, then sank into a canvas chair and watched them grow frosty as Vince poured clear liquid over ice cubes. Gin during the week, something she usually avoided. Perhaps it would loosen their tongues and fracture the shell of emotional reserve that had formed around them, between them, in recent weeks. No, what a bad idea! She'd be sure to say something hurtful. But maybe the gin would erase or at least ease her sense of meanness, of selfishness.

"I'm sorry," was all she could think to say. Emily Gutierrez, Vince's once-indomitable mother, was suffering from congestive heart failure. She was at home in her big house, confined to her bed and dependent upon nurses and various family members, nearly all of whom offended her by the fact that they were walking around and breathing without pain. Emily was looking at helplessness and hating it.

"She's always been such a fighter," said Vince with a deep sigh. "She can't find a way to fight this, and it's making her frantic."

"Mm," said Meg. Emily, listing as breath would permit the sins and failures of her seven children, was particularly vehement about Vince's recent marriage. Vince, who alone of her brood had settled here in his hometown and had even become Port Silva's chief of police, was Emily's pride and joy. Vince deserved a young, adoring wife who would first of all take his name, and then devote herself to providing him with home-cooked meals, home-ironed shirts, and a homemade baby or two. The fact that Vince, at fifty, had absolutely no desire for fatherhood was in Emily's view irrelevant.

At least, Meg thought with a sidelong glance, Vince had always *said* he was perfectly happy with a working wife and a teenaged stepdaughter, both of whom still called themselves Halloran.

He intercepted the glance. "She resents you the most, Meg, because you're the most like her, the way she was. Strong, independent." He drained his glass, rose to pour a refill, and sat down again. "So I want you to go ahead with the trip you've planned with Katy. You're punch-drunk, lady, and you need a rest."

Meg, her eyes filling and threatening to spill, was again disgusted with herself. Vince shouldn't be worrying about *her*. "I don't want to leave you alone. And whether she likes me or not, Emily needs help."

"I talked to both my older sisters today, and they're making plans to come. And with school out, Cass can spend more time at Mama's house. It'll be good for her to get better acquainted with her aunts." Vince's sixteen-year-old niece, Cassandra, who had come to live with them the previous fall, was working off years of outsiderness in several ways, the most recent of which was her fervent devotion to her grandmother.

"And God knows Katy needs to get away from Cass," Vince added.

"She certainly does."

"And you've promised her this trip."

Meg nodded. Whether she felt pleasure or guilt or both at the prospect, it was a promise that needed keeping. Her daughter, Katy, at almost fourteen was restless in the limbo between girl and woman and sick to death of being shepherded by her stepcousin, Cass. Katy was in love with wolves.

"So take her to Washington State, to that wolf rescue place she's been talking about. I'll miss you, both of you, but it will make me feel good to know you're enjoying yourselves. And then go ahead with the visit to that friend of yours who lives up in Modoc County—what's her name?"

"Lauren Cavalier." Lauren Macrae, as she was then, had been a student of Meg's in Tucson, before Meg's marriage to Dan Halloran.

"Pretty neat to keep up with a teacher for something like fifteen years," said Vince. "Must only do that with a pretty neat teacher."

"Lauren was special," said Meg. "And I was young, with no responsibilities to anyone but myself. I haven't actually seen her for years, but we've kept in touch; I write letters, and she makes phone calls."

Vince stretched out in his chair and cocked his bootheels on the deck rail. "What took her from Tucson, Arizona, all the way up to the very northeast corner of California?"

"She was born there, on the Macrae family ranch near a little town called Stony Creek. When she was orphaned in her teens, she came to stay with her aunt, her father's sister, in Tucson." Pleased to see Vince relaxing, Meg settled back more comfortably in her own chair and sipped her drink. "Sam Cavalier, Lauren's husband, is a nature and wildlife photographer, and for a few years she traveled all over the world with him. But when their second child was born, she and Sam decided a permanent home would be a good idea, so she settled back in on the ranch."

"You know," Vince said reflectively, "there was something on television not long ago that made mention of Modoc County. One of those pop public-affairs programs, 'America's Most Wanted' or 'Where Are These People?' or something like that."

Meg's evenings in recent weeks had been devoted to paper grading, with no time for television. "I must have missed that. And Lauren didn't mention it."

"Maybe I'm mixing locales or something, Meg." He gave his head a rueful shake. "Mind like a sieve, as my mother would say. Anyway, what's Katy going to do with herself while you and Lauren talk over old times? I'm pretty sure she won't find any wolves in Modoc County these days, just cows."

"From what I've heard—and read—about Sam Cavalier, he could be secretly breeding wolves in some distant and obscure corner of his ranch," said Meg. She paused to sip at her drink. "Katy's dying to meet him; he's her hero, and she has his wolf pictures plastered all over the wall of her room. Actually," she added, "I believe he's become something of a *national* hero, a major advocate for wilderness restoration in general and wolf recovery in particular."

"I guess the poor guy didn't have much choice." At Meg's questioning look, he shrugged. "With a name like Sam Cavalier, what're you going to do? Sell cars?"

"Quite right; he and the wolves were made for each other. You know, Gutierrez, I've never seen a wolf. Coyotes, sure; I've seen them, heard them, lost a couple of cats to them. So far as I'm concerned, coyotes are just an inevitable, somewhat irritating part of the western landscape. But now my desk is piled with these books about wolves that Katy is insisting I read as soon as I get my final grades in. What I myself had planned for this summer was to reread Faulkner."

"Jesus. Read about wolves. I understand they mate for life; that's behavior I approve of."

"I think it's a myth, Gutierrez. With wolves, anyway. But I agree, it's a nice myth. Is there any more gin, or shall we just go to bed?"

His familiar, white-toothed grin was short-circuited by the sound of the telephone. Police business or family? she wondered as she watched him get to his feet and trudge into the house. Not that it made much difference.

⋄ 2 ⋄

The eyes were green, not cat-green but a light, cool gray-green with a few flecks of brown. The color wasn't much different from that of her own eyes, just a bit lighter, or made to seem so by the black socket rim that stood out against silvery fur like skillfully applied eye-liner.

"Please, let's keep together; lone individuals tend to alarm the wolves."

Meg started guiltily but took a quick final look before hurrying to catch up with the human pack of some twenty Wolf Haven visitors. That wolf didn't look alarmed to her, he looked—thoughtful. As if *he* were the one coolly observing an adversary familiar from history and mythology. And she was becoming ridiculously anthropomorphic here, much more so than the keepers, of whom she had expected such an attitude.

The tour guide, a rangy, blonde young woman in a Wolf Haven tee shirt, khaki shorts, and hiking boots, turned to face her followers, waiting patiently while the photographers among them got their shots. The dirt path was edged by a waist-high chain link fence that provided a buffer zone several feet wide between the wolf-watchers and the eight-foot fence enclosing the actual wolf pens. Like everything else here, this safety feature was meant to protect the wolves.

"This wolf is Nonie, a female just over a year old," said the young woman. Nonie, whose coat was mixed silver-gray and tawny above a cream-colored underbody, paced and watched, keeping a few feet back from the wire of her pen.

"Why is she by herself?" asked Katy.

"We're trying to find a mate for her," said the guide. "Nonie was one of a litter being raised by a university wildlife study project. There were five pups, and she turned out to be the omega animal. They didn't have room to keep her separate, and they were afraid she wouldn't survive if left with her litter mates. Since she'd never lived in the wild and wouldn't know how to support herself there, we took her in."

"Omega?" asked a middle-aged man.

"Opposite of the top animal, the alpha. For whatever reason, Nonie was at the bottom of the litter's, and so in this case the pack's, social order, and as a consequence she took some very rough treatment. But she's a sweet lady, and she'll be fine once we locate a companion for her."

As the group moved on to the next pen, the guide explained that Nonie, in the wild, would probably have hung around on the outskirts of the pack until she was able to make herself useful and gain some acceptance, or she'd have moved out on her own once old enough and possibly found a mate to start a new pack. "Thus enlarging the gene pool," added the guide.

Social animals, social order . . . and social outcasts. How nice that our species have so much in common, Meg thought as she looked back at Nonie. Hang in there, lady.

The guide was clearly knowledgeable, and the other members of the group clustered close to listen when she spoke. Meg, comfortably weary after the three-day drive from California to Washington, was enjoying the dozy quiet of this place, the smell of dust dampened by an off-and-on light rain, the varieties of animal character she was seeing: aloof dignity, polite curiosity, indifference (one almost-black animal, stretched long to nap, opened an eye briefly, decided he wasn't interested, and closed it again). In one of the spacious pens a leggy, light-gray old gentleman came stiffly to the fence as if to greet callers. His shaggy little wife promptly bustled over, shouldered him toward the back of the pen, and watched him away. Then she faced the visitors and kept her eyes on them as she squatted to urinate.

Was that a comment? Meg wondered. Or simply an instinctive claim of territory? One thing she was sure of:

Never again would she look at a German shepherd and think it might be a wolf.

"I guess you can't let them have puppies." That was Katy again, a half-question.

"Right, we can't. For one thing, we don't want any more captive wolves. The other thing is, the pups are so cute that visitors want one for their very own; we don't want to encourage that, either. But these wolves are not neutered," she added. "They're only sterilized. We have a vet who does vasectomies and tubal ligations."

One man snorted at this, earning himself a quelling look from his wife and frowns from the rest of the group.

When they had returned to the locked gate through which they had entered, the guide turned to face them. "We are grateful for your interest and your support," she said. "Ideally, there would be no need for a Wolf Haven, because no one would steal puppies and try, and fail, to make pets of them; no one would shoot parent wolves and orphan their young; and study projects that used animals would train them afterward for release into the wild. Ideally, we would realize that this country is big enough to maintain a reasonable wolf habitat, big enough for wolves and men to live as distant, respectful neighbors. Thank you."

She lifted her head and gave a low howl. One wolf answered, then another and a third. Then what must have been a dozen of the animals pointed their muzzles skyward, rounded their mouths, and said, "Aouwooooo," in a chorus that stirred the hairs on the back of Meg's neck.

They had agreed from the start that this was to be Katy's trip. She had planned the itinerary and stopping places; she had reserved the right to veer off if an interesting detour caught her fancy. That was why their swoop south from Washington through Oregon to northeastern California had come to a temporary halt after less than two hundred miles, and why Meg now stood on a high bluff near Hood River, Oregon, looking down at the mighty Columbia River with her hands over her ears. Who could *live* with wind like this? As she watched, two figures detached themselves from a group beside the river, and a moment later Katy came running up the hill, a lanky boy of sixteen or so on her heels.

"Mom! Aren't they awesome?"

"They are," Meg agreed. Windsurfers darted about on the water's surface like a horde of brilliant dragonflies. How did they keep from running into each other? How did they stay upright, in this wind, on that swiftly flowing river? "Um, Katy . . ."

"It's okay, Mom, I'm not going out."

"I'd loan you my board, honest. But it would be better if you'd get some practice first, like on a lake someplace." The boy tossed back a sheaf of wet yellow hair and nodded to Meg, then turned his gaze back to Katy. "Next summer, maybe? I'll be here."

"Maybe," said Katy with a shrug. "Thanks."

"Well. Okay." With another nod, he straightened, turned on his heel, and headed back to the river, an absurd stick-figure in his black wetsuit.

And bless you for your good sense, thought Meg. "What was his name?" she asked as she and her daughter matched long-legged strides toward their car parked nearby.

Katy shrugged again. "Chris, I think. Boy, I'm starved; okay if I eat the pastrami?"

"Sure." Meg handed over the keys, and Katy loped the rest of the way to the car, to open the trunk and root around in the cooler chest. At three months short of her fourteenth birthday, she was five feet eight and probably not through growing. The long legs were elegant now rather than coltish, the rear sticking out of the trunk was subtly rounded; when she stood up, budding breasts made pointy little mounds against the fabric of her loose tee shirt.

Katy, however, was resolutely ignoring all these changes and what they portended, refusing to talk or even, so far as

Meg could tell, *think* about them. Maybe, thought Meg not for the first time, she should have bought her daughter Barbie dolls instead of a first-baseman's glove.

"How far?" demanded Katy a few minutes later, through a mouthful of one of the deli sandwiches they had bought that morning in Olympia, Washington.

"To Bend, about 150 miles. That will leave us 225 to Stony Creek tomorrow."

"Too bad I can't help with the driving," said Katy wistfully.

"Two years to go, kid. But that's all right; I love to drive."

"Um, Mom, did you call Vince?"

"Oh. No." Meg adjusted her sunglasses and sat straighter in her seat, to peer at the road ahead. "Look, there's Mount Hood."

"Mom?"

"Katy, he spends his lunch hour at his mother's, and I don't want to call him there." Truth to tell, she was reluctant to reconnect with everyday life. For the moment, for the day, she was just a body moving contentedly through space— nobody's teacher, nobody's wife. She didn't even feel much like anybody's mother.

"I'll try to get him tonight, okay?" she said, and chose to ignore Katy's reply, a less-than-polite shrug. The closeness she and her daughter had always shared had diminished over the past year or so, partly as a natural result of Katy's getting older but partly, Meg felt, because she herself had been preoccupied with her own life. If she had an agenda for this trip, it was to make the whole thing a trial run for what would one day be a new relationship between the two of them: woman to woman rather than woman to kid. She didn't intend to spend valuable time pointing out bad attitudes.

Katy swallowed the last of her sandwich and licked mustard from her fingers. "What about Mrs. Cavalier, did you call her?"

"Ye-es," said Meg slowly. That had been . . . odd, at least. Lauren Cavalier had been asking her to visit Stony Creek for literally years, most fervently since the birth of her second child and her more or less permanent return to the ranch. But today she had sounded ragged, distracted. Meg had been on the verge of suggesting a postponement when Lauren caught herself and began to crank out cheerful, hostessy noises.

"She sounded tired," Meg said now to her daughter. "Her husband . . ."

"Boy, just imagine being married to Sam Cavalier," interrupted Katy, her blue eyes alight. "I can hardly believe I'm going to get to meet him. I think maybe I'd like to be a photographer, if I'm not a forester," she added. "Or a veterinarian. But he is this totally awesome-looking guy, Mom, in pictures anyway. Did you ever meet him?"

"Once, at their wedding. I'd forgotten, but you're absolutely right; in a rugged-outdoors way, he's probably the most attractive man I ever saw in my life."

"Except for Vince. And Daddy," added Katy, in loyalty to the father who had died when she was small.

"Except for them. Sam isn't there now, Katy; he's off in Alaska, I think it is. But Lauren says she expects him any day." And there was the source of her young friend's weariness, surely. Life with a five-year-old girl and a nearly two-year-old boy would wear anyone down to a nub. Not much help to be had on an isolated ranch, probably, and Lauren's aunt, Frances Macrae, was somewhere around seventy and reported by Lauren to be growing frail.

Katy finished the last bite of sandwich, drained her Coke can, and reached behind the seat for the book that was her current bible: *The Wolf: The Ecology and Behavior of an Endangered Species*, by L. David Mech. The dog-eared paperback was nearly as thick as the Faulkner novel Meg had surreptitiously tucked into her own suitcase.

In recent days Meg had become an involuntary, though not unwilling, pupil of Dr. Mech. She had learned, for instance, that wolves hunting something as big as moose worked very hard at considerable risk and were successful only about 10 percent of the time. That a pack was a highly organized unit, with an alpha male and an alpha female at the top and every-body well aware of his own rank and of the fact that a move up would require a challenge and probably a fight. That the single litter usually born in a given pack was cared for not only by the mother and father, but by aunts and uncles and older siblings as well.

All of which was the interesting stuff, no doubt why she remembered it. She hoped Katy didn't have statistics in mind for today. Or more about killing techniques.

"Mom?" Katy hadn't opened the book. "This Lauren. You said that when you were teaching in Arizona, and she went to your school, she lived with you. How come?"

"Because she was determined to stay in Tucson for her senior year in high school, and the aunt she was living with—Lauren's parents died in an accident when she was four-teen—had decided to retire and move back to the Stony Creek ranch full time, instead of just spending summers there.

"Lauren was seventeen when she came to stay with me," Meg went on, "but she looked younger, all long legs and big feet and this mop of curly, carrot-red hair. She acted wild and tough, but she really wasn't." She was, however, just recover-ing from an abortion, a fact she'd revealed to Meg with a kind of shamefaced dignity. She had been both dumb and unlucky and had dealt with the result the way she thought best; Meg was entitled to know that and to know that she, Lauren, was determined not to make such a mistake again.

And there was no reason for Katy to know any of this. "The aunt was a good woman, but she was older, had never married, and was all wrapped up in the brother, a year younger than Lauren and reputed to be spoiled rotten. Any-way, Lauren was very smart and a nice person; we got along together just fine, and she sailed through her senior year with straight A's. After which she went on to graduate from Stan-ford and marry Sam and have two beautiful children whom you'll probably get to baby-sit."

"Listen, you're talking to the *premier* baby-sitter of Port

Silva Junior High; I can handle it. What happened to the brother?"

"Who?"

"Lauren's rotten brother."

"Nobody knows. He disappeared about ten years ago."

"He must have been grown up by then," said Katy.

"Just twenty-one, I think. He was extremely handsome, and very wild, and Lauren said he wouldn't work on the ranch and hated living there. She thinks he just ran away, probably because he was in trouble of some kind." As Meg recalled from Lauren's reports at the time, a local girl had turned up soon after Bobby Macrae's disappearance insisting he was the father of her unborn baby. "And he's never bothered to let anyone know where he is."

"Weird," said Katy. "Maybe he'll come home while we're there."

"Oh, Katy, let's hope not."

◦ 3 ◦

Dusty pine trees, dusty sagebrush, and empty stretches of heat-baked land: south-central Oregon was called high desert, and Katy could certainly see why. Dusty herself, as well as sweaty and tired, she perked up for a moment as they actually crossed into California, but of course the landscape changed not at all.

Katy sighed loudly, not that her mother noticed, and pulled the AAA map from the door pocket. There was the little town of Stony Creek, a dot on the map just to the west of this narrow slice of green that looked to be protecting California from the featureless mud-yellow of Nevada right next door. Warner Mountains, that slice was, and she hoped the green was real. And mountains should be cooler.

"Do you see where we are?"

Her mother's voice jolted her out of her semi-stupor; Meg looked tired, too, and hot, frowning as she reached up to lift her heavy hair off the back of her neck. "Um, yeah," Katy told her. "And I see the turnoff, too."

"Good. Watch and tell me when."

"Okay." Katy squinted at the tiny numbers. They had made a late start this morning, had dawdled in a shady spot with lunch and now, well into the afternoon, were still about twenty miles from their destination.

After a while, what looked like a painted lake appeared on the right, nothing stirring its flat blue surface. On the left, cows grazed on land that ran at a slight tilt right up against rocky, scrub-covered foothills; cows took over on the right side as well after the lake ended. Fields not full of cattle were this deep, quivery green, their lushness broken only by long lines of pipe balanced on enormous wheels, probably sprinkler systems of some sort on a very large scale. Field pasture pasture field pasture pasture. On and on.

"Katy?"

"Huh?" Katy blinked and brought herself back to reality just as a sign reading "Alturas, pop. 3,000" flashed past.

"Oh, sorry, Mom. I got hypnotized by green or something, forgot to watch where we were." She rubbed her eyes and spread the map out on her knees. "Alturas is about fifteen miles on from where we wanted to go. Sorry."

"My fault." Meg straightened her shoulders wearily. "The driver is supposed to be paying attention. Tell you what. This is the county seat, biggest town in the county; we might as well have a look at it."

"And get a Coke?"

"Why not. Or even a beer for your poor, tired mom." Meg stopped at what turned out to be the intersection of Highway 395 and 299, and turned right onto 299; the corner sign announced that this was now Main Street.

"This is the biggest? I think I can see clear to the other end," Katy remarked. There was a small supermarket on this side, a gas station across from that. Scattered, mostly one-story buildings lined the street, some of them flat and clearly commercial, others houses that appeared to be stores now. A long building on the left . . . Modoc High School. A huge gray monster on the right, looking like a fake castle. A restaurant, a motel, another motel; swimming pool there, Katy noted with envy. As they made slow progress into the town, the buildings got closer together and she thought older. "Funny buildings," Katy said. "What're they made of, concrete?"

"Stone, it looks like. I think Alturas dates from about the same time as Port Silva, the 1870s or '80s, but this part of the state is relatively free of earthquakes, so they can build with brick and stone. On the north coast you need materials that flex, like wood and stucco."

Katy caught a flash of color and leaned forward to look. "Hey, murals! Boy, that cow looks ready to jump right off

the wall. And there's a deer, on the other side of the street."
Huge, brightly colored paintings decorated the sides of a
number of buildings along the wide, clean street.

Auto traffic was light; no one honked at them as they
crawled along, sightseeing, in the curb lane. There were people out and about on the sidewalks, going someplace but in
no big hurry to get there. Katy spotted a bunch of kids, high
school kids, she thought, sheltering under the awning of a
boarded-up old drive-in and talking to a muscular man in a
white tee shirt.

Then came a vacant lot, and then a clothing store, a drug-
store, a Sears outlet, a tire store. A used-book store that
looked interesting. A three-story stone structure that seemed
to go on for practically a whole block, hung with signs that
said it was hotel, bar, restaurant. A vid shop. Just before the
town dwindled back into highway and pastureland, they
passed a cluster of smaller buildings set in a grassy lawn.

"Mom, look; that's a county museum. Maybe I could get
some maps or something."

Meg sighed, made a neat U-turn, and pulled into the small
parking lot beside the museum. "Okay, but I think I'll walk
while you talk. Meet you at that coffee shop two or three
blocks back on this side. The Bluebell, I think it was."

Three straight hours behind the wheel was too long; Meg's
legs were stiff, and there was an ache between her shoulder
blades. She locked the Honda and set off down the sidewalk
at a pace fast enough to create the illusion of a breeze in air
that was motionless and very warm, the sun packing a surprising punch for so late in the day, so early in the summer.

The Bluebell had dark plastic blinds over its windows and
looked cool inside. In a newspaper rack beside the door she
found only two copies left of a weekly tabloid newspaper
called the *Modoc Messenger*, published Thursdays and today
was Wednesday. Never mind, it was local and something
to read.

As she settled into a high-backed booth, Meg assessed her
own weariness and ordered iced tea instead of beer; she had

finished most of a second tall glassful and most of the news-paper by the time her daughter arrived. Katy had a stack of maps and pamphlets, a shiny-covered paperback book that had surely not been a freebie, and a pleased expression.

"Hi, sweetie. Coke?" Meg asked, beckoning to the waitress.

"Yeah. With lots of ice, please," she added as she slid into the booth.

"So," said Meg when the drink had arrived, "what's up?"

"It's a nice museum; I got some good stuff. Their historical society publishes books, and this one is a history of the Warner Mountains." She flourished the volume, a large-sized paperback with a photo of horses and miners on its cover. "They've got like samples of *everything* from the past hundred years. Antique clothes and dishes and quilts, and Indian stuff, and old tools and machines. And old diaries and pictures."

Katy paused to down about half of her Coke. "I saw this one picture, of some dead animals stacked up; they looked like wolves to me. I asked the woman in the office about it, and she said yes, there were wolves here originally, in the Warner Mountains. And guess what?"

"You can still hear them howl on nights when the moon is full?"

"Oh, Mom, don't be silly. No, but a couple of years ago, some people around here wanted to bring wolves back! You know, like the plans in the Rocky Mountains, restore the gray wolf to its historic habitat. She, Mrs. Kinsella, says one of the people involved was this famous photographer named Sam Cavalier!"

Somehow she did not find this news surprising. "So what happened?"

Katy's face turned briefly glum. "Well, the plan didn't get very far. Turned out to be not very popular with lots of people who'd lived here a long time."

Meg suspected it wouldn't be very popular with the major-ity population of this area, either: all those cows. "It's a controversial idea, Katy. A lot of energy went into eradicating wolves in the West."

"I know. It was disgusting." Katy sighed, took a long swallow from her glass. "What's in the paper?"

"Something very . . . interesting," said Meg slowly. "It seems that this coming weekend is the tenth anniversary of the disappearance of Lauren's brother, Bobby. So there's a big story—see, here are several pictures of him. Interviews with people who were around at the time, people who knew him. And reports of various sightings of him over the years since."

"Weird," said Katy, pulling the paper around to scrutinize the face in the pictures. "He's mega-good-looking, isn't he?"

"I suppose you could say that." Meg thought she knew, now, why Lauren had sounded frazzled; this kind of attention could only be painful to the surviving family. "Drink up, kid, and let's go. Lauren will be wondering what's happened to us."

Outside, they blinked for a moment in the glare and then set off for the car. Katy thought the air felt even warmer after fifteen minutes in the cool coffee shop; she clutched her belongings in hands already sweaty again and wondered aloud whether the ranch house would have air conditioning, or at least fans.

"Fans, I'd imagine," said her mother. "It's an old house. Look out!"

The doors they were passing, doors to the old stone hotel, had burst open suddenly, spilling out a blast of cold air and a stumbling, laughing man. Flailing about with both arms in an attempt to regain his balance, he slammed into Katy and nearly knocked her down.

"Oops! Saved by a pretty lady," he crowed, and brought his arms down and around her, pushing his sweaty forehead into the side of her neck.

"Get away from her!" snapped Meg.

"Let go!" Katy twisted and thrust with her elbows to break his grip; he giggled and let go of her so slowly she could feel the shape of his hands as they slid. Under a damp fringe of light brown hair his face was narrow, the features sharp. Ratty, she thought in confusion as she untangled her own feet and grabbed her mother's outstretched arm. Except she liked rats.

"I'll ask you ladies to please excuse my friend." The man behind the stumbler was taller and broader, with a round head that he tilted to one side as he gave them a rueful, gap-toothed grin. Muscles bunching under the tight white tee shirt, he gripped the other man's elbows to lift him clear of the ground, then set him on his feet again.

"He's a nice enough little fella most times," the larger man added. "Just had a bit too much beer on a hot day. Right?"

"Yeah, yeah," muttered the smaller man, eyes on the ground. "Sorry."

"Right." The bigger man draped an arm over his friend's shoulders . . . an arm that reminded Katy of a picture in an anatomy book, ropes and knots of muscle and twining blue veins. Not veins, she realized after a moment, but a tattoo: writhing blue lines from sleeve hem to wrist. A very long snake.

"Come on, Katy," said Meg, who had bent to scoop up the dropped book and pamphlets without letting go of her daughter's hand.

"That . . ." Katy, tugged along at a good clip, looked back over her shoulder to see the men disappearing back into the hotel. "Do you know what that dickhead did? He squeezed my butt! With both hands!"

"Welcome to the world of the adult female," said Meg, continuing her leg-stretching pace.

"Mom!"

"Sorry, sweetie. I didn't really mean that. But the first, best thing to do about a grabby drunk is get away from him, fast."

"So what is this, like he's the predator, I'm the prey, and I have to run away?"

Eyeing her daughter's red and furious face, Meg acknowledged wearily that what they had here was a learning experience, fairly cheaply purchased. A fine chance to discuss one of life's crummier facts.

"Do you want to be the predator, chasing things down and killing them?" She set Katy's books and papers on the roof of the car and propped her own rump against the door. All her life Katy had been bigger and stronger than most of her peers: another phase about to come to an end.

"No. But he's got no right to touch me, and I'd like to break his rotten face!"

Katy's fists were clenched. Meg reached out with her left hand to grip her daughter's slim wrist, brought the fist up, and held her own clenched right fist next to it. Almost the same size. "Think of . . . of Vince's fist, beside those," she said, and Katy looked and then jerked her hand away.

"Even a woman as big as I am, as big as you're going to be," Meg said quietly, "cannot stand toe to toe and slug it out with a grown man." She shoved her hands into her jeans pockets and lifted her chin.

"Believe it, Katy. So what you do, you save some time from soccer and basketball and swimming, and take the judo class I've been suggesting. It won't make you the physical equal of a man; nature didn't set things up that way. But it will give you break-away skills and the ability to temporarily disable an opponent."

"I don't want to disable him. I want to dismember him."

"Quite right. Leg over there," Meg said, with a gesture to the right of the parking lot, "and another leg there, maybe."

"Arms draped over the fence," said Katy.

"Why not?"

"Head propped on the rim of that dumpster," Katy went on, with the beginning of a grin shaping her mouth. "Except for the eyeballs; what we'll do with them is . . ."

Meg winced dramatically as she slid into the driver's seat. "Katy, you'll gross me out in two seconds. You can sing it to yourself in the shower, if we can find Lauren's place."

∘ 4 ∘

The tiny town of Stony Creek, which they had somehow missed an hour earlier, spread shallowly to either side of the highway. Houses were one- or occasionally two-story, wooden or stucco, with wire or chain link fences surrounding small front yards. Porches, Meg noticed; big old trees in front yards, with chairs underneath. Petunias and climbing roses and snapdragons along the fences. There was a gas station at a cross street, and a Frostee with a parking lot. A wooden house serving as library, open Monday, Thursday, and Saturday. A very small grocery store, and down a side street Meg could see the white bell tower of a church.

"I guess we were too tired to notice," said Katy as the little town disappeared behind them.

"So it seems," said Meg. "So let's watch this time; the Macrae ranch is about three miles north."

They drove slowly, eyeing a serene and unpeopled landscape in which green, not-quite-flat fields ran up and around small buttes and rocky outcroppings and clumps of trees to touch rolling hills. After almost three miles they spotted what they'd been told to watch for: a pair of high wooden poles holding aloft a crosspiece from which swung a carved wooden sign: "Macrae Ranch." There was no gate between the posts, only a cattle guard; they rattled across that and made their way up a long drive bordering a lush alfalfa field whose green was deepened here and there by shifting cloud shadows.

The drive curved toward a tall white house nearly hidden in trees, and behind that a large, solid-looking barn fronted by a corral, the barn not the traditional red but a mellowed brown. Only two vehicles were parked before the house in a graveled patch big enough for half a dozen: a dark blue Chevy king-cab pickup truck and a red Jeep wagon.

Meg pulled the Honda neatly parallel to the Jeep, got out and stretched, and then walked around the front of the car to join Katy. The house was old but immaculate, with white-painted wood siding in a style that Meg thought was called shiplap. The roof was cross-gabled, the gable fronts covered in fish-scale shingles; tall windows had segmented upper panes but were simply framed. This house would offer them cool, high-ceilinged rooms; soft, comfortable chairs. Iced tea. No, showers first. *Then* they'd be presentable guests worthy of nice chairs and cool drinks. A sound familiar but out of place penetrated her weary mind: a revving engine, coming from behind the house or from somewhere in the surrounding screen of brush and trees.

"Katy!" Meg's dry throat could produce only a harsh caw as she lunged forward to snatch at her daughter's shoulder. Katy, who was already throwing herself backward, fell against Meg and both nearly went down as a car roared past, windshield a blinding blaze of reflected sunlight.

"Dumb asshole!" Katy pulled free to turn and glare after the offending vehicle. Not a car but an old blue panel truck, Meg noted. Dusty and dented, with words only partly legible on its rear doors: something something, and below that in larger letters, "Construction." The truck rattled across the cattle guard, slewed right onto the road, and was gone.

"Katy, are you all right?"

"Boy," she replied, her voice thin and high, "I guess this is just my day to get knocked down or something."

"What's happened? Oh, sweet Jesus!" The tall woman rounding the corner of the house skidded to a stop, sun setting her red hair aflame and touching her white face with color. "Is it . . . Meg? Oh, God, I'm sorry."

"Lauren," was all Meg managed to say before the other woman enveloped her in a hug.

"Oh, Meg, I'm so glad to see you. And this must be Katy, and she's so beautiful!" Lauren Macrae Cavalier released

Meg and reached for Katy, who stepped back and lifted her chin, eyes shooting blue sparks.

"Who was that asshole? He almost ran us down!"

"I know, I'm sorry. But the main thing is you're all right, you're not hurt. Come inside now and let me give you something to drink, and we'll . . ."

"Lauren?" The front door opened, and a gray-haired woman stepped out onto the porch, which ran across the entire front of the house and curved around to the right side as well. The woman's tall body was stooped, and she gripped a cane in her right hand. "Lauren, what's going on? I heard a car."

"Nothing, Aunt Frances. It's just Meg and her daughter, Katy; they finally got here. They need showers, and drinks, and something to eat."

Frances Macrae leaned on her cane, her thrust-forward head trembling a bit as she inspected the newcomers. Meg smiled broadly, to hide her shock at the cavernous eye sockets, the deep lines carved by—what, pain? sorrow?—in crepey skin. In the eleven years since their last meeting, at Lauren's wedding, Frances Macrae had passed from mid-life vigor to withered old age.

"Meg Evans—no, I'm sorry, of course it's Halloran. I'm pleased to see you again," said Aunt Frances, her voice at least still strong. "And Katy, I'm happy to meet you. Please come inside out of the heat and dust."

They followed Aunt Frances into a small vestibule and through a wide entryway into a living room with patterned area rugs on dark wood floors, a stone fireplace flanked by low couches and a pair of wing chairs, and in the far wall a bay window with a padded seat. The older woman stopped, turned as if to speak to Meg, then looked at her niece instead.

"Lauren, I was calling you; where were you? It's almost five o'clock and those children need to be fed."

"I know, dear. I was working in the garden, but I was watching the time."

"Weren't you talking to someone? I thought once I heard voices."

"I was singing, Aunt Frances." Lauren's eyes found Meg's and held them in a gaze that pleaded for something. "As I'm sure you remember, Meg, I have a voice like a crow's. So I sing only when I'm alone, mostly outdoors."

Aunt Frances's frown relaxed, and she lifted her free hand in an apologetic gesture that revealed the gnarled joints of arthritis. "Please forgive a whiny old lady. The babies are almost too big for me to lift anymore, and it makes me worried and bad-tempered when I know they're going to need something I might not be able to manage. Lauren, why don't you see to the children, and I'll show our guests to their room."

"It's not really a working ranch at the moment," said Lauren as she set a tray of pitchers and mugs on a low table. The heat of the day faded quickly at Stony Creek's altitude of forty-five hundred feet, and the four of them were gathered around the fireplace and its small but crackling fire for after-dinner coffee. "So—coffee, sugar, cream, hot milk, cinnamon, nutmeg. What is everyone's pleasure?"

Black for Meg and Aunt Frances. Café au lait for Lauren and for Katy. More growing up here, thought Meg; Katy had never before expressed the slightest interest in coffee. Aunt Frances, who had sipped red wine steadily through dinner, was now quietly topping off her coffee mug from a small cut-glass decanter. Stretched out in an ugly but obviously comfortable recliner, the elderly woman looked more relaxed than at any time since the Hallorans' arrival; probably alcohol eased the pain of arthritis.

"My brother ran five hundred head of Angus, as a rule," said Frances. "After he died, I hired a manager, of course. The children and I worked with him and his crew summers." She sighed and sipped her coffee. "When I retired from the university, I took charge myself, with the intention of gradually turning the operation over to Bobby. But that didn't work out."

"When Sam and I moved here for good two years ago," said Lauren as she settled into a chair, "we sold the cattle and leased some of the land to a neighbor, for alfalfa, until Sam decides what he wants to do. We don't even keep a milk cow anymore, just a few hens for eggs."

"Don't you have horses?" asked Katy in mournful tones.

"Oh, are you a horse person? I haven't ridden much since Johnny was born, and the two best horses, Sam's horses, are in a summer pasture in the mountains. But we have a nice, easy, middle-aged mare, Daisy, that we bought mostly as a learner for Sara. And a youngish gelding named Max; he's lazy, but he'll smarten up if you're firm with him."

Meg had been silently surveying the room, with its built-in and well-filled bookshelves, its two Oriental rugs, the gleaming grand piano. In addition to a well-lighted arrangement of some of Sam's work—mountain landscapes and shots of bears and mountain lions as well as wolves—the walls bore a vigorous seascape in oils, several delicate botanical watercolors, and a pair of Japanese prints. These furnishings fit together as if they'd been in place for a while; presumably the ranch had paid its way well in the past.

Aunt Frances must have caught Meg's thoughts. "In my father's day, a small to medium-sized ranch could provide a very decent living for a family willing to live on the ranch and work hard. But Sam thinks that time is nearly over. He thinks the government will eventually phase out all public-land grazing, and that will be the end."

"Fortunately for us, Sam makes good money," said Lauren in dry tones. "And so did his maternal grandfather."

"This spring Sam had shows in New York and Washington, and there's one scheduled for fall in San Francisco," said Aunt Frances proudly. "And his last book has just gone into a paperback edition. The Bookstore in Alturas has it in its window display."

"Where is he now?" asked Katy.

Lauren merely shrugged and continued to stare into the fire. "In northern Alaska," said her aunt. "He'll have had one of his old flying buddies drop him—Sam flew helicopters in Vietnam. Anyway, the pilot sets him down with his cameras and supplies. Then he's on his own until the plane returns, perhaps two weeks later. Or a month."

"Try two months," muttered Lauren. A sharp cry from the upper part of the house caused her to lift her head; its repetition brought her to her feet. "Johnny. I'd better go try to soothe him before he gets really wound up."

"Johnny is very sensitive," said Aunt Frances with a sigh. "He has these terrible nightmares."

Meg wondered how you knew a baby less than two years of age was having nightmares. The little girl, Sara, was a five-year-old replica of her long-boned, red-haired mother, full of giggles and energy. The boy, also tall for his age but chubby with it, had a big, round head, an outthrust lower lip, and a vocabulary consisting of one word: no.

"He misses Sam. Boys need their fathers, as I certainly know too well," Aunt Frances added, with a glance at the mantel where a phalanx of family pictures included several of the nephew she had raised and lost. "I tried very hard to help Robert grow up—took him out to get his first buck, helped him find the right horse for the rodeos, tried to teach him how to run a ranch. But I just wasn't able to keep his attention.

"And Lauren . . ." The older woman drew her mouth tight and shook her head. "Of course, I never married, so I can't speak from personal experience, but I believe Lauren was much happier when she was able to travel with her husband. Now, cooped up here with two babies and an old woman, the poor girl just gets all flighty and irritable. She needs Sam to keep her in hand, keep her out of trouble."

Katy had been unusually quiet all evening—subdued, Meg thought, by road-weariness and by the day's less pleasant encounters. Now she straightened in her chair, clearly ruffled by this poor-helpless-female attitude, and Meg tossed her a quelling glance: Save it, sweetie.

"And the truth is, I don't know why he's had to be away so much this last year. Sam is very attractive; I surely hope he hasn't—" At the sound of footsteps on the stairs, Aunt Frances flushed guiltily and closed her mouth.

"He's settled, for the moment," said Lauren. She moved to a tall cabinet beside the fireplace. "Brandy, anybody? Or Kahlua, crème de menthe, Drambuie?"

"I was just telling Meg and Katy how sensitive Johnny is," said Aunt Frances as Lauren dealt choices around, including a drop of Kahlua in cream for Katy. "And how much he looks like his Uncle Robert."

Meg, who had risen to accept her Drambuie, passed the mantel now and paused to look. The largest photo of Lauren's brother was an eight-by-ten in black and white. He stood against a rail fence, elbows cocked back over the top rail. His clothes were dark, probably black: boots, jeans, shirt, and a high-crowned hat. Gleaming against the black felt was a hatband that looked to be silver: pale metal links supporting hammered, half-dollar-sized disks. Conchos, like those on a belt Meg had worn when she was a girl.

"He doesn't!" Lauren snapped. She set a brandy glass beside her aunt and poured an inch of amber liquid into it. "Johnny's hair is dark like Bobby's, Aunt Frances. But otherwise he's the image of Sam: blue eyes, curls, even the beginning of Sam's big, square jaw."

Meg moved her gaze to another photo of Bobby, a head-and-shoulders shot, and inspected the arrogant young face there; it was fine-boned and almost delicate, the eyes obviously dark under winging dark brows.

"He looks like Bobby to me," said Aunt Frances stubbornly. "I see him sometimes, you know—Bobby, I mean—going around a corner just before I get there, looking back at me and laughing. And he's been coming home in my dreams lately. Perhaps it's a signal, because the time is right," she said to

Meg. "Monday was his birthday, his thirty-first, and on Saturday it will be exactly ten years since his disappearance."

"Friday," Lauren corrected her gently. "And if he's coming home, let's hope his character has improved. I'm sorry, Aunt Frances, but I don't remember Bobby as a very nice person. When I was twelve, he shot my dog," she said to Meg.

"Lauren!" exclaimed her aunt.

"I had this big old dog named Cody, got him when I was six or seven, and he really loved me. Bobby didn't like dogs. One day Cody disappeared, and after he'd been gone five days Bobby told me he'd shot him. He took me out and showed me where he'd buried him."

As Katy gave a squeaky gasp of indignation, Frances shook her head. "But that's not the way it happened at all, Lauren. Your father shot the dog because he'd begun to kill sheep. He didn't tell you, because he thought it would be easier for you to think the animal had run off.

"I know that Bobby could be thoughtless and unkind," she added. "But it wasn't entirely his fault. And he'd have changed. I'm sure he has changed."

Lauren unclenched her jaw and rearranged her face into the politely noncommittal. "It's nice to have faith. Now, we should work out some things for us to do. It's really too bad you couldn't get here a week earlier," she said to Katy. "You could have seen the junior livestock show and then the rodeo, the Warner Mountain Roundup."

"My fault," said Meg. "Too much work at the end of the school year."

"Well, maybe next year," said Lauren. "So let's see. Katy should have a horseback ride tomorrow, Meg can rest up from driving, and then she and I can have a long talk over old times."

"Then, Friday night," said Aunt Frances, "there's the pot-luck supper at the Stony Creek Community Church, with a town meeting afterward. You and Katy must come to that, Meg, and get a real glimpse of small-town life."

"Port Silva isn't exactly a metropolis, with twenty-five thousand people including the university students," said Meg.

"Stony Creek has about three hundred," Aunt Frances informed her. "And they'll all be there Friday, along with the nearby ranchers. There's to be a discussion of a proposed county ordinance to institute some local control of federal land use."

"Oh, God, I'd forgotten about that," said Lauren. "Things will probably get heated. Maybe we should just stay home and play gin or something. Besides," she added, hugging herself as against a sudden chill, "I heard just today that Marv Jakel is back in town. He'll be sure to show up for the meeting."

"You mean they've let that disgusting animal out of prison?" Frances yanked the lever that brought her recliner upright.

"He'd completed his sentence. And Verna has been very sick, so they're all . . . home, for a while. People were talking about it in the store this morning," she finished.

"Verna Jakel, Marv's mother, has terminal cancer." There was unconcealed satisfaction in Frances Macrae's voice. "I've heard she's gone from two hundred pounds to about ninety and hardly ever gets out of bed now."

Katy was more interested in the previously mentioned Jakel, the one who'd been in jail. "What did he do, this Marv guy?" she asked, wide-eyed.

"He murdered an old woman!" said Aunt Frances. "Betty Burrus, her name was, but everyone called her the Wolf Lady. She had a place north of here, up against the mountains, where she kept wolves and wolf-dog hybrids that she found, or that people brought her."

"It wasn't murder, it was involuntary manslaughter," said Lauren wearily. "She was nearly ninety years old, and her heart gave out when she tried to stop him from shooting her wolves."

"Shoot . . . Why? Why would somebody do that?"

"Oh, Katy, you'll have to talk to Sam. Humans have

always hated and feared wolves; it must be in the genes or something. And livestock people, ranchers, hate them the most. This man, Marv Jakel, is a stupid and unpleasant person, but I think some of the ranchers put him up to the shooting or at least egged him on. There'd been some calves killed, and people suspected Miss Burrus's wolves."

"Did they do it?"

Lauren shook her head. "I don't know. There was a pack of feral dogs around here at the time, I understand. But Marv killed the wolves, and Miss Burrus died, and he went to jail for four years on the manslaughter conviction."

"All of them belong in jail, every Jakel ever born including the women!"

"Aunt Frances, they're not all . . . not all the same. Not all that bad," said Lauren.

Listening to the defensiveness in her friend's voice, Meg saw again, in her mind's eye, the rear of the panel truck that had nearly run her and Katy down as they arrived at the ranch: "Construction" in big letters, legible; other words smaller and dust-dimmed, one beginning with J. Jakel?

• 5 •

"Good morning, Meg. Did you sleep well?"

"Very well, thanks." This was politeness rather than truth. She had been awakened several times in the night, by stiff muscles and once by what sounded like cars.

"Just give me a minute and I'll fix you some breakfast." Lauren poked a last spoonful of something that looked like oatmeal into her son's mouth; then she wiped his face, lifted him from the high chair, and set him on his feet. Johnny wrapped one arm firmly around his mother's jeans-clad leg and glared up at Meg: Stranger go home.

"Just coffee," said Meg, who preferred to start her mornings slowly and hardly ever with oatmeal. She turned her gaze away from the baby's truculent face and looked instead at Lauren, who didn't appear particularly rested, either. Nor particularly happy. Meg's middle-of-the-night notion, that perhaps the noise was Sam coming home unexpectedly, didn't seem worthy of exploration. "And maybe some toast, in a few minutes. But I can do it myself."

"Sounds good to me." Lauren's move toward the stove and the coffee pot was hindered by her son. "Okay, Johnny, enough." She swept him up and carried him across the room to a toy-cluttered corner.

"There you go, hook the train cars together and give the little people a ride," she told him. "Meg, where's Katy?"

"Infants fuss," said Meg. "Teenagers sleep. On and on and on, unless someone tips the bed over."

Lauren grinned and straightened, wiping her hands on her jeans before smoothing back the wisps of curly hair that had escaped from her single long braid. "I can hardly wait. But here's the deal: Do you think Katy would be willing to get up to go riding? The cool of morning is the nicest time, and I'd enjoy being on a horse again. If," she said with a glance over her shoulder toward the toy corner, "you and Aunt Frances wouldn't mind baby-tending for a couple of hours."

"I'd be delighted," said Meg, her second polite lie of the morning. "And so will Katy. I'll get her up."

Thirty minutes later, Meg stood with her arms on the top rail of the corral fence, next to Sara, who took the same pose at the next rail down. "Mommy's riding my Daisy," said the little girl in sorrow.

"I know." Katy was up on Max, a bright bay with black markings, a high head, and a measuring look in his eye; Max didn't seem a bit lazy to Meg. Katy had spent a month at a horse camp the previous summer but had had little chance since then to practice her skills. Trust to good basic reflexes, Meg advised herself now. And limber young bones.

"There's your Aunt Frances," she said, as the older woman came onto the back porch and waved at them. "Want to go have breakfast?"

"I ate *hours* ago," said Sara. "I'm going to feed the chickens and then play with my kitty."

Meg watched the leggy little girl dash off toward some outbuildings. This was not a city, after all, with perverts lurking in bushes and discarded drug paraphernalia a possibility in every sandpile. And Sara was obviously a child accustomed to entertaining herself.

Frances's movements were slow and stiff this morning, and the skin beneath her eyes hung in dark half-circles. Booze might provide temporary relief from pain, but as Meg had discovered during the first year of her widowhood, it raised hell with sleep. "Sit down," she suggested gently as the two of them moved into the kitchen. "I'll get coffee."

Frances sank into a chair at the table. "Thank you. The worst thing about arthritis is that it prevents a full night's sleep. Well, maybe that's not the worst thing," she added with a grimace. "It also prevents my riding into the mountains, or drawing."

Meg winced inwardly at this. Frances Macrae had been a botanist and illustrator, going far into the desert or the mountains to collect rare plants or simply draw them on site. Her name was on many well-known textbooks and field guides, and her watercolor studies had the quality of art.

"Thank you," said Frances again as Meg set a mug before her. "I'm just a tiresome old lady these days, bored and depressed and nearly housebound, a constant burden for poor Lauren. That's why your visit is such a blessing; Lauren has talked of nothing else for weeks."

Meg found the serrated knife and began to slice bread for toast. "It's kind of Lauren to take Katy riding," she said over her shoulder.

"Lauren is a kind person," said Aunt Frances crisply. "She has an intense need to please—very sweet, but an unusual quality in a Macrae. It tends to make her too easily led."

And a pox on the Macraes. Meg snapped the toaster slide down with more force than was necessary and mourned that long-ago orphaned Lauren, trying her best to please an aunt who considered the impulse itself a character flaw. Half-orphan Katy had been incredibly lucky in Vince, bless him. He was wonderful with her, full of affectionate admiration mixed liberally with good sense and an occasional dose of caustic wit. Carrying plates of buttered toast to the table, Meg made a vow to call Vince tonight.

"Yow!" said Johnny from his corner. He clambered to his feet and came charging across the room to fling himself at Meg's denim-clad legs. As she bent to steady him, he realized the legs were not his mom's, and his eyes widened and filled with tears.

"Here you go, little kid," she murmured, and lifted him to the lap of his great-aunt, who clasped him close with wordless, soothing murmurs. His wail of dismay reduced itself to a snort as he rubbed his curly head against the older woman's shoulder.

"Mommy!"

Both women glanced first at Johnny. "Mommy!" came the cry again, closer, and pounding feet sounded from outside. "Mommeee! There's a wolf out there and he's all bloody!"

"Sara!" Meg ran for the front door and caught the little girl as she came flying up the steps. "Where, Sara? Show me," she demanded, and Sara flung an arm wide to point toward the road.

The animal, smallish and tawny gray, had been eviscerated and tied, or wired, onto the fence beside the ranch entrance road, spread-eagled there like a drying pelt. Once Meg got past the general gruesomeness of the scene, she noted the light-boned frame, the pointy face and large ears, and knew the creature was definitely not a wolf. Sara, coming down the driveway after her cat, had spotted the body and run screaming; she was still crying, her head buried in Meg's neck and her long legs wrapped around Meg's waist.

"He's a coyote, Sara, not a wolf. And he's dead, so he's not hurting anymore." There was a piece of cardboard strung around the animal's neck, words printed on it in broad, black strokes: What We Do to Wolves in Modoc County.

"That's disgusting!" snapped Aunt Frances, who had stopped some distance back from the fence and was holding on to Johnny with both hands. "How *dare* anyone make such a display on Macrae property! I'm going to call Sheriff Douglas and demand that he come immediately to remove that . . . obscenity.

"Hush, Sara," she added in only slightly softer tones. "That's just a coyote. They're vermin and nothing you should cry over."

Meg wasn't sure what made wolves valuable, coyotes not; was it simply the rarity principle? Probably there was more to it than that, and probably Katy would know. Since the little girl had stopped crying, Meg set her on her feet.

Johnny, it turned out, did know another word: doggy. And he was making a determined effort to get his hands on this one. "Let me carry him to the house for you," Meg suggested to Aunt Frances. "Then you can telephone the sheriff, and I'll come back down here and watch for . . . anybody displaying suspicious interest, I guess."

"Yes, good." Frances let go of the struggling child and sighed with relief as Meg caught him up. "And Sara can come along to help watch him. Sara's a good little mother, aren't you, dear?"

Sara's lower lip thrust itself out in silent mutiny, but she said nothing, merely hunching her shoulders and falling into line as they trooped up the drive. Meg put Johnny down among his toys in the kitchen and hurried off, taking care to close the door tightly behind her.

The sun was high now in a sky of mellow, gentle blue dotted with a few puffy little clouds; the air was so dry that Meg's nose felt tight and her hair had the texture of straw. No traffic on the road; so far, so good. Perhaps she should station herself casually in front of the carcass and hope no passerby found her interesting enough to stop for.

That was a dumb idea. For one thing, she couldn't stand still. The sun was too hot, the silence too . . . oppressive. She strained her ears and heard a far-off engine, maybe a tractor. A bird song. A buzz as a huge fly darted past her face. Right, there were flies around the coyote carcass. But a quick survey of the surrounding area revealed no additional gathering of insects, no hovering crows or other carrion-eaters; where was the rest of the animal?

Meg thought he—or she; Meg herself certainly couldn't say without getting a lot closer than she intended to—was a fairly fresh kill, not just a dead animal someone had stumbled across and decided to use in novel fashion. Someone had taken the trouble to find the coyote, to kill it and gut it somewhere else, and then bring it here.

A pickup truck roared past on the other side of the road, pausing not at all. Meg resisted the impulse to duck into the brush and instead stood and watched it diminish with distance; the driver wouldn't have had to slow down to see that the coyote still hung there. She glanced at the animal again herself and was reminded of a picture that was a standard in books on the American frontier: Not one dead wolf but a whole row of them hung like old coats along a prairie fence. Yes indeed, we have to stamp out anything that wants to eat what *we* want to eat. Or what we want to sell.

Which was what she, or anyway the Macraes, were supposed to be reminded of by this display. Sam Cavalier must have something new going on about wolves around here, or perhaps he was merely continuing to push the original wolf recovery project, probably his idea in the first place. And good luck to him, but Meg was suddenly quite sure she didn't want to meet the people who had expressed their opposition in this bloody fashion. It was clear that she had thoughtlessly brought Katy into the battlefield of a war that was none of their business, not at this personal, your-way-of-life-or-mine level.

How soon could they get away? She had more or less promised her daughter a quick trip into the Warner Mountains; if they did that tomorrow, and then accompanied Lauren and her aunt to the meeting . . . might be a boobytrap there she hadn't been told of, but again a promise was involved, and maybe the fact that the event was being held in a church would keep everybody peaceful. Then she'd think of a reason to get them on the road home the next morning, Saturday. Not nice to abandon Lauren, who seemed rather needy at the moment, but it was after all Lauren's war—or anyway Sam's.

She shoved her hands into her jeans pockets and paced the drive, each step sending up a little puff of dust. Katy had been gone for less than an hour; with luck she wouldn't return until the sheriff or whoever had removed the evidence. Another pickup went by in a hurry, its driver not so much as glancing toward the Macrae place. Maybe she and the coyote were invisible.

Over the next ten minutes, one more truck drove right by;

a big sedan paused and a round-faced woman peered in her direction before driving on. Finally a big gray pickup, not old but dusty and showing signs of hard use, turned into the driveway and rolled slowly past her, the driver giving a half-salute with his left hand without lifting his muscular arm from the edge of the open window. There was no insignia on the truck, but the man carried an attitude of authority that Meg recognized. He had to be the sheriff.

A few minutes later the truck came back, to park at the end of the driveway. "Are you Sheriff Douglas?" she asked as the man climbed out.

"No ma'am. Well, I'm Earl Douglas, but I'm not the sheriff right now, that's Lou Vukovich. You Mrs. Halloran?"

"Margaret Halloran, yes." He was taller than Meg, probably an inch or two over six feet, with a broad, meaty torso and long, solid arms and legs. In boots, Levi's, and a blue chambray work shirt over a tee shirt, he looked like a very large working cowboy. Inspecting him, she realized after a moment that he was doing the same with her.

"Halloran," he repeated, frowning. "Thought for a minute I might have seen you someplace, but Halloran doesn't hit me quite right. You maybe a cop's wife?"

"I'm married to Vince Gutierrez, chief of police in Port Silva."

"That's it. You were with him at a conference in Sacramento one time. Pleased to meet you," he said, holding out his right hand. He tipped his big head to one side and surveyed her from heavy-lidded brown eyes. Under a thatch of grizzled tight curls he had a long, weathered face, the face of an intelligent bloodhound. "Vince and me go back about twenty-five years," he said as he released her hand. "We were rookie cops together in L.A."

"Ah. But you're not a cop now?"

"Not exactly." He cast a glance at the coyote corpse, then reached into the back of his truck for a pair of wire cutters. "Just a . . . well, maybe not exactly friend, more like a famil-

iar public servant. I'm a local boy, born here and moved back
some years ago. Frances Macrae either forgot I didn't get
reelected last year, or she just don't care."

He strode through dry grass to the fence, to give the coyote
a preliminary tug. "Stiff. Must have been put here last night.
Nothing real illegal, though; there's no season for coyotes."

"This is a pretty nasty way to leave a message," said Meg.

"Right." He snipped wire from around each of the animal's legs, then lifted the rigid form and carried it to his
truck, to toss it in the back. "Probably kids. Nothing much
to do in the summer; they hear their folks complaining about
ol' Sam the Wolf Man and decide to play this little trick. You
know Sam Cavalier well?"

Meg shook her head. "I'm a friend of Lauren's; I met Sam
only once, years ago. But I thought his wolf recovery idea
had been dropped."

"I guess it has, but he's a determined man, Cavalier. One
thing, somebody told me he's been talking about turning the
ranch here into a wolf sanctuary."

"Oh, my," said Meg.

"Yeah. Well, I'll take this critter off to the dump. Tell Miss
Macrae, okay? And tell Vince hey from me when you talk to
him. If you're going to be in the neighborhood for a while,
maybe we could get together for a drink."

"Thank you." He was standing so close Meg could see a
small white scar on his jaw and catch the faint tang of healthy
sweat. Conscious of a sense of intimidation as well as a
heightened physical awareness that was equally unwelcome,
she took an involuntary step backward and then felt silly.
"I'm not sure how long my daughter and I will be staying."

"Well, I'll probably see you around."

"Anyway, he cut the thing down and put it in his truck and
didn't seem to mind having been called away from whatever
he was doing." The horsewomen had returned after the

excitement was over and just as Meg was beginning to worry about them. Now, with lunch finished and everybody else napping or reading, Meg and Lauren were enjoying a glass of wine on the vine-shaded side porch.

"Aunt Frances thinks she owns the county," said Lauren. "And quite a few of the people around here seem willing to go along with her on that."

Meg lowered her voice. "Lauren, I was shocked at how much she has aged."

"I know, it's awful. Bobby did that to her, his disappearance." Lauren stretched her long legs out and propped the backs of her sneakers on the porch rail. "He'd made her life miserable for years, the rotten little creep. You'd think his absence would have been a relief."

"Um." Meg was sorry she'd blundered into this obviously painful topic.

"She was always kind to me—tolerated me, I guess you'd have to say—but Bobby just owned her, heart and soul," Lauren said with a grimace, "the same as he had my mother. That first year, when everyone kept saying he'd surely come back, was just dreadful. Sam and I were traveling a lot then, but I came to see her as often as I could, and each time she was at least five pounds lighter with about a hundred more lines in her face.

"Then she seemed to adjust for a while, until Sam and the lawyers decided we had to have Bobby declared dead. She finally agreed to that, but it sent her into another decline; she just shut herself down, hardly left the ranch at all. Now there's this 'ten-year-anniversary' thing, and I'm honestly not sure she's going to survive it."

"I saw the article in the local paper."

"Oh, right. Up here Bobby Macrae is as famous as Elvis. He was one of the four featured 'mysterious disappearances' on a network television program a month ago."

"Oh, that's what Vince was talking about," Meg said. "I didn't see it."

"It was fairly sleazy. That may have been partly our fault;

we refused to be interviewed, so we're just backs of heads and hunched shoulders scurrying away from the camera like fugitives. Since then we've had requests for interviews from several newspapers and a couple of television people. And I know Aunt Frances has had some anonymous telephone calls, people claiming to have seen Bobby or to have a message from him. One I think actually claimed to be him, but she wouldn't talk about it. Meg, I think she really expects him to turn up."

"But you don't."

"He's dead." She let the words hang there for a moment, then lifted her shoulders in a shrug. "There's no way on earth Bobby Macrae would have left us in peace for ten years otherwise."

Meg sipped wine and eyed the profile of the younger woman. Lauren, and Katy too, had seemed weary but cheerful after their three-hour ride. A little high, even, with what Meg had assumed was the euphoria of exercise and fresh air. Now Lauren's shoulders were slumped, her mouth drooping.

"*I* should never have come back here, either," Lauren said flatly.

Meg held her tongue, and Lauren tossed her a sideways look. "So why did she, you ask? Good question. Because Sam wanted to. He said our kids had a right to know their heritage, to grow up breathing fresh air instead of exhaust fumes. He said family was the important thing and Aunt Frances needed us. He said we'd all be safer here, when he's away. It didn't seem to occur to him that some of us might be bored to bloody death!" She drained her wine glass, looked at it as if she might hurl it into the yard, then sat up and reached for the bottle instead.

"More?" she asked, and refilled both glasses without waiting for an answer. "But then Sam didn't know he was married to 'that Macrae girl' who was dumb and skinny-ugly and had a reputation with some people for being a slut. So he couldn't know how it would make me feel to have to live here again. Boys get away with that kind of shit; they grow up and get forgiven for anything short of murder. Girls. Never. Do." She punctuated each of her last words with a thump of the wine bottle on the porch floor.

"But actually, Sara loves it here." Lauren sniffed and then took a deep breath. "Johnny will, too, I suppose. And I don't mind it so much when Sam's at home. Dumb woman, put up with anything as long as there's somebody around with a hairy chest and a rumbly voice and she gets laid now and then."

She turned and met Meg's eyes. "I mean, look at you. You got married again, isn't that why?"

"No! Well, yes. But there were other reasons too. I like Vince; he's kind, and funny."

"Really? I don't think Sam has much sense of humor. But he's beautiful," she added with a grin. "Looks count, right?"

"And he's talented."

"Yes, he is. What a prize." She leaned back in her chair and sighed. "Meg, I apologize, and I promise not to whine anymore."

"What are friends for?"

"I don't know. I don't have that many. Oh, God, is that another whine?" She got up and came to put an arm around Meg's shoulders for a quick, hard hug. "I don't need *many*, just good ones."

◦ 6 ◦

"I'm getting pretty sick of cows," said Katy. "Scat! Get *out* of here!" She flapped her hands at the rough-coated reddish animal that stood broadside across the trail to stare at her from bulging, pale-lashed eyes set far apart in its wide white face. The cow, actually a large calf, waited a moment before flinging its head up and turning to lumber off after its fellows.

"What are cows doing in a wilderness, anyway?" Katy asked in indignant tones.

"I suppose it all looks the same to a cow," said Meg, watching where she put her feet. "Although we're not actually in the South Warner Wilderness; this is just the Modoc National Forest."

Leaving the ranch right after breakfast, they had taken the two-lane highway that spanned the Warner Mountains at the range's narrow waist, climbing through rolling, cedar-dotted foothills to top out at Cedar Pass, an elevation of some six thousand feet, and descend the steeper eastern slope through thick green stands of pine and fir to the little town of Cedarville.

From Cedarville they had ambled north in what was called the Surprise Valley, turning off into the Modoc when a likely gravel or dirt road presented itself, pulling over now and then to park and hike a bit. Meg was finding that this country, while not spectacular like the Sierra or the coast, had an appeal of its own; the wide blue sky with its shifting clouds worked a kind of magic on the land below, subtly altering shapes and muting colors.

"I wish we had our old van," said Katy, whose urge to explore had been frustrated by her mother's reluctance to risk her newish Honda sedan on trails that looked especially steep and rocky. "Or maybe Lauren and I could bring the horses up tomorrow; I bet I could get to some neat places on Max."

"Katy, I'm thinking seriously about going home tomorrow. Vince sounded lonely when I talked with him last night." Vince had in fact seemed weary and distracted; when she suggested cutting her trip short, he'd responded with a brief silence and then the information that his sisters were there as well as one of his brothers, all of them consulting about what to do with and for Emily Gutierrez.

Truth was, he hadn't demonstrated any great enthusiasm for her return, and she, not wanting to add to his worries, hadn't told him about the modern version of a range war she and Katy had stumbled into here. At the end of their conversation she had congratulated herself upon her virtuous restraint; by now she was feeling lonely and unwanted and very eager to be home.

"Mom! We just got here!"

"Sweetie, I'm tired. And I feel like an intruder."

"Lauren doesn't think we're intruders. She'll be really sad if we leave. Shit!" The expletive was directed not at Meg but at the pile of manure Katy's sneaker had just hit. "Boy, I'm never going to feel bad about eating a cow again."

"Okay, city kid."

Katy looked up with a glare that faded into a reluctant grin and then a giggle. "Right. Candyass, that's what the kids would call me. But this is *my* woods; it's U.S. national forest and I'm a citizen. I think deer belong here, and antelope and badgers and marmots, and mountain lions and wolves too. I think all those ranchers"—she waved her arm vaguely to the north and west—"ought to keep their cows at home."

"That would be my personal preference, too," admitted Meg. "But I'm not a person whose family has been living and working up here for a hundred years."

Katy's head came up, eyes narrowed. A born scrapper who at age ten got tossed out of summer Bible school for announcing that she thought turning the other cheek was a dumb idea, Katy believed it was immoral to back off from a righteous battle. In principle Meg agreed; in practice, as a veteran of many battles and more than a few of them lost, she was becoming a more reluctant warrior with each passing year. Whether this attitude stemmed from increasing good sense or simply advancing age, she wasn't sure.

"Mom. Just because something has been going on a long time, that doesn't make it a good thing."

"True. You're absolutely right. Okay, we've seen enough cows. Let's drive on out and eat our lunches at the big reservoir, or maybe at the wildlife refuge. The bird pamphlet I picked up says that the great blue heron is a permanent resident there."

"Boy, I'd love to get a shot of one of those guys," said Katy, patting the small camera she wore on its strap around her neck. "Okay, let's go."

"Well, shit," said Lauren as she hung up the telephone. "Excuse me, Meg. That was Johnny's sitter, who has some totally dumb excuse for not being able to come tonight."

"Why don't I just stay home with him?"

"Oh, no, please. Look, it's five-fifteen, and I promised to get there a little early and help set things up. I halfway expect Aunt Frances to change her mind about going; she's hardly left the ranch in months. If she does decide to stay home, Johnny can stay with her. If not, please just stuff everybody into your car and come along. Okay?"

Meg restrained a sigh. She was sunburned and relaxed, ready to put her feet up and read until bedtime. "Of course. We'll see you there."

At six o'clock Meg parked the Honda close to a grassy verge some hundred yards north of the white-spired Stony Creek

Community Church. "So. Here we are," she said, and pulled the latch that opened the trunk. "Katy, would you get the stroller out, please? Oh, Katy, for heaven's sake!"

"What?" Her daughter's face was open and innocent, a nice contrast to the sharp-muzzled wolf's head that stared from her chest. Katy was wearing her Wolf Haven tee shirt, and how on earth had Meg failed to notice in time?

"Oh, nothing. Never mind," Meg said, moving around the car to open the front passenger door. Frances Macrae had held to her resolve to come to the meeting. With Sam away, she'd explained, she felt she should make every effort to attend events like this. The implication, to Meg, was that Lauren's presence was negligible, or at least insufficient.

Frances had put on navy linen slacks and jacket over a white blouse, had fluffed up her iron-gray curls and applied a bit of pink lipstick and matching blusher. Meg had found the effect of color on the lined, pallid face less cheerful than macabre.

Now, watching Frances get carefully out of the car, Meg noticed that she had not brought her cane; she was, by God, The Macrae, and upright and painted to prove it. As Katy and the children set off for the church, Meg handed the older woman a foil-covered platter of chicken and picked up a Tupperware bowl of pasta salad, stifling a sigh. She had spent a good part of her adult life avoiding potlucks.

Singly or more often in family groups, people were coming from all directions to the side yard of the church, an enormous grassy field with a baseball diamond at the far end. At the field's forward edge, a vine-covered wooden trellis sheltered long tables covered with white paper; Meg found space for their dishes amid the many already there, then reached into a nearby barrel to snag a can of beer. Aunt Frances took custody of Johnny and his stroller, which would at least give her something to hold on to or even lean on; Katy, released from that responsibility, set off into the crowd with red-haired Sara on her heels.

And it was a crowd. A good half of Stony Creek's population of three hundred must be here, together with more than a few ranchers if the boots, straw hats, and sunburned faces were what they seemed. Children darted over the grass like noisy rabbits; a gaggle of teenagers lounged on the church steps. The grownups stood about in loose and shifting knots, calling to each other with waves and smiles. Small-town America on a nice summer evening, thought Meg, lacking only a latter-day Norman Rockwell to immortalize it. Where were the forces of disorder?

Frances took a deep breath and moved in stately fashion into the scene, Meg following in her wake. There were nods, and polite greetings, and a few introductions of "Margaret Halloran, a family friend."

She met Irma and Avery Prescott, a tall, solidly built pair of ranch owners. Shirley Claymore and her husband whose name Meg didn't catch, ranchers as well, but smaller than the Prescotts and less prosperous-looking. Jake Somebody in a straw hat that he doffed with a sweep. A carpenter, an elementary school teacher. A soft-voiced blonde woman who wrote children's books. None of them was named Jakel, she noted. These people talked about the weather, about a coming hot-air balloon festival, about plans for highway improvement and the need for a stoplight on the highway where it passed through Stony Creek.

As they moved from one small group to another, Meg had the feeling that animated discussions were being shut down, conversation becoming overly polite, even stilted, at their approach. Because of Frances, or because of Meg the outlander? Whatever the reason, there was no mention of grazing fees or federal rules within shot of her ear, nor of wolves either. And not one single reference to Bobby Macrae. She smiled and nodded in her turn and was grateful when Lauren appeared as the clang of the church bell set off a rush to the food.

At seven-thirty the bell sounded again, and a barrel-chested man in a seersucker suit announced that the meeting would begin in fifteen minutes. Meg collected the Macrae/

Cavalier leftovers and sent Katy to the car with them. Then she swallowed the last of her second can of beer and went to join the long line to the rest room.

Sun still washed the rapidly emptying field, but the air was growing chilly. Meg spotted Katy and waved to her. Lauren was nowhere in sight, but here came Frances from the direction of the parked car with Johnny in tow. Probably, thought Meg, he'd finally rebelled against being strapped in the stroller; he'd been working up to a major fuss over its restraint as the meal ended. The little boy's feet were dragging, his head bobbing; he'd be asleep in somebody's lap soon.

Meg was still twenty feet away from Frances when another woman crossed between them, to plant herself in the older woman's path. Meg saw the newcomer's challenging stance, saw Frances's head come up and her face freeze.

"Get out of my way, you slut."

"Miss Macrae, ten years is long enough for hard feelings; it's time for you to talk to us, to think about what's owed us. You keep hanging up on me on the phone, I got no choice but to come where I can catch you." White-blonde head erect, green eyes fixed unblinkingly on Frances Macrae's face, the woman reached sideways to grasp the shoulder of a skinny boy nine or ten years old. The boy's back was rigid, his head down.

"This here's my Bobby," she went on, "your *other* grandnephew. Look, Bobby, here's your cousin I told you about, only boy cousin you got. I heard his name's Johnny."

"I owe you nothing, Ruthie Jakel!" Frances bent to lift Johnny and straightened, clutching him close, her face mottled red from exertion or fury. "I say just what I said ten years ago: Your bastard is no Macrae. Get away!" she snapped at the older boy as his awkward feet and his mother's push sent him lurching toward her and Johnny.

Moving forward to put herself between the two women,

Meg saw the boy flinch as if he'd been slapped. Pale and freckled, with lightish burr-cut hair, he had his mother's high forehead and long nose; his jaw was broader, however, and his eyes were a dark hazel.

"And who the fuck are you?" Ruthie Jakel was shorter than Meg or Frances, with sloping shoulders that seemed too narrow to support the breasts swelling out of a low-necked blouse; her dark skirt clung tight around skimpy hips and stopped high on thin legs. Eyes narrowed to slits, lips pulled back from big teeth, her face had a hatchet-blade quality that Meg found faintly familiar.

"Here, let me have him," said Meg quietly, taking Johnny from his aunt's arms. "My name is Margaret Halloran, and I'm a friend of the Macraes. You'll have to excuse us; we need to go in and find seats."

The green eyes opened wide, and the woman drew breath to speak, but Meg gripped Frances's elbow and guided— pushed, actually—the older woman toward the church. Ruthie Jakel, standing there with one arm around her son's shoulders, was in a state Meg knew from years of trying to prevent battles in school yards: trembling on an edge and willing to let her fury sweep her to physical attack. Frances couldn't handle that, and Meg didn't want to.

◦ 7 ◦

The meeting was to take place in the main body of the church, where two rows of plain wooden pews were separated by a center aisle. In the open area before the raised section containing pulpit and altar, an ordinary speaker's lectern had been set up.

Frances, who had pulled free of Meg's grip once they were inside, paused in a side aisle about halfway to the front. Her color was better, her shoulders squared and her chin up. "This should do," she said to Meg. "You save seats for us, and I'll find Lauren."

Meg scanned the crowd for Katy, spotted her just coming in the door, and gave a beckoning gesture. Then she took the aisle seat in the nearest empty pew, sitting at a slight angle so that she could see most of the room. Two years of living with a cop and here she was, automatically watching the house and measuring out her route to the door.

The people who had mingled cheerfully outside seemed to be separating themselves like faintly hostile wedding guests as they filed in and found seats: ranch people on her side of the room, townspeople across the aisle. Both groups were low-voiced, most faces wearing expressions of noncommittal politeness—perhaps because they were in a church.

A third and smaller cluster, coming in at the last minute and taking seats toward the rear on the townie side, was less restrained. These people looked different, too: mostly slim, tanned rather than weathered, and dressed by L. L. Bean or Land's End rather than Sears or J. C. Penney.

"Modoc County's new rich folks," said a voice from close by; Meg looked up to see the children's writer, Abby Fowler, in the pew just ahead. Abby had sat with the Macrae/Cavalier group at dinner, her demeanor and conversation lightening the atmosphere considerably. Now Meg lifted an eyebrow: explain, please?, and Abby went on, speaking softly.

"There are two new second-home developments here in the east county: Wildcat Ridge, in the Surprise Valley, and Goose Lake Heights, on this side of the Warners. Well, they started out as second-home, but some people are settling in as year-round residents."

"Not ranchers."

"Oh my, no. Mostly retired people, although not necessarily what you'd think of as retirement age. They come here for the rural atmosphere, I think—and for golf, and hunting. That very tall man with the long arms is a former baseball pitcher, from Texas. The guy with the blow-dried silver hair is somebody from television, soaps or commercials or something."

"Mm. Looks familiar."

"And the round-headed guy with the reddish fringe? That's Dr. Emmett Smith; he bought a worn-out ranch southwest of Alturas and runs a clinic there, for rehabilitation of drug addicts. But he doesn't live there; he and his wife and their little boy live in Goose Lake Heights."

Meg's view of the doctor, his much younger wife, and their frail-looking small son was blocked as Katy came in from the other side of the pew, Sara right behind her. Johnny twisted in Meg's lap and said, "Kee!" in delighted tones.

"Hey, little kid," she said. "Look, here's your mama." Lauren and Frances settled in beside Katy and Sara, Johnny was handed across to his mother, and everybody faced front as the barrel-chested, seersucker-clad man, Pastor Harrington, rapped his knuckles on the lectern.

"I welcome all of you fine people to tonight's citizens' meeting of Stony Creek and adjacent Modoc County," he said in a resonant bass voice.

Meg half expected him to begin with a prayer; instead, he called on the town secretary to read the minutes of the previous month's meeting. Then came announcements: a fund would be set up to help renovate the county swimming pool used by Stony Creek; the bleacher refinishing job for the ball field would begin next week—a reminder to those who had offered their labor; several families were in need of funds or other kinds of help.

As the minister's soporific voice paused, the squeak of door hinges and then the clatter of footsteps on the wooden floor caught Meg's not-very-attentive ear. Sensing a stirring along her own pew and possibly elsewhere as well, she straightened and turned to see Ruthie Jakel come quickly through the open half of the double door, pulling her son along by the hand. A man came in after her, a ferret-faced male version of Ruthie a few inches taller. With a jolt Meg recognized the man who had accosted her, or really Katy, in front of the hotel in Alturas two days earlier.

Ruthie settled into an aisle seat near the back. Her brother—Meg assumed that was who he was—put a hand on her shoulder and bent close to say something to her; she shook her head but moved over to make room for him in the pew.

"Mom!" said Katy, who had followed Meg's glance.

"Ssh. I know."

"What are *they* doing here?" Not Katy this time, but a woman in the row behind them, directing the harshly whispered question to the man at her side.

"You just keep quiet!" he snapped, and added, in gentler tones, "Last thing we need to do is stir up Jakel meanness." Meg heard other rustlings and whispers in the room, saw other heads turn and then turn back. Lauren, and beside her Frances Macrae, did not turn at all.

"Now," said Pastor Harrington, "we'll get to the main topic of tonight's meeting." He yielded the lectern to a long-jawed, weathered man clutching a fistful of note cards. As this man, clearly a rancher, looked out at his audience, there was a shifting in the pews and a shuffling of feet—a difference in the air, as if the room's atmospheric pressure had increased.

"You all know me," he said in a reedy voice, "George Biggers. My family's been here almost a hundred years, ranching the whole time; we been grazing the land around here from before it was a forest reserve."

Exhalations and murmurs of agreement came from the crowd, along with one audible groan and, from the rear, a hiss that was quickly broken off.

"Like most of the family ranches, we just about make it from year to year. And every year recently I have this extra knot in my gut, waiting to see what somebody in Washington is going to try to do to me *this* time. Like last year, remember? What they had in mind just out of the blue, like, was to quadruple the goddamned grazing fee, charge about eight dollars a month for every damned cow. Sorry, Pastor Harrington," he added quickly, as the clergyman stiffened in his place in the front pew.

"Then there was that dumb proposal somebody made, and the government actually considered—bringing wolves back here. So we got by on that one, but next thing was the Forest Service wanting to reduce the number of cows on the land so there'd be more browse for deer. That's still under consideration, way I hear it."

"They talked about enlarging the wilderness area, too," called a voice from the ranch side of the audience.

"Right, along with changing the rules so there'd be no grazing, none whatsoever, on any land designated as wilderness." Biggers's ruddy face grew darker, and he leaned forward on the lectern.

"So what I propose is, we encourage our board of supervisors to proceed with what they've already talked about, a county ordinance that says the federal government can't come in here and change land-use rules on us without our approval. Plenty of other western counties are setting up laws like that, and I think we should get our ass in gear and do the same thing."

The air rang with cries of "Yeah!" and "Damn right!" from the ranchers' side of the aisle.

"Wait a minute." This from the other side of the room,

where the former pitcher rose to his full, gangling height. "Some of us don't ranch. Some of us would like to see more wilderness and better hunting."

"Some of you ought to go back where you come from."

"Excuse me?" In the moment of silence that followed this outright rudeness, the words rang like two strokes of a bell.

"Excuse me," said Katy again, standing up, "but these changes you're talking about, they're meant for the national forest land?"

"They sure are, young lady, national forest and Bureau of Land Management, our land right here."

"But it isn't your land. It belongs to the government of the United States and should be for the use of all citizens. Shouldn't it?"

As voices rose all around, Meg thought with resignation and some surprise that Katy's tone, at least, had been polite.

"Young lady," said Biggers, waving the room to near-silence, "we had a grazing permit since the beginning. That permit is family property, and reducing or canceling it reduces my income and the real value of my ranch. No government agency should be able to do that; it's called 'taking,' and it's not legal. We got a right to this land because we been using it."

"If that were the universal rule," came a voice from the back of the room, "the land would belong to the Modocs and the Paiutes. They were using it first."

Another teenager, Meg noted, from the rich-folks' group: a shortish, round-faced boy with a deep voice and a precise delivery.

Predictably, there was another furor of angry voices. Suddenly a whistle split the air and silenced everyone; a shaggy-haired young man standing against the far wall took two fingers from his mouth and nodded. His jeans and denim jacket were old and not very clean, his face two or three days away from its last shave.

"If we want to keep on ranching here—and that's what I

for one mean to do—we'd be smart to pay attention to what the kids are pointing out," he said. "The land *is* federal, and in this country, it's historical fact that the majority can take what it wants. Wait a minute," he said loudly as voices began to rise again.

"Maybe you haven't noticed," he went on after a moment, "but ranchers aren't a majority in the U.S.A. or in California either. And cows don't vote. So I think we'd be dumb to try to pass a law that will be useless and not valid; it'll just get people pissed off at us."

"Bullshit! What this law is gonna do, you dumb-fuck son of a bitch, it'll secure the value of our property, maybe even *increase* it!"

"Marvin Jakel, I will not have blasphemy or foul language in the Lord's house!" Pastor Harrington's thunderous voice and fierce glare brought a silence so deep that Meg thought people must be holding their breath.

Harrington moved to the lectern, waited until rancher Biggers had settled into a pew, and then presided firmly over further discussion, judicially calling out names from either side. Words like "subsidies," "carpetbagger," and even "eco-freak" were spoken, but in tones approaching civility.

After some fifteen minutes, the pastor said, "Now, just one more. Miss Macrae?"

Frances got stiffly to her feet. "You all know who I am; the Macraes have ranched here as long as any family in the county. Now I'm old, and I see the damage we've done. As a botanist, I can testify to the fact that many plant species that flourished when I was a girl have been lost as the land was overgrazed and heavily managed for grazing. Now I listen when younger people say we should try to put things right. We should all listen."

She sat down abruptly, and Meg heard from behind them the muttered phrase, "Senile old woman!" before Pastor Harrington moved smoothly back into control. "All right, folks, we've exchanged some information and some opinions. Do you want to take a vote, so that we can tell the supervisors what our feelings are about the ordinance they are considering?"

The ayes were more numerous than the nays, or at least louder, so he called for a vote and counted hands with the help of the secretary. Scanning the raised hands, Meg judged that the people in favor of an ordinance outnumbered those against by about two to one. Frances, Lauren, and Abby Fowler were among the latter.

People began to move, to murmur and rumble and get to their feet. Meg saw the shaggy-haired young rancher who had counseled restraint slip out the side door, and she saw Marv Jakel get up quickly and follow.

Katy stood before her seat, chin high; Sara, beside her, was struggling to keep her eyes open. Meg got to her feet and was about to say, "Let's go," when she saw Lauren hand her sleeping son to his great-aunt and hurry off down the center aisle. Frances's "Lauren!" went unheeded.

"Here, I'll take him," Meg said, and collected the child before stepping into the side aisle and the traffic flow that led to the door, open wide now and admitting a chilly evening breeze. She thought people were eyeing Katy and decided that was Katy's problem, so long as no one actually grabbed her; issue a challenge, you should expect some of the responses to be hostile. Nevertheless, she had her attention tuned to their immediate surroundings and so did not notice as soon as her neighbors the yells and then screams coming from outside.

"Mom, what's happening?"

"I don't know. Come on, but stay behind me, you and Sara both."

A moment later they were outside the door, where a ring of onlookers was milling around two—no, three—struggling figures. Squinting against poor light and swirling dust, Meg saw Marv Jakel swinging wildly at the shaggy-haired young man, who had planted his feet and was swinging back. The third man—Jakel's companion from the hotel encounter, Meg thought but wasn't sure—was bouncing around like a gadfly or maybe a referee. Now he lunged forward as if to separate the other two and succeeded only in bumping Jakel's opponent and knocking him off balance. Suddenly Jakel exploded in a flurry of hard punches to his opponent's head and followed with a straight-armed, battering-ram blow to the belly that bent the other man nearly double.

He hung in midair for an instant, as if dangling from a giant hand that gripped the back of his belt; then, feet tangled in those of Jakel's friend, he went down. Jakel delivered a thudding kick to the fallen man's ribs, and the third man, seeming to stumble forward, brought his boot sharply against the unprotected head.

Several men moved forward from the watching crowd, one of them calling, "Okay, enough now." As people shifted, Meg got a glimpse of Ruthie Jakel, one hand gripping her son's arm and the other covering her mouth.

Then there was a uniform, a young woman who had to be a deputy sheriff. As Jakel landed another vicious kick with his pointy-toed boot, she swung her baton and caught him on the right shoulder. "Knock it off! Right now!"

Jakel turned and grabbed at the baton, but she was quicker, rapping the side of his head lightly and then stepping away. "Quit it. Now."

"All right!"

This crow of satisfaction from her daughter was followed by a deeper-voiced "Yeah!" that brought Meg's glance around for a moment. Katy, hands on Sara's shoulders, stood beside somebody—ah, the round-faced teenaged boy from the second-home group, the one with the respect for history.

The man on the ground was curled tight, arms over his head; Meg could see the lower half of his face, and it was bloody. Jakel hesitated, muttering something Meg couldn't make out; his friend, who had moved well clear of the action, folded his arms on his chest and watched in silence. Ruthie was backing slowly away, hand still over her mouth; now she turned and disappeared with her son into the dusk. Not very sisterly, thought Meg.

"Back off," said the deputy, shifting her baton to her left hand as she laid her right palm against her holstered pistol. "Way off."

"Well, what the fuck," snarled Jakel. He moved to stand beside his friend, and a woman came from the crowd to kneel beside the man on the ground.

"Names," said the deputy.

"Hey, honey, what's *your* name?" Jakel's friend had a gap-toothed grin full of good spirits.

"Deputy Sheriff Garcia," she replied, "and I already got a call in for backup. Names."

"Marv Jakel," said Jakel sullenly. "And this here's—"

"Dick Williams," said the gap-toothed man. "Just a friend, ma'am, trying to keep two guys from hurting each other."

"And that's my baby brother, Chuckie Jakel, on the ground there," said Jakel with a twitch of his mouth probably meant as a grin. "This is a family matter, lady. Ain't nobody gonna press any charges here."

"It's Deputy Sheriff," snapped Garcia. She transferred the stick to her right hand again, backed off a few steps, and turned to look at the injured man.

It was Lauren who knelt beside him, Meg saw now with surprise. He had uncoiled himself and lay on his back, one leg bent up. Lauren was wiping blood from his face and murmuring to him something Meg couldn't hear.

"Sir, are you all right?" asked the deputy. "Do you want to come to Alturas with me, to the hospital? To make a complaint?"

"No. No thanks." He rolled onto his side and then pushed himself into a sitting position, leaning against Lauren. "I'll be okay in a minute." He was a version of his brother and sister shaped by a more generous hand, Meg thought, broader of face and shoulder, with well-set dark-lashed eyes and thick brown hair that curled. A nice-looking young man, or he would be when not bloody.

"Lauren!" Aunt Frances's voice was imperious. "Come up from there at once. Your son is exhausted and needs you to take him home."

As Marv Jakel and Dick Williams faded back from the crowd and then turned in rapid departure, Lauren got to her feet and came toward Meg. "Meg, will you please take everybody home?"

"I can, of course, but don't you think—"

"Lauren, I forbid you to do this!" snapped her aunt.

"Chuck is in no condition to drive. I'm going to take him home. Be good, Johnny, and Mommy will see you in a while." She reached out to stroke the baby's head before turning away.

"Lauren!" This, from Frances, was almost a wail.

"I'll probably be late, Aunt Frances. Just put the children to bed. Don't wait up; go to bed yourselves. I'll see you tomorrow."

· 8 ·

"Do you know that Marv Jakel guy?"

Katy, who had hoped to see the rat-faced man arrested or at least whapped another time or two by the lady deputy, kept her gaze on the departing figures for another moment and then turned to the boy standing beside her. "I ran into him once. He's a creep, and a killer."

His round face lengthened in surprise, and she felt she should explain. "He shot some wolves that an old lady was taking care of, and she died—of fright, I guess. So he went to jail."

"Oh, I think I heard about that," he said with a nod. "My name is Adam Kingsley. I've been living out at Goose Lake Heights for about six months, but I don't think I've seen you before."

"I'm Katy Halloran. I'm from Port Silva, out on the coast, and my mother and I are visiting at the Macrae ranch. My mom was Mrs. Cavalier's teacher a long time ago."

"I guess you came by way of Wolf Haven," he noted. "That's a new tee shirt, better than mine from last year."

"Yeah, we did, we took the tour twice. Isn't that a great place? I want to work there someday." She inspected him, a slightly pudgy-looking guy in broad-bottomed running shoes, baggy cotton pants, and a checked shirt worn open over a tee shirt. He was shorter than she was, like most boys her age; his face was ordinary except for big, light-colored eyes, maybe gray, with really long lashes.

She looked again at his tee shirt, expecting a wolf head but seeing only big letters. "E.R.O.P. What's that?"

"That's a group I'm just starting to organize. Eee-rop."

"What's it for? What does it mean?"

He dropped his voice half an octave and said, slowly and solemnly, "Equal Rights for Other Predators."

"Other—which other?"

"Other than man, the most successful predator of all."

"Hey, I like it! Can I join?"

"Sure. I bet there are Cokes left in those barrels. Let's get a couple, and I'll tell you what my plans are so far."

"Okay. Oh, wait. Where. . . ?" Katy felt a flutter of panic as she realized Sara was no longer beside her, panic that subsided when she saw that the little girl had joined Meg and Aunt Frances. "Right, I'm really thirsty."

Chin high and lips pressed tight, Frances Macrae voiced no further protest as Lauren helped Chuck Jakel to his feet and led him off, one arm around him in support. No one else said anything, either, and no one offered assistance. Then a child's weary cry broke the spell and set people into motion.

Meg cradled Lauren's half-asleep son and watched with dismay and a touch of admiration as the entwined pair faded into twilight gloom on their way to Lauren's truck. The emotional undercurrents surging around the churchyard were mostly unreadable to Meg the outlander, but she was quite sure that her friend had just pulled a load of trouble down on her curly red head.

Her own personal little tableau here—confused woman with children—didn't seem to be attracting any attention. Ranchers and townspeople were leaving, several of them pausing briefly beside Frances Macrae to murmur good-byes, or perhaps condolences. Frances replied with a brief nod to each speaker; then, as the flow around her thinned, she squared her shoulders and set off for the road and presumably the car, step a bit unsteady but head still high.

Meg glanced down at Sara, who looked almost asleep on her feet. "Sara, go with your aunt. I'll get Katy."

Sara trudged off obediently, and Meg scanned the yard for a moment before spotting her daughter. "Katy? Come on, it's time to go."

Katy said something to the boy she'd been talking to, then came across the grass at a trot. "Mom, there's this kid I met, he's been to Wolf Haven, too. We're having a Coke and talking."

"I see that. But we have to go; Aunt Frances is worn out, and the children are sleepy."

"See, he, Adam, has a car. He thought maybe I could stay for a while—it's not really late—and he could bring me home later."

Meg straightened, baby and all, and looked down at her daughter, at the wide-eyed, smiling face. "Oh, good one. Unknown person, car, nighttime, strange town—you must think your old mom is slipping, kid."

"Mom!" Her complaint was only mildly beyond the perfunctory; this was mostly a try-on. "He's a nice guy, I'll introduce you."

"Katy, I am much too tired. Just tell him . . . oh, I don't know what. Whatever. But come on."

"Meg?" It was Abby Fowler, laying a hand on Meg's arm. "I'm staying to help Pastor Harrington button things up here. I can bring Katy home when I leave in maybe half an hour; the Macrae place is right on my way."

"Mom? Please?"

"Well." Meg looked toward her car, where Frances was easing herself into the front and Sara climbing into the back. "Thanks, Abby. Katy?"

"I'll watch. I'll be absolutely all ready to go whenever Mrs. Fowler is."

"Okay. Abby, plan to come in for a glass of wine. I'm going to need one, and it's a lot more fun with company."

Johnny Cavalier, finally accepting the fact that his mother wouldn't be summoned by even his loudest cries, batted away his great-aunt's encircling arms and flung himself to the floor in his toy corner, where he continued to sob as if his heart were broken. Meg handed Sara a glass of milk into which she had stirred chocolate syrup and then turned to Frances, who looked as though she needed someone to hold *her*.

"Frances, don't worry," she began, and bit her tongue against further platitudes like "Lauren's a big girl" or "Lauren will be all right." She wasn't at all sure that either remark was true.

"Would you like me to make you a pot of tea?" she asked instead.

"Thank you, that would be nice." Frances shivered and hugged herself. "And we should turn the heat up. In fact," she added, pushing herself up from her seat at the kitchen table, "I'm going to go put my warm robe on. And just stretch out on my bed and listen to my tapes for a while."

"That sounds like a fine idea," said Meg heartily. "And I'll bring the tea when it's ready."

"You're very kind." Frances picked up her cane and moved slowly, not toward the hall and her bedroom at the front of the house but toward the living room. She returned in a few moments with the cut-glass brandy decanter in her free hand and had nearly reached the door to the hall when she turned, braced herself on her cane, and met Meg's gaze directly for the first time since leaving the church.

"We mustn't let Sam find out."

"Oh. No, of course not."

Meg prepared a pot of Earl Grey tea, took it in to Frances, and was trying to decide what approach to use with the still-sobbing baby when she heard a car pull up. Please God, she said silently, eyes ceilingward; a moment later Katy and Abby Fowler came in the front door and quickly through to the kitchen.

"Wow, Mom. What're you doing to that poor little kid?"

Johnny's head came up at the sound of her voice. With a hoarse cry of "Keeee!" he rolled to his feet and charged across the room, to wrap himself around Katy's legs and howl piteously. When she picked him up, he flung one arm around her neck, laid his head down on her shoulder, and stuck a thumb in his mouth.

"Now you'll have to hold him for hours," observed Sara sleepily. "And you better watch out, 'cause he bites."

"Could you, Katy, for just a while?" asked Meg. "There's a rocking chair in his room."

Katy departed with no more protest than a mild roll of her eyes, Sara following. Meg sighed, went to the sink to splash water on her face, and turned to greet Abby Fowler. "Lady, I am very, *very* glad to see you. White or red?"

"I'd say the only way to keep Sam from finding out is to get a vow of silence from more than two hundred people," Meg said to Abby a short time later, after repeating Frances Macrae's departing remark. "Do you suppose Pastor Harrington wields that kind of power?"

Abby shook her head before taking a sip from her second glass of wine. A Modoc County native who had lived away for many years, she was direct, friendly, and probably closer to Meg's age than Lauren's. The two of them had had an instant rapport, so much so that Meg had decided to set discretion aside in favor of getting some information. If she was in the middle of a potential conflagration here, she wanted to know who might be holding the matches.

Still, she tossed a glance in the direction of Frances's bedroom and cautioned herself to keep her voice low. "It was clear to me tonight that Frances Macrae is not alone in her dislike of the Jakel family."

"My father, God rest his honest soul, said that every community has its Jakels—people you don't mess with because the resulting trouble just isn't worth it." Abby Fowler sighed and stared into the fire Meg had built to take the chill off the big living room. "Object publicly to the Jakels' poaching or petty-thieving or their habit of letting their cows wander onto other folks' grass, you might find your cat dead on your front step, maybe your calves sick from bad feed. Or your barn burned; they were blamed for that once.

"Of course," she added, "that was a long time ago, when Marv senior was alive and Verna was healthy."

"What became of Marv senior?"

"Mm. I'd moved away by then, but my mother wrote me, sometime in the mid-seventies, that he'd died in an accident; got careless going over a fence with his shotgun, or so it appeared. He was a bad-tempered drunk, and even his own family didn't like him much."

"Lovely." Meg got up and poked at the fire, then went to look out the front window; with no light and no movement on the road, the driveway was simply a black tunnel to nowhere. "Christ, it's almost ten o'clock," she muttered. "Why doesn't that idiot girl come home?" She turned and strode across the room, to refill her wine glass and offer more to Abby, who declined with a shake of her head.

"Right, you're driving. And I wish I were. The other night Lauren said that the Jakels were not all the same, not all that bad." Meg paused in her pacing and looked hard at Abby. "Do you think she was talking about Chuck?"

Abby frowned and laced her hands together under her chin. With her small bone structure, fine pale skin, and fair hair, she looked a fragile twenty-five at most. "I don't know. Those people, Lauren and her brother and the three Jakel kids, were all close in age, and they lived on adjoining ranches. Out in the country, you tend to hang out with whoever is your age and lives less than three school-bus stops away.

"But the fact is, they were still in grade school when I graduated and left town. And I didn't get back here often; first I worked to put my husband through law school, and then I had to stay in the Bay Area to maintain shared custody of my son."

"Ah. I'm sorry."

"That I'm divorced? Don't be. Like the Jakels, lawyers believe in doing whatever you can get away with and then denying anything that can't be proved. This is not what any sensible person wants to live with." She grinned faintly and held her glass out. "Maybe just a touch, after all.

"Anyway, my son, Chris, went east to college last year, so I came back here; my parents are dead, and what's left of the ranch belongs to me. But I work hard, at home, and I don't get out and about much, where the gossip is."

And she was an honorable person, this small, clear-eyed woman, and didn't like gossip. No more did Meg, generally, but here in Stony Creek she was being expected to function like a member of the family without having the least idea of what the family was up to. She considered saying as much, then decided it wasn't necessary.

Abby sighed. "I think most people here would call Chuck Jakel the best of a bad lot. He went to junior college for a while at least. He got married and settled in Susanville and actually worked for a living."

"In construction," said Meg, remembering the panel truck and then wishing she hadn't. "He didn't look very prosperous tonight."

"Pastor Harrington told me that Chuck's marriage broke up and he, Chuck, is trying to get himself together and attempt to gain at least partial custody of his two little girls. He came back here to Stony Creek this past winter and has been living on the ranch." She paused, frowning. "If a basic recluse like me knows all this about Chick Jakel, you can bet Lauren does, too. And Meg, she's such a soft touch, an absolute sucker for a story like his."

Meg acknowledged this judgment with a nod. "His brother and sister don't seem terribly sympathetic to him," she said, remembering the look on Marv Jakel's face as he swung his boot into Chuck's ribs.

Abby shrugged. "I think the ranch belongs outright to Verna, and I've heard people say that Chuck is Verna's current favorite. Probably Marv and Ruthie are afraid that she'll leave everything to him. Apparently she is seriously ill."

"Frances says she has terminal cancer and can hardly get

out of bed." Meg remembered the look on Frances Macrae's face as she delivered this diagnosis. "Abby, Frances has more than a general dislike and distaste for the Jakels. She hates them."

"Oh, dear, I'm such a poor source of information. What you should do is find someone who was born here and stayed. I think there was a land problem way back. I think the Jakel ranch originally belonged to the Macraes, three or four generations ago."

"I suppose that might be motive enough," said Meg. "My family has never had any land, nor much of anything else; dynastic outrage is a bit beyond my personal grasp."

"Mine too," said Abby cheerfully. "I can't understand wanting to own anything more than what you can use."

"Mm." Meg's thoughts were again on the absent Lauren. She had returned here to live right after Johnny was born; Chuck had been here perhaps six months. Lauren was unhappy in Stony Creek, and vulnerable, but she did love her husband, and she did try to please her aunt. Meg decided that Lauren's connection with Chuck Jakel had to reach back to her earlier years here, her adolescence. Only that seemed sufficient explanation for tonight's defiant behavior.

"I suppose people in rural areas aren't quite so, um, puritanical as they used to be," Meg said, half to herself.

Abby chuckled as she set her empty glass aside and got to her feet. "You don't think so? Let me tell you, I would think twice—three times—before publicly scooping a handsome, injured young man up in my arms and trotting off into the dark with him. And I'm not even married."

After Abby had left, Meg made a circuit of the house to check door locks and occupants. Upstairs, Johnny was asleep, rump in the air and thumb in his mouth. Katy was asleep in the little armless rocker beside the crib; Meg woke her, or anyway got her up on her feet, and guided her into their room and into bed.

Sara, Meg discovered after a moment's fright, was asleep too, not in her lavender-gingham and white-eyelet canopied bed but on the rug beside it, a ratty old quilt wrapped around her like a sleeping bag.

Downstairs, Frances Macrae was propped against the headboard of her spooled bed, eyes closed. She still wore her Walkman headset, and the ruffled lamp on the bedside table cast a soft light over teapot, teacup, and the nearly empty brandy decanter. Meg considered stepping into the room to extinguish the lamp but decided not to risk waking the elderly woman. She looked warm and comfortable in her quilted robe and would probably wake sometime during the night, anyway.

In the living room again, wide awake herself, she poured another glass of wine and poked up the fire. Her book was in her room upstairs, but Faulkner did not strike her as a suitable companion to her edgy, prickly mood. The books on the shelves here were largely nonfiction: essays on current events and politics, biography, natural history, wildlife biology. The only fiction was either Russian or French, the latter untranslated; French had been Lauren's college minor. No mysteries or contemporary novels, no Victorians. Bah, humbug.

Meg made another circuit of the house, with a stop by the kitchen telephone. At home in Port Silva the machine answered, and she hung up without leaving the rude message that sprang to her mind. Where the hell was Vince, anyway?

She knew where Vince was, of course; either at work or at his mother's. But where the hell was Lauren, as the hour crept closer to midnight? Meg unlocked the front door and stepped out into cold darkness pricked by cold stars and no other light except that from the house behind her. Her car and Frances's Jeep were there to use, the latter a four-wheel drive; if she knew the area just a little better she could go looking, find the thoughtless, silly woman and bring her home.

She heaved an exasperated sigh and returned to the house. She didn't know where Lauren was, but she knew what she was doing, knew it with near certainty and a small, sharp bite of envy.

· 9 ·

Morning sunlight was coming at her from the wrong direction; had Vince turned the bed around while she was away? Meg squinched her eyes tight shut and slid lower into the weightless tunnel of her down comforter. No. Not her comforter but a heavier cover, a pieced quilt.

But definitely morning, and something had awakened her. She lifted her head to listen and heard a thump. Thump, pause, thump, pause. Nearby.

Then a voice: "Mama?" Meg groaned softly and made herself sit up. Johnny was awake, still in his crib, rocking it rhythmically against the wall as she'd seen him do the day before. As he had been doing now for some time, she thought. Which meant that Lauren had come in very late and was sleeping too deeply to hear her son's cries. Or that Lauren hadn't come home at all.

"Mama!"

For one mean, selfish moment Meg considered waking Katy, who'd been getting plenty of healthful sleep while her mother sat up until nearly one A.M. drinking wine and reading Russian short stories. But she had to get up anyway, right now, to go to the bathroom. And she had to find out right now about Lauren.

Lauren's room was empty, her bed unrumpled, and Meg could hear no sounds from the lower part of the house, detect no comforting smell of coffee. With a sigh she opened another door and said, "Hi, Tiger," to Johnny, whose face brightened only briefly at her appearance.

"Mama? Kee?"

"Not this time, little kid," she told him, and dropped the crib side and peeled him out of his sodden nightclothes

71

before he had time to organize himself for a real protest. "Good boy," she said. "Good Johnny. Oatmeal and toast and all that stuff, as soon as we get *these* pinned. And *these* snapped. And this pulled over that big curly head. Okay."

Downstairs was warm, because she'd remembered to set the thermostat clock the night before. She slid the baby into his high chair, found a banana in a bowl on the counter, half-peeled it, and handed it to him. The front door was still locked but not bolted, she found; in the graveled area before the house were her Honda and the Jeep. No pickup.

She closed the door and moved back down the hall, to Frances Macrae's bedroom door. Finding it slightly ajar, she pushed it wider and peered in. Frances was in the bed, snoring gently, the covers pulled so high that only a fringe of gray hair showed against the pillow; her pink robe lay across the foot of the bed. Meg pulled the door shut and hurried back to the kitchen.

"Oh, little kid. Where the hell is your mommy?"

Johnny lifted a banana-smeared face to give her a wide-eyed look that said he'd caught her feeling, if not her exact meaning. "Never mind," she said quickly. "Let's get you fed. Now where would I be if I were a box of oatmeal?"

She found oatmeal and pan, coffee for the pot, dishes and cups, all the while keeping up an inane running chatter at the little boy. Oatmeal she spooned into his mouth; toast she broke in two, one piece for each hand; milk she put in a cup with a lid that he promptly pried off. She cut an orange in quarters, as she'd seen Lauren do yesterday, put the pieces on his tray, and watched him suck on one while she poured herself a cup of coffee.

"Where's my mommy?" Sara stood in the doorway, dressed in jeans and tee shirt, red curls a wild tangle around her white face.

"Good morning, Sara. Can I get you some breakfast?"

"I need her to comb my hair. She *always* combs my hair." Sara's outthrust lower lip was trembling, and her round, blue eyes glistened with tears that would spill any minute.

"Sara, I . . . don't know where your mommy is, but I'm sure, that is I hope, she'll be home soon." Meg crossed the room to crouch in front of the little girl and bring their eyes more or less level. "I know you want to cry, but if you do, it will set your brother off and we'll both have to listen to him."

Sara palmed moisture from her eyes and sniffed, tossing a look at her brother. "He's a pig."

"He's pretty messy," Meg agreed. "Do you want oatmeal?"

"Yes, please." As Meg got to her feet, Sara marched to the table, transferred her great-aunt's cane from the back of her own tall chair to another nearby, then climbed up and sat. "With brown sugar and raisins."

As time crawled by, Meg drank coffee, and played with Johnny, and talked with Sara, and drank more coffee. Surely, she thought, we should report Lauren missing. But not me, I can't do that. Frances should do that.

Frances slept—or pretended to, thought Meg in a suspicious moment. But there was really no reason for her to get up; she was probably depressed and possibly hung over, and she wasn't strong enough to handle the children anyway.

Katy slept, for sure. Meg drank more coffee and wondered whom she could call. Abby Fowler, maybe? The minister, Pastor Harrington? But Sara insisted on dogging Meg's footsteps, following her even to the door of the bathroom. Sara shouldn't hear a conversation about her mother.

Just before eleven A.M.—as Meg was sure she couldn't sing another song nor read another story nor make one more truck go "Vrooom!"—there was the sound of a real engine outside, and the crunch of tires on gravel. Meg smoothed her hair with her palms and tried to will her face into a calm, forgiving expression. "You've scared us all to death, you silly bitch!" would not be nice for Sara to hear, although Lauren certainly had earned it.

The doorbell. Had she lost her keys? Meg hurried to open

the door and found herself facing a hefty man of about her own height who wore a brown uniform and an official face. Oh my God, I cannot do this, she thought, and turned to the child at her heels.

"Sara, why don't you go upstairs and wake Katy."

"Okay!"

Meg watched the little girl until she was out of sight on the staircase before turning to the uniformed man. Same uniform as that worn last night by the lady cop, but this man was something more than just a deputy.

"Undersheriff Ron Ortmann, ma'am, Modoc County Sheriff's Department. I'd like to talk with Mrs. Cavalier, Lauren Cavalier?"

Meg propped a shoulder against the doorpost, knees suddenly weak as her vision of a twisted and bloody highway scene faded. "Oh. Please come in." It wasn't until he had followed her into the kitchen that she realized she didn't know what to say to him. Frances would have to handle this.

"I'm sorry, but I'm just a . . . I'm Margaret Halloran, visiting from out of town. Lauren isn't here at the moment, but I'll get her aunt for you, Frances Macrae."

"Yes ma'am, I'd appreciate that."

"Frances?" When there was no response, Meg put a hand where she thought the older woman's shoulder might be and then sprang back as Frances Macrae rolled over in a flurry of blankets and sat bolt upright.

"What . . . ? Who . . . ?" Eyes so wide that white showed all around, Frances stared at Meg as if she'd never seen her before.

"Frances, it's me, Meg Halloran."

"Meg . . . oh. Of course. Meg."

"Frances, someone from the sheriff's department is here asking to see Lauren. I thought you should talk with him."

"Lauren. Where . . . ? Do you mean that sluttish niece of

mine hasn't managed to drag herself home yet? What time is it?"

Meg simply stared at the furious old face, and Frances snapped, "Well?"

"It's, uh, nearly eleven, Saturday morning."

"Saturday. Yes." She put a hand over her eyes for a long moment, then sighed and looked around the room and finally back at Meg. "All right. I'll get up and get dressed."

It was perhaps ten minutes before she appeared in the kitchen in jeans and a sweater, her face washed clean of sleep and of any trace of anger, her hair neatly combed. "Ronald Ortmann, how are you? And how is Jerry? Ron is a Modoc County boy, from Cedarville," she said to Meg, "and his youngest son has just won a full scholarship to Princeton."

He had risen from the table when Frances came in, and now he drew himself up to near attention, sucking in the belly that strained the buttons of his uniform shirt. "He's real excited, ma'am, counting the days and wishing he could leave tomorrow. Thank you for asking."

"He's a fine boy, and I know you're proud of him. Now, how may I help you?"

"Miss Macrae, I'd like to speak with your niece. Can you tell me where she is, or when she'll be home?"

Frances's grande-dame mask slipped, to reveal confusion and uncertainty. "I . . . perhaps it was a dream. I thought I heard her come home in the night. Are you sure, Meg, that she's not in her bed?"

"I'm sure." Meg pulled out a chair for the older woman and, once she was seated, put a mug of coffee in front of her.

"I can't understand it." Frances reached out a shaking hand, then thought better of it and used both hands to pick up the mug. "Lauren is so very dependable. This is not like her at all."

Ortmann stood even straighter and took a deep breath. "Miss Macrae, I've been told by several people, one of them a deputy sheriff, that Mrs. Cavalier left Stony Creek last night with Charles Jakel."

"Chuck Jakel, yes; you surely know him," Frances said in tones approaching her normal sharpness. "He'd been injured in a fight. She was kind enough to drive him home."

"But she never came home herself afterward?"

"Apparently not. But we all went to bed; she told us not to wait up. Sheriff Ortmann, I must insist on knowing why you people are interested in my niece. Is there someone you think—has there been an accident?"

"We don't know, ma'am. What we do know is that somebody blew Chuck Jakel away last night or early this morning. All we've been able to find out so far, the last time he was seen alive was when he drove off with your niece."

· 10 ·

"Blew away?" Frances pronounced the words with a kind of precise incomprehension, three syllables apparently as meaningless to her as they were for the moment to Meg.

"Yes ma'am." Just let fly with a load of number-two shot that caught him right in . . ."

"Hush!" Meg spoke so fiercely that Ortmann simply stared at her with his mouth open.

"I think it's time for children to be outside playing," she said in what she hoped was an ordinary voice as she moved to scoop Johnny up from his clutter of toys. The little boy was round of eye and unnaturally still, clearly aware of the tension around him. Not yet very verbal, he was in Meg's opinion very bright; it would be indecent to let him hear this bloody tale. About his mother, although the man hadn't said that exactly, had he? Had said, "blew away Chuck Jakel," not . . .

Sheriff Ortmann's "Uh, Mrs. . . . . Halloran, is it?" caught at her; she stopped to stare at him, clutching the squirming little boy tight.

Ortmann's face was a painful pink. "I'm real sorry," he said, and cast a quick look at Frances, who was making hard work of getting her coffee mug to her bloodless lips. "But I'd appreciate it if you'd stay, ma'am. What I'll do, I'll call in Deputy Garcia to help us out."

She was trying to breathe deeply but evenly, to not transfer any more tension to the child. This pink-faced man had come here, she remembered now, asking to *talk* with Lauren. Who thus had apparently not been dealt a load of what was it, number-two shot, in the night or early morning. She inspected this assumption for faulty logic.

"Mrs. Halloran?"

Logic, yes. She looked at his sweating face and read him as reluctant to be left alone with Frances Macrae, worried about her physical frailty or wary of her family clout. Or both. "Never mind; I'll get my daughter," she said.

Katy, bless her, came down at once with Sara and hustled both children out into the sunshine, pausing only long enough to ask for and receive a cup of very milky coffee. As the door closed behind her, Ortmann gestured Meg to a seat at the table, but she paused behind a chair, hands gripping its back.

"Sheriff Ortmann, you said Chuck Jakel. Was killed," she added. "What about Lauren? Is there any indication that she, that anyone else, was hurt?"

"There's a whole lot of blood, ma'am. And other stuff, too, of course, spread all over the dirt and gravel. We can't be sure it all came from Jakel. Not yet, anyway."

"Oh." Meg pulled the chair out and sat.

"But there's only the one body, you understand." He seated himself at the table and took a small notebook from his shirt pocket.

"Yes, of course we understand," said Frances, who had regained some of her color as well as her combativeness. "But the person you should be interrogating is Marv Jakel. Perhaps no one has told you that he had a public fight with his brother just last night. And the man is a convicted killer, after all."

"I understand how you feel, Miss Macrae, but—"

"Last night, Sheriff Ortmann, my niece performed a kind deed for a person in distress—inappropriately, in my view, but I know she meant well. And then somehow, somewhere, she ran into trouble. I think you should be out looking for her instead of pestering a tired old lady."

As the policeman assured Frances that he had already set in motion a search for Lauren and her truck, Meg managed to push aside images of blood-drenched gravel to follow her own train of thought, follow Lauren last night. She took

Chuck Jakel home, wherever home was, but probably it wasn't his mother's house, not while that sister and maybe even brother Marv and his buddy were staying there. Lauren took him somewhere, intending to stay with him for a while at least; that's what she, Meg, had thought last night, and so had Frances, although she surely would not say so.

"Where was he killed?" Meg asked suddenly, provoking startled stares and a moment's silence.

"He'd been staying out at this shack about half a mile from the main house." Ortmann was not pleased at being quizzed by an outlander. "Little place Marv senior built for himself a long time ago. His sister, Ruth, went out there this morning to talk to him, to Chuck, and found what was left of him laying there in the dirt, maybe ten yards from the door."

Meg opened her mouth and then closed it.

"Nobody else there or nearby, no blood and no signs of a struggle in the cabin," said the policeman. "But Jakel was naked. And the mattress had what sure looked to be fresh, um, semen stains," he said, averting his eyes from the elderly and presumably maiden lady sitting across from him.

"Ronald Ortmann, I resent what you're suggesting!" Frances snapped.

"Ma'am, I'm not suggesting anything. It's pretty clear a woman was there. Maybe we'll find prints, except there isn't much furniture in the place. What we did find was a few long red hairs."

"My niece is not the only redheaded woman in Modoc County."

"No ma'am. But she's the only one we know of that drove off from Stony Creek Community Church last night with Chuck Jakel. Look," he went on quickly, before the women had gathered breath to respond, "I'm willing to admit that Mrs. Cavalier ain't somebody I myself would think of right off as a murder suspect: well-liked young married woman from a fine local family, regular churchgoer, heard folks say she's a real good mother. Now, Sheriff Vukovich didn't grow up here in the county, so he might not see things from quite the same angle. But one thing I do know he'll agree with me on, what we got to do is find Mrs. Cavalier and talk to her."

Undersheriff Ortmann was somewhat smarter than he looked, Meg decided; at least his folksy little speech seemed to have mollified Frances for the moment. As he went on to question the older woman about Lauren's friends and resources, Meg clenched her teeth and tried to imagine a best-case scenario. Maybe they had sex, and afterward Lauren was struck by remorse and ran off. Had no knowledge of the murder and would turn up any moment and be horrified.

Ortmann's words broke in. "Now, about last night: You ladies both here all last night, were you?"

Meg's "Yes" and Frances's "Of course" sounded together.

"Either of you disturbed by anything at all during the night?"

"I was awake until about one, but I didn't hear anything," said Meg. "Then I went to bed and slept straight through until six-thirty." But a shotgun would have wakened her, she thought with a shiver. Had a shotgun, had murder, wakened Lauren from postcoital languor? And then what?

Frances was sounding embarrassed: ". . . had a bit more brandy with my evening tea than usual. I'm afraid I slept very heavily all night. Until you arrived, in fact."

"Okay. Now it's real important to pin down just what happened yesterday evening before Mrs. Cavalier and Chuck Jakel drove off; I believe Sheriff Vukovich himself is over talking to the Jakel family about that right now. As I understand it, you ladies were both at this meeting in Stony Creek last evening?"

"Yes," said Frances.

"And there was a fistfight there between Chuck Jakel and his brother, Marv?"

That pulled Meg back from her own painful speculation. "And his brother's friend," she told him.

Ortmann's stubby lashes blinked rapidly for a moment.

"Only mention I got of the friend, people thought he was trying to break things up."

Meg cast her mind's eye back to the scene in the churchyard and saw again the man's supposed clumsiness, saw his boot connect with the fallen man's head. "That wasn't my impression. I thought that was an act and he was really helping Marv."

"Yes ma'am," said Ortmann in neutral tones. "And what was the cause of that fight?"

"I have no idea."

"Jakels don't need a reason for behaving like heathens," Frances stated.

"How did the fight end?"

"It was broken up by Deputy Garcia," said Meg.

"And what did it seem to you was the condition of Chuck Jakel at that time?"

Reluctantly, she pulled that image into focus. "He was . . . conscious, but bleeding and clearly in pain. He'd been punched hard and knocked down and then kicked several times. He had to be helped to his feet."

"That the way you saw it, Miss Macrae?" the policeman asked.

"I didn't watch the fight itself. He did have to be helped up."

"By Lauren Cavalier?"

Frances sighed. "Yes."

"And she told you she was going to take him home?"

"As I've tried to make clear, my niece is hopelessly soft-hearted. She spent her childhood nursing injured animals, rescuing birds from cats. Pointlessly, of course; they always died." She pressed her lips tight for a moment. "Yes, Sheriff Ortmann, that's what she said."

"Did Mrs. Cavalier know Chuck Jakel well?"

Recalling the tender line of Lauren's body as she helped Chuck Jakel limp off to the truck, Meg was sure she had known him very well indeed.

"I assume she knew him when they were very young," said

Frances crisply. "Lauren and her brother attended Stony Creek grammar school along with the other local children. The summer after Lauren finished eighth grade, my brother and his wife died in an accident, and Lauren and Bobby came to Arizona to live with me."

"And then you moved back here."

"Three years later, with Bobby. Lauren stayed in Tucson to finish high school, went on to college, married a man she loves very much, and traveled with him and had two children."

Meg felt this was a tale made of selected truths, like a picket fence with gaps where stakes were missing. Frances had omitted, for instance, the fact that she and her two teenaged charges had spent their summers at the ranch; surely the local "bad-girl" reputation Lauren had railed against Thursday afternoon was not the kind that resulted from grammar-school pranks. And there was the abortion, performed just before Lauren was about to begin her senior year in high school and just after one of those ranch summers.

"I remember maybe fifteen, sixteen years back," Ortmann was saying, "I was working over in the west county at the time, at Newell, but I heard there was some bad trouble here with kids and drugs and like that. Seems to me there was Jakels involved, and wasn't there some Macraes too?"

Frances's chin quivered, and for the first time Meg saw tears well up in the faded brown eyes. "Not Lauren," she said almost sadly, and then paused to clear her throat. "She was in Arizona. It was Bobby, her brother. My nephew was a high-spirited and adventurous boy; the Jakels, Marvin and his sister and brother, were nothing but trash, but Bobby was always fascinated by them, and they used him. As to the incident you mention, no charges were ever brought against Bobby."

Oh, yeah, thought Meg. Dear Bobby was adventurous, while poor Lauren was too softhearted and easily led. Meg was developing a serious dislike for long-gone Bobby, and she wasn't at the moment absolutely crazy about Aunt Frances, either.

"Unh-huh," said the policeman. "Then when your nephew disappeared some years later, he was still pretty tight with some of the Jakels anyhow. And I believe you suggested at the time that they might have, uh, harmed him. So what about your niece, she feel that way too? Couldn't she maybe have had a grudge, all these years, against the family?"

"So she finally lured one of them off to kill him?" Frances gave a bitter little chuckle as she pulled a handkerchief from her sweater sleeve and wiped her eyes. "The problem with your theory, Sheriff, is that Lauren hated her brother. I think this stemmed from jealousy, mostly; Bobby was handsome and popular and she . . . wasn't. At any rate, she certainly would not have taken revenge on his behalf."

"I was working out of the office here ten years ago." Ortmann's voice was easy, but Meg thought his shoulders had tensed. "Mrs. Cavalier was in town at the time, and I talked to her. She never could give us any corroboration of her whereabouts at the time of her brother's disappearance."

"And neither could anyone else," said Frances sharply.

"Right, I know that. But suppose that now, after ten years, somebody remembered something, or was in need and threatened to tell something . . ."

"Or suppose Bobby came back for his own revenge," said Meg suddenly.

"Don't be ridiculous!" snapped Frances. "You know nothing at all about this."

Not much, certainly. And wished she knew less.

After watching the pair of them for a moment, Ortmann nodded, picked up his notebook, and tucked it into his shirt pocket. "One last thing I need to know, Miss Macrae. Does Mrs. Cavalier generally carry a shotgun in her truck?"

"No, of course not. She goes grocery shopping in that truck, takes her children places."

"But she knew how to use one, had access to one?"

Frances stood up from the table, feeling along the back of the chair next to hers until her fingers found her cane. "Lauren may be softhearted, but she's a ranch woman; of course she knows how to shoot. In fact, she killed an old, sick raccoon just a few days ago. And as for access, we must own five or six shotguns, and a couple of .22s, and my brother's .30-06, and . . . oh, Lord, I don't know what else. They're all in a locked cupboard in the tack room in the barn."

"I'd better have a look," said Ortmann.

"Of course. The keys hang on a nail in the barn—on the far side of the second stud to the left of the door." Frances stepped away from the table, leaning on her cane. "And you asked for a list of Lauren's credit cards; I'll get that. Then you'll have to excuse me. I have a dreadful headache. I'm going to take some aspirin and go back to bed."

"Katy, I really wish you wouldn't." Moving about in a fog of sleep deprivation and shock, Meg spoke with less than her usual decisiveness, and Katy pounced.

"Mom, I told you. Not everybody at camp last summer learned to be a good rider, but I did. And we all learned to take care of our horse; we had to do it every day for the whole month or we'd get sent home."

"I know, but—"

"I can saddle and bridle a horse. I know how to get on and off without help, how to stay on. I even know how to fall off without getting hurt."

"And suppose you fall off somewhere out there and don't know the way back to the house?"

"I'll stay on the trails Lauren showed me. I promise I won't go too far. I'll ride old pokey Daisy; even a bomb wouldn't spook her. Mom, I'm really tired of little kids and . . . all this weird stuff that's happening. I really need to get out of here and be by myself for a while, and I'm not old enough to drive!"

Katy was on the edge of tears, and if she fell over, Meg

would surely join her. That would be useful; the two of them could just sit down here in the dust and cry the afternoon away. "*Damn* but I wish we could go home!" Meg pounded a fist on the top rail of the corral, and the mare came ambling over to see what was up.

"Yeah, but we can't. Somebody has to take care of those kids, and Aunt Frances is a wreck. So what about it, Mom? Can I go?"

It wasn't safe, out there all alone on a half ton of basically stupid animal. "Promise to be careful? Promise to be back two hours from right now?" asked Meg, looking at her watch.

Katy checked her own watch, said "Promise!" and took three long strides in the direction of the barn before turning, pushing her fists into her jeans pockets, and drawing a deep, shaky breath. "Mom? What do you think really happened?"

"Oh, sweetie, I don't know."

"Lauren is . . . really nice. She wouldn't shoot anybody." When Meg made no reply, Katy swallowed and lifted her chin. "Unless he tried to rape her or something, then she might."

"I suppose she might."

"But if that's what happened, why didn't she come home?"

"She might be frightened."

"Because she blew away some asshole that tried to rape her? Boy, I wouldn't be scared. I'd be glad!"

Meg took two quick steps forward and reached out to wrap both arms around her daughter and pull her close. "No, you wouldn't," she murmured, tightening her grip as one of them shuddered, or maybe it was both. "Not to have killed somebody, especially somebody you'd known as a . . . friend. Believe me, Katy, you wouldn't. Now you'd better get going, kid," she added in lighter tones as she let go and stepped back. "Because your two hours are ticking away."

• 11 •

"Oh, wonderful! Yes, I can find it. Abby, I apologize for interrupting your work but you are saving my life. I'll see you in a few minutes."

Meg replaced the receiver and went to look for Frances Macrae. Earlier, while the children and Katy were eating lunch, Frances had stomped the porch from end to end and back again, muttering under her breath as she drove her cane hard against the wooden floor. Now Meg found her in the kitchen, staring fiercely at the teakettle as she waited for it to boil.

"Miserable slut. Miserable draggle-tailed slut. Just a bitch in heat, always has been, always will be. Damn her!"

Frances's fury, contained during the policeman's visit, had returned full force. At least, thought Meg, she had kept her voice low and her words indistinct until the children went down for their naps.

"How could she do this to Sam? And what will he do? Suppose he decides to take Johnny away from us?" she demanded, swinging around to stare with hot eyes at Meg. "He could do that, of course he could. Maybe he *should*."

"Maybe he should spend more time at home," said Meg.

"And he'll find out about this, he can't help but find out. Poor Sam."

And what about poor Lauren? A pox on Lord Sam and on this sad, silly old woman. Meg gave a moment's thought to emptying or locking the liquor cupboard but decided that she wouldn't be gone long enough for major drunkenness to occur. "Frances, I'm going for a drive, and Katy is out riding. Will you be all right here for a couple of hours?"

"Oh. Well, I suppose so. The babies are asleep. I'll just

make some tea and . . . " Her eyes filled with tears, and her face crumpled.

"Please forgive me," she whispered. "I'm too old for all this."

"I know," said Meg helplessly. She picked up her handbag and began to edge toward the door. "I'll be back by two-thirty or three. Is there anything I can get for you, in Stony Creek or Alturas?"

"No. Please, Meg. Old people get selfish and angry because the power is gone suddenly, before you've finished. You feel inside yourself like the same person, but then you try to bend, or to move quickly, or you accidentally catch sight of yourself in a mirror. Or worst of all, you notice that the person you're talking to is looking past you and nodding and maybe smiling but isn't hearing you at all."

She took a shaky breath. "I will face my Maker and his judgment finally, like everyone else; but until then I am still Frances Macrae, not some generic old woman to be tied into a wheelchair and tolerantly ignored."

"No, of course you're not."

"Hah," snorted Frances. "Never mind, it will happen to you too. You don't think so now, but you'll see."

"*Now* we're entitled to a beer," said Abby Fowler, opening the back door of her tall and somewhat ramshackle house to usher Meg into the kitchen. Almost an hour earlier, after one good look at her caller, she had offered sunscreen and a hike, "a little honest physical exertion to get rid of the bats and cobwebs."

"Beer, absolutely." Meg sank into a chair at the long pine table and wiped her sweating face. Hard walking at forty-five hundred feet had hit her in lungs and legs both. "I live my life at sea level," she said in explanation as Abby, barely winded, set two bottles of Sierra Nevada Pale Ale on the table.

"So did I, for twenty years. Took me months to get used to this again." Abby tossed colored pencils and a packet of yellow Post-Its atop a stack of typed pages, scooped the whole pile up from the table, and set it on a counter nearby.

"Abby, if you want to get back to work—"

"Nope. This idiot editor has decided to have a last-minute fit because my eleven-year-old heroine's single mom is thinking of letting her boyfriend move in. I can only deal with her dumb suggestions in thirty-minute bursts. Honestly, I think I'll give up this juvenile stuff and write a novel about grown-up people."

"Where would you expect to find models?"

"Good question," said Abby, shaking her curly, fair head.

Meg took a long pull on her beer bottle and considered possible grown-ups. Not Frances Macrae, who seemed to be regressing to childhood. Not poor Lauren. And she was none too sure about her own status; there had been times, lately, when Katy had seemed the more sensible.

"Frances Macrae is furious at Lauren for behaving like a slut and seems barely interested in what might have become of her since," Meg said, and took another drink of beer. "Undersheriff Ortmann thinks she might have killed Chuck Jakel because of a family grudge. What do you suppose people in town think?" Abby had heard of Chuck Jakel's death and Lauren Cavalier's disappearance before Meg's arrival; Abby thought it likely the entire eastern half of Modoc County had heard.

"I bought groceries this morning and stopped at the bakery and the gas station," said Abby. "Of the dozen people I heard talking about it, about half think Lauren shot Chuck Jakel to avoid rape; the other half think some other person, probably Marv Jakel, shot Chuck and abducted Lauren. There's one who thinks Lauren's long-lost brother Robert Macrae was that other person."

Apparently there were locals who didn't view Lauren as a slut but had no difficulty imagining Chuck—or any Jakel?—as a rapist. "Lauren is a big, strong woman," Meg said. "Chuck Jakel was a medium-sized man who'd just been beaten up pretty severely. I don't think she'd have had to shoot him to stop him."

Abby frowned. "But there was no sign of a struggle, according to what I heard."

"According to Ortmann, too. Abby, suppose she and Chuck made love, no rape involved. And then suppose he wanted her to—I don't know, pay him blackmail not to tell? Or leave her husband for him? My God, this sounds like trash melodrama."

"So does shotgunning somebody," said Abby. "Either before or after whatever the fact was."

Meg was envisioning Lauren, rescuer of baby birds, trying to run away from herself after such an act. Just thinking about it made her stomach clench. "Abby, what kind of person is Sam Cavalier?"

"A hunk," said Abby. Meg looked up and was surprised to see the smaller woman's cheeks redden.

"Not long after I came up here, I took part in an authors' night at the Alturas library, and Sam was the other author, the famous one. At the time I was . . . vulnerable. Available, I'm ashamed to say."

"So what happened?"

Abby shook her head. "Nothing. I . . . God, this is embarrassing. I arranged to run into him several times after that night, and I'm sure he had to realize what I was up to, but he just politely ignored the situation. Look, Meg, this is not the kind of thing I usually do."

"Did you think he was simply not attracted to small blondes? Or maybe just very devoted to his wife?"

"Neither. Oh, I believe he's devoted to Lauren; I've seen him with her and their children, and he's quite husband-and-fatherly. And of course I found out eventually that she's a very nice person and is crazy about him, so I'm glad I was rejected. No, I think he's not much interested in women, or in anything but his work."

"Well, I wish he'd for Christ's sake come *home* and get on

with his husband-and-father number!" Meg pushed her chair back and got up to pace the kitchen, her sneakers squeaking on the tile floor. "If Lauren is alive—and you realize, don't you, that if she was abducted, she's probably no longer alive? If she's alive, she's in terrible trouble. I'm a total outsider, the sheriff's people don't strike me as particularly capable, and Frances Macrae is just . . . unstrung."

"Frances doesn't know how to get in touch with Sam?" asked Abby.

"She says not." Meg propped her backside against the sink counter and crossed her arms on her chest. "Somebody in town really thought Bobby Macrae had come back?"

"Oh, sure. Didn't you see the *Messenger*? I had a copy, but I'm pretty sure I threw it out."

"Last week's, with the story about the tenth anniversary of his disappearance? I saw it. And Lauren told me about the television program. She says he's dead. Frances says he's alive, but I don't think she really believes that."

"My Aunt Rose says people as mean as Robert Macrae don't do the world the favor of dying." Abby flushed again as she spoke, running a small, ink-stained hand through her already rumpled curls. "See, I've been doing some snooping after all, pumping my mom's younger sister; she lived in Alturas until three years ago, when she and Uncle Jay decided to retire to Sonoma. This is in the nature of research, you understand."

"I guess your Aunt Rose knew the Macrae family?"

"Sure. She says John Macrae, Lauren's father, was a hard man who married a silly wife. He apparently liked Lauren, who adored him and was a biddable kind of kid and looked like his side of the family."

"But he didn't like his son?"

"Aunt Rose says Bobby was too pretty, too lazy, and too sneaky for John. Bobby lied a lot, too, and got whipped for it fairly often, according to what Bobby's mom told her lady friends. She, the mom, worshiped her beautiful boy and was seriously disappointed in her gawky, red-haired daughter."

"Sounds sad and unpleasant, but not that unusual," said Meg.

"I guess. But Aunt Rose says Bobby was a real piece of work from the beginning. Cunning and charming and sneaky-mean, the kind of kid who led all the other kids into deep trouble and was conveniently somewhere else when blame got passed around. Finally there was a really bad incident, a fifteen-year-old girl gang-raped. Frances Macrae supposedly paid the girl's family off and shipped Bobby away somewhere for a while, but he came back."

Here were some gritty details of the story Ortmann had referred to, to Frances's discomfort. And although Bobby had come back that time, he was then only a boy. What could have pulled him back after an absence of ten years? Could he have learned somehow that his old cohorts the Jakels were back in the area, and decided to attempt some kind of reunion?

Pacing again, Meg collected her beer bottle and sipped at the now-warmish liquid. "Abby, why would Marv Jakel have killed his brother?"

"For the ranch, and for the grazing rights. Aunt Rose says that with Chuck gone, Verna will probably leave everything to her two remaining children. Or if she leaves it to one, the other will undoubtedly share. Ruthie and Marv were always thick as thieves, according to Aunt Rose; in fact, it's her opinion that Verna would be well advised to watch out for her own rear end now."

"Grazing rights. That's what all the fuss was about at the meeting."

"Absolutely. The forest reserve program here was set up in the very early 1900s to give some stability to the local ranching economy. If you own land that was designated as 'base' property to qualify for grazing rights back then, you probably got the rights along with the property, and you can hand them down or sell them with your land or your cows or both. We don't have ours anymore, because my dad quit ranching and sold. Before she got sick last year, Verna Jakel ran about three hundred head of cattle and had a permit to graze them in the Warners."

"And these rights are important?"

"Most of the family ranchers here couldn't make it without them, or at least they think they couldn't."

From somewhere in the house a clock chimed three times, and Meg jumped and looked at her watch. "Abby, thank you for refuge and for information. I'd better get back; the children will be up from their naps by now, and Katy's not there."

"How long will you and Katy be staying?"

Meg drained the last drops of her beer and set the bottle on the sinkboard. "About half an hour, I wish. No, we'll have to stay at least until Sam turns up. Frances is . . . frail, and we can't just abandon Lauren's children."

"Frances Macrae is a strange woman. If those two children are ultimately left to her, if Lauren doesn't come back and Sam doesn't take personal control, I'm afraid Sara and Johnny will have the same kind of misery Lauren and Robert did." Abby got up from the table. "Meg, may I help? Please call me if you need baby-sitting backup, or any other kind. My time and place are my own; I could have the children here, or come there."

"I bet you'd write a good grown-up novel," Meg said, putting an arm across Abby's shoulders for a quick hug. "And I think I'd like your son to meet my daughter someday. I promise I'll call if we need help."

"That's the deal, kid; take it or leave it," said Meg. "Abby says you may ride her mountain bike wherever you want, in daylight anyway; but when you ride on the roads you wear this."

Katy sighed loudly, made a face, and reached for the white helmet. "I'll look like a total wuss."

"Ah, but a mobile wuss," said Meg. "Maybe you should wear it to ride Daisy, too, pretend it's a polo helmet."

"Mom!"

"Merely jesting, sweetie." Meg grinned at her daughter's indignation, both of them reaching for reassurance in the familiarity of their who's-in-charge game. Meg had returned from Abby's house with mountain bike and helmet in the trunk of the Honda, to find that Katy had come safely home. But Lauren had not, nor had there been any word of her. Now all of them, the two women and Katy and the two children, clustered in the Macrae kitchen like storm-caught hikers waiting in a cave for the skies to clear.

The electronic trill of the telephone sounded, as it had been doing at something like ten-minute intervals; Frances sighed loudly and reached for the wall instrument near which she had positioned her chair, and Meg amended the stranded-hiker image. They were a bunch of shipwreck survivors huddled on an island, scanning the horizon for any passing mast; the telephone was a consistently misleading riffle out there on the water, friends calling with sympathy or curiosity but never with any news, any help. The children were uneasily quiet; Frances had opened a bottle of wine while remarking with some defensiveness that it was after four o'clock. Meg and Katy were trying to talk in normal tones and pretend they weren't wishing themselves thoroughly elsewhere.

"Did you meet anyone while you were out riding?" asked Meg.

Katy shook her head glumly. "Not even any cows. I did see some rabbits, and one coyote."

The telephone trilled again. And went on trilling. Everyone looked at Frances, who sat staring straight ahead, hands clasped white-knuckled on her cane as tears streamed down her face. "I can't," she whispered. "I can't listen to one more person say one more mealy-mouthed, insincere thing."

Meg rose quickly. "Frances, I'll deal with the telephone for the rest of the day. And with the children. You go stretch out on your bed and listen to your tapes." Frances's tapes, Meg had learned, were not music but books; she was presently listening her way through *Pride and Prejudice*.

The older woman clambered to her feet and hesitated. "And I'll bring your wine glass," said Meg.

She returned to the kitchen a few moments later to find Katy hanging up the telephone, a look of satisfaction on her face. Probably she'd said something rude. And so what, if it made her feel better. "Katy, why don't you take the cordless phone out on the porch and call Kimmie? And feel free to talk to her for as long as you like."

"Really?"

"Really." Meg got her own brief feeling of satisfaction as she watched Katy trot out the back door with the instrument in hand. Telling all to her best friend in Port Silva would occupy her for a good hour and cheer her up for longer than that. And they would charge the bill up to baby-sitting wages.

Sara was on Katy's heels in a flash, but Katy could deal with that. "Oops. But not with you, tiger," Meg said, grabbing Johnny just as he launched himself at the door. He yowled in rage and twisted to get his mouth, and his teeth, on her arm, but she saw that coming, too.

"Nope," she said, swinging him to her hip. "Tell you what, let's go out to the barn." There was a baby swing mounted in a tree right next to the corral, and the mare at least would probably come over to socialize. Anything to get them one step closer to nighttime, and bedtime.

· 12 ·

"I'm sorry, but Miss Macrae is not at home at the moment, and she is not interested in talking to the press," Meg said, and hung up the phone. Frances had so far resisted the installation of an answering machine, insisting the devices were impolite, but Meg vowed grimly now that she herself would, first thing tomorrow, go to town to buy or rent one. If she was so unlucky as to still be here.

She paced restlessly around the kitchen, then moved into the hall to glance out the front door. Only her Honda occupied the parking space now, Frances having taken her Jeep and both children—and Katy—to church. Not for the solace of worship or the wise counsel of the pastor, Meg felt sure; Frances was once again holding high the flag of the Macraes, showing herself in public proper and unbowed.

The long driveway was empty, too; perhaps all the friends and neighbors whose pies and casseroles now lined the kitchen counter had gone to church as well. Meg wasn't up to date on country courtesy, but it did seem to her that these offerings might better have been made to Verna Jakel. Their presence here seemed to imply that Lauren, too, was dead.

Oops, not empty. Here came a car, something small, green, and dusty; it reached the house, paused, then swung into a wide turn. Third gawker this morning, this time a dark-haired man who seemed to scan the landscape and the house before heading back to the road. Meg had an uneasy feeling that she'd seen this car before, perhaps earlier in the week. She opened the door quickly to peer after it, but not in time to read the license plate; she closed the door even more quickly, reminded of how isolated she was here.

Maybe she should have gone along to church. The house

was stuffy and overwarm, but any open window or door gave access to hot, gusty wind bearing a freight of dust. Frustration enveloped her like an itchy blanket; the reflection that leapt from the hall mirror as she passed seemed all long, craning neck and staring eyes, a creature spooked and ready to bolt.

Go to the barn and saddle a horse . . . ridiculous, she had no idea how to go about that. Talk to the horses, maybe. Or . . . go talk to someone more interesting, like Verna Jakel. Probably there'd be other callers, come to pay respects and talk over the life and accomplishments of the dead son.

Meg turned to the kitchen counter and after a quick survey found a casserole and a pie that were in throw-away aluminum dishes rather than family ware with a name taped to the bottom. Share with Verna, why not? Might get her in the door, anyway. To talk, to find out what might be happening. To move or provoke movement in something, someone else.

She scrawled a note to Frances and Katy and stuck it to the refrigerator door with a ladybug magnet: Gone for a drive, back soon. Then she locked the doors, collected her offerings, and hurried out to her car.

The Jakel place was south, not far; during their sightseeing tour on Friday, Katy had spotted the Jakel name painted large and black on the roadside mailbox. Some combination of apprehension and excitement tightened Meg's chest now as she turned into the driveway to approach a house that seemed a pinched version of the Macrae residence, of more recent construction but not aging as well, surrounded by packed dirt rather than the Macraes' lush grass. Someone, quite a while ago, had decided to paint the place but had run out of energy or paint; now a white front sat oddly on a faded, forest-green building.

For the moment at least there were no other callers; the only vehicle in the packed-dirt foreyard was an old Ford pickup with soft tires and a windshield thickly crusted with dirt and dead leaves. She shut down the Honda and listened to the wind move untrimmed bushes and several tall trees.

That truck had been there a while; surely it was Verna's, and thus Marv Jakel was probably not here, not right now. Nor Ruthie. Meg took several deep breaths. Thought for just a second of Vince and snatched her mind away from that image; he'd be amazed. No, but certainly furious. Never mind.

The porch steps creaked, and there was a figure behind the screen door before she reached it. She registered size and shape and said, "Bobby?"

"Yeah. What you want?"

"I'm Meg Halloran; I saw you at the church the other night, with your mother?"

"She ain't here."

"Is your grandmother at home?"

"Yeah, but she's sick."

By now he and Meg were face to face; when she said nothing more, he shrugged, unhooked the door, and pushed it open.

"I guess you can come in if you want."

Meg stepped directly into a dim living room; curtains were pulled across all the windows, and the only light came from a small floor lamp and a silent television screen. The air was thick with the odors of dust and medicine and something that was probably just the smell of a failing old body. Beneath everything else lurked the sour tang of beer.

"Bobby, would you put these in the kitchen?" She handed him the two dishes, and he turned away with them.

"Don't call him Bobby." The voice from the couch was low and harsh. "Don't want to hear that little prick's name in my house. He's Vern, Vern Jakel. And who the hell are you?"

"Margaret Halloran. I came to tell you I'm sorry about your son's death."

"You a friend of Chuck's?" An arm reached up to turn the lamp one notch brighter, and Meg saw the pillow-propped speaker more clearly. Empty skin made a bat wing of the extended arm and hung in creased folds on the woman's face and neck; she'd been big, and now she was skeletal. The green eyes glittered in a thicket of false eyelashes, and the thin hair was bright red to the roots; someone was helping Verna keep herself together. Ruthie, probably.

"Not really. I saw him at the meeting Friday night, and I thought what he said made sense."

"Chuck was a good boy." She spoke almost absently, but tears welled in her eyes and spilled down her face. She ignored them, except to blink rapidly for a moment.

"She was with the Macraes. Friday."

Meg, who had forgotten the boy, shot a look over her shoulder at him and then turned to meet Verna's narrowed gaze. "That's true. I'm a friend of Lauren's. She's a good person, too."

"Not by everybody's standards, she ain't. But I wouldn't have thought she was a killer. Boy, bring your grandma a beer."

Meg, standing and not yet asked to sit, spotted a tall, cane-topped stool against a wall. She pulled it into the circle of light and perched on it as Bobby/Vern came back with a sixteen-ounce can of Budweiser, popping it open before handing it to his grandmother.

"First time in my life I can drink this stuff and not put on a pound." Verna tipped the can for several swallows, then cackled and patted her flat belly. "Look at that. Verna Jakel, fit as a filly and ready to run." Her hand fluttered higher, to her equally flat chest, and dropped. "And I don't miss them things, either—make your shoulders ache just to carry around, and then there's always some damn guy trying to get his hands on 'em. You want a beer?"

"I wouldn't mind," said Meg, and Verna nodded to the boy.

" 'Course," she said, after another swallow, "I need to be a little bit careful, what with all my pills. You know what can happen to a person that mixes booze and pills. What'd you really come here for?" she asked suddenly, sharply.

Why had she come? The boy appeared at Meg's shoulder, handed her a can of beer, and then retreated; she had the feeling that he was backing away, like a servant to royals or like someone unwilling to take his eyes off the players. If she'd remembered the boy, she wouldn't have come. She opened the can and took a sip. "For a beer, maybe?"

Verna's gaze didn't waver.

"I suppose I'm looking for Lauren. Or for reasons."

"Lauren ain't here, and I got no time to worry about reasons." Verna dropped her head back against her pillows.

"I'm sorry. I shouldn't have intruded."

"Damn right," she whispered, closing her eyes.

"Miz Halloran, did you know my daddy?" the boy asked, still behind her.

Before Meg could answer, Verna's eyes sprang open again, flat green stones. "No, she didn't, and you listen to me. Your daddy was a mean, sneaky little son of a bitch, and I should know, because he practically grew up here."

"Momma says he was smart."

"Not smart enough. You get out of here now, go feed your rabbits."

As the screen door slapped shut after Bobby's exit, Meg said, "Your grandson seems like a nice boy."

"Yeah, and we know what happens to nice boys. Go on, get out of here and take your beer with you. I can't help you none."

Meg got to her feet but stopped as she heard the sound of a vehicle outside. Verna hitched herself higher against her pillows and lifted her head to listen. One door slam. Loud voices, male, the tenor raised in complaint and the other, deep baritone, growling in response. The engine roared. As the roar diminished in company with the metallic rattle of an unloaded truck, Meg looked again at Verna and saw her relax.

Marv Jakel opened the screen door moments later, flinging it back so hard it hit the wall. He strode in, muttering, and nearly ran into Meg. "Hey. Who the fuck are you?"

"She's a friend, come to pay her respects to your dead brother."

"Yeah?" Jakel brushed his hair back with both hands, squinting up at Meg uneasily as he did so. A little less than medium height, with a long neck and sloping shoulders, he had a raw-boned, stringy-muscled look and feet jittery from energy or nervousness, or some kind of stimulant.

"Yeah," said Verna. "Did you find a place for your friend to stay?" She laid stress on the word "friend," and Marv flinched and shook his head.

"He's no problem here, Momma. And this way we both got the use of his truck till I get one or get yours fixed up."

"He's a problem for me; I don't like the bastard." Verna's voice was subdued, and she glanced at the door as she spoke. "Maybe the both of you could stay down at the cabin."

"I don't think the cops will let us."

"Well, ask them, for Christ's sake! Now go get me another beer."

"Momma, you drink another beer and you'll be throwing up."

"So then you'll bring me a bucket, if you know what's good for you!"

Watching them glare at each other, Meg decided that Verna did not need assistance or protection and moved quietly to the door; neither of them paid her any attention.

Meg drove around for a while, enjoying the Honda's air-conditioner and wishing she'd been willing to push for those reasons. Like, why did fierce Verna Jakel, mourning her son, not display more anger at Lauren? Or why had Bobby Macrae practically grown up at her house? Clearly she did not admire him, at least in retrospect; had she been, earlier, captured by his physical appeal, something her two older children definitely lacked? Beauty was a deadly-dangerous quality, to the beholder and to the beheld.

Finally she returned to the Macrae ranch to find a sheriff's car just leaving as she parked in the yard. "Frances?" she called as she entered the house. "What's going on?"

"Oh, just more of the same." Frances had not yet changed from the blue linen suit she had worn to church, a skirted suit this time; her clothes were wrinkled and her demeanor one of irritation. "Undersheriff Ortmann has been pawing through our belongings."

"Pawing through?"

"He wanted to look at Lauren's things. They haven't turned up anyone who's seen her, and the police are assuming that she's gone into hiding somewhere. So he wanted to know whether she'd taken any clothes, and he asked me all about her friends and took her address book."

Katy was in the kitchen, wolfing down a plateful of something that appeared to consist of tortillas, chicken, chiles, and cheese. "That cop was a jerk, Mom," she said as Meg came in. "I asked him very politely if he shouldn't have a search warrant, and he just said, 'You be quiet, little girl.' He'd never make it in Port Silva; Vince wouldn't have the guy on traffic duty, even."

Vince. She had to call home and tell him what was going on, before he heard it from some other source. Meg picked up a spoon and stole a scoop from her daughter's plate. "How was church?"

Katy's face brightened. "It was kind of interesting; the organist played Bach, and there was this neat church song-book—"

"Hymnal," interrupted Meg, savoring the purely personal and uncomplicated guilt of a parent who had not sent her child to Sunday school.

"Hymnal, okay. And the songs, hymns, sounded like Bach, too, most of them. They were neat to sing, in parts, and Johnny liked them, too. He was just awful except when there was music. Anyway, I'm going back."

"Next Sunday, you mean?"

"No, today. There's like a bazaar this afternoon, on the lawn; I thought I'd bike in and take a look."

The church lawn, in broad daylight, should be a reasonably safe place. And energetic, sociable Katy surely needed a break from old folks and babies. "Fine," Meg said, and went to search the counter for the tortilla casserole.

"Did anything happen here before you left?" Frances had trailed her into the kitchen and spoke now with just a hint of displeasure—over her having abandoned ship?

"Nothing important." Meg handed her the notepad of messages, telling her as well of the several anonymous calls and the drive-by vehicles. "It's too bad there isn't a gate across the driveway," she added.

"There is a gate, in the barn. It's a great heavy thing that we couldn't possibly put up by ourselves, and besides, it's more of a nuisance than anything else. Anyone who wants to get onto the property can find another way in."

"Oh. Wonderful."

"What I should do," said Frances, "is call Sheriff Vukovich and insist that he send an officer out here to protect us until Sam comes home. I was accosted by two different sets of newspeople right on the church lawn, and I'm sure they'll turn up here soon."

Meg suspected that this sparsely populated county had a correspondingly small sheriff's department. "Frances, I think the officers are more useful looking for Lauren. I'll help you repel boarders here."

"I suppose you're right." The older woman, who'd been holding herself square-shouldered and high-headed, a picture of dignity in wrinkled linen, reached now for a chair and slumped into it.

"Oh, my. Oh, I'm very tired. And all this food . . . it was nice of people to remember Bobby, but I don't know where I'll find the energy to thank them all."

Meg stared at her blankly for a long moment. "Bobby? But surely this is all for Lauren?"

"But Lauren will be back, she isn't . . . she's been gone only a very little while, and Bobby—"

"Actually, I suppose all this kindness was really meant for you, Frances, and the children."

"Yes," said Frances with a sigh, as if a problem had been

solved. "It is the strangest thing, you know, how time compresses. Ten years ago and yesterday seem to follow right upon each other, the way Wednesday follows Tuesday. And some days I look out toward the corral and see my father standing there beside Lauren, just two tall, young, red-haired people. If you'll excuse me, I believe I'll go change clothes now."

The field beside the church had been turned into a kind of flea market, people selling handmade potholders and jelly and pies and lemonade as well as used books and kids' clothing and stuff, none of it very expensive. There were some informational setups, too—tables bearing pictures of local and state politicians, people getting signatures on petitions. Katy felt quite free to go ahead with what she'd planned, handing out flyers requesting donations to Wolf Haven.

She got a card table and a chair from an old guy who was renting them out for fifty cents and set herself up in a vacant corner next to a guy who was making balloon animals for a quarter each. Her little stack of flyers looked forlorn, and she was half watching the crowd, half trying to decide what she should do to attract attention—stand on her chair and wave her arms, maybe?—when the boy from Friday night stopped right in front of her table.

"Adam Kingsley," he said.

"I know that."

"I've got something for you," he told her, unrolling a poster. It was one of Sam Cavalier's wolves, a dark-coated animal standing in a field of snow and staring calmly from pale eyes at the camera.

"If we tape this to your table," said Adam, "people will know what you're here for."

"Good idea," she said, and so it proved to be. For the next hour she was kept busy explaining Wolf Haven to people, some of them friendly and some of them disbelieving or even disapproving. She drank lemonade that Adam brought her and kept her voice and manner polite and managed to hand out quite a few flyers. Some people remembered Betty Burrus and seemed willing to see the Wolf Lady's work go on, especially two states away.

"You got one of these at home, for a pet?" The man who had paused beside her table was sunburned from neck to midforehead but pale above and also below, she could see from the open collar of his shirt. Rancher, probably, and middle-aged, older than her mother.

"Oh, no. Wolves are frightened of people, and they need their own family, they have their own society. They don't make good pets at all."

"Seems to me you'd want to get your hands on one, the way kids do with any animal. If you can't make a pet of it, why does it interest you?"

"I don't need to pet them. I just . . . it makes me feel good to know they still exist and that there's this place where the ones that can't be free can at least be safe and treated like real wolves. They once hunted over most of the world, you know. The wolf was the most successful predator on earth except for man."

The man shook his head and put his straw hat on; then he nodded politely at Katy. "I still say it's a real strange interest for a pretty girl," he said, and moved away.

A lull followed his departure, and Katy pushed her chair back and stretched. She was antsy from sitting, and there were only a few flyers left. She should probably think about getting home, to see what might be happening. The people here clearly knew who she was or at least who she was staying with; several of them had even asked her to take their best wishes to Frances Macrae.

Wondering what had become of Adam, Katy looked up to see four kids around her own age coming across the grass, the leader a big girl wearing Levi's and boots and a cropped tee. The girl had a headful of frizzy, light-colored hair that she was tossing around like it made her gorgeous or something. Horse's tail, was what Katy thought, braided and then combed out for a show. Boooring.

"You don't belong here, you know," said the girl in a boring high voice.

"I don't live here," said Katy. Sitting and looking up was uncomfortable; she stood and moved around the table, skirting the bicycle she'd propped against its edge.

"Nobody wants you here, or that Cavalier guy, either."

"Hey, you ever hear it's a free country?" Katy stood to her full height, lifted her chin, let out the voice she'd been keeping low all day. She balanced on the balls of her feet, feeling . . . interested.

"Not for some dumb bitch who thinks my 4-H calf ought to get his throat torn out by one of *those*," she said, with a gesture at the wolf poster.

"Well, the wolf probably wouldn't do that. Wolves prefer deer, and there are lots of those around here. But what do you think is going to happen to your calf, he's going to live this long, happy life in green pastures and die of old age?"

"What're you talking about? What do you think happens to calves?"

"So," said Katy with a shrug. "The only wolves I know personally live up by Olympia, Washington, which is a pretty long trip even for a wolf. But if you're worried, you should just keep your calf at home until you want to eat him yourself."

"You don't know what you're talking about. Take your stupid picture and go back where you came from!" said the girl, reaching toward the poster as if to tear it away.

"Leave that alone." Katy moved in front of the poster. The girl swung an arm at her, a back-handed blow that knocked her sideways and brought her rib cage sharply against the corner of the table, which promptly collapsed.

Katy landed on her butt and then rolled up onto her feet in a lunge that slammed her right shoulder into her assailant's chest, right against a big fat boob. Her left forearm came up and across in a follow-through that was almost automatic, to catch the other across the throat. The girl squawked and stumbled back, got her feet tangled and fell, hard. Katy planted herself and stood straight, breathing hard and watching for what might come next. Sorry, Miss Brady, she said in silent, less-than-sincere apology to her basketball coach, who would have benched her for the rest of the game over these moves.

In a moment that probably lasted ten seconds but felt about an hour long, nobody said anything or even moved. Okay, thought Katy, and *she* moved, stepping forward to hold a hand out to the blonde girl. "Are you okay?"

"Sure." The girl took the extended hand, came to her feet, and the two of them faced each other for another long moment. The blonde girl was broader, Katy taller and longer-limbed.

"Sorry," they said in near unison, and the other kids, two guys and a girl, relaxed.

Katy's flyers had been scattered and the poster torn; bike and table were tangled together in a heap. She shrugged and began silently to gather things up. After a moment's muttered consultation, the blonde girl's friends departed, but she stayed and bent to help in the salvage operation.

"I'm Tracy Turner," she said as she straightened a metal leg and set the table upright. "And I still don't think this is a good idea. I don't see any need for wolves at all."

What about because they're beautiful? thought Katy. Because they're intelligent and hard-working and interesting? Because men shouldn't decide to destroy something just because it's troublesome, only God or whoever should be able to do that? "Lots of people believe the world needs biological diversity," was what she actually said. "Besides, do you want to live where there's nothing but people and cows and millions of insects?"

Tracy shrugged and grinned. "I don't mind, if I can have horses, too."

"How about you get horses, I get wolves?"

Tracy shook her head, more in lack of understanding than in disagreement, Katy thought. "Whatever. Well, I gotta go. And look," she added, "I don't usually hit people. Okay?"

"Okay."

"Hi," said a voice from just behind her that spun her around.

"You shouldn't sneak up like that," she snapped at Adam. "Where have you been, anyway?"

"I didn't sneak, I was just standing here watching. I was going to help if you needed it, but you didn't. I know why she hit you," he added, "and it wasn't about wolves."

Katy took a deep breath and noticed that her legs felt shaky. It occurred to her that what she'd done wasn't entirely about wolves, either. "Okay, why did she?"

"Because you're tall and stand up straight with your chin out and this 'Fuck you!' expression on your face."

There was no animosity in his voice, and Katy could read none in his face. "Well," she said, "maybe I could practice, in a mirror or something, and change my expression."

"Maybe." He didn't sound convinced. "You want another lemonade, or a piece of pie?"

"Thanks, but I'd better get home."

"Can I give you a lift?" He gestured toward the curb, where a little open-topped car shot teal-blue rays back at the sun. A Porsche, she thought, a newer model than Vince's.

"No thanks, I've got a bike. Adam, are you really old enough to drive?"

"I'm eighteen," he said with a shrug. "Don't look so pissed; it's not like I'm some older guy putting moves on you. I have a very high I.Q., but my shrink says I'm socially retarded."

"Right," said Katy. She stuffed the remaining flyers into her backpack, suddenly very tired. This place was full of seriously weird people.

In silence, he helped her fold the table and carried it back to its owner while she followed with the chair. "If it's okay, I'll call you tomorrow," he said as she picked up her bike. "At the Macrae ranch, isn't it?" He put out his hand, which so startled her that she took it.

"See you." A brief, businesslike shake, and then he turned and trotted off to his car.

Weird, she thought again. But in sort of a nice way. She looked at her watch and felt the events of the last two days collect around her like a jangle of discordant sound. She needed to get back, to find out whether Lauren had turned up, or maybe even Sam.

At the edge of the road she paused, sighed, and slid the helmet off the handlebar. The dumb thing made her feel like a Martian, or some kind of big-headed insect.

"You sure you got enough energy left to ride that thing?" drawled a voice. It took her a moment to locate the speaker, who was leaning against the door of a white pickup truck parked in the shade of a tree. He stood with big, curly head tilted, arms crossed in a way that showed off the snake tattoo: tail wrapped around one wrist, open-mouthed head on the back of the opposite hand.

"Hey, why don't you toss the bike in the truck here, and I'll give you a ride home. Young lady like you shouldn't have to put that ugly helmet on her pretty head."

"I'm not a young lady, I'm a kid." Although his face was in shadow, she could see his eyes clearly, big eyes with lots of white showing.

"Not for long, you're not." The eyes were on her like hands, like his friend's hands the other day. Katy was suddenly conscious of her old Levi's, washed to thinness and tight in the crotch, of the way her sweat-dampened tee shirt clung to her chest. Ignoring the flutter in her belly, anger or fear or something else she didn't recognize, she pulled the helmet on and buckled its strap, then threw a leg over the bike.

"Thanks, but I don't know you."

His chuckle drifted after her as she pedaled away.

· 13 ·

Later on Sunday afternoon, when all of them were clustered once again in the kitchen, Sam came home. At the sudden rattle of tire-flung gravel and then the slam of a door, Frances and Meg and Katy turned toward the front of the house like a trio of pointing bird dogs while Sara leapt to her feet and shot out of the room.

"Daddy!" The word ended in a drawn-out shriek of glee, and Meg reached the front door in time to see the man step from his dusty car and scoop Sara up in his arms. Not a car but a Jeep, the twin of Frances's wagon in black or maybe gray; something about it made her think of a police vehicle. She turned and headed back for the kitchen, his heavy footsteps behind her on the porch and then in the hallway.

"Sam, where have you . . . you look . . . Sam, you remember Lauren's friend—"

Frances's stammered phrases were finally drowned out by Sara, who was riding high against her father's shoulder with both arms wrapped around his neck. "Daddy, Mommy's lost! She didn't come home and you need to go find her!"

Sam Cavalier's face was one you'd expect to see in a museum diorama labeled "Mountain Man": sparse flesh drawn tight over the heavy frontal bone, Slavic breadth of cheek, solid jaw. Today the blue-gray eyes had the bleary look that comes from drink or exhaustion, and the Levi's and flannel shirt bore the creases and grime of many days' wear. More unexpected to Meg was the glint of silver in the curly, shoulder-length mane of dark hair and on the unshaven cheeks. Sam Cavalier had to be in his early forties, and he looked his age.

"I know, darlin' girl." He spoke to Sara, but he looked at Frances and Meg. "But Daddy's here now, so you can stop worrying." He gave the little girl a hug and set her down. "Frances, good to see you. And here's Meg Halloran, know you anywhere. And . . . Katy, is it?"

Sam came forward to shake Katy's hand and then Meg's, and Meg was surprised, as she had been years earlier, to find that he wasn't unusually tall, probably no more than her own five feet ten if allowance was made for the heeled western boots. Even travel-worn and worried, the man filled a room and gave the impression of being larger than life.

"Sam," Frances began again, and he shook his head.

"I know, Frances. One of the sheriff's people stopped me at the highway turnoff and told me what's happening. She seemed to think I should go along to the office with her, but I said I was going home to see my family first." He lifted his chin and narrowed his eyes, and Meg thought that poor Deputy Garcia, if that's who it was, had been much better matched against Marv Jakel and his buddy.

"Undersheriff Ortmann—or Sheriff Vukovich, I should think—can just come here to talk to you," said Frances. "Sam, you look exhausted."

"Alaska's a long trip. Say, where's my—" He spotted Johnny, who sat upright and silent in his high chair. "Hey, tiger! Come say hello to your old man!" Sam grabbed the little boy and swooped him ceilingward, then settled him into a cradling crook of arm. "Frances, I'm sorry," he began, and then yelped "Ow!" as Johnny sank sharp teeth into the flesh at the base of his thumb.

"You little shit!" Sam set the baby down hard and put his own blood-smeared hand to his mouth. Johnny rolled to his feet and ran full-tilt across the room to fling himself against Katy's legs. Howling, he clung there and glared at his father, who was glaring back. For a moment Meg imagined that she could see testosterone swirling around the room like blown smoke.

At eight that evening, Katy winced at the sound of the door-bell but kept the rocking chair moving in slow, steady fashion. The baby on her shoulder twitched just the tiniest bit, pushed his face deeper into her neck, and went on sleeping. She'd rock him a while longer anyway; the last time she thought he was ready and got up to put him in his bed, he came awake with a roar.

Crazy little kid had decided he owned her or something. Right now she didn't mind; he smelled good and his skin was warm and incredibly smooth against hers, the curls that tickled her face soft as kitten fur. Poor little guy, she told him silently, your mother better come home to you pretty soon.

His daddy wasn't going to be an acceptable substitute, that was for sure. Katy inhaled another lungful of warm baby and remembered how this sweet little mite had looked in the kitchen earlier: feet braced, fists clenched, a two-foot-tall Charles Bronson ready to take on his father and the whole 49'ers offensive line. Boys, big or little, were just weird.

Voices. Katy turned her head slightly, to get more distance between her ear and the baby's breathing, and realized that she could hear people talking in the living room. Where . . . oh, right. She hadn't remembered to close the heater vent here, something she was supposed to do when putting the baby to bed; Johnny's room was right over the living room and must share a heating pipe.

One voice was unfamiliar to her, deep and twangy and not very distinct. The sheriff, probably; he'd been expected. Then words she couldn't make out, but it had to be Aunt Frances, in the high, sort of whiny tone she used when Sam was around.

Sam Cavalier's voice she would recognize anywhere. It was deep but clear rather than thick, and he spoke more slowly and softly than Vince, for instance, or her mother, either.

Actually, his voice sounded crisp right now, and she could make out most of what he said, about not having seen Lauren for almost two months but he talked to her frequently on the phone. Rumble rumble from the other man, and Sam Cavalier talking about how he'd met Lauren while she was still in college, and how she believed in him and his work. How she was a loving wife and mother.

It was very strange, sitting up here in this dark room with his baby in her lap and listening to this man she'd admired practically forever. When Sam came into the house this afternoon, Katy remembered being disappointed. He was just . . . ordinary, dirty and smelling of sweat, moving like his back hurt and maybe his feet, too. Not as big as she'd expected, and older, with gray in his hair.

But he'd noticed her right away, noticed everybody in the room and concentrated on each of them. He had these light-colored eyes in this very suntanned face, so you could really tell when he was looking at you, and you couldn't help looking back.

She'd lost track of what they were saying, and now there was more rumble rumble and then Sam again, louder or sharper or something. His wife was fully committed to her marriage and her family. She was not a sexual adventurer. He paused, and Katy stopped the rocker, suddenly afraid that its small sound might be audible in the room beneath. She would hate it if Sam Cavalier ever spoke to her in that tone. If *anybody* ever did.

Sam went on. Lauren's weakness was her soft heart; obviously the dead man had taken advantage of that and so had pulled her, knowingly or not, into some trouble of his own. If his wife was still alive, she was in terrible danger; the sheriff should have his whole department out looking for Lauren Cavalier.

If she got up, Katy wondered, would they hear her footsteps? Never mind, she'd just keep holding Johnny, poor little kid. Convinced or maybe consoled by the idea that Lauren was only hiding, temporarily, after defending herself, Katy had pretty much stopped her thinking at that point. Had been caught up in the strangeness and excitement, she supposed, and in everybody's efforts to keep things as nonscary as possible for the little kids. Dumb dumb dumb! she said silently to herself now, and remembered story after story in the newspaper, on television, about things that happened to women.

Meg was listening, too. The hours following Sam's arrival had been not-in-front-of-the-children stuff, enlivened only by Johnny's forthright determination to have nothing to do with his father; after dinner, as the children were readied for bed, their father had disappeared into the outbuilding he used as studio and darkroom. When the sheriff arrived as arranged, Sam Cavalier's thoughts about Chuck Jakel's death and Lauren's disappearance were still known only to Sam.

So Meg had cleared the dinner table and loaded the dishwasher, watched but not helped much by Frances. She had called Port Silva to be greeted, of course, by the answering machine and had left a brief message about recent events and a promise to call the next morning. She had opened the door to the sheriff's arrival and had gone out to fetch Sam.

Then, shiny-faced with virtue, or so she imagined, she had settled herself at the kitchen table to sip wine and play a little quiet solitaire. And eavesdrop. Why not?

Hearing Sam's responses to the sheriff, Meg wondered at first whether he was simply protecting his wife's reputation, and his own. If he was being honest, then he was either ridiculously self-confident or seriously lacking in imagination. Or more probably he simply hadn't paid attention, she thought, remembering Abby Fowler's description of the man as wrapped up totally in his work.

His sorrow now, the pain in his voice, sounded real enough. Meg set a seven of clubs on an eight of spades, looked blindly at the result for a moment, and then swept all the cards together. And listened to Sam as he answered Sheriff Vukovich's questions about his recent whereabouts.

Alaska, commercial airline from Klamath Falls, Oregon, via Seattle to Anchorage. Then a trip north by chartered puddle-jumper and weeks spent more or less alone in the bush. Finally, back out via a prearranged pickup charter. The pilot, a friend, brought him back by stages to the lower forty-eight, finally this morning to Klamath Falls, where he picked up his Jeep wagon and drove straight home.

Katy, upstairs, was grieving and worrying now instead of listening. But her ears hadn't been trained as had her mother's by the subterfuges, mistaken beliefs, hopeful but unlikely projections, and downright lies put forth by year after year of high school students. Sam Cavalier's voice, in relating his travels to the sheriff, was soft again, warm, convincing. Meg wondered if he might be lying.

"Meg, the kids and Frances could not have survived the last couple of days without you and Katy. There isn't any way I can thank you enough. At least let me get you another glass of wine."

Meg didn't really want any more wine, but she wanted to talk to Sam, or have him talk to her. She nodded acceptance, thanked him for the glass he brought, and watched him sink wearily into the chair across from her. In the flickering light from the fireplace, his face was haggard and sad.

"Did the sheriff have anything hopeful to suggest?" The two men had finished their session outside, Sam ushering the departing lawman to his truck and then the pair of them standing around out there, in sight but well beyond earshot, for probably fifteen minutes. Meg thought Sam had initiated the move, in order to talk without Frances's increasingly testy participation. The old woman, frustrated and not completely sober, had promptly tottered off to bed.

"He trotted out a few items, mostly to placate me. They are looking for Jakel's two brothers-in-law, a pair of rough types who are very protective of their little sister and reportedly had threatened to break his arms and legs if he attempted to see her or her kids."

"Ah."

"And they've talked to Jakel's brother, of course. My reading of this is that he can't prove where he was Friday night, but nobody's really very interested in him. The sheriff believes that Lauren and Chuck Jakel had a fight and she shot him, period."

Meg couldn't think of anything to say. Sam drew one big hand down over his face, as if to wipe away fear, or anger, and looked at her. "But I can't believe that, I just can't imagine it. Meg, did she say anything to you about, oh, how she's been feeling, or any plans she might have had?"

Meg chose her words carefully. "She said that she was lonely and wished you could be home more."

"God, I know she misses me. And I miss her, but she couldn't travel with me once we had the kids. They were her idea, you know; she was absolutely fixated on the notion of having babies."

"Most women are," replied Meg. "We're programmed by nature along those lines, I believe."

"I guess. I mean, I *know*. And I'm not sorry, I love my kids. Meg, did Lauren say anything to you about this Chuck Jakel?"

Not exactly. What Meg said was simply "No."

"Apparently he'd been in the area for some months, but I'd never met him. And she never mentioned him to me."

"But haven't you been away for most of that time?"

"Well, yes, I guess so, but I couldn't help that. And I called her whenever there was a telephone I could get to." His voice was faintly defensive. "Ever since I was a kid, moving around with my dad from post to post in the Forest Service, I've known what I wanted to do with my life, how I needed to use my talent."

"I know. I've seen your pictures."

He made a dismissive gesture. "The photographs are a living, but beyond that, a means to an end. Wilderness preservation is my real vocation. Lauren always understood that, or said she did."

Meg made a noncommittal noise, and Sam sighed. "But about this Chuck Jakel, she must have known him when she was just a kid. What did you think, Meg, when you saw her leave with him Friday night?" He leaned forward into the firelight, his eyes boring into hers.

"I thought she certainly knew him well enough to want to help him. No one else was offering to."

"Well, she'd do that for practically anybody."

"True."

"Lauren never talked much about her earlier life. I know she had a hard time after her parents were killed; she really loved her dad. Frances . . . well, she's a good woman; but she just wasn't cut out to be a parent. I think she was too tough on Lauren and much too easy on the boy, Bobby. Useless little prick lived off his aunt, couldn't stay in school, wouldn't work the ranch or get a job." Sam's voice held the disdain of the committed for the undecided.

"Bobby Macrae was the kind of creep who liked to use his fists on women. Lauren was scared to death of him, until I caught him hitting her one time and put a stop to that for good. But she never said anything about anyone else bothering her. So if there was danger here for her, I didn't know it." He turned to stare at the fire, and a last flare from the dying embers cast his face in harsh relief. "I should have, shouldn't I?"

It was after all a dramatic face, so the tragedy-mask expression was not necessarily purposeful or insincere. Meg looked away and saw instead Lauren's confused, unhappy countenance, remembered her attempts to make light of her own misery.

"Yes, I think you should have," she said.

With a sigh that was half groan, Sam straightened and rubbed the back of his neck. "God. I have to get some sleep so I can go out tomorrow and look for her. Meg, will you stay? For another day or two, at least? I know Frances isn't easy to get along with, but she obviously respects you. And Katy has got my son's number in a way I never could. If you can spare the time and energy, the two of you, we really need you."

"What're you mad about, Mom?"

Katy's sleepy, worried voice startled Meg, throwing her back eight or ten years.

"I'm not mad at you, sweetie." The answer was as old as the question, both a regular part of their earlier lives.

"What, then? Did you hear something more about Lauren?" Her daughter was no longer a small child seeking only comfort and the assurance that she was loved, and this was a problem even a loving mother couldn't soothe away.

"No, there's nothing new." Meg pulled her sweater roughly over her head, then crouched to untie her shoes. "Your mother, Katy, was born with her fists clenched and hasn't managed to grow up, I guess. When something awful happens, something I can't do anything about, I get mad."

"Me too. Sometimes I want to *hit* somebody."

"Poor baby, you are your mother's daughter." Meg shucked her Levi's off and tossed them onto a chair. "You'd have done better to take after your daddy, a kind and thoughtful man who was always interested but hardly ever angry."

"Yeah, well, it's maybe safe for *men* to be kind. Lauren is a kind person, and it doesn't look like it did her much good."

The fierceness of Katy's voice raised the hairs on the back of Meg's neck. She shut her teeth on an about-to-escape platitude and said, instead, "No, it doesn't."

"When Sam said she wasn't a sexual adventurer, did he mean she didn't go out there to have sex with that Jakel guy?"

Two eavesdroppers in the Halloran family, it seemed. "I think so."

"But what difference does that make now?" Katy's head was propped against a pillow, the gleam of her eyes visible from across the room.

Good question, thought Meg. "I don't know."

"Do you think she did?"

Oh, shit. "Friday night I thought it was a possibility."

"Oh. Well, okay, but that's still not the important thing. The important thing is, where is she now?"

"Katy, you're absolutely right."

"Listen, I want to know everything that happens. I don't want to be one of the kids."

"I understand. Now try to go to sleep, sweetie. Sam asked us to stay here for a few more days, and I more or less agreed that we would."

"Yeah, okay. I love you, Mom." Katy pushed the pillows flat and burrowed down under the covers. "G'night."

"Good night, love."

Meg tossed her bra and panties after her Levi's, decided to keep her socks on, and padded across to the closet where her nightgown hung. There was a full-length mirror on the door; she'd forgotten that and wasn't quick enough in averting her eyes. After forty, not even good genes and good health were proof against the pull of gravity; once-firm breasts began to droop, abdominal muscles had to be voluntarily tightened against a faint low sag. Thighs would go next, probably; she found the long flannel gown and pulled it on and down, concealing the evidence.

And apparently the libido was doomed to fail, too, probably be dead completely by the time she was forty-five. Sam Cavalier was certifiably gorgeous in a totally masculine way. Lauren couldn't even talk about Sam without going dry-mouthed; sensible Abby Fowler had made a fool of herself over him.

But she, Meg, had stood under Sam's blue-eyed gaze tonight without bothering to pull her shoulders back or her belly tight. Had felt not the slightest tingle. Had thought, irritably, that here was a larger and thus more troublesome version of headlong, demanding, two-year-old Johnny.

In the dim light from a small lamp on the dresser, her face looked weary and bad-tempered. Fair enough, that was how she felt. Meg turned out the light and padded over to her side of the bed, sliding in carefully so as not to disturb Katy.

· 14 ·

" . . . so it's been three nights and two days, and she hasn't been seen or heard from. Sam took off early this morning to explore several places he thought she might have headed for if she was trying to hide." Moved by guilt, arrogance, or mistrust of the sheriff and his people, Sam had refused to reveal exactly where he was going, and he had instructed Meg and the rest of the household to say, if asked, that he was just out driving around.

"Well. Doesn't sound good, Meg." Vince's voice against her ear carried the impersonal sadness of someone who has seen more than his share of what people do to each other.

"I *know* that." What she knew, or was beginning to feel, was that time was turning against the most straightforward version of events, a killing in self-defense. Remorse and humiliation might have sent Lauren Cavalier into headlong flight but should not have kept her out there away from her children, not for this long. What Meg had hoped was that Vince in his cop's wisdom might have some magical alternative to suggest.

"If she doesn't turn up or get in touch pretty soon, it begins to look more like a third person, at least, might have been involved," said Vince.

"I know," she said again. Their present emotional distance hadn't impaired his ability to catch her unspoken thoughts; she found this startling, and unnerving. "She's probably dead, which strikes me as a pretty severe penalty for a little illicit sex."

"I'm sorry."

"Yes. Me too." Meg brushed damp hair off her forehead and tried to position herself so that she faced neither the blazing sun nor its reflection in the glass of the phone booth. Having decided she had to tell Vince the whole of what was going on, she had been reluctant to do so from the Macrae telephone. Standing here under glass in midmorning heat was making her regret such delicacy.

"What's the weather like in Port Silva?" she asked.

"Oh, the usual. Some drizzle this morning, probably a gang of slugs in the garden. The sun is breaking through now, and it's supposed to get warm later, radio says high sixties. Meg, what about the husband, this Sam?"

Meg, who'd been thinking with an unnatural wistfulness of drizzle and even of slugs, blinked and tried to pull her thoughts back to this hot, dry place and its problems. "Sam Cavalier. What do you mean, what about him?"

"You know as well as I do that the usual . . . Okay, Saturday night this long-haul trucker, guy named Grubb, came home to Port Silva and found his wife had gone out with some other guy and left their three little kids home alone, oldest one was seven. Not for the first time, either. When she came in at three A.M., he shot her and the kids, and then himself."

"Oh, Vince. Did you know him?"

"Oh, yeah." He took a deep breath. "My point is, murder is pretty often a family affair, particularly in small towns."

"Sam couldn't have . . . harmed Lauren. The shooting and her disappearance took place sometime late Friday or early Saturday; he didn't get back into town from Alaska until Sunday afternoon." Meg paused, remembering her moment of doubt as she listened to Sam tell the sheriff of his travels.

"No, I don't think so," she continued. "I've talked with him, Vince, and I believe he cares about his family, but . . . but not that much, not that way." She groped for a fairer way to phrase what she wanted to say. "His real passion is for his work, and for the wilderness."

"Mm. Anyone else showing interest in Cavalier?"

"Interest? Oh, you mean as a suspect. I don't think so. The sheriff—a man named Vukovich, who has a border-states

twang and looks as if he didn't get enough to eat as a kid—
Vukovich came out and talked to him Sunday night for quite
a while. Which I found a bit odd," she added.

"That he came there instead of having Cavalier come in?"

"That and the fact that it was the sheriff out working an
investigation. I thought they spent their time shaking hands
with voters and riding in parades."

"Sparsely populated rural counties like Modoc probably
can't afford a sheriff who's just an administrator and politi-
cian, particularly now when money is tight everywhere. Hey,
there's somebody you could look up if you get in trouble—
old buddy of mine named Earl Douglas. We put in about fifteen years together in L.A., and he was sheriff up there in
Modoc until the last election."

About to tell him that she'd already met Douglas, she took
in the import of his remark and said, sharply, "I wasn't planning to get in trouble."

"Right," he said. "Meg, it worries me to have you up there
in the middle of . . . whatever this turns out to be. Why don't
you and Katy head out for, oh, Plumas County? Call Bob
Wiley at Wiley's Realty in Quincy, say I want him to find you
a cabin for a few days. Or you could go out to Mama's place,
the Gutierrez family camp, if you don't mind roughing it."

No invitation to come *home* to safety, Meg noted, nor any
suggestion that he might join them. "I didn't bring camping
gear. No, we're both useful here. Sam asked me if we could
please stay another day or two."

"Suit yourself. But get in touch with Douglas, okay? He's a
little on the rough side, used to be very quick to play grab-ass
with good-looking women—although I don't think many
objected. But he's not likely to try anything with you. Nothing you can't handle, anyway," he added.

Oh, right. Either he'd have no urge to grab *my* droopy old
ass, or he'll know a barracuda when he sees one. Meg swallowed these thoughts along with a deep breath and asked,
politely, "How is Emily?"

He made a sound somewhere between a sigh and a groan.

"Generally pissed off, at life and us and the doctors. They want to send her to San Francisco for surgery, latest techniques and a good chance for recovery and a more comfortable life. She just grits her teeth and shakes her head. And clutches her chest. Says she'd rather die in her own bed than in some hospital."

"Surgery is scary.

"Yeah. But Bettyjean is working on her, says she'll go along and special her after the operation."

"Ah." Vince's oldest brother, a widower with grown children, had recently acquired a new wife, a nurse twenty years his junior. Bettyjean had big round eyes, big round boobs, and a personality whose sugar content would cause cavities. Emily Gutierrez had taken an immediate liking to her.

"I guess I forgot to tell you Rich and Bettyjean arrived," Vince added. "They're staying here. I moved into Katy's room and put them in ours."

Suddenly this odd, isolated place seemed more tolerable to Meg. "Well, that should keep you from being lonely. Please tell Emily that Katy and I are thinking of her. I'll say goodbye now; I want to go to the newspaper office in Alturas to look at some back issues."

"Meg, don't go looking for trouble," Vince said sharply.

"As usual, you mean? Don't worry. I'll do as you suggest and keep in close touch with good ol' Earl Douglas."

She hung up the receiver, then sighed and shook her head. By the time she had punched out all the numbers for another credit-card call, he had apparently left the house. "Vince, I apologize for being bitchy. I love you," she said to the answering machine, and hung up again.

The *Modoc Messenger*, a weekly paper with coverage devoted mostly to the eastern part of the county, was housed in a flat-roofed stone building on the edge of Alturas's downtown area. Meg spent an hour in a back room there and emerged dusty and grimy-fingered but not much wiser.

The Macrae family had been mentioned frequently over the years, mostly in a social context: visits, celebrations of anniversaries, donations to local causes. Then came the deaths of John and his wife and the return to the area of the mildly famous artist-scientist, Frances. After that the items settled back into local-flavor bits, like Lauren's champion 4-H calf and Bobby's appearance in a junior rodeo.

Jakels had appeared less frequently and less favorably, Meg noted, Marv senior turning up in the occasional police report for driving under the influence, or for a domestic altercation, Verna once for a face-off with the Forest Service over the number of cattle that had been turned onto the Jakel grazing allotment. At the age of sixteen, Ruthie Jakel had been an unsuccessful Rodeo Queen contestant; in her picture she looked poised and totally in command of a very large horse.

In 1978 the area had a spate of arrests of teenagers for drug use and drinking. In a late-August issue Meg came across the story of a party in the mountains, at a cabin owned by the Macrae family, that ended with a rolled pickup truck, a brush fire, and a fifteen-year-old girl found wandering naked and disoriented, claiming abduction and forced drugging and rape. The only participant named in the story was Marvin Jakel, Jr., who had the misfortune to be of age.

In the next issue the girl was declared to have changed her story. There had been no coercion and no drugs, just a drunken party that she had joined willingly. She had no memory of what had actually happened. The deputies had found drugs only in the possession of the hapless Marv Jakel, a small stash of marijuana. Jakel was arrested and charged.

And that was it, except for a mention two weeks later of the fact that Robert Macrae had decided to spend his senior year not at the local high school but at an exclusive prep school in southern California. Cause and effect, crime and if not punishment at least adjustment, all perfectly clear to the locals, Meg supposed.

She scanned headlines, social notes, and police reports covering the next four years: Frances occasionally, Bobby in two drunk-driving arrests, Lauren when she graduated from college and married. A year later came Bobby's disappearance, which didn't make headlines in the beginning because it developed as a story so slowly.

The night of his disappearance, June 21, Bobby Macrae had a fight in a bar with his frequent companion, Miss Ruth Ann Jakel—a loud and physical fight. Because of this falling-out, and because he'd been quarreling with his family for some time and living at the ranch only sporadically, several weeks passed before either family or friends began to take his absence seriously. When he finally was declared missing, the sheriff's department was faced with a very cold trail. The investigation was mentioned with gradually diminishing emphasis over the next few months' issues of the *Messenger*.

Probably she could read on for occasional "whatever happened to" stories or mentions of sightings, but Meg was weary and thought she'd spent time enough and to little purpose. She'd learned only two facts that struck her as significant: At the time of Bobby's disappearance, both Sam and Lauren were at the Macrae ranch for a brief stay before a trip to South America; and all three of the younger Jakels were in the area, the boys living at the ranch with their widowed mother and Ruthie in an apartment in town.

Meg nodded thanks to the teenaged girl behind the reception desk and took a deep breath before opening the door to the noonday heat. Wide Main Street and its colorful murals had little charm for her today, and the people on the sidewalks were going about their business with rapid strides and closed faces. Meanwhile, back at the ranch—she swallowed a silly giggle as that phrase crossed her mind—it was no doubt grim as well as hot, everybody grieving and worrying and waiting. If she were a truly good mother she would hurry back to provide some relief for Katy.

"Mrs. Halloran?"

"Oh!" Meg jumped at the touch of a hand on her arm and found herself looking into the weathered, concerned face of one of the people she'd met Friday night at the church. "Mrs., um, Prescott?"

"Irma, please. I saw you from across the street and wondered whether there'd been any news. About Lauren."

Meg shook her head. "Not up to two hours ago, anyway."

"I'm just so sorry. Everybody is." Irma Prescott was several inches shorter than Meg, with broad shoulders and a build that was solid without being fat. Her short hair was iron gray, but her blue eyes were clear and sharp; about fifty, Meg thought, and probably good for another forty years at least.

"Lauren was—excuse me, *is*—such a nice person, sweet is what I'd say, except it's an odd word for somebody six feet tall with flaming red hair, wouldn't you think?"

Meg merely nodded, and Irma nodded in return. "Everybody respects Frances, of course, always has. And Sam is, oh, pleasant, I guess, for somebody who's so famous. But Lauren is a person you can't help getting fond of. I just pray somebody finds her before she does herself harm."

Does *herself* . . . Meg followed this notion back to its source. "Do most people believe that Lauren shot Chuck Jakel and then ran away?"

"Well, sure! Most I've talked to, anyway. Of course, she shouldn't have gone home with him, not with a Jakel . . . but a woman's entitled to defend herself. Or to change her mind, come to that," she added with a little shrug. "Don't you think so, Mrs. Halloran?"

"Please, my name is Meg. And yes, I do." Chances were this woman had lived here all of her fifty years and could be far more informative, should she choose, than a weekly newspaper. "Irma, I was just going to look for a place to get a glass of iced tea and a sandwich. May I buy you lunch?"

The Bluebell Coffee Shop produced nice big sandwiches on bread that hadn't come out of a plastic wrapper, and potato salad in which the potatoes had maintained their shape and flavor. Meg gathered up the second half of a towering construction of bacon, lettuce, and tomato and took a big bite, her eyes on her companion. Just keep talking, please, she urged silently.

"Nobody I know ever got close to Lauren's and Bobby's mother, Angie. She was this real pretty little thing and not strong enough for most ranch work, or so she said. And she was Catholic, so she went to Sacred Heart here in Alturas instead of Stony Creek Community. I myself was some younger than Angie, and my oldest, Wayne, was five years younger than Bobby Macrae." Irma popped the last bite of corned beef on rye into her mouth and reached for the big bottle of Blue Heron ale, to top up both mugs.

"I haven't heard anyone say anything good about Bobby Macrae—except for Frances, of course," said Meg.

"No, I guess you wouldn't." The ale, a local product with full flavor and, Meg suspected, a fairly high alcohol content, had left a smear of its creamy head on Irma's upper lip, and she paused to use her napkin. "Frances was absolutely besotted with that boy, wouldn't let anyone offer help or suggestions, wouldn't hear a bad thing about him.

"But he wasn't her fault, really. After all, he was something like thirteen, fourteen when his parents died. Already running with the older kids, generally raising Cain. My mother had a name for him: Limb of Satan."

Irma spoke the final words in a rush, as if she meant them literally; then she flushed and looked away. "Oh, shoot, probably that's the beer talking. I don't remember much about the time John and Angie were killed. I was pregnant with what turned out to be a third boy and didn't know where we were going to put him or how we were going to feed him. I probably listened to Ma too much, or some of her church friends."

"Somebody told me that when Bobby was little, he spent most of his time at the Jakels' place."

"Shoot, you ever know a little boy wouldn't prefer a pigpen to a palace? Verna Jakel let all those kids run wild as the dogs and chickens. Ate whatever they wanted, took baths in the creek or not at all, slept out or in. Pastor Truman, he was at Stony Creek Community then, he used to go out and try to pray with Verna about raising little heathens, but she always went her own way."

Meg finished the last of her sandwich and salvaged a few shreds of bacon that had fallen to the plate. "Weren't the Jakels and the Macraes related in some way?"

Irma gave her a straight, probing look, and Meg concentrated on the ale bottle, dividing what was left in it evenly between their two mugs.

"Well, not exactly." Irma sighed and took a healthy swallow of ale. "Frances's and John's uncle Arthur, who was a couple years younger than their father, went off to fight in World War I and got gassed. He came back to the states, spent some time in a hospital in Tennessee or Kentucky or some such, and came home with a wife. Set up housekeeping on his half of the original ranch."

"Ah," said Meg.

"Problem was, the other Macraes thought the girl was trash, wouldn't have anything to do with her. Then pretty soon Arthur died, and the wife, Daphne her name was, brought her relatives out to help her. She didn't live long herself, had TB. And she didn't have any kids. So she left the ranch to her cousin Esau Jakel. And there they are to this day, the Jakels."

She drained her beer mug and set it aside. "And if Frances Macrae should find out I'm talking like this about her business, she'd come at me with a horsewhip."

Meg grinned at Irma, who outweighed Frances by about fifty pounds. "Not if she knew what was good for her, she wouldn't."

"Well, that's as may be."

"Irma, what did you think when Bobby disappeared?"

"Thought he'd finally run across somebody as mean as he was and misjudged him, like. We weren't here at the time,"

Irma added. "Ave and I took our three boys camping that summer, to Yellowstone and the Grand Canyon and Glacier Park. Wayne was sixteen, last time he was ever willing to go someplace with his folks."

"My daughter is nearly fourteen, and I'm not sure she'll have time for me two years from now." Meg finished her ale and mentally straightened her shoulders. "Thanks for the company and conversation, Irma. I'd better go see what's happening at the ranch."

"Tell Frances Macrae, and Sam Cavalier too, that Ave and I and other folks will be praying for them. For Lauren, that is."

"I'll tell them," said Meg, wishing she had a way to tell Lauren, who thought herself a local pariah.

"And if you want to know more about the time Bobby disappeared, the person you better talk to is Earl Douglas. Earl's out of office now, used to be sheriff; but ten years ago, he was undersheriff and did all the real work."

· 15 ·

A white van closely followed by a white sedan passed Meg in the opposite direction as she neared the ranch, giant letters on the doors of both registering only as K V something something as they sped past. Television, probably; the van had some strange-looking gear on its roof. And here came another vehicle, this one turning out of the ranch driveway. For a moment she thought it was Frances in her Jeep; then she registered dark gray rather than red and saw the breadth of the shoulders behind the sun-splashed windshield. She waved at Sam Cavalier, but he was intent on the road or his own thoughts and didn't see her.

An American-made four-door sedan bearing the seal of the Modoc County Sheriff's Department was parked on the road beside the driveway. Reproaching herself for having stayed away so long—God, it was nearly 1 P.M.!—Meg turned off the road and then braked hard as she saw a brown-uniformed figure coming toward her.

"Officer Garcia? Has there been trouble?"

"No ma'am, not really." Deputy Garcia was perhaps five feet six, slim and quick-looking; Meg remembered her work with her baton in the churchyard. Her face under a tumble of dark hair was narrow, tanned, and alert.

"I came to take Mr. Cavalier downtown to talk with Sheriff Vukovich, and these television guys were here. So I waited until Mr. Cavalier was through with them, and then he asked me to wait a while longer to see if you might get home. He's worried more newspeople might come and hassle Miss Macrae."

"Has something turned up about Lauren? Mrs. Cavalier?"

"I can't say, ma'am." Eyes on Meg's face, she relented

slightly. "Nothing major, no body or anything. The boss just wanted to talk to Mr. Cavalier again. Uh, you *are* Mrs. Halloran?"

"Margaret Halloran. I'm visiting with my daughter, Katy."

"Right, I met her. Nice kid. Look, this is none of my business, but could you maybe talk to Miss Macrae and try to get her to watch her mouth some? She's saying stuff about the Jakels that could get her in trouble."

"I'll try. Thank you, Officer Garcia."

The young woman sketched a half-salute as Meg drove on to the house.

Frances's Jeep was there, in company with a little teal blue number. A Porsche, Meg noted as she climbed out of her Honda—a Carrera, the version with the soft top. If this belonged to a reporter, the television must be network level.

"Mom!" Katy came running from the kitchen as Meg stepped inside the front door. "Where have you been? They arrested Sam!"

"No, they didn't." The words came plaintively from a boy trailing several steps behind Katy. Of medium height and looking less than that in baggy jeans, loose shirt, and slump-shouldered stance, he had a mop of shaggy brown hair over a face that was round and undistinguished except for a pair of beautiful gray-green eyes.

"Oh, Adam, shut up!"

"Katy, they don't arrest you by asking you to come downtown in your own car maybe sometime soon if you can manage it. Hi, Mrs. Halloran. I'm Adam Kingsley," he added, and put out a hand in gentlemanly fashion.

"Hello, Adam." The name struck no chord of memory, but the face, or perhaps the stance, was familiar; she thought this was the boy who'd been talking to Katy at the church Friday night, the one who'd offered to drive her home. So the Porsche must be his, although he looked hardly old enough to own a license, much less such a car.

"Sweetie, I suppose they had some information for Sam."

Meg framed Katy's worried face between her hands and kissed her forehead. "And probably some more questions.

"Sorry I was gone so long," she added. "Where are Frances and the children?"

"Aunt Frances is sitting out on the side porch," said Katy in low tones. "See, Sam let these TV reporters in, with their lights and cameras and stuff, and gave them an interview. I got to be on for a minute!" she added, forgetting her worries long enough to grin. "Just my face, no words. But Aunt Frances didn't like having them here and was really rude. I thought she was going to hit one guy with her cane."

"We made her some tea afterward," said Adam.

"And the kids are having their naps," said Katy with a gesture of weariness. "Sara is okay, I think. But Johnny's wild. He just howled and howled until he wore himself out."

"Katy, you've pulled your shift," said Meg. "I'll take over now, and you can go enjoy yourself for a while."

"Come home with me, and we'll go swimming," suggested Adam. "The pool is big, and there's a tower if you like to dive. I have a feeling you're a good diver."

"Thanks, Adam, but I think I'd like to stay here until Sam gets back," said Katy.

No to a ride in a Porsche convertible? to a chance to show off her considerable skills from a high board? Meg inspected Katy's troubled face and deduced that her daughter had fallen under the spell of Sam the beautiful. And Adam was far from beautiful, although he seemed nice enough.

"Katy, the Modoc County Sheriff's Department strikes me as fairly civilized. They probably do not indulge in—" Meg snapped her mouth shut on a remark about rubber hoses, remembering how it felt to be fourteen and in love. "Sam Cavalier is a grown man and not somebody who'd be easy to push around. I don't think you should worry about him; I think you should go have some fun."

Then motherhood kicked in: Lordy, am I sending my daughter off in a high-performance sports car with a boy or in fact a young *man* about whom I know nothing at all? When there's probably a murderer in the neighborhood?

"For a few hours, anyway," she added hastily. "Adam, where is it that you live?"

"In Goose Lake Heights. With my sister, Nancy, and my nephew, Brendan, he's five. And my brother-in-law, Dr. Emmett Smith."

Smith. The drug-clinic doctor Abby had pointed out the other night. Sounded perfectly respectable.

"Welll . . ." said Katy.

Adam stood quietly, looking from one Halloran to the other.

"While you're away," Meg said to her daughter, "I can have a long talk with Frances."

"That's a really good idea," said Katy. "Okay, Adam, I'll go get my suit."

Meg waited a moment and then spoke softly to Adam. "Katy is a fine diver, but she has too much nerve and competitive spirit for her own good. Please don't get her into a heavy-duty diving contest."

"Oh, I won't be any challenge to her. I'm a coward, especially about heights and the risk of pain."

Meg stared at him.

"But I'm a very careful driver. The Porsche was my father's idea; when I dropped out of school, he thought I needed something that would help me develop a new self-image. But the fact is, going from zero to sixty in five and a half seconds isn't something I really need to do. I'd have been perfectly happy with a nice little Toyota truck."

Frances was dozing on the porch, stretched out in a lounge chair with her head and shoulders in the shade, her lower body in the sun. It wasn't an easy sleep; a shoulder twitched as if shaking off a fly or a hand, the mouth pressed tight and then relaxed, dropping slightly open. It might be a kindness to wake her, thought Meg—an idea she dismissed almost the moment it struck her.

The house was quiet but less hot and stuffy than the day before; several windows were open, and a big ceiling fan stirred the air in the living room. The floors and other flat surfaces were dusty, Meg noticed, and the chairs and couches were rumpled and set askew. It was a home showing signs of its mistress's absence.

And so far as Meg was concerned, it could stay that way. She was not impelled to dust, nor to arrange furniture, but to prowl and think. If Lauren had gone into hiding, probably her sanctuary was not nearby; the sheriff or Sam would have located it, or some local person would have seen her and reported the fact.

So, somewhere else, but where? Palo Alto, where Lauren had gone to college? Or Berkeley? Meg remembered the occasional postcard from there, some years back. Magazines on a long table were national; a stack of newspapers contained only the local *Messenger* and the *New York Times*. A bookcase shelf reserved for travel books gave the world as a possibility, but Meg found a handful of guides to what must be almost neighborhood for the Cavaliers: Death Valley, Anza-Borrega out of San Diego, Mendocino County, Humboldt County. Wonderful California, only about a thousand miles long.

Giving up on the living room, Meg tipped her head to listen for any sound from Frances. If she woke, she would probably call out or make some kind of noise. She certainly wouldn't get up the stairs silently. Meg kept her own steps soft and quiet as she climbed the stairs to continue her prowl. She should feel guilty about this, she told herself as she pushed open the door to the room shared by Sam and Lauren, stepped inside, and gazed around. And did feel dreadful for just a moment, not for violating social rules but because of the photographs, most of them probably Sam's work. Wedding pictures, pictures of Sam and Lauren on mountainsides and snowfields and lakeshores. Pictures of the children separately and with Lauren. Several wonderful color shots of Lauren alone, smiling, laughing, mugging for the camera. The pictures made Meg's throat hurt.

There was also, on the tall chest, an older, candid color shot of a lanky, red-haired man leaning against the corral fence: Lauren's father, probably. None of his wife. None of Bobby.

The deputy searched here, Meg reminded herself. Nevertheless, she pulled open drawers in the bedside tables, peered into the recesses of the small desk. A thin sheaf of personal letters inspired hope for a moment but proved disappointing; three of them were from Meg herself and two from Sam. A clutch of postcards occupied the same receptacle: two Monet reproductions signed with a squiggle, a Venice Beach boardwalk scene from someone named Rae, and two from a Beth depicting Trinidad Head. These last gave Meg a pang; Trinidad on the north coast was as beautiful as Port Silva and even foggier.

She found nothing resembling a diary or journal. No appointment calendar; probably the cops had taken it as they had the address book. No snapshots of people who might be friends. This room was dusty, too, and cluttered with Sam's discarded clothes and his open, not-yet-unpacked suitcase.

She slipped out the door, stood listening hard for a moment, then moved very quietly down the stairs and across the hall to Frances's bedroom. The door was closed, but it opened under her touch with no sound, which was a good thing because Frances herself was sitting—and Meg certainly hoped sleeping—on the porch just a few feet to the left of the curtained French doors on the far wall.

The room was as she'd remembered it from an earlier glance, a veritable picture gallery. The longest of the inner walls was lined with corkboard, four-foot-high panels of the stuff mounted flush against each other eighteen inches from the ceiling, framed top and bottom with narrow wood molding. Photographs, in black and white as well as color, were fixed to the cork with pushpins.

High on the left were faded brown photos from early in the century—mostly of a tall, bearded man in rough clothes. Below these she found shots of a small child who looked like Lauren but aged over a dozen or so poses into boy and then young man. Lauren's father, Frances's younger brother?

For the rest, most of the photos were of Bobby, from in-the-cradle age to obviously adult, or as adult as Bobby had managed to get. Meg took her time moving from picture to picture, trying to see the soul, or spirit, or intelligence, behind that beautiful face. Nothing came through to her.

He was the key, though, she was sure of it. What did you do? she asked silently. What happened to you, and why is it still happening, still creating misery?

Silly, and pointless. Talk to people, not pictures. Meg sighed and glanced at the rest of the pictures. Bobby's total was going to be surpassed, eventually, by Johnny's; poor little kid had obviously spent much of his brief life looking at a camera.

Sara appeared only four—no, five—times. Meg made an indignant mental note to suggest to Lauren that . . .

Shit. Her throat was hurting again, and her head as well, from trying to reach conclusions with no facts at all. This was just the dusty room of a testy, complicated old woman, smelling of potpourri and cologne but also, a little, of old age, like the room where Verna Jakel drank beer and waited to die. Neat closet, clothes evenly spaced on their hangers, sweaters in compartments in a hanging bag; sneakers and dressier shoes on a rack, Western riding boots standing on their own. Expensive black shoulder bag hanging from a hook, keys dangling from its front pocket.

A clatter came from outside, followed by an angry mutter. Meg tried to move on her toes as she fled the room, pausing to pull the door shut behind her. "Frances? I'm coming," she called softly from the hallway, hoping that the noise hadn't disturbed the sleeping children.

"I'm all right," Frances replied. "I simply dropped my cane. Where is Sam?"

"Uh, I believe he's in town."

"He's not back from the sheriff's office yet? Ridiculous!" Frances planted her cane and pulled herself laboriously to her feet, waving away Meg's outstretched hand. "He's told them everything he knows. Why can't they leave him alone?"

"Probably they need his help. Besides, when a wife dies or disappears, the police always look her husband over pretty thoroughly; statistics force them to."

"Ridiculous," Frances said again. "Harassment is what this is; I'm going to call my attorney."

"That would probably be a good idea." Meg followed the old woman into the house, an ear cocked toward the upstairs, where blessed silence still prevailed.

"Well. Perhaps I'll wait until Sam comes back and let him decide," said Frances. "Meg, I believe there's a bottle of wine open in the fridge. Could I ask you to pour me a glass? And one for yourself, of course."

"Not for me, right now. But I'll get one for you."

Frances nodded and headed for the living room, where she settled into her recliner but kept it upright. She took the proffered wine with a sigh of pleasure. "Thank you."

Meg perched on the arm of one of the wing chairs. "Frances, does Lauren have any good friends in town?"

"Well, she sees people at church. And she volunteers at the library; I'm sure she meets people there."

"Is there any woman her own age she spends time with?"

Frances shook her head. "I don't think so. She's quite busy here at home, with the children. And the garden."

"What about the children she played with when she was a girl? Have any of her close childhood friends stayed here?"

Frances lifted her chin. "I have no idea who her childhood friends might have been. I visited the ranch no more than once or twice a year while Lauren and Bobby were small, and my stays were always brief. When John and Angie were killed, I returned here only to bury them and collect the children. If there were playmates around then, I don't remember them."

"But—"

"Margaret, why are you quizzing me? What is this all about?"

About Lauren. And Bobby. And a series of events for which the term *coincidence* seemed woefully inadequate. Meg said none of this but asked in conversational tones, "Frances, why do you think Bobby ran away?"

"To punish me," came the answer at once, in a near-whisper.

"But why?"

"He wanted the ranch sold, so he could have his third in cash. Sam and Lauren refused to sell, and so did I. I wish I hadn't," she added.

"Couldn't one of you have bought him out?"

"I didn't have the money."

"Couldn't Lauren have done it? Or rather, Sam?"

"Not right then. Sam's income from his work was just beginning to exceed his expenses, and he didn't come into his mother's money until he was thirty-five." Frances blinked, set her teeth, and drew breath through them with a sound like the hiss of an angry snake. "You're as bad as those reporters," she said coldly. "One of them suggested to me that Bobby had come back and murdered his sister. I won't have any more of this, from them or from you."

"Frances, who was the father of Lauren's baby?"

Frances stared at her, openmouthed, for a long moment. "Her—what on earth do you mean? Sam is the father of Lauren's children."

"No, I mean the baby she didn't have when she was sixteen. The abortion. Did she tell you who it was?"

The older woman got out of the recliner with surprising speed. "Lauren never had an abortion, unless it happened during that year she stayed with you and as a result of your lack of supervision. *I* didn't want to leave her there, with a single woman far too young to have good sense."

Meg stared into the angry brown eyes, trying to remember. It was Lauren who'd told her of the abortion, as if she felt

Meg was entitled to know that fact, that black mark against someone who would be sharing her home, but she'd volunteered nothing further. Meg and Frances had met, at school and later at Meg's apartment, but . . . she didn't remember Frances's being present at the time of Lauren's confession. Had it been a fiction concocted for some obscure teenaged reason?

"I will not, I absolutely will not have this kind of talk in my home, in Sam's home. If you persist with this filth, I'll ask you to leave and—"

Meg had been hearing, and ignoring, a series of thumps from above. Now the thumps were drowned out by a roaring wail of rage and misery; Johnny was awake.

"Oh, dear," whispered Frances, her shoulders sagging. "Oh, dear."

"Finish your wine, Frances. I'll get him."

Katy surfaced, shook her short hair out of her eyes, and swam to the edge of the pool. She pulled herself up and out in one smooth motion, tugged down the seat of the black tank suit that had fit her only two or three months ago, and trotted across the deck to the umbrella and lounge chairs.

"This is an awesome pool," she said to Adam as she flopped into a chair and reached for her tall glass of lemonade.

"You're an awesome diver." Adam had swum for a while, without much grace or enthusiasm. Then he had retreated to the shade of the umbrella, probably a good idea because his skin was really pale. "Doesn't it scare you, to stand up there and then just throw yourself off into space?" he asked.

"Nope. Well, a little," she amended. "That's part of what makes it fun."

"Not for me. I can't do it. I can't go off that tower even feet first."

"No reason to do it except for fun," she said. "So if it's not fun for you, you shouldn't do it."

"Q.E.D.," he said.

Katy had a fair idea what that meant but chose not to test it. Instead she stretched lower in the chair and turned her head lazily against its padded back, gazing around her. Enormous pool. Green, green grass that seemed kind of empty without cows on it. *Big* houses set at odd angles on land that looked as if somebody had hand-patted it here and there into little hill shapes. The houses weren't quite far enough apart for their size, and they were . . . show-off houses. *Ostentatious*, that was the word.

The one right across the pool, for instance, was made of brick with white trim. It had square posts two stories tall across its front, holding up a porch roof that was too high to provide any protection to somebody standing at the door. So there was a little separate lower roof for that. A plantation house in cow country, it needed trees and . . . vines, maybe.

"Ugly, huh? Money but no taste," Adam remarked, looking at the brick house.

"The problem is, it doesn't fit very well. Your sister's house is nice, though," she added.

Adam swiveled his head around to glance at the vaguely southwestern house behind them. "It's okay. It fits the landscape fairly well, and it's big and comfortable."

"How come you live with your sister?"

Adam shrugged. "My mother took off years ago, my old man is always busy or traveling, I like northern California a whole lot better than L.A. And I like my sister and Brendan."

Katy had met the Smith family when she and Adam arrived, and she had found Nancy pleasant enough; the little boy, Brendan, was so quiet after Johnny Cavalier that she wondered, a bit, whether he was healthy. Probably with that oily, never-stop-talking father, he couldn't get a word in. "How about your sister's husband?"

"Emmett's not as bad as he looks. He was a doctor in a fancy detox clinic. Drugs," he added in response to Katy's questioning look. "Nancy had been on one thing or another since her freshman year in high school, really messed herself up. Emmett got her straightened out."

"Oh." Katy felt chastened, for a moment; then she decided that Adam wasn't putting her down but was simply relaying information. She finished her lemonade and got to her feet.

"I've had a really good time, but I ought to be getting home."

"They probably need you, that little kid in particular." Adam followed her across the pool deck, across the grass and quickly across the asphalt road, then up a flagstone path that had been dampened recently and was cool underfoot. Beside the broad, recessed doorway a Rottweiler lifted his head from his paws and twitched his stump of a tail vigorously, then even harder as Katy leaned down to pat his broad head.

"See, even Erik likes you."

Katy gave a moment's wistful thought to her own dog, an enormous, shaggy Komondor named Grendel. Lots nicer and a whole lot smarter than a Rottweiler, and probably he was missing her. Inside, she trailed Adam across polished floors with patterned rugs, up a broad staircase, and down a hall to his room, his apartment really.

The biggest room had rugs and a couch, chairs, a padded window seat. It also had floor-to-ceiling bookcases, crammed full, a big-screen Mac computer and several million dollars, it looked like, of music system.

There was a bedroom as well, and a tiny, closetlike kitchen. And the biggest bathroom she'd ever seen in a house, where she changed out of her suit while trying to convince herself not to be intimidated by all this *stuff* Adam owned. She returned to the living room with her chin out and her eyes narrowed, and stalked around to inspect books and pictures. He had more wolf books than any library she'd been in, plus tons of books on other animals. Glancing over the photos, she stopped short and stared at a familiar face: the guide from Wolf Haven. Well, two familiar faces, because Adam was in that one, too.

"That was one of the teams for the howling survey last year, in Idaho," Adam said.

"Wow." Katy's awe of his possessions was lost in her envy

of this achievement. Wolf Haven trained volunteers for these surveys, but you had to be eighteen, alas. "So, how many wolves did you find?"

"Only five in our sector. Seventeen altogether, I think, but it looked like all of them were singles. I think it will turn out to be the same in Washington state, just a few loners that wander in from British Columbia and then go back. Except probably in Glacier, wolves aren't going to get back to breeding level in the western United States without help."

"Not here, for sure. Too many cows. Hey, here's some neat stuff; where did you get these?" She began shuffling through a stack of paperbound booklets, some with drawings of wolves on their covers: "Central Idaho Wolf Recovery," published by the Forest Service. "Northern Rocky Mountain Wolf Recovery Plan," published by U.S. Fish and Wildlife.

"Those are government publications; anyone can get them," said Adam.

The Northern Rocky Mountain book, spiral-bound in plastic along its side, had been dog-eared and highlighted. Katy leafed through, finding that wolves had been protected in Montana since 1975 and in Idaho since 1977; that fish and game departments had once been under orders to acomplish the "extermination of wolves, coyotes," and so forth. "Oops," she said aloud. "Listen to this: 'Wolf recovery areas should not be superimposed over major livestock-producing areas.' I'd say that pretty much takes care of Modoc County."

"I guess," said Adam with a grimace. "In this county the human population is about ninety-six hundred, and this year there are fifty-nine thousand cows here. But some people, including Sam Cavalier, think the situation is temporary. Cavalier says the romance of the range was made up by rich guys with political connections who wanted their government subsidies to continue, and that open grazing of beef is a waste the public at large won't put up with for much longer."

"But if people want to eat beef . . ." Katy cast an assessing look at her new friend; was that pudgy body vegetable-fed? "Adam, do you eat meat?"

"Even if I didn't," he replied huffily, "I think other people should be able to. And wolves should. And dogs. But there are ways to produce beef without filling the national forests with cowshit."

"Absolutely!" said Katy, and then remembered her conversation with Tracy Turner and the remarks of some of the others on the church lawn. "But I don't know how you'll convince the ranchers."

"It will have to be political, eventually."

"So what are you going to do, run for president?"

Adam shrugged. "I thought about it for a while, after I decided I really didn't want to be a mathematician. And I read a lot of political history. But the problem is, I'm not tall, I'm not good-looking, and I'm not charming."

Katy tipped her head and gave him a careful, thorough look-over. "Well. Probably you could do something about the charming part. And you're smart, that should count."

He shook his head. "I think smart's a handicap, if it shows. But I just had this terrific idea." He folded his arms on his chest and looked at her with his eyes wide and serious. *Earnest* was the word, she thought, and wondered if he was setting her up for something.

"In another, oh, twenty years the country will probably be ready for a woman president. One like you're going to be, tall and good-looking. And I could be the behind-the-scenes husband."

"Running things, you mean?" Katy shook her head. "Wrong, Adam. Really, reeeeelly wrong. Maybe I'll be tall and good-looking—"

"And charming."

This stopped her for only a moment. "No way, definitely not charming. But smart. If I ever get to be president I'll run things *myself*."

"Yeah, I bet that would be a problem," he said, grinning. "I guess I'd better revise my plan."

"What you'd better do is stick to wolves." Katy picked up her swim bag, cast a last look at the bookshelves, and pulled out a volume, another, and a third. "Okay if I borrow a couple of books?"

Nancy was somewhere else, presumably with Brendan. Dr. Emmett nodded to them from one of the big downstairs rooms as they passed. Adam's Porsche had been parked under a roof like a carport at the side of the house, so its leather seats were cool against her legs.

"You want to come swimming tomorrow?" he asked as he drove slowly down the private road.

"I don't know if I can. Depends on what's happening."

"Right," said Adam. "So I'll call you tomorrow, if that's okay."

The road wound gently around to the gated entrance, where a very large black man stepped out of the gatehouse to smile and wave them through.

"I've never lived where there was a guard on duty," said Katy.

"That's Walter; he used to play for the Raiders. People with lots of money have to take precautions," said Adam. "Especially if they've got kids."

· 16 ·

"Oh, good, here you are," said Meg in the voice that had brought numberless adolescents to heel. "Now you can tell us what happened this afternoon."

Sam Cavalier, who had just come downstairs after reading a bedtime story to Sara, looked both startled and slightly offended. Who is this woman to be questioning me? was the import of his glance, and Meg had a reply right at hand if needed: the very one who has been taking care of your children and cosseting your elderly aunt and generally busting her butt around here and is entitled to some information.

"Well, I was going out to the studio—"

"Yes, Sam. Come right now and tell us what's going on," said Frances.

Sam gave the faintest of shrugs and came into the living room, where the women and Katy were having after-dinner coffee, Katy with a book in her lap. He had returned home late that afternoon with a nasty abrasion on his jaw, offering as explanation only the remark that he'd had a run-in with Marv Jakel. He had then disappeared into his studio, where he remained until summoned to dinner.

His jaw was swollen now and should ripen by tomorrow into something approximating an eggplant. "Nice bruise," said Meg. "Good thing it happened after you'd done your television number." He had been impressive in his brief appearance on what turned out to be the evening news from Reno—strong and earnest, pleading for any word about the young wife and mother whose picture he displayed.

"Oh my, yes," said Frances. "Sam, why did Marvin Jakel hit you?"

Sam blew out a long breath and sat down in one of the wing chairs. "The bastard spewed out this stream of filth about my wife, right there on the courthouse steps. So I hit him, he hit back, and unfortunately one of the deputies came out and broke us up."

"What did he say?"

"Aunt Frances, you don't want to know," he said, shaking his head and casting a glance in Katy's direction.

When their only response was an expectant silence, he slouched lower in the chair, stretched out his legs, and spoke rapidly, miserably, to his own boots. "He said Lauren had been screwing Chuck, and screwing him over, practically all his life. Said she had no right to shoot him Friday night just because he expected her to . . . do what she always did." He slid another sideways look at Katy, his face coloring; Meg decided that it wasn't only her daughter's youth that was bothering him, it was her status as his wholehearted admirer. A man discussing his wife's fairly public unfaithfulness doesn't look much like a hero.

"Katy," said Meg, bracing for a battle, "you've had a busy day. Why don't you go to bed early and maybe read for a while?" To her astonishment Katy simply stood up, folded a finger into her paperback book, said a quiet good-night, and departed.

"Marvin Jakel is a degenerate, and you should not dirty your hands on him," said Frances.

"Well, *I'm* glad you hit him, and I wish I'd been there to do the same." Meg wanted to go further, to defend Lauren, but she didn't know enough, she hadn't been close enough, and Lauren's morals were deeply and basically none of her business. "What I think," she said, "is that Jakel is trying to deflect suspicion from himself. I've heard that Chuck was expected to inherit the ranch when his mother died."

"There won't be anything left to inherit but debts," said Frances in tones of satisfaction. "Who told you that about Chuck?"

"I don't remember," Meg lied. "Sam, what line is the sheriff's department pursuing now?"

Sam sighed and let his shoulders slump. "Sheriff Vukovich should be out chasing rustlers, or maybe cows. He still thinks Lauren is the killer, but he keeps asking me where she is, trying to show how clever he is by sneaking in these repeat questions when he thinks I'm not paying attention. Vukovich obviously believes I helped her escape, or at least that I've heard from her and know where she's hiding."

"That's ridiculous," snapped Frances.

"Certainly seems that way to me," said Sam. "And he's playing the same kind of game with my whereabouts before Sunday—snap questions that he's asked half a dozen times already."

"I'm glad I didn't vote for that man," said Frances. "You shouldn't talk to him again without an attorney, Sam."

"Don't worry, Frances. He's just flailing around because he's frustrated. And by God, so am I! One more day like today, and I'll be punching out cops."

"Have they come up with any evidence?" asked Meg.

"Nothing that sounds very important. The road to the cabin is just a pair of ruts, not much good for tire prints. Besides, Ruthie Jakel drove down there Saturday morning. Chuck Jakel had spread gravel around the cabin, to keep dust down, so there were no clear tire prints there, either."

"What about a gun?"

Sam shrugged. "Marv and Ruthie *think* Chuck had a .22 rifle and an old shotgun. The rifle was found in the cabin, but there was no shotgun."

Oh, yes—the ubiquitous shotgun. Here in ranch country, the potential murderer need not even bother to bring his own weapon because his potential victim is sure to have one lying around. Meg pushed that chilling notion aside. "Has the sheriff said, or do you know, whether Marv Jakel or Ruthie can prove where they were Friday night?"

"Well, I did talk for a few minutes to that nice little lady deputy, Grace Garcia." Sam's brief smile had canary feathers at its edges. "Their only alibi is their mother, and she's pretty vague about Marv. Seems Verna is sure Ruthie was in by 10 P.M. or so, and she *thinks* she heard Marv come in sometime around midnight. Estimated time of death is several hours later than that."

"Verna is a liar, and on drugs as well," said Frances.

"Grace did say that Verna is taking lots of medicine and is believed to be washing it down with beer," Sam replied. "So her credibility is not going to be right up there."

Seeing no need to contribute her bit of support to this, Meg watched Sam and Frances exchange looks of—what, superiority? pleasure in the approaching demise of somebody neither of them liked? Wishing she had a polite way to escape, Meg heard the doorbell and remembered that she had in fact arranged one.

As Sam stood up and said, "Who the hell—?" and Frances sputtered something about not seeing anyone, Meg looked at her watch and headed for the door.

"I'll get it," she said over her shoulder. "I think it's probably for me."

She flicked on the porch light and then opened the door to former sheriff Earl Douglas, who stood at ease with his hands in the pockets of a bomber-style leather jacket.

"Evening, Meg. It's chilly tonight; better bring a coat," he said as he stepped inside.

"I'll go get something and say good-bye to my daughter," she said. "Why don't you chat a moment with Sam and Miss Macrae?"

It was still a pickup truck, high to climb into and bouncy on its underloaded springs, but at least it had bucket seats, high-backed and deep and comfortable. And no gun rack across the rear window, a circumstance that gratified her. She didn't feel up to riding around with a shotgun just behind her head.

As they left the driveway for the road, Meg tossed a glance at the man beside her. He was certainly big enough to command respect, his six-two or so of height backed up by a thick chest and long, solid arms. Add to this his easy bearing and the good-old-boy look of that long face, and you had a man hardly anybody would want to get mad at. Meg settled back into her seat and felt herself begin to relax for the first time in days: jaw, neck, shoulders.

She must have sighed aloud, because Douglas grinned without taking his eyes off the road. "Pretty tense in the Macrae household, I bet. You must be more than ready for a nice, quiet drink in a nice, quiet bar."

"I certainly am," she said with some force. That was at least half the reason for her late-afternoon telephone call to the big ex-sheriff; without a change of scene or pace, she'd soon be shrieking at unexpected noises or baring her teeth at chance remarks.

"You planning on staying much longer?" her rescuer asked.

Her jaw tightened involuntarily, and she made herself yawn to relax it. "I don't know. I don't see how I can leave just yet."

"Suppose not," he agreed. "Miss Frances Macrae is a little bit like royalty around here. People admire her and respect her, but that's different from offering to come in and help out. And Cavalier's got no relatives, I believe I heard?"

"I think that's true." Lauren had told her that Sam's parents were dead and that he had no brothers or sisters.

"Well, it's real kind of you to stay. And I was surely glad to hear from you; be nice to talk with somebody new about life someplace else." He shot a sideways glance at her, the corner of his mouth quirking up. "Or were you thinking to pump the old country-boy ex-sheriff, find out what he might know about the local murder investigation?"

"Could I have that nice, quiet drink anyway, while I decide?"

He laughed aloud, a two-note bark that rang like gong-strokes in the metal chamber of the truck's cab, but he didn't pat her knee as she had half expected he would. Maybe Vince was wrong in estimating that she could handle this man. Maybe she wouldn't even try.

Douglas drove out of the little town of Stony Creek in a direction Meg thought was southeast. Soon he pulled into a big parking lot before a single-story wooden building with a roof that sloped forward over a long railed porch. A sign over the double door said, in blue neon, "Charlie's Place."

"Weekends, Charlie's can get kinda strenuous," Douglas said as he parked at the outer edge of the sparsely filled lot. "But on a Monday night, it's more or less civilized."

He came around the truck as she stepped down and reached past her to slam the door. Meg shrugged her coat—a long sweater, really—closer around her shoulders and put her hands in its pockets as they set off toward the building. A step or two ahead of Douglas, she was the first to hear the low, bitter voice.

"Son of a bitch, son of a bitch, son of a bitch, fuck!" A woman's voice, thought Meg, and then she saw the woman or at any rate her short-skirted rump and long bare legs as she bent to reach into the open hatchback of a small, light-colored car. Meg stopped, and Douglas, behind her, put a hand on her arm; the woman straightened, teetered back on four-inch heels, and tossed a jack to the ground.

The little car had a very flat rear tire, Meg saw. Then the woman, sensing their presence, half-turned, and Meg recognized Ruthie Jakel.

"Well, shit, what're the two of you gawking at? Just fuck off, okay?"

A pair of floods attached to the porch roof of Charlie's Place threw a low, glancing light over the lot, and as Ruthie turned her head to glare at Douglas, Meg saw that the left side of her face was puffy and bruised.

"Who beat you up, Ruthie?" asked Douglas softly.

"Mind your own business. Nobody beat me up, I just fell down." She turned and looked at her car. "And I'll probably fall on the other side of my face unless I can get some help here. You too important to change a tire for a lady, Sheriff?"

Douglas grimaced as he looked at the oiled dirt of the parking lot and then at his own trousers. He had dressed up for the evening, Meg noticed belatedly, wearing not Levi's but tan wool gabardine slacks of a trim western cut. Very susceptible to grease, those would be.

Douglas was glancing around the lot. "Think I'll delegate this one, Ruthie. I see a couple of younger, stronger guys are here, used to be my deputies; bet they'll be glad to perform a civic duty and help out a lady. Be right back, Meg. Oh—forgot my manners. Meg Halloran, Ruth Jakel."

Muttering under her breath, Ruthie bent to retrieve the jack and then squatted to try to position it under the rear axle. "You could get the handle out of the back, okay?"

"Okay." The rear of the car was a tumble of blankets and pillows and a sleeping bag or maybe two. Meg fished around along the edges and came up with the foot-and-a-half-long tire iron. "Got it," she said, and moved back around the car to where Ruthie still crouched.

"I want to tell you," she said quietly, "that I'm very sorry about your brother."

"Yeah. Me too." Ruthie didn't get up, just squatted there and turned her head, so that the light from the bar fell on her face. Her left eye was merely a slit in puffy, darkened flesh, and her lower lip was swollen and split—the damage fairly recent, Meg thought. From more than one blow, and it must have hurt a lot. Meg shuddered and gripped the tire iron with both hands.

"Can I—is there anything I can do to help you?"

"Sure. Give me a million dollars and a couple one-way tickets to L.A. or someplace." Ruthie leaned forward to give the jack another shove, teetered on her heels, and regained her balance with a hand against the car's flank. She rested her forehead against the hand, her shoulders a tight line that spoke of both defiance and despair.

A chilly little wind sprang from nowhere, penetrating Meg's sweater and sending an empty beer can into a rattling roll past her feet. She heard no human sound except Ruthie's breathing and her own. Dark cars crouched on every side like silent, waiting animals, and overhead the high sky was black and moonless.

Hands gripped her elbows from behind, and Meg careened back through time to another parking lot, another hard grip. She shrieked and pulled free, spinning around with the tire iron high; only Douglas's quick footwork saved him from a blow.

"Jesus!"

"Oh, shit. I'm *sorry*." She let the tire iron fall to the ground and put her hands to her face, fingers pressing against her eyelids.

"Okay, it's okay. I shouldn't have grabbed you. Jocko, you help Miz Jakel change this tire. I'm gonna take Mrs. Halloran in for a drink."

"Sure."

Meg took a deep breath, dropped her hands, and saw a lanky, fair-haired young man bend to pick up the tire iron. She wanted to say something, but her mouth was cottony-dry.

"Come on. Okay if I hold on to you now? Just friendly, okay?"

Meg found her voice. "Don't you patronize me, Earl Douglas."

"No ma'am! I am not doing that. Look, I can tell you've been real scared sometime, I been there myself a time or two. And I want to say, I sure admire your reflexes."

"Yours are pretty good, too."

"I sure am glad of that. Now, let's go inside and find a corner where we can both sit and shake."

Charlie's Place was cavernous, with a long bar and a scatter of tables as well as wooden booths along the walls.

In a corner booth Douglas ordered Wild Turkey for himself, a Bombay martini for Meg, and kept silent until the drinks came.

"I remember hearing something last year," he said when the barmaid had left. "That some guy grabbed you and held you hostage."

"Yes, I was kidnapped from . . ." Meg took a deep breath and rejected the comfortable distance of the passive voice. "A man took us, Vince's niece and me, from a parking lot. He subsequently raped her. What he did to me was terrorize, humiliate, and beat me." She tasted her drink. "When I saw Ruthie Jakel's face tonight, I was suddenly back in that place, looking in a mirror."

She took another slow sip of icy gin. "But it's a year later, that man is safely locked up, and I'm having a nice drink in this nice, quiet bar. How on earth did you hear about it?"

"Once a cop, I guess. We just like to watch what's going on. When Vince's name turned up in the story, that really caught my attention. We had some good times, him and me," he added with a grin. "When we were just uniforms in L.A. Used to shoot cutthroat pool, try to outdrink each other, steal each other's women."

"Vince?" said Meg, who knew her husband as a peaceful man and a very moderate drinker.

"Oh, yeah. I could hold my liquor better, probably because I'm bigger. But the women always went for Vince. He was just too damned good-looking."

"But weren't you both married? Do you mean the two of you hustled each others' *wives*?"

"Oh no, no ma'am." Douglas shook his head and then grinned again. "Well, I might've, but not Vince; he's a much nicer guy than me. Nope, the stealing was before and after being married."

Meg came to attention. Vince's brief first marriage, nearly twenty-five years in the past, was something he never talked about. "What was his wife like?" she asked.

"She was a liberated southern belle, that's what." Douglas's mouth drew down in distaste. "From Georgia, Virginia, someplace like that. Sexy little yellow-haired number with this soft voice and these big blue eyes, real cute. Had a mouth like a sewer when she got mad."

"Good heavens," said Meg. "She doesn't sound at all Vince's type."

"Well, she liked his looks, one thing. And I always thought she liked the fact that he was more or less brown; like I said, she was liberated and made a point of proving it."

"So what happened?"

"She wanted him to go to law school, like he'd been saying he might. When he decided he'd rather stay a cop, she divorced him quick as that." Douglas snapped his fingers. "I thought he was lucky," he added. "And so did he, I think. After a while."

Quite a long while, thought Meg. Rotten little southern bitch. "What happened to *your* wife?"

"First one, nice lady too, left me because I screwed around. Second one, we both screwed around until we both got bored, and then she left. It took me a long time to grow up from being an asshole; I guess I'm still working on that."

"Some people don't even try," she noted. "Douglas, who do you suppose beat up Ruthie Jakel?"

"Jocko—the deputy I got to change the tire, Jocko Riordan—says her face was already messed up when she came in here for a drink, alone, maybe an hour ago. One thing you can be sure of, she won't talk to the law about it; Jakels got a rule about that."

"Could it have been her brother? He had a fight with Sam Cavalier today."

Douglas shrugged. "In their younger days, Marv wouldn't have dared lay a finger on her. But he's just put in four years in prison, where he probably added considerably to his collection of bad habits."

"Do you think he could have killed his own brother?"

Douglas folded his big hands around his drink and cocked his head at her. "Sure he could. So could a whole bunch of other folks, including Lauren Macrae, although I'm damned if I see why she would have."

"That's what I think, so I really need to know—" Douglas was shaking his head slowly, and she sighed and closed her mouth.

"Honest to God, Meg, I can't talk about the specifics of Lou Vukovich's murder investigation—even if I knew 'em. If I pick up on anything major, I'll let you know there's something up, and you, or more likely Cavalier, can push Vuke on it."

"Will that do any good?"

Douglas lowered his head, and his voice. "He's nobody's top cop, and he's not real smart. But he likes living here and being sheriff, so he'll try not to step on important toes. Just tell Cavalier not to get too shitty with him; the man's got a big ego and a thin skin."

Terrific, thought Meg. Sounds like Sam's twin, except Sam's smart. But probably not smart enough to be polite.

"He doesn't like me much," Douglas was saying, "so I more or less stay out of his way. If there's something I think Vuke needs to know, I leak it through one of his deputies. This is my neck of the woods, too, and I like it."

"Douglas, do you have an opinion about Lauren? Where she might be?"

His good-humored face took on a somber look. "I don't. See, we got mostly trees and cows up here, not streets and houses. Middle of the night, there'd be nobody to notice a blue pickup truck helling it off into Nevada. Or somebody wants to hide a body, or even a truck, there's plenty of room."

She knew all that; why was she wasting time? "Okay, I accept that you can't talk about the current case. But what about one ten years back? Tell me, former undersheriff Douglas, what do you think happened to Bobby Macrae?"

He inhaled in the middle of a swallow and spent a moment sputtering into his handkerchief. "Shit, waste of good bourbon. You are a very pushy lady, you know that?"

"You're not the first person who's noticed."

"I bet. Well, what the hell. That was all ten years ago, and you're a certified friend of the family. What did you want to know?"

"Did you think, at the time, that he was dead, or that he'd simply left?"

"At the time, I thought he'd just run off to avoid marriage or a paternity suit or some other problem he'd stirred up for himself. Not to say I knew him well," added Douglas, pausing to sip bourbon. "I was born here, but I went into the service right after high school and hardly gave this place a thought for the next twenty years."

He drained his drink abruptly and signaled the barmaid. "Same again," he said, and Meg, about to protest, realized that her glass was empty. Well, she wasn't driving, and clearly the former sheriff wasn't worried about his own blood-alcohol content. She pulled a bowl of snack mix closer and began to pick out the nuts and small pretzels.

"I hadn't figured on coming back ever," he told her. "But I was feeling pretty useless after my second wife took a walk, and L.A. was getting uglier and dirtier every day, seemed like. So when I heard about an opening in the Modoc County Sheriff's Department, I bought myself a pickup truck and came on home."

The barmaid set fresh drinks before them. "Anyway, Bobby Macrae. It was a cold trail by the time we really got on it. The last person known to have seen him was Ruthie Jakel. The two of them spent the evening of June 21 drinking right here, except it was called the Bar None then. They had a big fight—cursing, screaming, even punching each other, according to about twenty people who saw it. Then she ran out, and he ran after her, and everybody was real happy for the quiet."

Meg nodded. "I read some of this in the newspaper. Ruthie said their fracas in the bar was just the worst of several recent 'disagreements,' so when he didn't turn up the next day, she assumed he'd just gone off to sulk for a while."

Douglas bent his head and swirled his glass, clinking the

ice cubes; in the dim light from the wall sconce illuminating their booth, his thatch of curls gleamed like a scrolled silver helmet. "Ruthie was driving that night," he said, "because Macrae had put his truck in a ditch the day before, and it was in the shop waiting for a new axle. She says he caught up to her in the parking lot and tried to get her car keys, but she fought him off. So he cursed her; said he didn't need her anyway, he'd hitch a ride; and he took off down the highway. She says that was the last she saw of him.

"The feeling I got when I talked with her," he added, "she was happy enough not to have to deal with him for a while—until she realized she was pregnant, anyway. Then she started pounding on his aunt's door."

"He never got home the night he and Ruthie had their fight?"

"Not so far as anyone at the Macrae ranch knew, or so they said. Although it's not real far; he could have walked it. Miss Macrae told us that Bobby often slept in the barn if he got in late. And he hadn't been coming home a lot anyway—been spending his nights with Ruthie or with other friends.

"Anyhow, nobody in his family was much worried, either. Turned out he'd been fighting with them for months, mostly over division of the ranch, as I recall. Their idea, at first, anyway, was that he'd finally given up and just gone off mad."

"Frances says he did it to punish her."

Douglas shrugged. "We never did find anyone who'd given him a ride that night, and by the time we got a full investigation under way, nobody had an alibi. Ruthie had her own place in Alturas, little cottage off an alley where nobody noticed any comings or goings. Marv said he was sleeping off a drunk in his own barn. Chuck was—I don't remember, but it was uncorroborated."

"The newspaper said Sam and Lauren were here," Meg said.

"Let's see if I can remember." He frowned and brushed a hand over his hair. "Cavalier, he was out in the Warners on horseback, with a bedroll and his cameras. Didn't get back till some days later. Lauren ... had gone off shopping someplace, Reno I think, and got home late. Yeah, and was real quiet coming in because she knew Miss Macrae was leaving early the next morning for one of her plant-gathering trips, also in the Warners. So nobody actually *saw* anybody else."

"Weren't there any workers on the ranch?"

He shook his head. "None live-in, anyhow. And they'd moved all their cows out to the allotment the week before; that's one reason Lauren came home, to help with that.

"Anyway, from a couple of other guys young Macrae had had some trouble with, same kind of thing. No alibis, no evidence. No body."

He lifted his bourbon for a slow, thoughtful swallow, and Meg remembered her own drink, diluted somewhat now. "Just like Lauren," she said.

"Not quite," said Douglas. "This time there is definitely a body."

She kept forgetting that. The young man who'd looked like a nice boy, who'd been shabbily dressed and unshaven but had spoken with good sense. Who had had a wife once, and children—she remembered mention of children, but her head was swimming with gin and weariness. Nice curly-haired boy whom Lauren had cared about—oh God, and surely couldn't have killed, however logical everyone thought that was. So who would, and why?

"Are you okay?" Douglas was leaning forward to look into her face, his own face drawn into a frown of concern.

"Douglas, do you think it's possible Bobby Macrae has come back? To kill Chuck Jakel and maybe Lauren too?"

"Well, probably not. People disappear on purpose and never come back. Or maybe they're found and dragged back. But disappear, hide successfully for ten years, and then sneak back for revenge? I just can't see it."

"Oh. Too bad." She tipped her glass up, swallowing the

last of the watery gin and taking some small bits of ice into her mouth. "Mm. Douglas, it's getting late, and I'm suddenly very tired."

"No wonder. Come on, I'll take you home."

He held her arm as they crossed the parking lot, making a large, comforting presence; Meg thought it was like being escorted through the woods by a friendly bear. Monitoring her own responses as if she were listening hard for a faint and distant sound, she could discern no remnant of her earlier terror.

They moved past the second parking row, past the empty space where Ruthie Jakel's little car had been, and Meg was suddenly angry with herself and her ill-timed panic. Of all the people involved in both the old trouble and that of the present, Ruthie Jakel was the most promising source of information, and she, Meg, had missed her best chance to explore that.

Douglas ushered her into the truck, climbed in himself, and put a cassette in the tape deck: Oscar Peterson, sounded like. Lovely. She leaned her head back and closed her eyes.

There were still lights in the lower part of the house, in the living room and Frances's bedroom, but the upstairs was dark. Douglas drove slowly across the gravel, pulled to a stop, and was out and around the truck before she had unfastened her seat belt, to hand her down.

"You okay now?" He took hold of her shoulders as he inspected her face in the light from the truck's open door. "Chances are you won't flash back that hard again."

"I'm fine. Thank you."

"And listen. You find yourself wanting to poke into things, call me, okay? Kind of like reverse A.A., I'll buy you a drink and help you resist the temptation to snoop. This time we know there's somebody killing people, and if I let you get into trouble, Vince Gutierrez will hang me up by my—well, you just take it easy."

"I'll . . . try. Thanks for a nice evening."

He hooted quietly at this, then pulled her into a hug—bear hug, she thought—and planted a loud kiss on her mouth.

"We'll do better next time."

She let herself in with the key Frances had given her, and Sam came into the hallway to meet her.

"Meg, hello. Did you have a nice evening?"

Lovely, just ducky. "It was fine."

"Your husband called. Katy took the call, but I believe she said you weren't to call back."

"I see."

"Would you like to sit and talk for a while? I can't seem to get sleepy."

There were probably things she should ask Sam, but she was too tired to organize her mind. Most likely too tired to be polite, too. "Thank you, Sam, but I don't think I'd be very good company."

"Oh." He hung his head, like a little boy who'd been disappointed. "Won't you please have a glass of wine with me, or maybe a cup of coffee? Frances just ranted on about her pet hates, the Jakels, and drank too much brandy. And Katy—well, I didn't think I should burden her with my troubles."

"Good. Thank you," said Meg.

Cavalier, misunderstanding her, said, "Wonderful," and pulled a bottle of white wine from its ceramic cooler on the hearth. He had poured a glassful and handed it to her before she could get her retreat under way.

So, five minutes. She took a sip she didn't really want and found it tasted peculiar after the gin.

"So—how do you know our ex-sheriff?" asked Sam. Since she had merely perched on the arm of a wing chair, he remained standing, one arm resting on the mantel.

"He's an old friend of my husband's."

"Did he tell you anything useful?"

Meg was unaccountably irritated that he would suspect her of using personal connections for snooping. "He's a cop," she snapped. "Cops don't tell you things, they ask you things."

"Oh," he said. "Sorry."

"He did say that Sheriff Vukovich doesn't appreciate interference, from him or from anyone. He says we shouldn't irritate the man."

"Bullshit! He's a public servant, after all, and not a very good one in my opinion."

Well, she'd done her best there. One of the should-asks occurred to her. "Sam, do you think Robert Macrae is dead?"

"Hell yes, he's dead! Look, Meg, I know you're trying to help, and believe me, I'm grateful, but please leave that alone. Even Frances has finally accepted reality. And Lauren was always about three-quarters scared of that little prick; last thing she needs is—" He gulped a breath and put a hand over his mouth, tears making his eyes brilliant. "I keep forgetting."

"I know." Meg stood up and set her glass of wine on the nearest flat surface. "Sam, I'm going to bed. I'll see you in the morning." She was away before he could answer, into the hall and quickly up the staircase.

Their bedroom was dark and still. Meg undressed as quietly as she could, then crept around the bed and slid in. Settled herself on her right side, arm under the pillow. Thought there was a great deal of tension here somewhere—her legs? neck? No, it was coming from beside her, a reproving stiffness emanating from Katy in waves.

"Katy?" she whispered. "Katy, what did Vince say?"

"He just wondered how we were. I told him fine."

"And he didn't want me to call back?"

"He was going to Grandma Emily's house to spend the night."

"Oh."

Katy turned over suddenly and came up on one elbow. "Mom, why did you go out with that man? And let him kiss you?"

"Katy, he's a friend of Vince's, and that was just a friendly kiss, because I'd been . . . worried."

"You're too old to be out kissing men."

"And you're too young to know anything about it!

Katy, I'm not doing anything wrong. Don't make a big deal of this."

Katy turned again, presenting her rigid back. "I love Vince. I love our house and the way we live. I don't want things to change."

Me neither. Oh, shit. "Katy, I love Vince, too. If things should change, and I hope they won't, it won't have anything to do with Mr. Douglas."

"Sure," said Katy bitterly. "Thanks a lot. I'm going to sleep now."

"Me too," said Meg, but that was a lie, or at least a miscalculation.

· 17 ·

"I have nothing whatever to say to those people or any others." Frances Macrae's tone was as absolute as her words.

"Frances, that attitude is self-defeating." Sam set his mug down so hard that coffee sloshed onto the table. "Shit. Excuse me," he muttered, and applied a paper napkin to the puddle with a hand that shook. Sam Cavalier's face seemed gray today, except for the bruise on his jaw and the bruise-colored circles around his eyes.

"Look," he went on in desperately reasonable tones, "the press is our best hope. If we're to find Lauren—one way or another," he added after a quick glance at his daughter, "we need to have everyone looking for her. Screaming at reporters and threatening to have them arrested for trespassing is not going to win you any friends."

"I don't need friends. This is my property, and I can refuse entry to anyone. I want you to get the gate out of the barn and put it up, with a lock."

"That will make our own coming and going a real pain, Frances."

"I don't care. I'm not going anywhere."

The two of them bickered on, trying and sometimes failing to keep the real topic of their discussion shrouded in euphemisms or meaningful glances. Meg, who had slept so poorly that every muscle in her body was complaining and even her teeth felt fragile, only half-listened as she got up to refill her own coffee mug. Katy had attended to Sam's coffee, but she was behaving this morning as if her mother were invisible.

Fight that battle later, Meg told herself as she sat down again. Or maybe never, maybe there was nothing sensible to

162

be said. Katy believed her mother was behaving badly, and Katy was at least partly correct in that judgment.

"Why not a statement?" she asked the room at large.

Everyone but Johnny looked at her.

"Frances, I think you're wise to avoid an interview. Newspeople asking questions tend to be provocative; that's their business. But there's no reason you shouldn't sit down at your desk and compose a few simple remarks about Lauren and her disappearance, and about Bobby too, if you like, and give it to the *Messenger*. That way, no one will nudge you into saying something you don't mean."

"I never say things I don't mean."

"But you might say something that would get you into trouble, like a slander suit."

The older woman responded with something that sounded like "Humph."

"Terrific idea," Sam said. "You go write it, and I'll take it to town." The telephone rang, and Sam, seated nearest the wall instrument, reached up to get it.

"Just tell them I'm preparing a statement," said Frances.

"Macrae Ranch," Sam listened a moment, his cold face warming slightly. "Katy, it's for you, a guy named Adam," he said, holding the phone out to her. "Here what, five days? And you've already lined up a boyfriend? Quick work."

Cheeks ablaze, Katy shook her head. "He's not my boyfriend, he's a friend. I'll talk to him in the hall."

Sam waited until he heard her muttered "Hello?" before replacing the telephone on its hook with exaggerated care.

Adam Kingsley, polite and apparently nonthreatening but somehow . . . odd. Meg downed the rest of her coffee and knew she should eat something but found the thought of actually putting food in her mouth revolting.

"Sam, do you know anything about this family? Adam is the brother-in-law of a Dr. Emmett Smith, who I've been told runs a clinic for drug addicts. They live in Goose Lake Heights."

"He's a local—well, celebrity is probably the wrong

word," said Sam. "But there was a lot of press coverage and even a mention in *Time,* or maybe *Newsweek.*"

"I must have missed it."

Frances took up the tale. "He came here from Los Angeles, where he'd run a successful rehabilitation program for drug abusers, and bought a ranch south of Alturas with the idea of setting up a similar place that would be well away from the temptations of a big city."

"A private clinic?"

"Basically, yes—a place for the children of the wealthy to shed their bad habits in some comfort. But before he received county permission, he agreed to reserve a number of scholarship spaces, you might call them, for people from the area," said Frances. "Some of our more paranoid citizens fought the whole thing, convinced their backyards would become havens for lurking dope fiends, but his clients or whatever you call them seem to be well supervised."

Sam shrugged. "I'd bet anybody who gets a weekend pass just skips Alturas and heads straight for Klamath Falls or, better yet, Reno."

Katy came back into the kitchen, her flush dimmed to a healthy pink. "Adam's going to pick me up at eleven, and we're going to drive to Blue Lake; he says it's pretty, and they don't put cows there until September. And then we'll probably go back to his house and go swimming."

Meg sat straighter and met her daughter's gaze; Katy, after a moment, lowered her chin and looked away. "If that's okay, Mom."

"Well, I suppose—"

"Mom!" Katy's eyes went wide, her voice high. "What's the matter with Johnny?"

All of them turned to look at the high chair, where Johnny had been silently, sullenly running several small cars back and forth through the food he had rejected. His jaws were moving now, side to side rather than up and down, and a trickle of blood ran from the corner of his mouth down his chin to his shirt.

"Holy shit!" Sam leapt to his feet and then stood still, hands dangling helplessly. "Frances, what the hell is wrong with that kid?"

"He's just chewing his new tooth, probably," said Sara, who had come running at Katy's near-shriek. "That's what he always does."

"What he *sometimes* does," corrected Frances. She reached across the table and dabbed at the blood with a paper napkin. "Poor baby."

Johnny paid no attention, just stared grimly ahead at nothing in particular and kept grinding.

"Holy shit," said Sam again. As Katy moved to deal with the blood-smeared child, Sam sat down at the table and put his head in his hands. The telephone rang a moment later, and he reached for it without looking.

After a moment his face tightened, with narrowed eyes and clenched jaw. Meg couldn't distinguish the speaker's words, but the tone was flat and authoritative.

"All right." Sam slapped the receiver back onto the wall and stood up. "You all will have to excuse me. It seems Sheriff Vukovich has thought up some more questions and wonders if I would mind stopping by to talk to him."

"Oh, Sam," said Frances.

"Goddamn it! If my wife had to go out there and get herself fucked, which the physical evidence makes pretty clear she did do, why the hell couldn't she just let it go at that? Why did she have to shoot that poor bastard?"

Meg set her teeth so sharply that she bit her tongue.

"I don't believe she did—shoot him, that is," said Frances.

"Right, okay. Sorry," said Sam. "I'd better get going."

"Sam, please call Tom Alderton," Frances said quickly. "He could meet you there."

"I don't see any need for a lawyer yet. Don't look for me to be home before evening; soon as I finish with Vukovich, I'm going to go out looking for Lauren again."

◦　◦　◦

"When will you be back?" Meg asked her daughter.

"I don't know." Katy looked at Adam and then back at her mother. "Does it matter?"

And how much would a smack in the mouth matter, sweetie? Like right now? Keeping her own mouth firmly shut, Meg simply raised her eyebrows, and Katy flushed.

"Unh, like maybe three o'clock? That's about when the kids will get up."

"Fine. Adam, will there be people at home at your house?"

"Oh, yes ma'am, Mrs. Halloran. My sister and my nephew, and if my sister should have to leave, the housekeeper will be there. Mrs. Halloran, I want to tell you what I told Katy, that I'm not this older guy trying to put moves on her."

The person under discussion rolled her eyes skyward and turned bright red.

"I see," said Meg, since nothing else came to mind.

"So I just want you to know she's safe with me. Well, except for acts of nature."

She simply stared at him, and he hurried on. "You know, like floods or lightning or earthquakes. There wouldn't be much I could do about those."

"Except try to keep out of their way," Meg suggested.

"Yes, I certainly would do that. So I don't want you to worry."

"Thank you, Adam."

"You're welcome."

"Have a good time, both of you."

There were children to be watched and tended to, meals to be prepared as endlessly usual, and messes to be cleaned up. Sam—Meg was trying to be understanding about Sam but without much success—had gone off assuming someone else would take care of all these boring tasks. Frances had settled down at her desk, in the closed-door privacy of her own room, to compose her statement for the press.

Johnny, having thrown the predictable fit at Katy's departure, now lay on his belly in his toy corner trying to sob and at the same time chew on a knot of ice cubes tied in a dish towel. Sara had sensibly taken herself outdoors, beyond earshot and baby-sitting range, but Meg decided the little boy would be safe for a moment and went to her car to get her tape player and the bag of cassette tapes. There was no music in this house except for what could be picked up on a small battery-powered radio, mostly country-western and soft rock.

Surprise: Johnny was still there when she got back. Poor little wretch. She selected a tape from the bag, slipped it into the player, and pushed the play button, settling the light little headpiece into place over her ears. *Da da da dum* went the music, tape apparently in the wrong box and not the Schubert her friend Charlotte Birdsong had loaned her but the Beethoven Fifth, old warhorse, too bad. Never mind, she thought, and looked at the room she stood in—crumbs on the table and something gritty on the floor, squashed unidentifiable mess on the high chair tray, dishes in the sink with nasty gunk clinging to them. Through the music she could hear the baby snuffling and muttering to himself around his icy teething aid.

And could feel time slipping again. Here she was, a woman who'd been bitching and snarling against the onset of middle age, experiencing an involuntary and unwelcome replay of the mother-of-young-children bondage of, God, years and years ago. When she got out of this mess she would definitely take up hang gliding or skydiving.

Meg swept into the sink whatever dishes were still on table and counter and used a sponge to give surfaces a desultory wipe. Ah, Lauren, where are you? This is a bad time to bolt, when you have babies; maybe all times are bad and people always get hurt, but this is the worst. They need you, and Sam is worse than useless, and I need to go home!

For a moment she was caught by a notion: Take the children and all their gear, stuff them and Katy into the Honda, and head for Port Silva. Then she remembered that her not-very-big house, Vince's house actually, was presently occupied by Vince's family.

The music. She stopped and stood very still. How could she have thought warhorse? She listened, and stared at nothing through a shimmer of tears, and then heard a sound out of key with the music.

Johnny was sitting up, staring at her, and howling. Hungry, probably. Miserable, certainly. Red-faced and snot-nosed and brokenhearted.

"Oh, baby." She crouched before him, wiped his face. Took the cassette player from her belt and set it beside him, took the headphones from her own head and put them on his. "Oh, baby. Listen."

His eyes went from squinched to wide, and he stared at her. After a moment he closed his mouth and put his fat, dirty little hands up, but just to touch the earphones, pat them very gently. Cup them close. And listen, eyes even wider.

Be nice to think Beethoven could calm any savage two-year-old breast, but she doubted it. Nevertheless, for the moment at least this two-year-old was transfixed. Okay, baby, I need it, too, but less than you. Now I'd better fix you and your sister some lunch.

Maybe music produced endorphins, she thought later, as she tiptoed away from Johnny's bedroom. Whatever those were . . . supposed to make you feel better, anyway. Probably that was an inelegant way to think about great music, as the equivalent of a good drink or a good joint or maybe sex but with no physical side effects. Doesn't make you drunk, doesn't make you pregnant; watch out or they'll ban it.

Let's see, what's first on the list of the temporarily free woman? Right, Vince. She dialed her own number, to be greeted by the answering machine. Okay, no big deal, she could handle that. After the beep she told Vince in fairly sprightly tones that she was fine, Katy was fine, they both missed him. Lauren had not been found, no one had been arrested, she, Meg, had spent some time with Earl Douglas and really intended to heed his, Vince's, admonition that she take care. Bye for now.

As she replaced the receiver, her mind swung back to Earl Douglas—Douglas, Charlie's Place, and Ruthie Jakel. Meg had missed her first opportunity with Ruthie, but that was no reason to give up.

There was only one Jakel in the telephone listings: Verna. Meg punched out the numbers, trying to decide what she would say if Verna herself answered. Or worse yet, Marv.

Damn, another answering machine. "You have reached the Jakel . . ." Then a muttering voice, a click, and a tentative-sounding "Hello?" that was male but not adult: Ruthie's son, presumably. "May I speak with Miss Ruth Jakel, please?" Meg said.

"Just a minute." Squeaks and rustlings followed, and then the same voice, very distant: "Mom?"

"Yeah?" said a woman, a moment later.

"Ruthie, this is Margaret Halloran."

"Who?"

"Lauren Cavalier's friend. We met at the church Friday night, and again last night at Charlie's Place, in the parking lot."

"Oh, yeah, the tall lady who would love to help us unfortunates. What do you want now?"

"I'd like to talk with you. Can you meet me somewhere?"

"Well, I wouldn't like to talk with *you*, thank you very much! And don't call here again, you hear me?"

"What if I could put in a good word for you with Frances?"

"With—why would you do that?"

"I was a single mother myself, once."

"Oh, right, and that makes us sisters or something. Listen, lady, you can just fuck off."

"Fine, but I think you're missing a bet. I'll be at the Bluebell Coffee Shop in Alturas in thirty minutes, if you change your mind."

"Wait!" There was a dull silence for a long moment, probably because Ruthie had her hand over the mouthpiece. "Not the Bluebell. Go out past Charlie's Place about half a mile to a joint called the Grotto. It's a dump, but you'll be okay if you stick to booze and don't eat anything. Maybe I'll be there."

Meg replaced the receiver and looked at her watch. She'd give it the thirty minutes she'd mentioned, in the hope that Ruthie would get there first.

She went quietly upstairs to change from shorts to jeans and a loose cotton shirt and to subdue her long hair into a French braid. Just a touch of lipstick, a little cologne, her turquoise earrings. She picked up her purse, and a light sweater in case the Grotto had serious air conditioning, and tiptoed past the bedrooms where the children napped and down the stairs, to the kitchen and the back door.

"Frances?" she called to the figure standing in the doorway of the barn. She waved, and Frances waved back and came to meet her.

"What is it? Has something happened?"

"No, but I'm going out for a while. If you like, I'll take your statement to the newspaper."

"Oh. Oh, yes, that would be kind of you." She set off for the house and went around to the side porch and the French doors that let into her bedroom. "It's right here on my desk."

Meg took the envelope and put it in her bag. "I have some errands, Frances, and the children may wake up before I get back. Can you manage?"

"I think so. I feel quite spry today, and Sara can help me get Johnny up. Thank you for taking care of this for me, Meg; I don't know how I'd have managed the last few days without you and Katy."

Meg mumbled something and made her escape, feeling sneaky and vaguely guilty; the feeling lasted to the end of the driveway, where it was replaced by mild apprehension and a stir of excitement. For her, any kind of action was preferable to waiting around. "And that's what they'll put on your tombstone," she said aloud.

Blue Lake was nice, Katy decided. Not spectacular like Tahoe, or awesome like the ocean, but nice. Friendly. She sat down on a rock, leaned back against another, and turned her face up to the sun.

"Maybe you should put some more sunscreen on," said a worried voice from the next rock.

Katy kept her eyes closed but frowned. "Stop that, Adam. You're not my mother."

"I'm your friend, and I don't want you to get skin cancer."

"I will not get skin cancer. I have dark skin and it tans very fast. I *have* sunscreen on." She opened her eyes and turned to look at him. He wore a broad-brimmed hat in addition to sunscreen, and a long-sleeved shirt as well. But he was a good hiker and stronger than he looked, and he knew a humungous amount about birds.

"Adam, have you ever had a girlfriend?"

"Nope."

"Why, are you gay?" This was a subject that interested Katy quite a lot. So far as she knew, none of her classmates was gay, but maybe eighth grade was too soon for anybody to be sure what he was, or she.

"No, I just had bad luck. I started college when I was fifteen, two inches shorter than I am now and pretty fat. Girls were definitely not interested."

"Is that why you quit school?"

"I didn't quit, exactly. I got a degree in mathematics and decided I didn't want another one—or two, which is what my father had in mind. My son the Ph.D.

"Anyway," he added, "I like girls. It's just that I'm not ready to do anything about it yet."

Katy thought this over for a few minutes, squinting to watch a tall white bird that Adam said was an American egret stalk the lake's edges in search of food. It sounded smart, and sensible. Wait until you're ready.

The egret's head shot forward and down and then snapped back up with a flapping fish. Adam got to his feet and adjusted his hat. "I'm hot. Let's go home and have a swim."

"We could swim there," she said, gesturing at the lake. "Or wade, anyway."

"Ugh. I'd rather the pool. And I'm hungry; we can get something to eat at home."

"Katy, little kids aren't supposed to be in the pool without an adult."

"You're an adult," she said. "Isn't he, Brendan?" she said to the child who was clinging to her back. "Adam is a grown-up, and *I'm* a very good swimmer. And you like the water, don't you? Keep your head up, now, and hold on," she added, and tipped herself forward to tread water.

As Adam and Katy were finishing their sandwiches in the green-and-white breakfast room, Nancy Smith had come to the doorway and beckoned to Adam, saying something about a telephone call. A short time later Adam returned to say that Nancy had been called away and that he had promised to watch Brendan, who had just been put to bed for his nap.

But Brendan, craftier than he looked, stayed in bed only about five minutes after his mother's departure. Then he popped into the room like something on springs and said he really *needed* them to play with him.

Skinny little kid that he was, he was fairly strong; Katy found that out when he wrapped his arms around her neck. He wasn't clumsy, either, just hadn't been taught to do things. Nancy, Adam said, was afraid of the water.

"Okay, Brendan, I'm going to stand up now," she said, and did. "And I'm going to shift you around so I can hold on to you, and we'll jump and splash." When she had him in her grip and he had one arm around her neck, she said, "Okay, hold your nose now, and here we go!"

"Shit, Katy, my sister is going to have a fit," said Adam from his perch on the lip of the pool.

"Then you'd better come in, too, to spread the blame around. We're going to teach Brendan how to float."

"I think you've had enough, little kid," said Katy half an hour later. "You did really well; I think you must be part duck." She swung Brendan up onto the pool deck and climbed out to rub him down with a big towel that she then spread out on the grass beside the deck. "Now you're going to lie here in the sun for a few minutes and get warm again, okay?"

"Okay. Quack quack," said Brendan, and he flopped to the ground and spread his skinny white arms and legs out.

"Adam?" Katy went to sit on the pool edge and dangle her legs. "Where did your sister go in such a hurry?"

"Emmett called and said he needed her at the clinic."

"Clinic?"

"Emmett has this big ranch south of here that he's turned into a rehab clinic for addicts," said Adam. When Katy just looked at him, he hunched his shoulders high as if in pain, or self-defense. "His patients are young, mostly, from families with lots of money. They don't all want to be there. Just recently some of them have been sneaking out, and it looks like they've found a local supplier. Emmett is really worried."

"Has he talked to the police?"

"Katy, I don't know. And please don't you talk about it to anyone. He has to worry about the law, and about the families as well."

"Oh, right. I'm sorry." She got to her feet. "It's getting late. I'd like to dive a couple times, and then I really should go home."

"Okay." Adam climbed out of the pool and peeled off the wet tee shirt he'd been wearing against the sun.

"I *need* an ice-cream cone," said Brendan.

"I need an ice-cream cone." Brendan spoke this time from the rear of the Porsche. Since Nancy had still not returned, Adam had left her a note and packed her son into his own special harness in the back of the little blue car.

Now Adam frowned. "All there is in Stony Creek is a soft-vanilla place, like eating cold liquefied sugar. Katy, is it okay with you if we take a little longer and go into Alturas?"

"Sure."

Ten minutes later Adam found a spot at the curb half a block past a pink and white storefront. The door of the place stood open and was flanked by a pair of benches where several children sat eating and dripping. "I'll go ahead and see what they've got," said Katy.

A thermometer on a building across the street read 94 degrees. Katy hadn't experienced 94 degrees since the last time she visited her grandparents in Tucson. She swiped her hair back from her sweaty forehead, then shoved her hands into the rear pockets of her shorts and looked over the list of flavors painted on the shop window. Maybe she'd have sherbet, sharper and more cooling than ice cream.

"Hey, it's the pretty lady with the long, long legs."

Katy jumped and looked up to meet the grin of the curly-haired man with the snake tattoo. He wore a long-sleeved white shirt today, open over a black tank top and khaki shorts. His own legs were muscular and tan, lightly furred with curly hairs that gleamed golden in the sun.

"Or pretty kid, I forgot. How about I buy you an ice cream, double chocolate maybe?"

"Thanks, but I can buy my own." He hung his head in mock sorrow, and she couldn't help returning his grin.

"Won't ride in my truck, won't eat my ice cream. What's a

poor guy to do?" A car horn from the street brought his head up; he waved in the direction of the sound without taking his eyes from Katy. Funny eyes, she thought; they were a light brown that was almost yellow, and there was a wide space between.

"You be good now," he said softly. "And I'll see you later." He turned and jogged off to the truck that was double-parked just up the street.

"Katy?"

She jumped again. "Adam! You scared me."

"Who was that guy?"

Katy shrugged. "I don't know his name. He's just a guy I've seen around."

· 18 ·

The Grotto Bar and Grill occupied half of a single-story, flat-roofed building that couldn't possibly be as old as it looked. Slightly newer than the building, probably, was the lumpy, false-rock front glued to the Grotto half. Given a choice, Meg thought she would rather spend her time in the adjoining auto-parts store.

She pushed the door open and stepped into a shadowy interior where two big ceiling fans were slicing their blades through air thick with the smells of burned fat, old beer, and tobacco smoke. Since the windows were painted over or covered with dusty wooden shutters, the room was somewhat cooler than she had expected. She took off her sunglasses and found herself facing a bar and a row of mismatched stools; the tables and chairs ranged along the opposite wall appeared to be discards from a number of very old kitchens. A high counter beyond the far end of the bar marked the cooking area.

"Help ya?" The man behind the bar put a finger in his paperback book and twiddled bushy eyebrows at her. He was large and not young, with a round face under a thatch of wiry gray hair. His Hawaiian shirt, a riot of palm fronds, hibiscus blossoms, and billowing surf, brightened his corner considerably.

"I'm supposed to meet someone here. Ruth Jakel," she added, as he simply cocked his eyebrows up another half-inch.

"Ruthie? Well, make yourself to home, lady. You got your pick of places to sit." His gesture took in the whole of the room, which she now realized was empty except for two men at the most distant table.

"And what can I get you to drink?"

176

She settled onto a stool and eyed the signs over the bar mirror. "Corona?"

"Yes ma'am." He pulled a long-necked bottle from the refrigerator behind him, popped its cap off, and set it before her. "Glass?" he asked, and without waiting for her reply plucked one from a rack, set it on the bar, and poured it half full.

"Thank you." In the dimness, and after Ruthie's warning, she'd have preferred to drink from the bottle. She took a cautious sip.

"Had lunch? I could do you a nice burger with fried onions."

"Thanks, but I've eaten."

"Well," he said, obviously feeling it would be impolite to abandon her to her own company.

"Hey, Larry!" came a voice from the rear table; Larry sighed, said, "Coming," and pulled two bottles of Budweiser from his fridge. Meg took another swallow of her beer, which tasted just fine, and after a moment turned his paperback around for inspection. Not a thriller as she had suspected, but a Harlequin romance.

"You like them things, too?" Larry had been quick with his beer delivery. "My girlfriend buys half a dozen at a time, and she got me hooked on 'em. Me, I don't like these modern ones as much as the historical kind. I figure I learn a little something from those."

The door opened to admit a burst of bright light and a silhouette that proved to be Ruthie Jakel. She stood for a moment, probably adjusting her vision to the dimness; her permed, almost-white hair seemed to glow.

"Hey, Ruthie. I been making your friend here comfortable while she waited for you."

"Hey, Larry." Ruthie looked around the room before approaching the bar. She wore her usual spike heels, a pair of tight-legged black jeans, and a black tank top. Her bare arms and shoulders were very pale, and she shivered as a downdraft from one of the fans touched her. She kept the battered side of her face turned slightly away from the bartender, and he, although he couldn't have helped seeing it, made no comment.

"Well, I got here," said Ruthie flatly. "Let's go sit at a table. Larry, I'll have my usual. Mrs. Halloran here is buying."

Meg carried her beer to a table about midpoint along the wall. Ruthie followed, dropped into a chair, and was silent until Larry had set down a bottle of Budweiser with an empty glass upended on top of it, and a shot glass of whiskey.

Ruthie poured her beer, tossed back the whiskey with a shudder, and then took a long swallow of beer. "Okay," she said. "What makes you think you can get Frances Macrae to take care of Bobby and me?"

"I don't necessarily think that. I simply said I'd talk to her about it."

"Hey, big deal. I been trying to talk to her about it off and on for almost ten years."

"She doesn't like you. She does like me." This was not entirely true, Meg knew. Frances regarded her with a wary respect rather than liking. Too complicated to get into here, that was.

"So why would you help me?" Ruthie narrowed her green eyes and thrust her long jaw forward.

"Is your son really Robert Macrae's child?"

"Hell yes!" The word ended in a long hiss, and Ruthie had another swallow of beer without taking her eyes from Meg's. "Listen, Bobby *wanted* us to have a kid, he made me quit using anything. He figured it would soften the old bitch up or something. Which you can see about how well that worked," she added bitterly.

"Do you know how the Macrae property was divided?"

"Sure. The old man, John senior, left two-thirds to John and Angie, one-third to Frances. I guess he was smart enough to figure she was never going to get married or have kids. Then when John and Angie were killed, their shares went equally to Bobby and Lauren, but they couldn't touch the property until they were twenty-one. Frances was in charge until then."

"Do you think Bobby is dead?" Meg asked.

"I told you, he wanted the kid, he wanted to marry me." Ruthie lifted her chin, squared her shoulders, and took a deep breath that threatened to pop her large breasts out of the low neck of the tank top. "He wouldn't have gone off and left me, or not for more than a few days, anyway, to scare me. So he's dead, but his kid's alive, and it's only right he should get what belonged to his father."

"I'd be inclined to see it that way," said Meg.

"So, back to the original question. Why would you even try to help me?"

"Because I want to help Lauren."

Ruthie gave a harsh caw of laughter. "You're some late for that."

Meg sipped her beer. "Do you think Lauren killed your brother?"

"Sure, who else? She was there, he gets shot, she's gone." Ruthie shivered and hugged herself with both arms. "Chuck had this idea the three of us, him and me and my Bobby, could work the ranch and maybe get it back into paying shape. Bobby was really looking forward to that; he's all broke up over Chuck's death." She drained her beer glass, then set it down hard on the table and called to the bartender. "Larry? Do it again."

Meg said nothing, sipping her beer as Larry brought another round for Ruthie and another Corona for her. She put a twenty on the table; he wigwagged the eyebrows at her to indicate he'd get it eventually. Ruthie tossed back her second shot, and Meg kept looking at her.

"Well, shit. No. No, I just can't see her shooting him, does that make you feel better? God, she was always such a total baby! Just a born victim, you know? Hard to believe she could shoot anybody. Particularly not Chuckie, Lauren always really liked Chuckie."

"So who did? And what happened to Lauren?"

"I don't know and I don't know! And that's the truth."

"Could your older brother have killed Chuck?"

"Not on his own he couldn't." Ruthie's mouth twisted into a sneer that she quickly covered with one hand. Then she blinked and took a deep breath. "Dumb question. If I knew, I wouldn't tell you."

"Okay. Tell me about Bobby Macrae, what kind of person he was."

"He was handsome. You seen pictures of him?"

Meg nodded.

"Then you know. And he was a man real early."

"He was younger than you."

"More than two years. But by the time he was fifteen he was like . . . Well, I'd been with guys ten years older weren't as good."

Ruthie Jakel, seventeen years old and already the veteran of numerous back seats and motel rooms, thought Meg sadly. Probably not looking much different from the way she did now at twice seventeen, her only assets these improbable breasts and a certain raw nerve. Balanced against the ferrety face and the Jakel name and reputation. No wonder she'd been eager to seduce the baby son of what passed locally for gentry.

"And he thought *I* was special, too," said Ruthie, as if she'd caught Meg's thoughts. "I lived in Susanville for a while after I graduated, and then Redding. But wherever I was, he always came after me."

"I see," said Meg. "Besides sex, what did you like about him?"

" 'Like' isn't the right word. He just always . . . made things happen, that's all. Hey, Larry?"

Meg tried to marshal her thoughts, her questions. At the rate Ruthie was drinking, she couldn't stay coherent much longer.

Larry brought the whiskey—rye, he said, when Meg asked—and beer for Ruthie, but Meg waved off another Corona and waited for him to reach his bar and his book.

"What else?" she asked again. "What else do you remember about Bobby Macrae?"

Ruthie took only half the whiskey this time, then set the glass down. "Bobby Macrae would do anything."

"You mean he was brave?"

She shook her head. "No, no, no. Not in any physical way, anyhow. He hated getting hurt, and he never got in fights unless the other guy was a lot smaller. Or a woman. Bobby was stronger than he looked, and he kind of liked letting a woman know that. No, what I mean is he didn't care about rules, or what d'you call 'em, taboos? Or what anybody thought. He would do *anything*."

She looked at the whiskey glass but picked up her beer instead, drank deeply, and then leaned forward. "I'll tell you something *nobody* else knows. But I didn't say it, you understand? No way. What it is, Bobby killed his folks."

"His . . . parents?"

"Right. Big mean ol' John and silly little Angie."

"But he was only a boy!"

"Thirteen. But smart. And tired of them. He told me he fixed their car so they'd have an accident. And they died. So there. That's the kind of thing Bobby would do." She took a deep breath and rubbed her bare upper arms with her palms.

Meg felt chilly and picked up her sweater to drape it over her shoulders. "Do you think it's possible that he's still alive? That he's come back here to make trouble?"

"God, I hope not!" Ruthie quickly tossed back the remainder of her rye. "No, look. I got this kid. He's not as handsome as his father, but he's nice, a really nice kid. And smart. All I can do for him, I work bartending, or check-out in some little nonunion store, or fixing hair; I went to this beauty college for a while."

"You have a ranch, or your mother does."

"No she don't. The bank's got most of it, or somebody, she won't let me see the papers." Ruthie hunched her shoulders. "Ma is just . . . out of it. Well, you know, you were out there. She's gonna die pretty soon and she knows it, that's all she thinks about. With Chuck gone, she'll probably let Marv and that fuckin' buddy of his do whatever they want, sell what's left of the place. Listen."

She reached across the table with both hands and gripped Meg's nearest arm, her right arm. "Please. Talk to Miss Macrae. I don't want any million dollars, just enough to get a start someplace else, maybe buy a house for Bobby and me. Tell her."

"I will." Meg picked up her beer glass to pull her arm, and her glance, away from Ruthie Jakel. She had little real hope that Frances would listen, and this made her feel small and nasty, a liar if not a betrayer. "I promise."

Ruthie stayed where she was as Meg stood up, dropped a ten on top of the twenty, and slung her bag over her shoulder. "Thanks, Ruthie."

"For nothing," the other woman said quickly. "One thing, though."

"Yes?"

"Bobby Macrae would have shot Chuck. He hated Chuck. But . . ."

Meg waited, and after a moment Ruthie looked up.

"But if it was Bobby, he'd have shot Lauren, too. Right then, right there."

Larry, hunched over the bar and his book, looked up as Meg opened the door. "You come back now," he said.

Meg waved at him and stepped out into a blaze of sunlight. She walked slowly toward her car, welcoming the warmth on the tension-ache in her neck and shoulders. Maybe if she simply stood here for five minutes the sun would melt not only the ache but also the gothic atmosphere Ruth Jakel had conjured up.

The early-sex part of Ruthie's tale was shocking for only a moment; after many years of teaching high school, Meg was well aware that many if not most fifteen-year-old males were sexually capable and desperately eager to prove it. But a thirteen-year-old parricide? A person who ten years after his death or disappearance still inspires what looks like fear in a tough woman in her thirties?

Tough, maybe, but not very smart, she reminded herself. And perhaps inclined to dramatize the past against the drabness of her present life. At least Ruthie had confirmed Meg's reading of Lauren's regard for Chuck Jakel, and made more likely his status as the father of Lauren's unwanted baby. Poor Lauren, then and now; Meg was swept by a wave of pity so intense it approached nausea.

In this heat, even the one beer she'd actually drunk had left her feeling thick-headed. As she rolled down the driver's-side window and then walked around the car to do the same with the other, she found herself unable to believe that the Bobby Macrae Ruthie had described was alive and in the neighborhood.

"Wait ten years to get even for . . . whatever?" she muttered as she pulled out of the dusty lot. "Without the pleasure of threatening in advance? or gloating afterward? Not bloody likely."

And that was the question she'd failed to ask: If Bobby Macrae was dead, how did he get that way? Who killed him? Not that Ruthie would have answered. Meg glanced at her watch and sighed. Nap time was long over, and while Katy would not have forgotten her promised return time, she might very well have decided to ignore it.

"Good heavens, is that safe?" Meg asked a short time later. Hands gripping the top rail, she stared into the corral and saw Sara Cavalier thump her bare heels against the round, dun-colored sides of the mare, Daisy. Daisy responded only by continuing to do what she was doing, ambling around the enclosure.

"Of course it is," said Frances tartly. "That mare is virtually unprovokable. And she's sensible; if Sara falls off, which is unlikely, Daisy will be very careful not to step on her."

"I'm surprised you were able to lift Sara," said Meg.

"I didn't have to do anything but bridle the mare," said Frances. "And lead her to the fence so Sara could climb on. Sara certainly doesn't need a saddle for this kind of thing. She's a real Macrae, with those long legs."

Real Macrae. This could be a good time to broach the subject of Bobby Jakel, while Frances was relaxed and cheerful. "Frances—"

"Johnny ride horsie." The little boy, who'd been gloomily building the dusty dirt into mounds and then flattening each with a blow from his palm, now got to his feet and made a headlong dive for the corral.

"No!" Frances made a grab at him and missed. "No, Johnny, I told you, you're too little!"

Meg stepped between the child and the corral, blocking him with her legs. He stopped just short of her, turned with more agility than she'd have expected, and ran off to the side, sturdy legs churning and dust flying. "Okay, little kid, work off some of that energy," she said, and followed behind him at a distance of about two paces. She could save her persuasive efforts on Ruthie's behalf for later, perhaps over evening drinks.

Finally, after one headlong fall and several detours, his pace began to slow, and his interest was caught by a collection of heavy wire frames, pieces of fences or cages or something, propped against the side of the barn. Not something she'd noticed before, and definitely not something a toddler should be playing with or on. Meg reached out a long arm and snagged the back waistband of his denim pants. "Enough, slugger. Frances," she called over her shoulder, "why don't I take him in for his bath, and you stay here with Sara."

"What a good idea. Thank you."

Meg lifted the squirming little boy, propping him on her right hip.

"No!" he roared, glaring at her.

"Yes. And listen, little kid. If you bite me, I will pinch you.

See?" she said, tweaking his plump upper arm just the slightest bit. "Bite? Pinch. That's the way it goes."

"Bite. Pinsch," he repeated.

"By George, you've got it."

"Kee!" he said next, much more happily, and Meg sighed with several kinds of relief as she saw her daughter coming across the grass. Katy's cheeks glowed pink under their tan; her thick, short hair was still damp; and Meg read the stain on her tee shirt as her favorite orange sherbet. Clearly Katy at least had been doing all the right vacation stuff.

"Hi, sweetie. Did you have a nice time?"

"Yeah, I did." Katy's smile was a polite throwaway.

"Did Adam?"

"Adam? Oh, yeah. He's not gay."

"Oh. Good. I suppose." And how did she find that out? "Katy—"

"Boy, that's a really grubby baby, huh, Johnny? Here, I'll take him and give him his bath." Katy held out her arms, and Johnny practically leapt at her.

Well. Two rejections for the price of one, thought Meg as Katy carried the baby off toward the house. She'd forgotten their estrangement, hers and Katy's. And she was surprised at how sharply lonely she now felt.

· 19 ·

For Meg, cooking was not a creative act but an ordeal, resulting in irritation, burned fingers, and a general sense of inadequacy. Besides, she was having trouble with reality, or with differing realities. This spacious kitchen, with its tiled counters and red-poppy-flowered curtains, its greenhouse window full of little terra-cotta pots of herbs, was so distant from bloody murder, or from Ruthie Jakel and the Grotto, as to induce vertigo.

"My, but that smells good," said Frances, who was seated at the kitchen table with a glass of wine.

"Can't go wrong with garlic and onions," said Meg, who knew that she could. "Frances, I think you should call Lauren's list of baby-sitters and try to find someone to come in daily until . . . things are straightened out. Katy and I need to think about going home."

"Oh, dear. Meg, I've tried. One girl is spending her vacation on the coast with her married sister, another is in summer school full time. And the remaining two didn't give any *reason* they couldn't come, but I think their mothers wouldn't let them. I think we are being regarded as either criminals or victims, and in neither case do people want their children to work for us."

What is this "us" stuff? Holding her tongue and her temper, Meg dumped browned hamburger and assorted vegetables from two skillets into a big pot where tomatoes and juice were about to come to a simmer.

"I'm sorry, Meg." Frances's tone was woeful. "I know we're a burden to you and Katy."

The only decent answer was a lie. "Of course you're not, we're glad to be able to help. It's just that eventually we will be needed at home. What about an adult, Frances? Isn't there some older woman in town or on one of the ranches who would appreciate earning some extra money?"

"I can't think of anyone that I'd be willing to have here all day."

Whooo. Bondage. Meg went to get a glass for herself; there was plenty of wine in the house, at least. Red for a change, to go with the spaghetti—she *thought* she'd seen a package of spaghetti in the pantry.

Drinks. Evening or nearly. This was when she'd planned to raise the topic of Ruthie Jakel. Meg was searching for an opening phrase when the back door opened and Katy came in with a basket of greens. Sara was right behind her, towing Johnny by the hand.

"Look at the cute little lettuces, Mom." Katy took the basket to the sink and dumped it. "And really nice green onions, and I found some radishes. But the tomatoes are still green."

Before Meg could reply, the front door opened; a moment later Sam Cavalier came into the room, walking as though he hoped to hear bones crunch beneath his boots. With a grunt probably meant as greeting, he yanked open the door of the fridge, pulled out two bottles of beer, opened one, and set the other on the counter within reach.

"Sam, are you all right? Have you been with the sheriff all day?" asked Frances.

"Only about half of it." He drained the bottle in half a dozen gulps, set the empty aside, and reached for its replacement.

Meg was dying to know why, to know just what the sheriff had wanted with Sam that kept him several hours. What has he got on you? would be a good question. She eyed him and decided reluctantly that such a question right now would earn her a right to the jaw or at least its verbal equivalent.

Sara was less experienced at reading atmosphere. "Daddy, where have you been?"

"Out looking for your bloody damned mother!" he snapped.

Sara's bright face went dull and slack. She let go of her brother's hand, and he plopped down on his bottom and began to howl.

At dinner Sara, still looking wan and worried, sat as close to her father as her chair would permit, practically under his left arm. Meg dished spaghetti and sauce at the stove, then handed plates around. Katy brought the salad bowl to the table, then settled herself on Sam's other side, not quite so close.

Meg found to her surprise that she was hungry. Everyone was, it seemed, except Frances, who between sips of wine was pushing strands of pasta around on her plate. Even Johnny came out of his doldrums and dug into his bowl of chopped-up spaghetti with spoon and fingers.

"Nothing," said Sam softly as he picked up his fork. "No sighting, no news, no word. Nothing from any of her friends. Zilch. That's that for the moment, and may I please have some salad?"

Katy made a brave try at conversation. "Adam has every wolf book you've ever heard of," she said to Sam, "including yours."

Sam nodded and made a noncommittal noise.

Katy, determined, tried again. "He's planning to set up this new environmental organization called E.R.O.P.—Equal Rights for Other Predators. See, he had these tee shirts made up." She gestured at her own chest, where the four black letters edged in green marched against a white background. "I like the idea, but I told him the name is maybe too cute?"

"Maybe he should spend his energies going back to school," suggested Meg.

"Mom, he already has a degree in math." Katy's voice was faintly patronizing.

"At eighteen? Good heavens."

"I guess Adam's a genius or something," Katy said. "Actually, he's thinking about going back to college to become a biologist. But I told him he should leave the biology to people like me, and study to be a lawyer. To represent the biologists when they get into trouble."

"You're planning to be a biologist now? And in trouble?"

"Yeah, I think so. I mean, you can't get anything important done in the world without getting in trouble. It looks like to me, anyway."

Meg exchanged glances with Sam, who had stopped eating to listen.

"Makes the future look more interesting than I was hoping for," Meg told him.

Katy sat straighter, pleased by the success of her conversational gambits. "Oh, Mom? Were *you* in trouble today? Is something wrong with the Honda?"

"Not so far as I know. Why?"

"Well, we were driving along and I saw the Honda parked outside this auto-parts store."

"Katy, I don't think—"

"The thing is, Adam says that place, Mackey's Parts, is okay for trucks but not for foreign cars."

"Adam is right," said Sam. "And even for trucks you'd better know what you're doing."

Every face but Johnny's was turned toward her. Okay, she thought. Here's the opening, just dive right in. Safety in numbers.

"I wasn't in the parts store," she said, picking up her wine glass. "I was in the bar next door."

"You were in the Grotto?" Sam's eyebrows climbed very high.

"I was having a drink with Ruthie Jakel."

As Sam blinked in astonishment, Frances drew a noisy breath through clenched teeth. "I don't want to hear that name, not at my own dinner table."

"How on earth did you meet . . . her?" asked Sam.

"She was changing a flat on her car at Charlie's Place when Earl Douglas and I got there the other night," said Meg. "She knew I was a family friend, and she wanted to talk to me about pleading her cause with Frances." Not an untruth, Meg told herself, but simply a rearranging of the details.

"Whore!" said Frances, and Katy dropped her fork and stared.

"What cause?" asked Sam.

Did he really not know? "She wants her boy acknowledged as Bobby Macrae's son," said Meg.

"Ah. That old story," said Sam.

"Lies," said Frances. "She's a tramp and a liar, like all her family. She simply wants money."

"Well, she does," admitted Meg. "She says he, her son, is a nice, smart kid and entitled to better than she can provide for him. I thought she was sad. I also thought she was telling the truth."

"I know this looks like a purely moral issue to you, Meg," said Sam. "A woman wanting the best for her son. But we have to be very, very careful about the legal implications of any action we might take. Our long-range plans for the historic Macrae ranch—"

"She destroyed *my* son." Frances caught her breath at the last word but did not bother to correct it. "She fastened on him like a leech, like a succubus, when he was no more than a child."

"Mom?" said Katy "What's a . . . ?"

"Later," said Meg quickly.

"I don't believe she *knows* who fathered that boy." Holding herself stiffly erect, Frances turned only her head to glare at Meg. "And you have no right to go meddling in our family's business, tossing our good name around in filthy bars."

Oh, lord, thought Meg, looking at the ravaged face and shaking hands, she's so old, she looks so ill. And I'm here striking moral poses and making deals with her life. "That's true, and I'm sorry, Frances. I had no right at all."

This apology appeased Frances for the moment. She pushed her chair back and got to her feet. "I'm very tired; I think I'll lie down for a while. Meg, thank you for dinner."

And from now on please confine your efforts to the

kitchen, hm? Fair enough, thought Meg, and she humbly offered to do the cleanup so Katy could help Sam sort negatives in his studio.

". . . Well, I'm keeping you talkin' here and you sure didn't call to chat with *me*. Vince, honey?"

"*Vince honey?*" drawled Meg moments later, in response to her husband's "Hello."

"Meg. Don't start," he said softly.

"Did you get my message?"

"Oh, shit. Meg, I'm sorry, but somehow the machine got erased."

"Bettyjean isn't very mechanical, as I recall."

"That's true."

"How much longer will she and Rich be staying?"

"I don't know."

"Vince, what's wrong with you? Oh. She's standing right there, is she?"

"Yes, that's right."

"Well, tell her to go away."

"Meg, I don't like to do that. How are things with you? Is there any news of Lauren?"

"Lauren has not been seen nor heard from, Katy is fine, I am fine. All of which I said in my message. How is Emily?"

"Stubborn but coming around, we think. Oh, thanks, Bettyjean. Bettyjean just made me a cup of tea," he told Meg.

"Well, enjoy. And call me when you can find a moment. I myself am going to go call up Earl Douglas so I can have a nice, intimate conversation." She replaced the phone gently.

It was past eight-thirty, and the house was very quiet: Sara and Johnny asleep, Frances resting or perhaps sleeping, Sam and Katy in the studio. Too late to call Douglas, probably, but she'd go up and get his number from her purse anyway.

The telephone rang when she was halfway up the stairs, but she ignored the sound and continued on her way. The second ring was interrupted; Frances must have taken the cordless unit into her room and answered from there. Meg waited a moment for a summons, but none came. Not Vince.

She could call Douglas and go out for a drink. She could call Vince back. She opted instead for a shower, then put on nightgown and robe and lay down on the bed to feel miserable—for herself, for Lauren. For Ruthie Jakel and her hapless son.

"Mom? Come on, move over. You should get under the covers."

Meg groaned, sat up, and peered through sleep-fogged eyes at the face of her watch. Ten-thirty.

"Katy, is everything all right?" Dumb question, she thought.

"We quit for the night. I'm going to bed, but I think Sam is going to have a beer."

"Oh. Maybe I'll go down for a few minutes."

She stopped by the bathroom first, to wash her face with cool water and rub it hard with a towel. She could hear noises downstairs, the kind you make when trying to move around quietly. If Frances hadn't taken the wine bottle to bed, maybe she'd have a glass.

"Oh, I'm sorry. Did I wake you?" Sam was pacing the living room with a bottle of beer in his hand; another waited on the mantel.

"No. But why don't you take your boots off, and then you'll be safer. Or at least quieter."

"Right." He dropped to a chair and pulled off his boots. "I guess if anybody had telephoned with news or anything, somebody would have come to the studio to tell me."

"I suppose so, but I've been asleep." She thought he looked calmer than he had earlier, the worry and frustration less evident. Feathers smoothed by several hours in the company of his devoted admirer, Katy. Don't be bitchy, she told herself; but the fact was, she didn't much like this man. And she did wonder what it was that kept the sheriff leaning on one of his more illustrious constituents.

"In fact, I'm still foggy," she said. "I think I'll get a glass of wine and try to reorient myself."

She returned in moments to find that he had leaned his head against the chairback and closed his eyes. "Funny thing is, I'm trying to envision Lauren's face, and I can't get the focus right. It's months since I've seen her, and you don't . . . look that hard at people you're used to. People you think will always be there. I should go upstairs and get a picture."

Meg sat down in the other wing chair and rested her wine glass on her knees. "Have you had any other thoughts about what might have happened?"

He simply shook his head.

"What about the sheriff's people?" She waited, and when no reply came, said, "They're concentrating rather heavily on you. Do they still believe you're hiding Lauren, or have they something more in mind?"

He opened his eyes and stared directly at her for a long moment. Then he got to his feet, retrieved the beer bottle from the mantel, and opened it. "Let's just say they're deeply interested in where I was, when."

She sat still and followed him with her eyes as he paced the room. Lacking the height or bulk of, say, Earl Douglas, he had hiker's legs with well-muscled thighs, and his neck and shoulders were thicker than she'd realized. Right now he was working his shoulders like someone too long restrained.

"They're fascists, I told you," he muttered. "Just like all cops."

"Oh?"

"What? Christ, I forgot you're married to a policeman. Look, I'm sure your husband is a very nice guy, but so far as I'm concerned, most people who choose to spend their lives wearing uniforms and ordering other people around are not healthy." He shrugged and tipped the beer bottle to his mouth.

"Why are they keeping after you?"

"No reason except I'm convenient, and rousting me is easier than doing the job."

"Did you call your lawyer?"

He shook his head without looking at her.

"It's pretty hard to travel without leaving a paper trail, especially by air," she said as if to herself. "I imagine even private pilots have to file flight plans or something."

"Yeah, they do." Sullenly.

"Is that what happened? You lied about your travels and got caught?"

"Something like that."

He wasn't looking at her but was working those shoulders again, tensing and relaxing the long muscles. Probably she should finish her wine and go to bed. "Sam? When did you really get back to town?"

He turned to glare at her; when she didn't look away, he wilted and sank into his chair. "I got back *here* Sunday, when you saw me. I got to Klamath Falls ten days ago. From British Columbia via Spokane. That's traceable. Then I went into the Sierra, by myself. No records. And nobody's business."

Meg stared at him, seeing maps. "British Columbia?"

"I stopped for a visit; I have friends there."

"And you have a wife here, who thought you were in Alaska."

"Look, I don't live my life in a suit and tie or on a businessman's schedule. Lauren's always known that. And I can't always check in; places I go, there aren't a lot of telephones around."

"Right. I guess A.T.&T. hasn't yet made it across the frozen tundra to Klamath Falls, Oregon."

He straightened his spine, gripping the chair arms as if to hold himself in place. "It doesn't appear that Lauren was waiting here patiently right by the telephone, does it? You know, Meg, Frances was absolutely right; you're way out of line."

"Well, excuse me and I'll go pack my bags this very minute. What did you tell the cops on your second pass?"

"Nothing. It's none of their business where I was, unless they have evidence to prove I was here. And I wasn't."

Meg stared at him, at the narrowed eyes and the thrust-out jaw. Lauren had said her husband had no sense of humor, so presumably he wasn't kidding. "That's a remarkably silly attitude," she said.

He shook his head and sank back into the chair, staring at his outstretched feet and reminding her of any number of sophomore boys. "You know what they, the cops, think? They've got these two notions they just won't give up on. They think I have a woman, that I spent my unaccounted-for time off in the woods or someplace screwing. Then they think I came home unannounced, caught Lauren and her lover, and killed both of them."

When she made no reply, he pounded a fist on his knee. "But don't you see? Why would I come home and blow my wife away for doing the same thing I'd been doing? Does that make any sense to you?"

"Maybe not, but it happens every day."

"Not to me." He leaned forward and put his head in his hands. "Sure, I'm a hunter; I kill for meat. And I'd shoot somebody in self-defense, or to protect Lauren or my kids. But I wouldn't shoot some guy just because he'd taken my willing wife to bed. Wouldn't shoot her, either—I'm not that kind of guy.

"But I think they're going to arrest me anyway. The idea of being locked up scares me shitless, you know?" The face he lifted from his hands was wet and very pale.

"I suppose it would." So talk to the police, tell them where you were, admit whatever it was that you were doing, and with whom. No point in saying these things, not to that face; the man clearly saw himself as some kind of martyr. Meg got to her feet and Sam did the same, watching her.

"Look, could you please not say anything to Frances about this?" he asked in uncharacteristically humble tones. "She's barely holding together as it is."

"I think that's a reasonable request," she replied.

"God, Meg. Thanks." He moved close and in a weary gesture put his arms around her, pulling her close and leaning his head against hers with a deep sigh. Her spasm of fear at being gripped was so brief he didn't read it.

"You're welcome," she said, and waited a moment before pulling free. There was nothing sexual in his embrace, nor any menace, but there would be hell to pay should Katy wander down and catch this scene.

• 20 •

"Mama?"

"Not yet, baby." Meg thought Johnny was making this request by rote, without any real hope. He was sleeping later and later, this morning until nearly seven-thirty. And he didn't struggle or try to assert himself as she stripped off his wet nightgear and gave him a quick wash; he just lay there almost limp, looking off to one side. Could a child this young, she wondered, become depressed?

Or perhaps he was physically ill. Better have Sam or Frances make an appointment with his pediatrician. She swung him out of his bed and cuddled him close for a moment. "Come on, little kid. Your Aunt Meg will make you breakfast."

Each day the bizarre becomes a little more normal, she thought as she moved about the sun-washed kitchen. The jagged edges get a little less rough, the unacceptable fact more . . . approachable. But not for Johnny; he just keeps missing his mom.

He chewed on toast stolidly, accepted several bites of oatmeal, and then began to turn his head away from the spoon. Finally she put his milk cup and a partly peeled banana on the high-chair tray and backed away, to drink her own coffee and let him eat or not, as he wished. Definitely better call a doctor.

Where the hell was his father, anyway? In a spurt of anger she hurried to the front door, stepped out onto the porch, and glared in the direction of the studio where Sam had said, last night, that he intended to sleep. She could see from here that the door was closed tight, the single small window that faced the house closely curtained.

And there was a gap in the parking area. Frances's Jeep was still there, but its harder-used gray twin was gone. Sam Cavalier, damn him, had managed to go off on his own again, leaving the women and *his* children to fend for themselves.

Johnny! she thought, and hurried into the house. But he was still in his chair, glumly squishing banana through his fingers. Meg cleaned him up, set him in the corner with his trucks, and poured herself another cup of coffee. Could Sam have run away? she wondered. Given his standoff with the police and his fear of being locked up, flight might have struck him as an eminently sensible act. He was used to being on his own in the wild, and there was a lot of unpeopled space in Modoc County.

And not all cops were fascists, nor stupid. If the sheriff read Sam Cavalier as an arrogant, self-centered man who resented his wife's infidelity, the sheriff was not far off. Question was, would Sam have taken his resentment that extra step, like the truck driver Vince had told her of in Port Silva? It seemed the sheriff didn't think so, quite yet. Neither did she, quite yet.

Her gaze fell on the wall calendar, and she frowned at it for a moment. Wednesday, today was Wednesday. "I am going home Saturday at the very latest," she vowed softly. First she'd try to find, or help Frances find, some help here; maybe Irma Prescott could locate someone for them. And if that failed, or if Frances Macrae resisted, she would just take the children with her, by God. Call Vince, tell him to move his relatives out.

"Can I have some oatmeal?"

"Sara! I didn't hear you come in. Of course you can."

"Where's my daddy?"

Oh, shit. "He, um, I think he went for a drive."

"Is he going to come back?"

"Yes," Meg said firmly, cursing Sam Cavalier in her heart. Sara, she decided as she watched the child scramble onto her tall chair, was looking unkempt. Her neck wore a grayish ring of dirt; her hands were grubby and her fingernails black-rimmed; her wild, bright hair was lank and dull-looking.

Oh, Lauren, I'm not doing very well by your children. Meg put a bowl of oatmeal on the table and bent to hug the little girl. The telephone rang, but she ignored it. "I'll get the raisins and brown sugar. Do you want toast?"

"Yes, please. Aren't you going to answer the phone?"

"Don't worry, there's an answering machine now, in the hall. Or your Aunt Frances can answer if she likes; she has the portable in her bedroom."

"Aunt Frances isn't there."

"What?" Meg looked at her watch. Frances hadn't been up this early at any time since the Hallorans' arrival.

"She went out way long ago."

"But her car is here." As Meg moved into the hall, the answering machine buzzed, whirred, and settled back to its unblinking red zero; whoever had called had hung up without leaving a message. Frances had reported answering several calls like that yesterday: a live line and someone at the other end who waited for a moment without saying anything and then hung up.

Meg rapped gently on Frances's door, and when there was no response, she opened it. Empty bed with covers thrown back, teacup on the bedside table. The small cut-glass brandy decanter, with less than an inch of dark amber liquid remaining; Meg had filled that decanter herself, yesterday, at Frances's request. The curtains over the French doors moved gently, and Meg pushed them aside to find the doors slightly ajar.

"She went riding," said Sara as Meg came back into the kitchen. "Hours and hours and hours ago. On Daisy. I bet she's looking for my mommy. I bet she's going to shoot the people that took her away."

"Sara," Meg began, and then sat down across the table from the little girl. "Did you see her go?"

"Yes, I think so," said Sara. "I need the strawberry jam."

Meg got the jam from the refrigerator. "Sara, was it still dark?"

"Oh, yes. But I can see in the dark, I see my mommy in the dark all the time. Besides, I went out and talked to Max, and he told me. He was mad that he didn't get to go."

Meg got up and went to the back door, to step out onto the porch. The grass, sprinkler-watered late yesterday, was steaming faintly in the morning sun, but there was a haze of dust in the air already. She squinted toward the corral, saw one horse. No, two; a second had just come out of the barn.

And from behind the barn but outside the corral fence came a slight, tall figure, moving stiffly with the assistance of a cane.

"Frances?" Meg called, and waved.

Frances lifted her head, slowed her not-very-rapid pace, and veered in the direction of Meg and the kitchen.

"Frances, where have you been?"

"I beg your pardon?" the old woman said crisply.

"Sara . . . thought you'd gone riding," Meg said lamely.

"Oh, what a sad, lovely idea. Actually, I suppose I could manage a few turns around the corral, like Sara." Frances stopped and leaned on her cane to catch her breath; Meg thought she looked exhausted, eyes bloodshot and dark-ringed in her crumpled gray face. Maybe it would be possible to run out of brandy and forget to buy more, let the old woman get some real sleep.

"No, I woke a short while ago with a dreadful headache and this dream that the horses were out. At least, I thought it was a dream, but it was just so *vivid*," Frances added as the two of them reached the porch. "So I decided to go down and make sure.

"And then I stayed to talk to them for a bit, to Max and Daisy," she added, brushing at her sweater and jeans and then dusting her hands together. "I do like horses."

Meg let the older woman precede her up the porch steps and into the kitchen. "Good morning, Sara," Frances said. "Good heavens, child, you look like a grubby little gypsy. You need to have a bath and have your hair washed."

Sara put her hands protectively to her head. "No. I hate hair washing."

"I know, dear. Maybe we could wait until Katy gets up and have her help you."

"Saturday?" Katy had mumbled the word around a mouthful of toast. Now she swallowed, licked her fingers, and said, "Well. Yeah, okay, that'll be neat. I think I've turned into the kind of person who needs to see the ocean fairly often." Then, after a sip of milk, "But what about the kids?"

"Shh," said Meg. "If things aren't cleared up by then, we might take them with us." She turned at the sound of the telephone, but Frances had picked it up in the hall.

"Wow," said Katy, her eyebrows high. "That will be . . . interesting. But I guess we can do it."

They both fell silent, contemplating the hurdles facing them. It was a moment before Meg became aware of Frances's presence.

"That was the sheriff," said Frances. She stood in the doorway, her head erect but trembling slightly. "He wants Sam."

"Oh." They had been over this already, Meg and Frances. Sam had said nothing to either of them about where he was going, and neither knew when he'd left.

"It seems someone has found a body, in the national forest up toward Triangle. They want Sam to come to look at it, at her."

Meg put a hand over her mouth, feeling several cups of coffee pulsing bitterly against the back of her throat.

"I said I could come. But they said no, it had been out there more or less in the open, in this heat, for quite a few days. The sheriff obviously thinks women, particularly old women, are a frail and useless lot."

"I—" Meg shut her mouth, unable to say, "I'll do it," unwilling to hear herself say, "I can't."

"No, they'll look out for Sam," said Frances. "I feel quite

sure this is not Lauren, that she's alive somewhere. But we won't let poor little Sara hear about it. Are you ready to come help us, Katy?"

Not Lauren, of course not. After a wide-eyed and subdued Katy had gone upstairs with Frances, Meg looked around her, decided to ignore the dishes, and sat down on the floor to pull Johnny onto her lap. He struggled briefly, then leaned back against her with a sigh, shoving a thumb into his mouth. "I forgot to bring the tape player down; I'll get it for you in a while," she whispered; for the moment she wrapped both arms around him and rested her cheek lightly against his soft curls, rocking slightly, humming a children's song whose words eluded her for the moment.

The telephone's trill jolted her out of a near trance. Frances and Katy were still upstairs with Sara, she thought; she'd been halfway hearing giggling and splashing. Maybe the sheriff again, and she'd like to talk with him.

She set Johnny gently aside, scrambled to her feet, and managed to reach the telephone on the wall at the start of its fourth ring. "Hello?" she said breathlessly.

There was no reply. "Hello?" she said again, more impatiently, and then, "Who *is* this?"

Silence, followed by a long, descending sigh, on a single syllable somewhere between "ah" and "oh." Then a gentle click, and the dial tone.

"What on earth?" she said, very softly. She replaced the telephone and went back to the toy corner, where Johnny sat watching her. She sat down on the floor again, propped her back against the wall, and looked at the baby without seeing him.

"Mama?" he said.

"Shh," she said, replaying that soft sound inside her head. Then she blinked and focused on his face. Jutting lower lip; big, dark blue, accusing eyes. Meg leaned forward, took his face between her hands, planted a kiss on his button nose.

"Maybe. Maybe," she repeated absently, and got to her feet again.

"I can't tell anyone about it," Meg said to Abby Fowler for the second time. The first time had been about an hour earlier, when she arrived at Abby's house full of excitement and wild conjecture. Now, after a dusty but satisfying hike in the foothills, she sat on one log with her back propped against another and watched Abby pour iced tea from a thermos.

"I'm an earthbound kind of person; I don't have visions or receive mystical messages. But I swear I could *feel* Lauren at the other end of the wire." And see her bright head tilted to listen, pale face intent and then eased. "Nevertheless, I have no proof, no evidence. It would be dreadful to give people false hope. Thank you, Abby, that looks wonderful," she said as she accepted a cool plastic cup.

"But I am sure. I think," she added, and sipped the chilled tea—nice, dark, lemony stuff.

"You said there'd been other calls like this?" asked Abby as she settled on the other end of the log with her own cup.

"As Frances described them to me, they were just the same except for that . . . word, or whatever it was. Open line, nothing said, disconnect. No heavy breathing or banging down of the receiver."

"And what you think is that this time Lauren recognized your voice and was relieved to find you still there."

"Yes ma'am." Meg sipped again and shrugged. "At this moment in my life I may not be a shining example of perfect mental health, but I am certainly several long flights above Frances Macrae in that category. And above Sam Cavalier too, in my humble opinion. If it was Lauren, she now knows for sure that Katy and I haven't run out on her children."

"Mm. It sounds—reasonable."

"Yes, it absolutely does! Oh, God, Abby! That body in the forest has got to be some other poor woman, not Lauren. Lauren's alive!"

"But not necessarily well." Abby spoke uneasily, clearly not relishing the role of doomsayer.

"I know, I know." Meg leaned her head back and closed

her eyes, enjoying the feel of dappled sun on her face. There were insects droning nearby, and a bird trilling a complicated liquid song. Smells of sun-warmed grass and piney trees. Peace and quiet, or closer than she'd come to it in several days. She opened her eyes and sighed. "But I've given this a lot of thought, and it seems to me that the worst thing she could be guilty of, the very worst, is killing in self-defense. That's awful, dreadful, but something you can live past and get over."

"Eventually, I suppose."

"With help," said Meg firmly. "I just wish she'd talked to me when she called, or let me talk to her. Or that I could find where she's holed up." Meg shifted her rump into a more comfortable dip in the log and stared up at the blue sky. Blue, clear, and unmarred by structures or wires. "Telephone records!" she said suddenly. "Of calls to friends out of the area. With a self-employed husband, she'll have kept the bills for taxes. Abby, I bet I can find her!"

"*If* that was Lauren on the phone," cautioned Abby. "And if you do find her, what will you do?"

"Tell her what's happening here. Ask her to come home, I guess."

"Mm. And do you tell the police you've found her?"

"Well, I . . . Damn," said Meg. "No, I wouldn't want to do that. I haven't heard anything about your present sheriff to make me think he's to be trusted."

"Lauren Cavalier is a grown woman, Meg. I'm a coward, I know, but I'd be very, very reluctant to interfere in this. I'd leave things to her."

"You're suggesting I exercise caution and restraint instead of jumping in to straighten everything right out? You sound just like my husband. And you both have a point," Meg added with a sigh. "God! I hate being sensible. Waiting. Is there more tea?"

As Abby rose to refill their cups, Meg flexed her shoulders against the log behind her, trying to get at a niggling ache along her spine. "Abby, what is the east county grapevine saying now? Who's the favorite suspect, Sam? Or Lauren?

"Neither. Marv Jakel is being hauled into the sheriff's office daily, at least, for questioning. He's at the top of everyone's list."

"Good."

"And number two is Bobby Macrae."

"Christ on a crutch."

Abby spread her hands and shrugged. "It's not every little town that has its own ghost, a person whose picture actually was on television."

"He's not a ghost, he's a revenant. Or a vampire," said Meg.

"There's a writer from some magazine I never heard of pursuing the Bobby Macrae saga," said Abby. "I was in the library in Alturas yesterday when the guy came in, and I heard him questioning the woman on duty, who told him she was too young to have known Bobby Macrae."

Recognizing the storyteller's approach here, Meg sat forward. "And then what?"

"Then he left, and she saw me; I'm in there quite often, and we've talked. She beckoned me closer and told me that in fact she was dating Bobby Macrae up to the very day he disappeared."

"Dating? But what about Ruthie Jakel?"

"This woman—her name is Lisa Murtaugh—says that Bobby was tired of Ruthie Jakel and made rude fun of her to other people, or at least to Lisa. He said Ruthie had been chasing him for years and he was trying to dump her. Lisa actually had a date with him the night he disappeared, but he called her where she worked and said he'd have to take a rain check. And that was the last she ever heard from him."

"Good heavens," said Meg. "Did she tell the sheriff's people about this, when they started looking for him?"

Abby shook her head. "She was only seventeen and living at home, and her parents had absolutely forbidden her to have anything to do with Bobby Macrae because he had such a rotten reputation. My reading is, she was excited by him and his reputation and enjoyed the thrill of sneaking around to see him, but once he was gone, there was no thrill to be had and quite a lot of serious discomfort if anyone found out."

"I wonder if we should tell the sheriff now," said Meg.

"It strikes me as pretty old business," said Abby.

"I could ask Earl Douglas, see what he thinks. I've been meaning to call him," Meg added, and got to her feet. "Time to head back, I guess."

". . . really my aunt, but she's a lot younger than my mom so we're more like sisters. Anyway, when I was over there baby-sitting her kids the other night, she told me she knew Bobby Macrae, she was just a year behind him in school. And she says he was this totally rad person."

Tracy Turner paused in her tale to slide a swimsuit strap down and crane her neck to examine a plump pink shoulder. "Look at that, I'm going to have to put a shirt on. God, you're really lucky to be so dark."

"I just get tan really quickly." Katy told her. "Rad how?"

"Well." Tracy looked around quickly, but there was no one nearby. "See, my aunt says there was this math teacher everybody absolutely hated, old guy that never gave *anybody* A's. And he flunked Bobby Macrae in algebra, I think it was. And then," she said, and paused dramatically, "his house burned down!"

Katy stared at the blonde girl for a moment. "You mean he, Bobby, burned it down?"

Tracy nodded and swept her long hair back on both sides so it lay over her shoulders like a bright cape. "Only a few people knew, kids that he told."

"Awesome," said Katy, sensing that this was the kind of response Tracy was expecting. Katy didn't want to talk or think about Bobby Macrae, or Lauren, or dead bodies, and mostly Tracy Turner and her friends were turning out to be fairly nice kids and were not hounding her about all that stuff. Instead they called her Wolf Girl and asked her questions running from the humorous to the really dumb, but the basic tone was friendly.

And the pool was nice. Run by the county, it was not much larger than the one at Adam's place and was neither new nor spotless. But there was nice grass all around it, for sitting or lying on, and a fairly new board with enough bounce for a back dive. Katy felt a sprinkle and looked up to find a lanky, pale-haired boy flicking water at her.

"What I want to know," said the boy, whose name was Mike, "if you were raised by wolves, who taught you to dive?"

Katy sighed and rolled her eyes skyward in the same good humor with which she'd been addressed. "See, a wolf pack is very well organized. Everybody has to work, and everybody has his own job that he learns to do really well.

"Now, my pack lived in river country," she went on, "with deep canyons, so there was always a wise old wolf that knew how to dive—for fish, of course. Our pack's diver, an elder named Three-Paws, was training me as his replacement when the humans came and stole me back."

Mike and Jason clapped; a boy named Ty sat back on his haunches and gave a howl. "Not bad," said Katy, and she tipped her head back and howled as Adam had taught her.

"Don't *do* that," said Tracy with a mock shudder, looking around at her troops for approval.

"Yeah, you might be calling them in, for all we know," said Jason.

"I wish," said Katy.

"Hey, I can see 'em now, barreling down 395 from Oregon, looking for their leader."

"Not Oregon," said Katy. "They *might* come from Washington, or Idaho, but most likely from British Columbia." She looked across the pool to the clock on the changing house and was startled to find that it was almost four o'clock. She'd pushed Meg some in order to have this afternoon to herself, but she really didn't want to tip the balance to the point where they were actually fighting. "Hey, it's getting late. I better go."

The others scrambled to their feet as she got up. "You coming skating tonight?" asked Ty, who was taller than Katy and almost as brown.

"Skating?" She fished her shorts from her backpack and pulled them on over her suit, which was only slightly damp.

"Just south of Stony Creek there's this old county fairground," said Tracy, "where they hold some of the junior livestock events. What they do, they set up this livestock pavilion for roller-skating Wednesday nights in the summer."

" 'Course, you can usually still smell the livestock," said Jason.

This earned him a playful slap on his bare shoulder. "No, but there's soft drinks and music, and you can rent skates," said Tracy. "It's fun. If you want, call my house and Tom and I can come and get you."

Tom Turner was sixteen to his sister Tracy's fourteen, a curly-haired, happy-looking guy who made Katy remember how often she'd wished for a big brother. "Thanks," she said. She shoved her feet into her sneakers and then crouched to tie the laces, since she'd be biking. "I'll probably come if I can."

Jason and Ty walked her to the gate in the chain link fence that surrounded the pool area. "Hey, maybe I'll see you tonight, okay?" said Ty.

"Okay," said Katy, and left the barefoot pair of them there, where the grass ended and the hot tarmac of the parking lot began. Kids were still arriving in twos and threes, and a few were leaving, climbing into cars or onto bikes. Two or three guys and a couple of girls hung around the gate talking and smoking cigarettes. There was another group under a big tree at the far end of the parking lot, mostly guys.

As she reached the bike rack, the far group broke up and its members drifted off to their cars. One of them stayed where he was, looking in her direction; he lifted a hand to shade his eyes, and she saw the flash of blue on his arm.

She tossed a look toward the pool gate, but Ty and Jason

had disappeared. Well, so what? She wasn't afraid of this guy, or of anybody. And she really hated the way girls were supposed to be ready to scream and run at all times. With her shoulders square and her chin up, Katy pulled her bike from the rack. She unhooked the helmet, settled it on her head, and swung around to face the snake man, but he was gone.

Meg's car was there, but Sam's was not. Katy wheeled the bike around to the back of the house and found her mother and Aunt Frances sitting on the shady porch. Sara lay on her belly in the grass, with a coloring book; Johnny sat beside her, looking weird with headphones on.

Meg looked up and saw her and had her mouth halfway open when Katy shook her head vigorously. She pointed to herself and her swimsuit, made a two-handed motion like rain falling over her head, and mouthed the word "shower."

Meg nodded, and Johnny, thank God, didn't notice. Wondering what he was listening to, Katy tiptoed in the back door and up the stairs.

The house was quiet, the upstairs warm and stuffy. She opened a window in their bedroom, grabbed her shampoo from the suitcase, and headed for the bathroom and the shower.

It might be fun to go skating tonight, she thought as she scrubbed the chlorine smell from her body and her hair. She'd present the idea to her mom and see how it flew. Katy's experience with roller-skating involved helling down a sidewalk on in-line skates; she'd never tried the four-in-a-square kind, in a rink, with music.

She turned the shower off and toweled her short hair roughly; then she wrapped the big towel around herself, picked up her clothes, and headed for the bedroom. At the top of the stairs she paused, cocked her head and opened her mouth the way you do when you're listening hard. Only the very faintest murmur of voices reached her from the open kitchen door.

In the bedroom she tossed the towel at a chair, enjoying the feel of the warm, gently moving air on her bare skin. She ran a comb through her hair, put some lotion on her face. Picked up her dirty shorts and collected the tee shirt she'd worn earlier, carried them to the closet, and stuffed them into the laundry bag. Then she pushed the closet door shut and stood facing the mirror to inspect her body.

Very big feet, something people had been pointing out to her for years. Her long legs weren't so skinny anymore, but they weren't fat, either. Her butt, though—she twisted around to get a look at it—was a whole lot bigger than she'd remembered. Gross. Was that what they were looking at, Ty and Jason and the other guys at the pool who'd kept eyeing her today?

She untwisted. Nothing there you could really call hair yet. And no real boobs, either, just two little pink bumps that might have been bee stings or mosquito bites. With luck they would turn into something like her mom's, big enough but not so humongous they got in the way. She put a finger against the right one and jumped when she found it was tender. Terrific.

So she wasn't there yet, but she was well on her way; it was happening, and there wasn't anything she could do to stop it. Katy sighed loudly and went to rummage in the suitcase for clean panties, shorts, and shirt. So far as she could see there was nothing really wrong with her; probably she'd be okay-looking but tall, which she'd always been but never minded because her mother was five feet ten and got along just fine.

Or so she'd always thought, anyway. Katy had a strong feeling that this was all going to be a whole lot more trouble than it was worth. Look where being female got Lauren Cavalier. And her mother, who had always been tough and sensible and somebody you could depend on, was behaving like a . . . she didn't know a word for it. Like she was hearing or smelling something that Katy's senses didn't get, and it was making her act . . . weird.

· 21 ·

"Mom, you *can't*," Katy wailed.

"I most certainly can. There's enough spaghetti sauce left for another meal for the rest of you, and I am weary of kitchens and small children. Please keep your voice down," she added, hoping to avoid disturbing the two small children who were playing peacefully for the moment just outside the kitchen door.

"But *I* need to go someplace tonight."

"Really? And where might that be?"

Katy unfolded a tale of Wednesday night roller-skating in a livestock pavilion. "It sounds like really fun, and I can't go there on a bike at night. I *need* you to drive me."

"Maybe Sam can take you; he says he'll be home this evening." As Meg had just reported to her daughter, Sam had called earlier with the news that the dead body was definitely not that of his wife, and that so far the sheriff did not seem ready to arrest him or anyone else.

"Sure, Sam *says*," replied Katy, in a tone that Meg read as somewhat disenchanted. A good development, in her view.

"Besides," Katy went on, relentlessly, "I don't think you ought to be going out on dates with that cowboy sheriff; it doesn't look good. What if Vince calls?"

"Katy, I've been here most of the day, and he hasn't called."

"Yeah, well, he's working."

Ah, yes, while I've been dancing and singing and generally making merry. "Anyway, this is not a date, just an evening meal with a friend."

Katy's lips parted, and Meg could see "Bullshit!" in her daughter's mind as clearly as if it were printed in red letters across her forehead. They stared at each other in hot silence for a moment, and then Katy's eyes filled.

She blinked twice and cleared her throat. "Well, it looks like I'll just have to hope Sam does come home."

"Adam called a while ago," Meg told her. "He asked that you call him back. Maybe he'd like to go roller-skating."

Katy blinked again and lifted her chin. "Maybe," she said, and turned on her heel to stalk from the room.

So, a draw at best. Meg returned to her post on the back porch, sat down and closed her eyes, breathed the smell of dust and grass, and thought of the ocean. She had dreamed last night that she was at home in Port Silva, sitting happily on the deck of the hillside house with Vince, who looked happy, too. They'd brought the portable CD player out with them and were listening to Haydn and sipping champagne. Gazing idly at the ocean, where the sails of small boats dipped like dancers in the sunlight. Holding hands and planning their vacation.

Then, in her dream, she'd looked down at the hand she was holding to find it broad, hairy, and taloned—a bear's paw, its pads leathery and hot against her palm. Woke her right up, that did.

Now she opened her eyes and scrubbed her hand against the leg of her jeans. In the peaceful scene before her, Sara and Johnny were sitting on the grass facing each other, and Sara was feeding her brother . . . grass, that's what. "Sara! Stop that, you'll make him sick."

"Maybe it will make him smell nicer, like a horse. He stinks."

Wonderful. Katy was no doubt on the phone by now, telling her woes to Adam Kingsley. This task was clearly Meg's. She picked the little boy up, carried him to the house, and was pleased to see his father coming in the front door.

"Your turn," she said, and handed the child over.

◆　　◆　　◆

"He didn't even *try* to bite me," said Sam Cavalier when he brought his son back downstairs. "Maybe he's decided to like me after all."

"He seems to be generally listless," said Meg. "Do you know whether Johnny has anything chronically wrong with him? Any illness that recurs?"

"So far as I know he's always been healthy; Lauren says he doesn't even get colds."

"So he's just sad," said Meg, feeling fairly sad herself. As the day wore on, her conviction that Lauren Cavalier was alive had begun to fade; a sigh on a telephone was pretty thin evidence. "Sam, what about Frances? She's what, early seventies? The last time I saw her she was in her sixties and looked forty-five. A tough, strong forty-five. Now she sometimes looks about ninety, and at least twice she's said something to me about time running out."

"I seem to remember that she had some kind of surgery four or five years ago," said Sam. "I never heard just what was involved, probably some kind of female thing. Nothing she'd talk to me about, you'll have to ask Lauren . . . Goddamn it!" he groaned, and sat down at the table to put his head back and squeeze his eyes shut.

"I'm sorry," she murmured. The dead woman in the forest had been quite tall, like Lauren, Sam had said earlier. But her hair, cut short, had been a light reddish brown, not Lauren's golden-carroty shade. "Is there nothing new from the sheriff?"

"No. I talked with the undersheriff, guy named Ron Ortmann, this afternoon. Vukovich wasn't around; I think maybe he's lost interest. I think they're ready to move on to other things. Just a Jakel dead, just another Macrae missing, who gives a shit?"

Surveying his haggard, miserable face, Meg was tempted to tell him about the telephone call. She was still trying to decide when Katy came in from the hall.

"Oh, Sam. Hi," said Katy. "Mom, I'm going out to dinner.

At Adam's house," she added quickly as Meg's eyebrows lifted. "He's coming to get me in a few minutes. We'll go roller-skating after."

"Ah. Well, I hope we will each of us have a good time."

This was not a date, Meg told herself firmly as she surveyed the dining room of the historic Alturas Hotel, an odd but appealing combination of Old West and city suave. The floor was wood plank; one wall was stone and another brick; an animal head Meg took to be elk, an iron stove, and a wall of faded old pictures were juxtaposed against solid small tables, dark red table linen, fresh flowers, comfortable chairs. Not really a date, more like stopping someplace for dinner with one of her colleagues—Jack Skelley, say—after a late faculty meeting.

Except that she and Jack usually restricted their drinking to a glass of wine each, and she always paid for her own. Earl Douglas, now coming back from the bar with fresh drinks, had recoiled in horror that was only partly mock when she offered to pay. Watching him move his big body easily between tables on the way to their larger table against the padded banquette, she decided that this evening out was probably a bad idea—and she was glad she'd agreed to it.

"I told Jerry to start bringing us food in twenty, thirty minutes," said Douglas, putting the glasses on the table before settling into the leather chair opposite her. "But if you get bored with the story of my life before that, we can whistle at him."

She simply smiled and shook her head before tasting her drink. "So, how long do you think you can stand being a rancher instead of a cop?"

"Oh, I'm still a cop; I expect I'll run again next go-round. The ranch is kind of a skimpy place as ranches go, just enough to keep me and my kid busy. When his momma got fed up with him and sent him to me two years ago, I was some worried about how I'd have time to keep the reins on a sixteen-year-old city boy with an attitude. So the fact is, I didn't try real hard to get reelected."

"But he's okay now?"

"So far, so good. He's put on five inches and forty pounds, he's found out hard work won't kill him, he's made some friends including his old dad. He's going to college in September, to Chico State; doesn't really want to, but I talked him into giving it a try."

"Are the Douglases one of the old original families here?"

"Pretty close, anyway. Macrae, MacAlpin, Campbell, Douglas just a little later: bunch of Scotchmen who fought with each other just to keep their hands in."

"And the Jakels arrived later?"

"Right. Arrived later and managed to grab a big piece of Macrae land."

"Irma Prescott told me about that."

"Did she." Douglas nodded and sipped his bourbon. "There is nobody on earth more stiff-necked than a Scotchman. And my granny said the Macraes were the stiffest of anybody and brought their loss on themselves. Of course, she could feel free to speak that way; the Douglases never accumulated anything much to defend. If we fight, it's for the pleasure of it."

"I have nothing against a good fight," said Meg. "But I don't understand grudges and feuds. I don't think Ruthie Jakel does, either."

"Ruthie?" said Douglas, and Meg told him of her meeting with Ruthie the day before.

"Maybe Ruthie's got tired of being part of the Jakel clan," said Douglas. "For one thing, if Chuck got her back here with this idea of them working the ranch, she's gotta feel seriously misled. Way I hear it, Verna's got mortgages up to her eyeballs. I also heard just a whisper that maybe Sam Cavalier has bought up some of the paper on the place."

Last night at dinner, Meg remembered, Sam had said something about "the historic Macrae ranch."

"Okay to start, Earl?" Without waiting more than two

seconds for an answer, the waiter who had appeared at their booth set a big soup plate in front of Meg, another before Douglas. "Cheese is on the table," he added, and departed.

"Here's how it'll come: minestrone, pasta, salad, then prime rib," said Douglas. "Not what you call *nouveau* California cooking, but pretty good."

Meg tasted the soup and decided he was right. "Earl, I understand that you can't talk about the murder investigation specifically. But may I ask you for some opinions?"

"Fire away."

"Sam thinks the sheriff is losing interest in the case."

"Might be he's got other things need his attention," said Douglas carefully. "Vuke's got forty-two hundred square miles to protect, a jail to run, a 911 emergency system that's gotta be covered twenty-four hours, all with a department that was too small to begin with and a budget so shot he can't afford to replace personnel he loses. So long as Lauren Cavalier is the main suspect and she's not to be found, there's not a lot he can keep committing his people to."

"If Lauren should come back, what do you think she'd be charged with?"

He shook his head. "I haven't seen the evidence, not the reports from the scene or the post-mortem on Jakel. And of course nobody's seen Mrs. Cavalier to know what shape she's in."

"Self-defense against rape? Involuntary manslaughter?"

He just shook his head again. Then he spooned up the last of his soup, set the spoon down, and looked at her. "Meg, have you had communication with Lauren Cavalier?"

"No." Meg refused to think of this as a lie. "But I believe she's alive."

"Okay. Let me suggest this. If you do hear from her, tell her to come directly to the sheriff, or even to me."

"Why?"

"Just do that."

"No. Not without a reason. *If* I should hear from her," she added quickly.

Douglas looked at her for a long moment, then reached for the carafe of red wine the waiter had just brought and poured their glasses full. "I've learned a few things about Sam Cavalier, and I'd say his first response to his wife—who it's pretty clear was screwing around or having a love affair or whatever you want to call it—his response might be not real friendly."

"The sheriff is just angry with Sam because he won't cooperate."

"Because he lied, you mean? I don't know anything about that beyond the fact that he did. But it's a fact that Cavalier's got a real bad temper; he's had serious fights with people in the wolf recovery movement." Douglas set his soup plate aside, and the waiter turned up instantly with two plates of penne with meat sauce.

"Cavalier has been working on this wolf recovery stuff for years, with people in Montana, Idaho, other places," Douglas said when the waiter had left. "But there's a feeling around that he's turning the whole business into a religion, a crusade. For one thing, he personally beat the shit out of a rancher up by Glacier who'd killed a wolf he claimed was threatening his sheep.

"And," Douglas went on after pausing for several bites of pasta, "he seriously threatened this guy from Alaska Fish and Game over a proposal they're making up there for legal wolf hunts. Told the guy he'd from now on really better watch his back when he's out in the woods."

Meg put her fork down and stared at him. This was a very different Sam Cavalier from the honest hunter and defender of his family she'd listened to the night before.

"Look, it's the truth. He is not welcome in some of these places anymore. There's people, government people and ordinary citizens, been working for wolf recovery for years and years. Wild-eyed raving maniacs do them no good whatsoever, and they know it.

"Hey, don't let me ruin your meal," he said, pausing for a sip of the wine. "Eat your macaroni, or whatever it is. As to wolves, I guess I'm in favor of them. But that might be because I've got pretty tired of people over the years."

"Not a good reason," said Meg. "But understandable. I was talking to a friend today, and she says the sheriff has been pretty interested in Marv Jakel. For the murder of Chuck," she added.

Douglas shrugged. "He's a sorry little bastard, always was, from what I hear. Probably meaner after serving time, like I said the other night."

There went the pasta, here came the salad. "Are the people here always this efficient?" she asked Douglas. "Or do they just want to get us out of here?"

"I'm a favorite customer," he told her with a grin. "Lousy cook; my son eats at his girlfriend's house often as he can get invited. This place and a couple others make lots of money off me."

The salad was mostly iceberg lettuce, but it was crisp and chilled. Meg crunched for a moment and then remembered something. "Earl, what about Marv's friend?"

"Who's that?"

"I don't remember his name. He was there at the church Friday night. Apparently other people thought he was trying to break up the fight between the two Jakel men; I thought he was pretending to do that while helping Marv."

"Nobody's said anything to me about him."

"Okay." Meg sat back and picked up her glass of wine, ready for a break in food intake. "Here's a man, maybe mid-thirties. Gappy teeth, probably never had orthodontic care. Has this quick grin that's gone at once. Watches around him, eyes always moving. About my height, not particularly ath-letic-looking, but has extremely well-developed chest muscles and biceps. Oh, and he has a tattoo down both arms from at least the edge of his tee-shirt sleeve: big blue snake."

"Ex-con," said Douglas at once. "Works out, is used to taking care of himself in the yard. This is a buddy of Marv Jakel's?"

"I saw them together twice. He seemed to be the . . . oh,

boss. The one in control. And yesterday, Ruthie was talking about Marv in a way that made clear she thought he was of no consequence, but then she said something about his 'buddy' in a different tone entirely. As if she disliked him and might be afraid of him."

"I'll tell Ron Ortmann to run a check on him, Meg. Suggest, I mean. Ortmann is a capable guy, easier to deal with than Vukovich. Maybe already looked into this, but if not, he will."

The prime rib arrived, a thick, deep pink slab that covered nearly the whole plate. Feed a family of four for a week, thought Meg as she cut into it. Wonderful.

She ate slowly and with pleasure, the problems at hand receding to a quiet distance and hovering there, ready to reclaim her in the future but not bothering her much just now. She believed Lauren was alive, and she might still decide to ignore Abby's advice and dig into telephone records to locate Lauren's friends. Sam, bad temper or not, would surely not harm a returning Lauren in the presence of Frances and his two children. Katy—God save us from judgmental teenagers, but for the moment Katy was safe with placid Adam.

Meg took a breather and watched Douglas alternating bites of meat and sips of red wine, pausing now and then for a forkful of baked potato. If he was killing himself with cholesterol and booze, he was certainly enjoying the process.

He looked up and grinned at her. "Better eat, or I'll leap on yours after I finish mine."

His forearms, under rolled-back shirtsleeves, were covered with a pelt of curly black hairs that continued over the backs of his hands and even the first joints of his fingers. The origin of her bear-paw dream, probably—that and the sheer size of the man, looming there across the table like the rest of the bear. Tall Meg was seldom looked down on physically by a man; maybe that factor was at work here. Was she responding to him as big and protective, something safe to hide behind? Or perhaps big as in a challenge?

She looked across the room, caught the waiter's eye, and beckoned. "Could I have some coffee, please?"

"Yes ma'am."

"You're quitting," said Douglas in tones of mild accusation.

"Admitting defeat," she countered.

"Look, I was kidding," he said. "About wanting that. Take it home to your kid."

"What a good idea. Katy will bless you."

The coffee arrived, an insulated carafe of it on a tray with two cups and a pitcher of cream. The waiter poured and retreated; Meg looked at her wine glass, decided to leave it, and picked up her cup. The coffee was gratifyingly dark and rich, its aroma head-clearing. It made her remember one more question.

"Douglas? I'd forgotten about something very odd that Ruthie said yesterday. She said no one else knew about it, but Bobby Macrae told her he'd killed his parents. That he'd done something to their car to cause their accident," she added, in response to his raised eyebrows.

"Jesus. At about fourteen? Sounds to me like the kid was just blowing smoke, but I'll try to get a look at the old files." He poured cream into his cup, then straightened and turned at the sound of raised voices coming from the adjoining bar. "Excuse me a minute," he said to Meg.

By shifting her chair a bit, Meg could see through the open double doors. Two men who had apparently just come in were talking to a third who was seated at the bar. The newcomers were in sheriff's department uniforms with full gear, but they seemed to be cheerful, slapping each other's shoulders and talking animatedly. Douglas approached, they widened their circle to include him, and there was more low-voiced but apparently good-humored talk. Then the two newcomers and their friend came into the dining room to take a booth against the far wall, and Douglas came back to their table, his face thoughtful.

"Well?" said Meg.

He sat down and emptied his coffee cup in several quick swallows. "How about dessert? Good cheesecake, home-made ice cream. Or maybe biscotti and brandy to go with the coffee?"

"Fine. If you'll tell me what's happening."

Douglas waved the waiter over, poured the coffee cups full, looked back at his . . . friends, she supposed. Former subordinates, anyway.

When the waiter had delivered biscotti and brandy, Douglas sighed and sat back in his chair. "It's odd, but probably not a big deal. Oh, nothing to do with you or the Macraes," he added quickly. "There was a kind of family riot out at the Jakel place, and Ruthie's kid called us. Them."

"Riot."

"Verna took a shot at Ruthie, or at least in her general direction. Says Ruthie was trying to steal her old truck."

"Why?"

"Ruthie says her brother Marv stole *her* car last night, that little hatchback. Says he took the keys away from her and drove off, hasn't come back. According to Jocko, Ruthie is scared of something and decided she wanted to leave town right away. She asked Verna for the truck, Verna said no, Ruthie decided to try to take it anyway."

"I saw that truck the other day. It obviously hadn't been driven in ages, and all the tires were soft."

"Verna didn't want it driven tonight. Fortunately she'd had a few beers, and she wasn't strong enough anyway to lift and aim a heavy old .22."

"So Ruthie wasn't hurt?"

"Not this time. If you don't mind, Meg, I'll take you home soon as we finish our coffee. No hurry, but I think I'd like to go out there and have a little talk with the Jakel ladies. See if maybe there's something they need help with."

Should she ask to go along? Meg decided not, decided that those two women would be more easy, more manageable, for a man, particularly one like Earl Douglas. "I don't mind," she told him, and dipped one of the chocolate-almond biscotti into her coffee.

"Your sister is sure a better cook than my mother," said Katy, scooping up a last spoonful of something that was too elegant and flavorful to be called beef stew. Adam had dished up the food, heated it in a microwave oven, and set it out on the round glass table in the breakfast room.

"Nancy doesn't cook," said Adam. "Mrs. Swenson made this, the lady who works for us here. In Los Angeles Nancy and Emmett used to order in from caterers all the time."

"Oh." Giving orders was one thing his sister seemed to be good at, anyway; Katy was still smarting from Nancy's lecture.

"It was nice of you not to yell back at her," said Adam, a born peacemaker. "She'll be sorry later, and she'll apologize. She just can't help being crazy where Brendan is concerned."

Katy thought Brendan was going to turn out to be a pretty weird person, if his mother continued to treat him like a . . . a balloon that might burst. A little boy made of glass. "Brendan looks perfectly healthy to me," she said.

"He is. But Nancy spent about five years trying to have a baby. When she finally did get pregnant, she just went to bed for nine months and prayed every hour, I think. Nancy converted to Catholicism when she married Emmett. Anyway, the odds are against her being able to conceive again, so she's very protective of Brendan."

"I'll say. Somebody might tell her it would protect him to learn to swim."

"I did," Adam said.

Katy got up and began carrying dishes to the dishwasher. As she tucked the last glass in, she heard a self-conscious cough from the doorway and looked up to see Nancy Smith looking at her. Katy straightened to her full height and looked back.

"Katy, I want to apologize for yelling at you. I worry too much about Brendan. And I know, from watching you and from Adam, that you're a capable person and weren't taking risks. Please forgive me?"

"Sure." Katy took the smaller woman's outstretched hand and returned its brief clasp. Nancy Smith didn't much resemble Adam; she had a pale face with small features and a narrow body with the bones very close to the skin. She looked a lot like her skinny little kid, in fact.

"Thank you," said Nancy. "Adam, I'm going to the clinic and I don't know when I'll get back. Mrs. Swenson will stay the night. Brendan would really love it if you and Katy could go up and say good night to him before you leave."

Fifteen minutes later they had tucked Brendan in and were on their way, with the top down on the little car. Sweet little car, Katy thought. Earlier, before dinner, she had gone riding around the grounds with Adam and had begged and pleaded and finally convinced him to let her try driving, out there on the private road where nobody would see them. She hadn't done very well, kept killing the engine; but she was sure the skill was there, waiting in her feet and hands and head, and she'd get it working before long. If she could have another chance . . .

No, unfair, she told herself, tossing a sideways look at Adam. It was getting dark, he'd been incredibly nice about the first time, and she wouldn't push it again so soon. Particularly when he was being equally nice about the roller-skating, something she was fairly sure didn't interest him. "Adam, you don't have to stay with me. There'll be kids there I know, sort of, and I'm sure I can call the ranch and have somebody come to get me after."

He shook his head without looking at her. "I'm not going to be any better at roller-skating than I am at swimming, and you can laugh at me if you want. But I'll enjoy watching you; you have a better time doing things than anybody I ever knew."

They found the old fairground, and the temporary skating

rink, without difficulty. It was just a big circular expanse of concrete, railed all round and open between railing and roof. Taped music sounded from speakers set on sawhorse tables, soft drinks were cheap, and there was no booze even for the surprising number of grown-ups who had turned out.

Katy talked briefly with Tracy, who had Jason and Mike in tow and was effusively glad to see Katy but seemed to want to keep both the boys with her, one on either arm. She saw Ty and had a sort-of race with him around the outer edge of the rink, an activity basically forbidden here. She skated with Tracy's brother, Tom, and found it was easy to hold hands and skate backward. She was polite to older people, some she had met before and some who simply knew who she was; she told all who asked that Frances Macrae was worried but okay and there was no news of Lauren.

Adam stumbled around the impromptu rink once, sat out for a while, tried again and did better. It wasn't that he was really awkward, Katy decided; more than he *looked* awkward. He was being a good sport, and she was having a wonderful time.

"Oh!" She'd been skating backward, looking toward the spot where Adam had gone to sit and rest after a fall, when an arm settled across her shoulders and spun her around.

"Hi, pretty lady," said the snake-armed man. The snake was mostly covered up tonight by a long-sleeved dark shirt, only the head and tail twitching from the backs of his hands. "You're pretty good. May ol' Snake have this dance?"

"It's not a dance," she said, but settled into stride beside him and let him take her hands in a cross-armed hold. The music was smooth and gliding, something one of the older people must have requested.

"I guess your boyfriend doesn't like to skate?"

"He's not my boyfriend," said Katy. This sounded like some kind of put-down of Adam, so she added, "I don't have boyfriends."

"Oh, sure," said her partner. "Here, you're a natural. Let me show you how this goes." He took her left hand in his, took her right and pressed his over it on her right hip. He clasped her lightly against him and lengthened his stride into a long glide, and her body followed his with the music. It was more like dancing than skating, and more like flying than either one.

The song ended, and she braked, pulling away from him. He turned smoothly and skated slowly backward, still holding on to her left hand. "See? I said you'd be good. How 'bout I buy you a Coke?"

"Katy?" Adam had come up beside them, moving with care and teetering just a little. "We should be going. It's almost ten o'clock, and I promised your mom we wouldn't be late."

Katy was instantly back in the Macrae kitchen, being told what to do like a little kid. By her mother who was fooling around with that big cowboy when she was married to Vince.

"Bullshit!" she said. "My mom probably isn't home yet herself. You do what you want, Adam. I'm having too good a time to leave."

· 22 ·

"Katy, what's the matter?"

"Nothing! Not one thing, okay?"

Meg stared at her daughter in astonishment. "Katy, I wasn't . . ."

"I don't want to call Adam back, okay? I'm pretty sick of Adam and everybody else, and if I want to spend some time by myself, what's wrong with that?"

"Nothing at all. I was just passing on the message."

"So okay, you did that. Why don't *you* call *Vince*? Call him and tell him we're coming home Saturday or even sooner."

"I'm not sure we can. I mean, I haven't talked to Frances or Sam yet about our leaving."

"Mom, you promised!"

"Sweetie, I didn't. I said we'd try."

"You don't want to go home. You'd rather stay here where you can mess around with that fat cowboy cop." Katy's eyes blazed blue with tears and anger. "Oh, never mind. Just never mind!"

"Katy, that tone is not acceptable."

"I am just really sick and tired of people telling me what to do!" said Katy in a near shout. Then the tears overflowed; she stifled a sob and ran out the back door.

Sara, who'd been on the porch, came into the kitchen and looked at Meg with wide eyes. "What's the matter with Katy?"

"I don't know." Katy had stayed out until almost eleven the night before, late enough so that Meg had begun to worry. She'd come in without Adam, had pronounced herself very tired to Meg and Sam, and had hurried off upstairs to bed. She'd been asleep half an hour later when Meg followed.

It certainly appeared that she'd had a disagreement of some kind with Adam. The possibility of a sexual assault struck Meg and then was quickly dismissed; in a physical contest, she'd bet on Katy over Adam anytime. More probably she was having her first bout with raging hormones. God, what a time and place for nature to strike.

"I'll go ask her," said Sara.

"No, don't. Why don't you go down and talk to the horses? Tell them Katy is upset, and they should be nice to her if she comes around."

"Yes, I'll tell them," said Sara with a nod.

The unnatural quiet of the house began to weigh on Meg almost as soon as the little girl had left, and she wandered through the lower rooms peering out windows without actually looking at anything out there. Sam had taken his electric presence and his loudly protesting son off to a late-morning appointment with the pediatrician in Alturas. Frances was having trouble with her arthritis but making no fuss about it; she had hobbled in for a breakfast consisting mostly of coffee and aspirin, had wished everyone good morning, and then had returned to her room and presumably her bed.

There was a clatter, a thud, and a sharp word of complaint from the ground-floor bedroom. Meg hurried to the door, rapped once, and pushed it open. "Frances? Are you all right? Oh, let me help you."

"Never mind!" Frances was on one knee beside the bed, red-faced. As Meg watched, she gripped her cane and the bed and pulled herself to her feet. "I dropped that cursed thing and then fell when I tried to pick it up."

"It" was her small black tape player, lying on the floor with its cassette spilling out. Before Meg could move to retrieve it, Frances lifted her cane high and brought it down in a blow that glanced off the little machine and sent it skittering across the floor.

"Here, I'll get it," said Meg, bending quickly to scoop the

player up before the cane came down again, on it or on her. It seemed undamaged; she pushed the cassette back into place and held the unit out to Frances.

"Thank you." Frances reached for it, her hand trembling slightly. It was a spotted, shiny-skinned old hand with blue-rope veins, knuckles swollen from arthritis, thumbnail ridged and thickened.

Frances had caught the look. "Isn't that dreadfully ugly? Ugly and no longer very useful. And I need the tape player because my eyes get tired so quickly when I read. I wonder what I'll do when my hearing fails; I think it's beginning to."

"Frances—"

"Disgusting, all of it. Has Sam come back yet?"

"No. His appointment was for eleven, I think."

"I'm sure there's nothing really wrong with Johnny. Perhaps a little stomach trouble, from that tooth he's cutting."

"Mm," said Meg. She had conducted a gingerly inspection of Johnny's mouth to find that the tooth, the last of four canines, was completely through and the gum no longer swollen. "I don't think it's teeth, Frances. I think he just misses his mother terribly."

"Lauren should be ashamed of herself," she snapped, obliterating the sympathy Meg had felt a moment earlier. "Meg, what is that noise?"

"Let's look." Meg moved to the French doors and pushed them open. A helicopter, she thought, and she and Frances moved along the porch, peering up through the trees, until they finally spotted the dragonfly shape.

"Oh, I just hate those things," said Frances. "Not even July yet, surely it's too early for fire season?"

"I don't know." The copter was very close and quite low. Surely if a fire were nearby, she would be able to see smoke, or at least smell it.

"Oh, good, here comes Sam!" said Frances, and the two of them stood watching as the gray Jeep pulled up and parked.

"Hi, Johnny," said Meg. The baby, draped over his father's shoulder, glanced at her and then turned his face away.

"Nothing wrong with him," said Sam as he led the way into the house. "Just feeling a little low, the doctor said. We're supposed to be nice to him and fix things he especially likes to eat." He gave the baby a gentle shake, then set him down on the fireplace rug. Johnny lay down and put his thumb in his mouth.

"He'll perk up when Katy comes in," said Frances, and Meg thought there was a trace of jealousy in her voice.

"Right. Ah, you got a copy of the paper," she said, spotting the *Messenger* tucked under Sam's arm. "May I see it?"

The front page of this first issue since the murder and Lauren's disappearance had a blurry snapshot of Chuck Jakel, a portrait photo of Lauren Cavalier, and another, slightly smaller, of her brother, Bobby. "Local Man Found Dead" proclaimed the headline; the subhead read "Mysterious Disappearances Plague Modoc County Family." Although the "apparent murder" of Charles Jakel was reported, the writer had avoided suggesting that Lauren Macrae might have been responsible; she was simply "missing and being sought by authorities throughout the state."

Inside, along with more Macrae pictures, Meg found a reprise of the old "sightings of Robert Macrae" story with three new updates, one in the mountains and two in Alturas. "Oh, listen to this," she said, and read the item aloud. " 'On Tuesday morning Mr. Willard Yarrow of Alturas saw a man he believed to be Robert Macrae driving west along Main Street in a dirty green car, one of the small Ford or Chevy economy models. Mr. Yarrow says the car bore a British Columbia license plate.' What do you make of that?"

"It's bullshit!" snapped Sam.

"Well, I don't know," said Frances. "We used to go camping in British Columbia when we were children. I think John and Angie took Lauren and Bobby on similar trips."

"When I was here alone Sunday, a car like that came up the driveway and then went away again," said Meg. "With a dark-haired man driving."

"Really?"

"Frances," said Sam tightly, "don't. You'll just make yourself sick. Tourists drive through Alturas all the time, and God knows any number of gawkers have come by *here* recently. Besides, Will Yarrow is a well-known drunk."

Frances subsided with a sigh."Soon there will be sightings of Lauren, I suppose."

Can't happen too soon for me, thought Meg. "Well," she said, "there's nothing about the trouble at the Jakels' last night. Clearly it happened too late to be covered."

"That isn't a big-city daily, after all," said Sam.

"What trouble?" asked Frances.

Meg folded the newspaper and handed it back to Sam. "Didn't we . . . ? No, that's right. I told Sam when I got home, but you'd gone to bed. Yesterday evening when Ruthie Jakel wanted to use her mother's truck, Verna objected and took a shot at Ruthie."

"Did—was Ruthie hit?" asked Frances in a near-whisper.

"I don't think so," said Meg. "I got the story secondhand, from Earl Douglas." Ruthie's son called the sheriff, she was about to add, but caught herself; no need to raise that painful topic.

"Do you suppose we should feed this child?" she said instead, and bent to scoop Johnny up from the floor. He made no effort to hold on to her nor to escape, and she thought he didn't feel quite so solid, so heavy, as when she had first lifted him a few days earlier. "Come on, Johnny-boy. We'll find you something lovely to eat."

But he wouldn't eat. Sitting stolidly in his high chair with his hands gripping its arms, he wouldn't even look at the soft, cheese-topped scrambled egg, the diced tomato.

"Beans 'n' wieners are his favorite." Sara, guided by an alert stomach clock, had come in a few minutes earlier and was now happily devouring her own eggs.

"Just leave it there, Meg. He'll eat," advised Sam.

Meg shot him a furious glance, but he was exploring the interior of the refrigerator in search of something for his own lunch. Meg found a can in the pantry, heated the stuff quickly, and took a small dish to Johnny. "Here you go, kid."

He shoved the dish off the tray to crash on the floor, meeting her eyes with a look of such baleful misery that her breath caught painfully against the back of her throat. "Oh, baby. What are we going to do with you?"

A sound that had been a distant rumble came closer, grew louder, and resolved itself into the whap-whap-whap of a helicopter rotor. Sam ran to the back door and out onto the porch to shake a fist at the sky.

"You sons of bitches, knock it off! What the hell are they doing, anyway?" he muttered as he came back into the kitchen. "Trying to drive every living thing out of its mind? Meg, leave him alone! Kids are like dogs; they'll eat when they get hungry enough."

A blast of rage swept her like a hot wind, searing her skin and taking her breath away. "You . . . idiot," she said in a voice that rasped. "Dogs don't always. Dogs have been known to die of broken hearts. You think a child is less sensitive than a dog?"

They were glaring at each other wordlessly as Katy came in from the front of the house, stopped in the doorway with a frown, and said, "What's the matter with everybody? And how come that helicopter's hanging around?"

"Oh, Katy, we need you," said Meg.

A slow hammering and a crooning wail brought all eyes to the high chair. Johnny was pounding on the chair's tray with both fists, eyes spilling tears and mouth drawn into a downward bow. "Kee, Kee, Kee," he wailed.

"Well, shit." Katy strode across the room and bent to look at him. "Hey, kid. Okay, I'm here. You want to eat, or what?" As Meg quickly dished up another serving of beans, Katy wiped the baby's face with a paper napkin, then pulled a stool up beside the high chair, perched on it, and picked up the spoon.

Meg turned to Sam, took his arm, and more or less

dragged him from the room, towing him out the front door onto the porch.

"What the hell do you think you're doing?"

What indeed, she thought wearily. Never viewing herself as particularly maternal, Meg had picked her way very carefully through the thickets of motherhood, blessing her own luck and Katy's admirable character. Now she seemed stuck in some kind of save-the-children role, a posture that was exhausting her and Katy both.

"Sam, I want you to look around for some household help. Katy and I need to go home."

"You can't!" He pulled free of her grip and turned to glare at her. "Look, that bastard of a sheriff is seriously pissed off at me already. Every day Lauren's not found, he gets that much closer to calling me a double murderer. Any minute now I expect him to throw my ass in jail, and then what?"

What, indeed. "I'm suggesting you make some reasonable preparation for that possibility," she said.

"Look, I don't know anybody—" A flare of sirens drowned his words, and he spun around to stare down the drive toward the road, where one of the sheriff's department's Chevy Blazers sped past, roof lights flashing. A moment later another followed.

"Holy shit," he muttered. "Listen. They're headed in the direction that copter came from. Toward the Jakel place. I'll go find out what's happening," he announced, and set off at a run for his Jeep.

Nearly an hour passed before he returned, his face an odd greenish color and his hair damp from sweat. Ruthie Jakel's car and Marv Jakel's body had been found. Jakel had been murdered, shotgunned like his brother. He, Sam, had been ordered to come downtown to talk to the sheriff. He thought he should probably take along a toothbrush.

He told them all this with his gaze resting mostly on Meg, his expression a mixture of "I told you so" bravado and accusation, as if she were somehow to blame.

· 23 ·

Everything was falling apart, Katy told herself in misery as she rocked, quietly, in the little chair beside Johnny Cavalier's bed. He'd been asleep now for maybe half an hour, but she couldn't think where else in the house she might want to be. Maybe she should go back down to the barn; there was something comforting about horses.

Aunt Frances had flown into a fury at Sam's announcement, using words Katy hadn't thought an old lady like that would know and thoroughly terrifying both children. After ordering Sam to call the lawyer and standing right beside him as he arranged for the man to meet him in town, Frances took her cane and went outside to pace the porch, back and forth. Even up here Katy could hear her, not her footsteps but the thump of the cane.

And Katy wanted, really really needed, to talk to her mom—had halfway tried to do that two or three times, catching Meg's glance and willing it to hold, but it never did. Finally she had realized that her mom was trying to give her lots of space, to not make her feel pressured. To not set up for a fight.

But there wasn't anything to fight about. It had taken her most of the morning to admit to herself that it was herself she was mad at this time, and with good reason. And her mom wouldn't be mad, she'd be . . . astonished. Disappointed. Scared.

She got up and tiptoed to the window, to look out into the heat and shimmery green fields and blued distances and wish for fog and the wind-whipped Pacific. She hadn't lied, not really; she simply hadn't said anything. Katy squeezed her eyes shut against the brightness and against that evasion.

Lying wasn't the point here, trust was—and besides, she *would* have lied last night if anyone had questioned her.

Her heart bucked at the sound of the telephone, but no one came to get her. What if Adam called again, to tell Meg what Katy had done the night before? He might do that, might consider it his duty or something; Adam was pretty straight-arrow. Almost, she wished he would.

Never mind. She'd broken a mega-major rule, but she'd been lucky and nothing really bad had happened. The unlucky part was now, when what she really wanted was to put her head in her mom's lap and get forgiven or at least understood. Maybe even punished, she wouldn't mind that. Problem was, with all the shit that was happening already, Meg didn't need one more mess to deal with, and Katy was simply going to have to feel rotten all by herself.

She moved close to the crib to look down at Johnny, whose face was streaked from crying. Even for her he had eaten only a few bites of lunch before turning his head away; she had not known that kids so little could get so sad. Mommy missing, daddy in jail, sounded like a song but it was real life.

As for Sam Cavalier, he was a selfish man and not a good father, and Katy had decided she no longer liked him very much. But could he be a killer? She decided humbly that she wasn't old enough or smart enough to have an opinion about that.

Meg was trying to make plans. If Sam should be arrested, actually charged with a crime, she couldn't leave. Yes, she could leave, but she'd take the children with her. But what about Frances? Gah.

The telephone jolted her, bringing her teeth together with a snap she thought might have cracked enamel. She moved into the hall, listened as the answering machine clicked on and droned its message and then took one: for Frances, a reporter whose affiliation Meg didn't hear as she turned to sprint up the staircase.

Telephone, and telephone records. Abby Fowler's belief that they should leave Lauren to come home on her own struck Meg as much less valid in light of the second murder and Sam's imminent arrest.

Sharp-eared Katy put her head out of the baby's room, but Meg just waved her off, put a silencing finger to her lips, and hurried into Lauren's and Sam's room. The small filing cabinet was not locked; she was pleased to find that its drawers moved easily and noiselessly.

Lauren had a nice, straightforward way of keeping things, in manila folders with penciled notations on the tabs. Fingers awkward from her attempt to be both speedy and silent, Meg finally found the "Telephone" folder tucked behind a fat one labeled "Taxes."

She moved to the desk and spread out the long-distance charge sheets, breathing shallowly and keeping her ears tuned: Frances's cane was still thumping out there. Line them up, look for numbers that appear frequently. A drop of sweat fell on the papers, and Meg paused, took a deep breath, and sat down at the desk. What she was doing was perfectly legitimate under the circumstances, and if Frances came in, that's what Meg would tell her.

There were quite a few repeats. Meg found a pencil and marked repeat calls within California or to nearby Oregon and Nevada; then she double-checked to see which ones had gone on for more than a minute or two. After ten minutes that felt like an hour, she had three numbers on a notepad: one in Palo Alto, five calls in the last three months; one in Westwood, which, as she recalled, was virtually part of Los Angeles, four calls; and one in Trinidad, on the north coast, six calls.

"Mom? I think Frances just came in," whispered Katy from the doorway, good natural conspirator that she was. Meg waved thanks, scooped the papers back into the folder, and shoved the folder into its place in the cabinet. She could explain her actions to Frances, but she'd really rather not.

"Oh, hello, Frances," Meg said moments later. "Here, let me help you with that."

Frances watched sourly as Meg twisted the lid from the jar of sun tea that had been set out earlier on the porch. "There's at least one call from a reporter on the machine," said Meg. "In case you want to do anything about it."

"I want to have a glass of iced tea on my porch, quietly," snapped Frances, and Meg prepared a tall glass with lemon and carried it out for her. Then she took the cordless telephone and her list of numbers into the living room.

At the Westwood number, Rae promised via answering machine to get back promptly to whoever was calling; Meg left no message but hung up and dialed the Palo Alto number.

"No, I don't have any idea where Lauren might be, as I told some deputy from your county several days ago." The speaker, a man, softened his voice slightly as he added, "But if I should hear from her, I'll tell her you called."

Chastened by the fact that the sheriff's department had been working after all, Meg nevertheless completed her task by dialing the Trinidad number.

"Hello?" said a brisk voice.

"May I speak with Lauren Cavalier?" said Meg.

The answer was a quick intake of breath, and then a click and dial tone.

Oh ho. Meg hit the redial button and got an answering machine. This time she did leave a message: This is Margaret Halloran. I'm a good friend of Lauren's and I really need to talk with her. Please call me at her number."

Meg carried the phone to the kitchen, set it on the table, and found herself keeping her eyes on it as she moved to the fridge to get a glass of cold water. Then she sat down at the table and continued to watch the instrument as if it were a dangerous sleeping animal. When it did ring she nearly knocked her glass over.

"Hello?" she said cautiously.

"Are you Margaret Halloran?" demanded the caller. It was

a woman's voice, youngish, with the flat vowels and slightly nasal quality of West Coast speech.

"Yes, I am. Who are you?"

"Isn't Lauren there?"

"I haven't seen her for almost a week," said Meg. "Have you?"

"That's none of your business."

"Since you bothered to call me back," said Meg, "you must know of me from Lauren. And she'd have said you can trust me."

There was a sigh at the other end. "Okay, sure, she did. And I hate dicking around, I'd rather just tell you. My name is Beth Sangster, and I've known Lauren since college."

Beth, who had sent a postcard of the beach at Trinidad. "Lauren has been with you?"

Silence.

"Please, Beth. She called me two days ago, but I didn't get to talk with her. Her children really need her."

"She . . . was here. She got here Saturday night."

"Was she all right?"

"Don't be stupid! She was dirty and tired and said she was thinking about killing herself."

"Did she say why?"

"She said somebody was dead and it was her fault. That's all. And I didn't ask any questions, I just told her suicide was a really bad idea. Then I fed her hot soups and fresh vegetables, and loaned her one of my cats to sleep on her bed, and took her for long walks on the beach."

"Where is she now?"

"I don't know. I had an appointment in Arcata Tuesday morning, and by the time I got home, around noon, she'd taken off in this old car my former boyfriend left here for the summer. There was a note on the table saying she was okay, or more okay, anyway, and she was going to go home and try to straighten things out."

Tuesday. From Trinidad to Alturas was probably not much

over three hundred miles. "She hasn't turned up at the ranch. Is the car dependable?"

"Oh, you have to talk to it nicely, but it usually gets you there."

"Has the sheriff's department called you?"

"Yeah. My cleaning lady told them I was out of town for the month. Look, what's happening now?"

"There's been another killing. The older brother of the first man who was killed."

A taut silence. Then, "Fuck."

"Yes. Beth, could you give me a description of the car, and maybe its license number?"

"I don't think I should do that. If she wanted to be shot at by the fuckin' Highway Patrol, she could have driven home in her own truck."

"All right." That partly resolved Meg's moral dilemma: If she didn't know, she couldn't tell anyone. "But if she comes back to you, or you hear from her, please tell her everyone is worried about her, particularly her little boy."

"Okay. One thing, though—I wish you wouldn't say anything to her husband. She really freaked when we saw him on TV Monday night, and before that she kept having bad dreams about him. I think she's scared of him."

Meg clutched the receiver more tightly as opinions and options began to tilt in her mind. *Scared* of Sam. "Did she say anything about her aunt?"

"The only person she actually said anything about was you," said Beth. "And listen. I never made this call." She hung up without another word.

Now what? thought Meg, replacing the receiver. There was nothing for her to do about this except wait. Wait and see wait and see wait and see. *Paciencia.* In your patience possess ye your souls. Damn and blast.

And no one to tell. Not Sam, so not Frances. Assuredly not the police. Mentally rummaging through the jumble of recent terrible events, Meg came up with an equally terrible fact: If Marv Jakel was killed sometime in the night Tuesday, Lauren could have been in the area at the time of his death. If Lauren Cavalier was not a killer, she certainly had the world's worst timing.

Meg jumped as the telephone rang again; she grabbed the instrument in the middle of its second trill. "Yes?" she said.

The speaker was secretary to the sheriff's department. Sheriff Vukovich and/or Undersheriff Ortmann wished to talk with Miss Frances Macrae and Mrs. Margaret Halloran soonest. A car would be sent for them.

"Just a minute," said Meg, and went to consult with Frances. No car, she said to the secretary a short time later; Frances would not, she said to Meg fiercely, be taken from her own house in a sheriff's car like someone being arrested. The two of them would appear on their own, thank you, within the hour.

"Mom?" Katy stood in the kitchen doorway, her face creased in anxiety. "What's wrong now?"

"Oh. Well, nothing more, really. The sheriff wants to talk to Frances and me, so we're going to town to see him. We'll need you to stay here with the children." Lauren is afraid of Sam, she remembered suddenly. And then: Yes, but Sam is downtown, in custody or nearly so.

"Why does he want to talk to you?" Katy's eyes were wide.

"I'm sure we're not suspects, Katy. I'm sure he just has some general questions." She closed her eyes and then massaged her eye sockets with her fingertips. Sand in there, felt like.

"Mom?"

"What is it?" When there was no reply, Meg opened her eyes and reached out to pull her daughter close, wrap both arms around her for a fierce hug. "Katy, don't worry! But stay close to the house while we're away, please—inside, even. We need to remember that somebody is out there with a shotgun. Now if you'll excuse me, I'm going to call Vince."

"Oh. Good."

• • •

Contrary to her usual practice, Meg called Vince at work.

"Meg, how are you?" His voice was cautious, and Meg's immediate response was guilt, followed quickly by irritation. No, don't, she advised herself.

"I'm all right. How are you?"

"Oh, so-so. Police problems have eased off a bit, now that the university has cut back for summer session. And the tourist rush hasn't really started yet. So everyone is taking a bit of a breather."

"How is Emily?"

"She's going to San Francisco for surgery on Sunday. That is, she's going down Sunday, and if things look good they'll do surgery later in the week."

Meg had a quick mind's-eye picture of Emily Gutierrez propped up in a hospital bed. Although she was a plain-vanilla New Englander by birth, a seventeen-year marriage to Esteban Gutierrez had somehow lent a stately Latin tone to Emily's own high-headed presence. With her long hair gone completely white and her features sharpened by age, Emily approaching the end of her eighth decade looked like an imperial of Spain and often behaved like one.

But before this illness she had occupied a hospital bed only in recovery from childbirth. Meg suspected that Emily was frightened of hospitals. That Emily was frightened and perhaps disgusted, like Frances Macrae, by the unlovely failure of her body. And although her life had been productive, successful, and often happy, probably she harbored, again like Frances, a bitter sense of business unfinished. Things yet to do.

"Was it her decision to go?" Meg asked.

"I . . . Christ, Meg, I'm not sure." Meg knew he was running a hand over his close-cropped, grizzled hair. "I hope it was, I hope we didn't just browbeat her into agreeing."

"Will you tell her something for me? Please tell her that if I were in her place—" Meg stopped and stared at the wall for a moment. Were pain and terror a good price to pay in a wager that a few final years could be more active? How much pain?

"If I were in her place, I wouldn't know what to do, either. Tell her I'm thinking about her, Vince, and I deeply wish her the best. Are you going to the city with her?"

"I"m not sure. I will if she insists."

"If you do go, will you please try to find an at-home sitter for Grendel? He just hates the kennel." Grendel, Meg's big Komondor dog, was probably already moping with both Meg and Katy away, and the kennel would be the final blow. For an animal weighing more than a hundred pounds, Grendel was very sensitive; like Johnny Cavalier, he had been known to stop eating.

"Wait a minute. Katy said you were coming home Saturday."

"I—I'd truly like to, Vince, but I'm not sure I can."

"Your friend hasn't turned up yet." It wasn't a question.

"No, she hasn't."

"Do I get a vote in this? My personal and professional opinion, in case you're interested, is that my wife and daughter should get out of the line of fire *right now*. Besides, Meg, I need you here. I *need* you to come home." Gutierrez's voice was tight, as if he were talking through clenched teeth.

"Look," he went on, "I don't know what's been happening to us. What I do know is that I slept alone most of my life—I don't mean sex, I mean sleeping and waking up—and it was okay, I didn't even think much about it. But now I hate it; every morning I wake up and the first thing I'm aware of is a sense of loss."

"Yes, I know." She cleared her throat to get the gravel out of her voice. "Vince, could you move Rich and Bettyjean out? To your mother's, maybe, or to a motel?"

"And then you'll come home?"

"I'm not making conditions or trying to bargain. It's just that I might have to bring two little kids with me. And maybe one bad-tempered old lady."

"Jesus. Okay, okay," he added quickly. "I'll do it."

"And there's this one other thing." Not about Lauren, she couldn't tell even Vince about that, but about Sam; he'd find out anyway and be justifiably furious with her. "The main reason I called was to tell you that there's been another killing—the brother of the first victim. And Sam Cavalier is being questioned and may very well be arrested; he'd had a fight with this man, for one thing."

There was a long silence. Pregnant silence was what Meg thought, first time she'd ever heard one. That she remembered.

"I see," he said finally. "You're sharing a house with a man suspected of murder."

" 'Sharing' isn't quite the way I'd put it."

"He lives in the same house."

"Well, yes."

"Meg—"

"I don't honestly think he killed anybody. I don't honestly think I'm in danger. Please, Vince, I'm not stupid, nor reckless. Not stupid, anyway?" she said into his silence.

"Not stupid," he agreed.

"I'm being careful," she assured him. "And I'll let you know if anything else happens. I miss you."

He sighed. "Good. Meg, I think I'd better call Svoboda back from vacation so I can get away and come up there. I'll let you know. And you keep in touch with Douglas."

"Mm. Okay."

They said quick good-byes, and Meg set the telephone aside and rubbed her eyes wearily again before getting to her feet. She stepped out the back door and saw Katy down at the corral, deep in what appeared to be conversation with one of the horses.

"Katy?" Meg waved, and Katy came to meet her halfway.

"Mom, is Vince okay? Is he mad?"

"Lonely. I told him we can't come home quite yet, and he said he might be able to get away and come here. I wanted to tell you that Frances and I will be leaving for the sheriff's office in just a few minutes. Be good, now," she added, and stroked a hand along her daughter's furrowed brow before kissing her smooth brown cheek.

· 24 ·

"Frances, I'll take you home. They can just wait for me."

"No, Margaret, you stay and talk to the sheriff. They wanted me to come here; now that I'm not feeling well, they can just take me home. Isn't that so, Deputy Garcia?"

"Yes ma'am."

The sheriff and the jail were housed in a tan stucco building that looked baldly modern and pinched beside the domed, neoclassic county courthouse that was its neighbor. On arriving, Meg and Frances had learned that Undersheriff Ortmann was busy at the crime scene, so Sheriff Vukovich himself would talk to Miss Macrae and Mrs. Halloran. Miss Macrae first, of course, which had left Mrs. Halloran twiddling her thumbs and cursing, mostly under her breath, on a metal chair just inside the front door.

Now Meg thought that Frances looked weary and frail, but then she always did. Whatever her true state, she'd be better off at home than here. "Frances, I may do some errands after I finish here. Keep Katy with you, please." For both their benefits.

"Yes, I will. And don't worry. I told Sheriff Vukovich that I was home asleep all Tuesday night, and that I was quite sure you were, too."

"Miss Macrae, we better get going," said Grace Garcia hastily. Meg watched the old woman take the younger one's arm and hobble off toward the door. Frail she might be, but she was not easy to fool or to push around. Probably the sheriff knew that now if he hadn't before.

Sheriff Vukovich, who'd been waiting in his office doorway, now ushered Meg inside and directed her to a chair. He was a tall man with bony shoulders held high as if to ward off backslappers, friendly or otherwise. His short, red-blond hair was combed firmly back; his pinkish face looked naked because his eyebrows and the lashes of his light blue eyes were so pale as to be nearly invisible.

"Mrs. Halloran," he said with a brief nod as he took his own seat behind the desk. "You won't mind if we record this? We got nobody to spare to take notes."

"I won't mind," she said, and he turned on a small recorder. He asked her full name, her relationship to the Macraes, the purpose and length of her present visit. Then he asked who had been at home at the Macrae ranch on Tuesday night.

"Everyone was at home. Well, except for Lauren, of course. The children went to bed right after dinner, and Frances soon after that. Katy, my daughter, worked in the studio with Sam until, oh, around ten. She went to bed, I sat up for a while and talked with Sam. Then I went to bed."

"Alone?"

She registered the nasty tone with interest; Vukovich *was* a son of a bitch, as Sam had said and Earl Douglas had hinted. Meg folded her hands in her lap and smiled sweetly. "No, with my daughter. We share a room and a bed."

"What about Cavalier?"

"I'm not the man's keeper, sheriff. He said he was going to sleep in his studio, and I assume that's what he did."

"But he was gone when you got up."

"He was gone by the time I got around to looking out, probably around eight-thirty."

"You leave the house at any time during the night?"

"No."

"Got any proof of that?"

"Not really. My daughter might have noticed if I'd gotten up, but she's a fairly sound sleeper."

"Miss Macrae says she slept heavily all night, but you were there when she got up and she had no reason to believe you'd gone out."

Meg gave him a minimal nod, aware that Sheriff Vukovich

wasn't going to entertain any doubts about Frances Macrae's truthfulness. But Frances had not been exactly on the scene when Meg got up; she'd been out talking to the horses. Horses that Sara said could talk back, but Meg doubted they'd talk to Vukovich.

"Well. Okay." He sat back in his chair with his elbows on its arms and steepled long fingers in front of his chest. "Now, about Lauren Macrae. Did you know about her relationship with Charles Jakel?"

"I didn't, and I still don't."

"Did she say anything to you about leaving?"

"No."

"Do you know where she is?"

"No," she said, resisting the impulse to embroider on this truthful statement and thus make it suspect.

"Have you had any communication with her since she left?"

"Not to my knowledge. There were several telephone calls from people who didn't speak but simply hung up."

"What about her husband, he have any contact with her?"

"I don't know. You'll have to ask him."

"I have," he said grimly. "Now, about the Jakel family. Did you know them before coming here a week ago?"

"No."

"I'm told you've been involving yourself with them. Pestering them is what Mrs. Jakel says."

Meg said nothing, keeping her face serene.

"According to Miss Ruth Jakel, you invited her out for a drink Tuesday afternoon. Why did you do that, if you didn't know her?"

"I was trying to find out what I could about Lauren. She and Ruthie knew each other when they were younger."

"You learn anything interesting?"

Meg had a mental picture of this man questioning Ruthie Jakel, in her own way as tough a subject as Frances. "She said Lauren had always liked her brother Chuck and was therefore unlikely to have killed him."

"She say who she thought did?"

"No, and I did ask."

"Mm. She tell you, Ruthie, who beat her up?"

Righty-ho, Ruthie was not talking. "No. But I got the feeling," Meg said slowly, "that she was frightened of her brother Marv's friend. Have you talked with him?" She was fairly sure he, or someone, had; the man had come out the door as she and Frances were arriving, paying them no attention as he headed for the parking lot.

"That's no concern of yours, Mrs. Halloran. Your comment will be noted."

"Thank you," she said with an inclination of her head. "Ruthie was also frightened of Bobby Macrae. But she said she didn't believe Bobby had reappeared after ten years and killed Chuck, because he would have killed Lauren, too, right then."

Vukovich frowned. "Robert Macrae is dead. These people who say they've seen him are just looking for publicity. Or they're crazy. Me, I got dead bodies and people missing right now; I'm not interested in ancient history."

Meg thought he was seriously wrong in that view but saw no point in saying so.

"Why did you go out to the Jakel place Sunday?"

"To express my sympathy over their loss."

His nose twitched at that, as if he'd smelled something unpleasant. "Mrs. Halloran, as a policeman's wife you ought to know better than to stick your nose into what's police business and none of yours." Vukovich stood up to indicate that the interview was over. "I believe you're helping out Miss Macrae with the house and the children? Might be a good idea for you to stick to that."

What, she wondered, would they do to a grown woman for flipping off a county sheriff? Lock her in some equivalent of the stocks? She wouldn't deliver the gesture, but neither would she reveal her tentative plan to take those children away from here. As she got to her feet, she said, "Sheriff Vukovich, have you arrested Sam Cavalier?"

"There, just like I said. None of your business. And I've got one last question—for the moment, at least—for you. Do you know—no, I'll put it this way: Where do you think Mrs. Cavalier might be?"

"I think she's alive but hiding somewhere, I have no idea where. Sheriff Vukovich, I hope you and other officers and agencies will be . . ." Reasonable? Kind? Controlled? She finally settled unhappily for "careful, if you find her."

"Oh, we will be. And you be careful, too, Mrs. Halloran."

She nodded and kept her gaze down, willing to finish on a humble note on Lauren's behalf. Miraculously, she'd gotten through the whole interview without telling a single lie—although she was probably fudging the definition in ways that Katy, for instance, would quibble with.

Meg looked around as she headed for the front door but saw no one who was even vaguely familiar. She sighed and stepped out into the afternoon sunlight just as Grace Garcia pulled up to the curb.

"Hello. Thank you for driving Miss Macrae home."

"No problem. She's real creaky today."

"Yes, she is. Officer Garcia, have you seen Earl Douglas around this afternoon?" she asked, gesturing to the building behind her.

"Oh, no ma'am. He and Vuke—the sheriff—don't get along, so Sheriff Douglas doesn't keep an office or anything here."

"Oh. Too bad. I tried to call him at home, but there was no answer."

"He doesn't always bother to turn on his answering machine if he's working around the place. If you want to drive out there, just go north on 395 for four and three-tenths miles, and then . . ."

Meg jotted the directions on a card, thanked Garcia, and set off for her own car.

Deputy Garcia's directions were exact and easy to follow, and the house, a plain, elderly wooden structure, was set fairly near the road. Meg noted that the siding could certainly have used a coat of paint, and the grass all around was ankle-deep, but there was a new redwood deck jutting out from the right side, the south side. Southern California influence, looked like.

Douglas's pickup truck was parked before the house. Meg put her Honda beside it and got out to breathe the expected smells: dust and damp grass and probably horses. Just like the Macrae ranch, where she hoped Katy and Frances were coping with the children and each other. Swung from the stimulation of conflict to the isolation of this still-alien landscape, she found fear and confusion lapping around her like a rising tide: two dead, one missing, line of fire line of fire line of fire. Lauren afraid of Sam, Ruthie afraid of someone; some frightened people simply ran, others killed, and how could you know who was which?

There was no response to the doorbell, but Deputy Garcia had said Douglas would probably be working outside. Meg stepped down from the porch and set off for the barn and corral some distance behind the house. Both were smaller than those at the Macrae ranch but were neatly kept, the barn freshly painted red and the fence rails white. Horse in the corral, gray with a wide forehead and an interested look. And an incredibly leggy baby, also gray. The mother horse put her head over the top rail and gave a questioning little whicker, and a moment later Earl Douglas appeared from behind the barn, carrying a big tool Meg decided must be a posthole digger.

"Hey, Meg," he said, wiping his dripping forehead with one forearm. "I was going to call you pretty soon. Give me a minute."

She waited, and tried to watch without seeming to stare, while he splashed water on his face and shoulders from a standing faucet. In this setting it was not his size that was riveting to Meg but the fact that he was simply the hairiest man she'd ever seen this much of, covered from neck to low-slung jeans front and back in curly gray-with-black fur. What would that feel like?

Never mind! said her conscience, to which her libido or whatever it was answered, Hey! horny's better than terrified. Better than comatose, too, which was approximately how she'd felt lately. Douglas lifted a blue work shirt from a corral post and shrugged it on, fastening several buttons as he came through the gate and closed it carefully behind him.

"I'm sorry to interrupt your work," she said, "but I've just had a frustrating and fruitless session with your successor."

"Thought you looked a little frazzled." Douglas paused to stroke the nose of the gray mare. "You know how some kids drag in a dog and then leave it for Mom to take care of? My boy brought home this mare, in foal. Ease up, lady," he said, not to the mare but to Meg. "I don't have a lot of information for you, but I can hold your hand and give you a cool drink in the shade."

Oh, good, she thought, swallowing a giggle as she remembered her bear-paw dream. She let him point her at the deck, where several chairs sheltered under a striped umbrella. Moments later he came back from the house with two glasses full of ice and a big jug of the ubiquitous sun tea.

"Used to be, I could work and drink beer all day." He filled the glasses, handed one to Meg, and then settled with a sigh into a chair. "If I was to try that now, I'd probably wind up nailing some piece of myself to whatever I was working on. So, what do you hear from Vince?"

His posture was easy, but his gaze was direct and unblinking.

"I talked to him this afternoon. He's lonely."

"I bet," he said, with a grin that narrowed his eyes.

"He's also very troubled by the fact that I'm living in the same house as a murder suspect. In fact, he told me to keep in touch with you."

"Ah," said Douglas. "Like I said the other night, he's a much nicer guy than me. Besides better-looking."

"Well, nicer, anyway," said Meg. "Nicer than me, too, which is why it's probably a good thing he's making arrangments to come up here."

"Ah," said Douglas again, with a quick grin and a shrug that would have done a Frenchman credit.

And that takes care of that, Meg told herself with a fairly small twinge of regret. Life was already much too complicated. She took a hearty swig of the icy, minty tea and said, "Douglas, you have heard about Marv Jakel?"

"Oh, yeah. I even saw this one, not that anybody would want to. Poor little bastard took a load of buckshot right in the face."

Meg swallowed. Nothing left of that ratty, mean little face. Except its near-duplicate in Ruthie. "I think the sheriff is about to arrest Sam Cavalier," she said, and waited for reassurance.

What she got was a long look and then, "Well, probably I'd do that, too."

Meg took a very large gulp of tea, wishing it were something stronger. In truth, the phone call from Beth Sangster in Trinidad had absolved Sam only of his wife's murder. "Um— can you tell me where this killing happened, and when?"

"No secret there; about twenty people saw the scene," said Douglas with a nod. "Jakel was in that little car, like he'd been sleeping in back with the hatch open, then woke up and sat up and blam. Car was parked by an old feed shed near a little creek and a stand of cottonwoods, place that looks like it's been used for camping now and then over the years."

"On the Jakel ranch?"

"Well, yes, but right near the fence between Macrae and Jakel. He'd have had to drive along the fence one side or the other. Piece of fence there by the shed was down, probably been that way a while."

"Apparently he was killed sometime Tuesday night?"

"Looks like."

When Sam was sleeping, or so he said, in his studio. After Ruthie Jakel was forced to give up her car and thus left without transportation. Or so *she* said. "Did you believe Ruthie Jakel's story?" she asked Douglas. "About Marv's running off with her car?"

He shrugged. "Her kid backed her up, for what it's worth. Which would mean she had no wheels, but I think they still have a horse or two on the place. There'd been horses by that creek fairly recently, as well as a few cows."

Murder on horseback? Meg looked at Douglas, but his expression was bland. "The friend, Marv's buddy, has a truck," she said. "I asked the sheriff about him, and he said it was none of my business. But when Frances and I arrived for questioning this afternoon, I saw that man leaving."

"Must be they talked to him and had no solid reason to hold him," said Douglas. He drank the last of his tea and got up to refill their glasses.

Possess your soul in patience, Meg reminded herself, and kept an interested, hopeful expression on her face.

Douglas sat down again and tipped his chair back. "Just in case you're interested, I found out the buddy is an ex-con named Dwayne Wilhite. He served time with Marv Jakel at Susanville, and the deputy D.A. I talked to says Wilhite should have been in a tougher place, for a longer time."

"What was he convicted of?"

"Involuntary manslaughter, same as Jakel. Turns out Wilhite had a bunch of prior arrests but no convictions, because witnesses never stayed around long enough to testify. That's what happened the last time; should have been a heavier charge, but they felt they had to bargain it down."

"What was he arrested for, the other times?"

Douglas shrugged. "You name it, he probably did it, mostly on a minor-league level. Drug dealing, robbery, assault. The guy's what you'd call an opportunistic criminal—comes across any chance to make a buck, preferably crooked, he'll do it right off. Somebody gets in his way, he'll beat the shit out of him. Or her. Basically figures rules or laws just don't apply to him."

"I wonder why he came here," said Meg.

Douglas shook his head. "Fellow like that wouldn't have a family waiting with open arms. Probably this was a temporary layover till something interesting happened along. Or maybe Jakel got him thinking they could cash in on Verna or the ranch some way."

"Could he have killed Chuck for that reason?"

"To free up his buddy's inheritance? That's a little long-range for Wilhite's type. Fact is, Lauren Cavalier's still the best bet for that killing."

Meg took a long drink of tea, not looking at him. She definitely did not want to talk about Lauren with this man, ex-cop very easy on the ex. Did they stay sworn for life? she wondered. "Did you ask anybody about Ruthie's story? That Bobby Macrae killed his own parents?" she asked after a moment.

"He plain didn't do that," Douglas said. "I got a look at the files. The Macraes were coming home from a meeting in Carson City, middle of the afternoon. Three different sets of witnesses saw them get hit head-on, on their own side of the road, by a long-haul trucker who fell asleep and drifted over the center line doing about eighty."

"I *know* Ruthie Jakel wasn't lying to me about that," said Meg.

"Looks like it was Bobby Macrae that lied."

"Weird," she said softly. There was a rustle in the trees lining the driveway, and she lifted her head to feel a breeze touch her face; the afternoon was winding down. Probably no one at the Macrae ranch had given any thought to supper; probably the two little kids had by now worn Katy and Frances down to nubbins. She wondered whether Sam was there, or locked up. She knew she'd prefer the latter; Vince's attitude had reminded her of what was really going on around here, and what could happen to innocent bystanders.

Meg stood up and put her shoulder bag in place. "I'd better go now and relieve my daughter the baby-sitter. Poor kid, she thought this was going to be a vacation."

He was on his feet quickly. "I'll be in touch."

"Will you call me, please, if something turns up? On Lauren, or about Sam?"

"If I can. You take care, now."

At the top of the deck steps she paused and turned. "I'm grateful for your help, and if I've been pushy about getting it, I apologize. I feel like some—some unarmed female in a war zone, hiding in the cellar with the children and hoping the marauders don't stumble over us."

"Why don't you pack up the kids and come out here to stay?"

She smiled at him; exchange one danger for another, albeit a less lethal one? "Thanks. But what I'd like to do is pack them up and head for Port Silva. Do you think the sheriff would object?"

"He might. Let me know when you're ready, and I'll ride—" Shotgun, he'd clearly intended to say. "I'll provide an escort."

· 25 ·

The only person Meg felt bad about deceiving was Katy. Frances continued to appear unconcerned, or at most irritated, by Lauren's absence. The children knew only that she wasn't there, and announcing to them that she was alive would set a new and terrifying frame around the fact of her absence. To Sara Meg simply said, as she'd been saying every day, that her mother would surely come home soon and was surely thinking of her.

And Sam—Meg focused her weary, bleary gaze on the man who sat at the kitchen table sucking like a sullen baby at a bottle of beer. A second beer at that, at ten-thirty in the morning. Sam's concern was clearly for his own skin, his own freedom, his own pursuits. If Lauren Cavalier wanted her husband to know that she was alive, she knew where to get in touch with him.

But Katy really cared about Lauren. Meg thought her daughter looked only slightly less woebegone today than yesterday, but she had at least recovered from her anger or whatever it was with Adam and was preparing for an outing of some sort with him this afternoon.

"Dumb bastard thinks *no* evidence is circumstantial evidence, some way," muttered Sam. "And he wouldn't tell me how long he plans to keep my wagon. That's what I get for being cooperative."

Sam drained the beer bottle and got to his feet. "If he was going to arrest me, why didn't he do it yesterday? I think he's trying to wear me down, that's what. Expects me to fall apart and confess. Well, he's got the wrong man, both ways." He strode through the hall to the front door, peered out, came back through to the kitchen and stood just inside the screen door, staring at the barn.

Johnny, lying on the floor with the Walkman headset on, was oblivious to the emotional turmoil around him. Sara, who'd been huddled in her tall chair at the table watching and listening, now sat straighter with a worried frown. "Daddy? Is somebody going to take you away, too?"

"What? No, nobody. I'll be right here, sweetheart. Maybe I'll take one of the horses out for a while," he added to himself. Then he turned abruptly from the door, running his hands through his hair with enough force, Meg thought, to be painful. "No, there isn't time. Pick me up at eleven, they said. Hope it's little Gracie Garcia again; maybe I'll talk her into fleeing the country with me."

"Daddy?"

"Your daddy is just going to town again, to talk to the sheriff," Meg said quietly to the little girl. "The way he did yesterday."

"Right, right. And the day before and probably the day after. Christ!" Sam dug his fingers into his hair again, and Meg could see that the sheriff's plan, if Sam had called it right, could possibly work. Sam Cavalier was on the edge of an explosion. She watched him pull another beer from the fridge and said, "Sam, I don't think—"

"Right, don't think, it's none of your business!" he snapped, and reached for the opener to flip the cap off the bottle. "What's your problem, you worried that booze will zap me back into murder mode, I'll start wringing necks all over the place?"

"No."

"That what you were thinking last night when you bolted all the doors? Locked me out of my own fuckin' house, who the hell do you think you are?"

"I'm sorry, Sam. I must have done that automatically, without thinking." She had bolted every door and locked every window after he went to the studio to sleep, and not by accident; and she'd been on watch most of the night, in case he should decide to break in. It had all seemed futile and silly at daybreak. Now, looking at his furious face, all she was sure of was that she hoped the deputy got here soon.

He tipped the beer bottle to drink without taking his eyes off her. "And what were you doing all night, packing? Getting ready to abandon us?"

Sara slid down from her chair and came to stand close against Meg's side, and Meg put an arm around her: Don't worry. "I have an idea that might work well for all of us, Sam," she said. "With your permission, I'd like to take the children home with me for a few days."

"With my permission," he repeated in high, mincing fashion. "Not bloody likely, lady. You're not heading off down the road with *my* kids so the whole town can say, 'Look there, by God! That Cavalier is one bad bastard, fuckin' guy must have killed his wife after all 'cause now they're taking his kids away from him,' and next thing—"

"Shut up, you fool!" snapped Meg, as Sara, trembling, gave a little yip of terror.

Sam blinked and tried to focus his gaze. "Sara? It's okay, sweet girl, Daddy didn't mean anything. Sara?"

She turned away from his reaching hand to bury her face against Meg.

"Sara, don't be like that," he said. When she did not respond, he turned his bleak gaze on Meg. "So okay. I'd like to kick your ass out of here, but I can't afford to do that. Believe me, though, I can make sure you don't take Sara and Johnny anywhere."

The doorbell sounded, and Sam flung his head up like a startled horse. "No, I'm not going to . . . Son of a bitch. What am I going to do?"

"Answer the door," said Meg.

He looked from her to the bottle in his hand, tipped it and drained it and set it down. "Right. On my way. Oh, don't think you can work an end run with Frances's help, Meg. She can't give permission, and she wouldn't, anyway, not without my approval." He turned on his heel and headed through the hallway to the front door.

"Morning, Mr. Cavalier," said a deep voice—not Gracie Garcia but Ron Ortmann, Meg thought.

Sam grunted something in reply and then said, "Hey, you guys finished with my Jeep?"

"You know, that's kind of interesting." Ortmann had come through to the kitchen, apparently to say something to Meg, but now he turned back to Sam. "Inside of that wagon of yours is nice and clean, like it got vacuumed out and scrubbed—"

"Which it did," interrupted Sam. "Which it always does after a long trip."

"Yeah, but the inside is all scratched and scraped, like you carried big metal boxes or something."

"Coffins, right?"

Meg remembered her first glimpse of Sam and his Jeep wagon, and her sense that the vehicle resembled a police car. Because there was a screen between the front seat and the back. And there were those wire frames Johnny had almost tumbled into, beside the barn. "Cages," she said. "Wire cages."

"Oh, for Christ's sake," said Sam, glaring at her. "When I drive in the mountains, I make it a point to pick up injured animals, maybe a crime but so what? And if you just toss an injured doe or even a big raccoon into the back seat, you're likely to get a nasty surprise down the road."

"Good point," said Ortmann. "Morning, Mrs. Halloran. Thought I better tell you and Miss Macrae there's a bunch of reporters out at the gate. I reminded them about trespassing, and I don't think they'll bother you. Okay, Mr. Cavalier, let's go."

"Thank you," Meg called after him, and stood where she was until she heard the door close.

"Mom?" Katy came hurrying into the kitchen, her back-pack swinging from her hand.

"Just another policeman, come to collect Sam for more talk," said Meg. His departure had reduced the tension level in the house by about half, she thought. She herself was too tired to be tense, or maybe just too tired to notice. Katy looked—better.

"Are they—?" Katy clearly meant to ask if they were arresting Sam but stopped as she caught sight of Sara.

Meg shook her head as she hugged the little girl close, then released her. "Sam is upset, and it frightened us for a few minutes. So, where are you and Adam going?"

"Just out into the woods, I guess. He was going to try to borrow Emmett's Rover, so we'd have something high with four-wheel drive."

"Are you supposed to make sandwiches or something?"

Katy grinned. "Rich people have their cooks do that stuff. Good thing we're leaving, or I might get used to hanging out with rich people."

Johnny, catching the sound of his favorite's voice, rolled over and sat up quickly. "Kee!"

Katy winced and then smiled. "Hi, little kid. How're you doing? What're you listening to today?" She knelt beside him, took the headset, and held it to her ear. "Mom! Are you trying to make a Deadhead out of this helpless child?"

"Just never mind. He likes it. Johnny has a very good ear for his age. Katy, are you okay?"

Katy shrugged and put the headset back on Johnny's curly head before getting to her feet. "I'd have to say this was a pretty shitty vacation. Maybe we need to go back to Port Silva and start over, in a different direction."

"Wolf Haven was fun."

"Yeah, it was. And Adam is nice, and Lauren—" She put a hand over her mouth and blinked hard. "Sorry."

"She is, Katy. She *is* nice."

"Right."

About to say more, Meg heard an engine, and then the sound of tires crunching onto the gravel at the front of the house. "Katy, I'd appreciate it if you wouldn't go too far into the woods today. Stay a little closer to civilization, such as it is. Please?"

"Well, okay." She cocked her head. "I think we're stuck with roads, anyway. I think that's the Porsche I hear out there, and it's got less than five inches ground clearance."

She was frightened, Meg admitted to herself as she picked up Johnny, who was howling in sorrow over Katy's departure. He swatted the headset away when she offered it, and she decided he'd had enough of that, anyway. Too much like hypnosis or brainwashing, pumping sound into the helpless ears of a two-year-old.

Not terrified, as she'd been several times during the night. Not panicky. But definitely more than worried. She looked at the clock to find it was much too early for lunch and the blessed haven of naptime; Johnny had stopped wailing but was lying limp in her arms, giving an occasional little hiccup-sob that was sadder than a howl.

"I want to go home with you and Katy."

Meg jumped, nearly dropping the baby. She'd forgotten about Sara. "We might do that, Sara—go to my home. But we mustn't talk about it, not yet. Do you understand?"

"Sure. I like secrets." Sara's face crinkled in a grin for the first time that day. Or maybe even longer, Meg thought guiltily. The little girl was so self-contained that she got lost in the background while everyone danced attendance on her brother.

"Good. Now, what shall we do with you two?" She could send them out to Frances, who was spending her morning glumly weeding and hose-watering the vegetable garden. She suddenly remembered the big piano in the living room, which she had nudged idly the other day and found to be locked.

"Sara, do you like to play the piano?"

"I can't do that. It's my grandmother's piano, and we always keep it locked." She hesitated for a moment, and then said somewhat furtively, "But I know where the key is."

"Sara, you are a very smart little girl."

•   •   •

"Meg, what on earth is going on?" Frances came inside the back door and put earth-stained hands protectively to her ears.

"Entertainment," said Meg. Sara was on the bench, Johnny standing with his nose practically on the keys, and the two of them were making an awesome noise. "Or would you like to take the children outside to play for a while?"

Frances would not. Frances meant to take herself to the far side of the porch and listen to another few chapters of *Pride and Prejudice*. "If I can concentrate," she added in pitiful tones. "Poor Sam."

"Mm," said Meg. She waited until the old woman had gone on her way, then hurried upstairs and collected clothes from the children's rooms, for washing. If Sam was not charged or at least held, if Lauren did not turn up before the day was over, Meg Halloran meant to commit child abduction, preferably with the help of Earl Douglas but without it if necessary.

Lauren. Call home call home call *home*. She offered this plea with silent fervor. She had a feeling, actually, that Lauren would call, that she'd been out there as long as she could stand it, whatever her reasons. Lauren would call.

And she should call someone herself, for herself. Not Vince, because he was too far away, and her own high nervousness would frighten him. Douglas, of course. She took the telephone out the back door, out of range of the piano and the groaning washing machine, and punched out Douglas's number.

At his "Douglas here," she said without preamble, "Earl, please. I need to know what's happening. I need to know if they're going to hold Sam."

"Meg, why—? Never mind. I'll find out what I can, get back to you."

"Thank you," she breathed, and hung up to wait now for two calls.

◦   ◦   ◦

By lunchtime there had been four calls, none of them from Lauren. Twice Frances, summoned from the porch, spoke in her rude and blessedly brief fashion to reporters, one from Reno and one from Sacramento. The third caller spoke in a gravelly whisper, identifying himself as Robert Macrae and then settling into a tirade of obscenities and threats. Some local creep stimulated by yesterday's newspaper stories, probably; Meg slapped the receiver down and went to wash her hands.

And finally Earl Douglas called to say that Sam Cavalier and Ruth Jakel were both high on the sheriff's list, with Sam at the very top. The ex-con, Wilhite, occupied slot number three considerably lower down, but Wilhite was nowhere to be found at the moment.

Vukovich would like to charge Sam now, Douglas added, but was meeting resistance from the district attorney, who saw inadequate evidence. Sam would probably be held to the end of the day and released.

Lunchtime, and Johnny, who'd expended both energy and concentration on the piano, ate quite a lot of bread and peanut butter and banana and drank a whole cup of milk before remembering he was sad. Meg looked at a beer in the fridge, resisted, swabbed the children and put them down for naps, looked again at the beer and gave in.

Nothing from Lauren by two o'clock. Her ears, on alert for endless hours, were so tired she thought they hurt. She smeared a piece of bread with peanut butter, resisted another beer, and wondered. If she did not hear from Lauren, if Sam was arrested, *should* she tell Vukovich about Lauren's friend Beth in Trinidad?

Probably she should. Probably she would, and that was going to make several people angry—including Earl Douglas, not to mention Vince. Gah.

Oppressed by the stillness of the house, she paced the porch quietly for a few minutes, ears cocked as always, and then remembered the cordless telephone. Yes indeed, there it was in the dining room, little light bars glowing. Hang the thing in her back pocket and she could move out a bit, maybe go down to the barn for the company of the horses.

Children sleeping, Frances in her room with the pot of tea she'd made a while ago. Maybe with brandy, too, but so what; Meg was a little envious but walked resolutely past the refrigerator from which beer and at least one open bottle of wine beckoned.

Outside, the air was electric, moving in odd puffs of wind. The blue sky rolled with fat clouds, and those to the south were interestingly dark; there'd been rain somewhere nearby, she could smell it. She heard birdsong, caught the flash of red chevrons as a blackbird streaked past. Saw something high and soaring on wide wings, maybe a hawk. Maybe a turkey buzzard. Reached the corral and said, "Hello, Max," to the bay, who tossed his head away from her reaching hand.

"So be that way, I'll talk to Daisy. Where is she?"

Inside, presumably. Meg climbed the rail fence, picked her way across to the open door of the barn. It was dim inside, but she could make out the high, rounded form near the far door. She said, "Daisy?" and the horse whickered softly.

"Good, good girl. Frances will be glad you're both here and safe." She stood just inside the door for a moment to let her eyes adjust to the dimness; dust motes danced in the light that came from behind her, and the high-roofed building set outside noises at a great distance and surrounded her with a silence that seemed to be a different species of sound.

Max behind her, Daisy ahead. Meg had a sense of another presence, someone waiting with held-in breath. She caught her own breath and took a step backward as she remembered the missing ex-convict, Wilhite. Another step back, and as she pivoted to turn and flee, there was a rustle to her right, and then encircling arms like an embrace and a rush of body weight that carried her off her feet and threw her full-length to the barn floor.

· 26 ·

"Meg, oh Meg, I'm sorry." Lauren Cavalier was trying to help Meg to her feet and hug her and at the same time pull her further into the depths of the barn. "But you were standing there in the doorway in plain view. Come on back where they can't see us!"

"Who?" Meg allowed herself to be led, trying as she went to brush dust and wisps of straw from her face and hair.

"Anybody. The children. I can't let Sara and Johnny see me like this."

Meg gave Lauren a good, long look and had to agree. The younger woman was not only gaunt and wild-eyed, she was filthy. Dirt smeared her face and her forearms; her shirt and jeans were crumpled and stained; her hair was lank and greasy, and she smelled.

Lauren read Meg's glance and pulled away. "I'm sorry. I've been sleeping out since . . . God, I can't remember. Meg, are they okay, my kids?"

"They're asleep right now."

This remark drew a very straight look from Lauren, and Meg's face grew warm.

"Sorry. Of course they're not okay; Sara's worried and Johnny is very sad. We've done our best, especially Katy, but it's you they need. Why don't you come inside, clean up a bit, and—"

"No." Lauren sat down on a bale of hay and tipped her head back, to rest it wearily against the wall. "I wouldn't have come back at all, ever, except for them. But first I need to find out what's happening, and then, maybe . . . Where's Sam?" she asked suddenly.

"At the moment, he's with the sheriff; he's being questioned but hasn't yet been charged. Lauren, how did you get here? How long have you *been* here?"

"What is today, Friday?" At Meg's nod, she sighed. "I guess I got back in the area the middle of Wednesday night; it was still dark but beginning to show some gray. Then after it got to be full daylight there was something going on, helicopters and like that, and I figured they were looking for me, so I just buried myself in a gully and stayed there until it got good and dark again. Last night. And I came here and hid."

"Why? Why didn't you just come in then?"

"I meant to, but I was scared; there was all that noise and I thought they'd probably shoot me on sight. Or Sam would."

"Lauren, where were you Tuesday night?"

Lauren pushed herself straighter against the wall and stared at Meg. "Tuesday. Oh, I remember Tuesday all right. The car I was driving started acting funny late in the afternoon, so I pulled into this awful little highway town a couple hundred miles west of here and stopped at a gas station. The guy there, the mechanic, said it was something easy, timing or something."

"So you've got a receipt? Or the mechanic can testify for you?"

Lauren was shaking her head. "I really don't think so. See, he said he couldn't do the work until after hours, so I got some snack stuff and stayed out in the woods until everybody else had gone home and he closed the station. When I came in, he grabbed my purse and took every cent I had. More than four hundred dollars, I think. And the bastard hadn't even fixed the car; it still ran rough."

"Lauren—"

"The really stupid thing was, I fought with him," she said, hugging herself with crossed arms that Meg realized were marked not just with dirt but with bruises as well. "He wasn't very big. But he was strong. Then I said I'd call the police, and he just laughed. Said I'd better hit the road while I had the chance, so I did."

"Oh, Lauren. You should see a doctor."

She set her hands gently against her rib cage and shook her head. "I don't think he broke anything. Testify about what, Meg?"

Meg coughed to ease the ache in her throat. "Marv Jakel was shot and killed sometime Tuesday night."

Lauren stared, open-mouthed. Then she pulled her legs up and hugged her knees. "Marv. God. Why would Sam shoot Marv?"

This story came less easily, but it was short and Meg finally got it all: Friday night just one week ago, Lauren took the injured Chuck Jakel home to his cabin and helped him into his bed and then gave in to his urging and joined him there. They made love, and then dozed, and woke and made love again. As she was dressing to go home, a car drove up and pulled to a stop facing the cabin but some distance back, with its lights blazing and its horn blaring.

"Chuck said something like 'that Goddamned Marv!' and ran out naked, yelling. I was terrified and just kind of huddled inside, and then there was this incredible blast. I couldn't—it was a minute or two before I got to the door, and then I saw the wagon, Sam's Jeep wagon, just back off and swing around and drive away.

"Then I went out and saw there was absolutely no question that Chuck was dead, so I got in my truck and left. Isn't it weird?" she said in a raw whisper, "that I could do that, just drive away? From Chuckie Jakel, the first guy I ever made love with? Well, maybe not love, but we were sixteen and his brother was after me, with my brother egging him on. Chuckie fought Marv and made him leave me alone, and then we were together for a little while, just two babies."

Creating an unwanted baby of your own. Meg said, "Lauren, the night Chuck was shot, did you actually see Sam?"

"No. The headlights were too bright. But there was a little bit of moon that night, and I could see his gray Jeep. So Chuck is dead and rotten old Marv too, and Sam's a murderer and it's my fault. Meg, could you sneak into the house, do you think, and get me a change of clothes? At least a change of underwear."

Meg's mind was dizzy with questions: Had you been seeing Chuck regularly since he came back here? Could Sam have known? How could he have known where you were Friday night? None of her immediate business, these. "Are you sure you don't want to come in?" she asked.

Lauren shook her head, her lip outthrust in the manner of her son, but trembling. "I'm too dirty. I think what I need is a cell someplace, with a concrete floor and no windows."

"All right. I'll get you some clothes, and if you don't mind, I'll tell Frances what's going on. If we take her wagon instead of my Honda, I think I'll be able to smuggle you past any reporters hanging around the gate."

There were myriad gaps in logic here, Meg thought as she hurried to the house and then crept upstairs to Lauren's room. In addition to her own questions, there was the one Lauren had asked and then forgotten: Unless he knew her whole history—and she'd said herself, earlier, that he didn't—why would Sam have killed Marv Jakel?

But it did make all kinds of sense to get Lauren to the sheriff, and to whatever safety custody offered. And to find her a lawyer. Meg added a washcloth and towel and a bar of soap to her armload and hurried back to the barn. She'd tell Frances what was happening right at the last minute, when Lauren was ready to go.

· 27 ·

"Katy, I really am sorry," said Adam for about the nineteenth time.

"Adam, be quiet!" Katy tossed a glance toward the creek bank where Brendan squatted, peering down into the shallow, slow-moving stream. "He thinks this is his very own picnic, that he's why we came here today."

"You were supposed to have a rest from baby-sitting," he muttered. "Besides, if you go home tomorrow, this is the last time I'll see you."

"I don't mind having him along; he's a nice little kid," she said. Dr. Emmett and Nancy were totally busy today; the dead person in the forest, who wasn't Lauren, had turned out to be a girl who had run off from the Smiths' clinic a week earlier. Dead of an overdose, Adam had said, or maybe some bad drugs. It was the kind of story that made Katy want to be out in the sunshine, and she thought Brendan should be, too.

"Well, I'm still sorry." Number twenty.

"Okay." Katy dropped to the blanket and stretched out belly-down; with her chin propped on her crossed arms, she could easily make out Brendan's red tee shirt through a thin screen of long grass. Adam, who could sound and act about five years old sometimes, was playing grown-up games today, talking about one thing when he meant something else entirely. He was apologizing for getting so mad at her the other night, and probably for following her all the way home.

She took a deep breath, hard to do in this position. "I'm the one who should apologize," she said. "It was very stupid of me to let Snake drive me home. It was nice of you to follow us, and actually I'd have to say brave; he's a big guy, and he might have gotten mad."

She turned to look at Adam, whose face had turned bright red. "I didn't know what else to do," he muttered.

"Well, anyway, nothing bad happened, to me or to you," she said, peering steadily into the grass. Just the one thing, not exactly bad: Snake had kissed her. Adam had probably seen that; she thought Snake had meant for him to see. Maybe wouldn't even have done it otherwise. She squinted and remembered the big wet mouth suddenly covering about half her face, the huge tongue ... Disgusting, and really strange.

"I can't tell my mom because she'd totally freak, and she's got trouble enough already," Katy said. "But I was stupid. I wound up scaring myself, and I won't do anything like that again. Not for a long time."

"Why did you?" Adam's question was serious.

Lots of reasons. Because she wasn't supposed to. Because it was dangerous. Because Snake made her feel strange, in a way she didn't understand but found interesting. She slid another glance at Adam and decided he was not the person to talk to about this. Her mother was, if they could ever get back home and back to the way they usually were.

"Don't you ever feel you just absolutely have to take a risk?" she asked.

"Nope, not really. I guess I'm just a seriously boring person. A dweeb."

Brendan's voice broke in before she could reply. "Katy! Come here right now, I see something!"

Katy got to her feet and went to look. "Where? I don't see anything. Oh, wait, now I do."

"I found a fish," said Brendan proudly. "What kind is it?"

"Beats me," said Katy. "Look, a whole bunch, little tiny guys. Whatever they are, they're just babies. Oops," she added, and grabbed the back of Brendan's jeans just as he began to slide down the bank. "Watch out, little kid. You don't swim that well yet."

He scrooched back, rubbed his eyes, and yawned. "I don't want to swim. I need to lie down. Did we bring Snoopy?"

"He's in the car. Come on."

"Doesn't look like we'll get another hike, at least not for a while," she said to Adam as Brendan wrapped both arms around his big stuffed toy and lay down on the blanket.

"We might as well have stayed at home by the pool," he said sourly. They had driven along the little highway that crossed the Warners, passed the crest, and soon after that turned off at a spot where a historical marker was paired with a picnic-table symbol. Four and a half miles down the gravel road, according to the sign, there was a historic cabin and a pioneer graveyard. The road itself wound through tall pines and offered, at irregular intervals, cleared, secluded spots with tables and sometimes a stove on a post.

Now Katy glanced around and shook her head. "No, this is a nice place. Nice tall trees, nice cool shade, and I love the sound of the creek."

"Katy, tell me stories," said Brendan in a froggy voice. "Tell me about your dog."

"His name is Grendel. He's big, even bigger than Erik, and he has this long, grayish white hair like dreadlocks. He loves me. Once when I was little, I got lost and he helped find me."

"Erik loves me, too. I think," said Brendan. "Now tell me again about your other little boy, about how he bites."

"Some bedtime story," she said. "Okay, his name is Johnny, and he's almost two years old, and when he gets mad at somebody . . ."

"I *need* a Coke," she said to Adam a few minutes later, and he fished one from the ice chest and tossed it to her.

"So, are you going home tomorrow?" he asked.

She sat down with her back against a tree and opened the Coke carefully. "I think so. My mom thinks they're going to arrest Sam, and she's getting really nervous. She wants us to go home and take the kids with us."

"Sam Cavalier is a superb photographer," said Adam in a stiffish voice, "and an invaluable advocate for wolves. Your mother can't really think he's a murderer?"

"She doesn't know. I don't know." Katy hugged herself against a shiver. "But somebody is."

"Never mind," said Adam quickly. "Katy, I have a secret. A good one," he added quickly. "Promise not to tell anyone?"

"Maybe. What is it?"

"I think I heard a wolf howl. Yesterday."

"Where? Around *here*?"

"South of here, in the Wilderness."

"But you aren't sure?"

"Well, no. I just heard it for a minute, and it startled me. It could have been a coyote."

"But how would a wolf have gotten here?"

"I don't know. But the great thing is, if wolves come back on their own, they're really safe. There won't have to be negotiations or agreements, or a management plan. They'd be simply an endangered species, fully protected."

The rumble of a big engine drowned out the creek, and they both looked toward the road. After a moment a white pickup truck jounced by, throwing up a cloud of dust. The driver, intent on the road, didn't look their way, but Katy thought she recognized the shape of his head, and she was pretty sure it was Snake's truck.

"What does that guy do, follow you everywhere you go?" Adam's voice was harsh, his cheeks an angry red.

"Hey, it's not my fault if he does!" she snapped. Snake, if that's who it was, had driven on. "Anyway, I don't see how he could have. We'd have seen him."

"Right. Sorry, but I don't like the guy, not one bit."

"Maybe he's just going down to the pioneer graveyard."

"Maybe." Adam didn't sound any more convinced than Katy felt. He popped open a Diet Coke and drank deeply. The two of them were standing there staring silently at the road when another engine sounded, this one higher in pitch. Moments later a small red car whisked by, bouncing along the ruts at a speed too high for safety or comfort. Katy saw blowing yellow hair, a sharp profile, a thin tanned arm. Beside her, Adam muttered something under his breath and ran forward to look after the red car.

"Adam? What's the matter?"

"Um, I don't know. But I think I'd better go call Emmett." He glanced around their clearing, at scattered belongings and the debris left from the picnic. "We passed a phone on the way in, about three clearings back. I'll run down there and make the call. Why don't you start pulling things together, get Brendan ready to go. We'll take off as soon as I get back."

"Why?" she asked, but he was already on his way and simply waved over his shoulder.

"Shit." She packed away the food and put the garbage in a plastic bag, stowed the chest and their books and odds and ends in the Porsche's trunk. "Brendan? Come on, it's time to go. You can sleep in the car."

He came half-awake and let her lead him to the open-topped car, lift him into the back, and fasten his harness. She tucked Snoopy in beside him, then looked around to see what she'd missed. The little clearing had lost its cozy, friendly feeling and seemed alien and lonely. The Porsche's key was on the console, where Adam had left it after moving the little car into the shade. Maybe she could . . . "Come on, Adam," she muttered.

"Where'd your boyfriend go?"

The startled squeak that she made embarrassed her. "He's *not* . . . He went to make a phone call." Snake was standing at the edge of the clearing, beside the road, but she didn't see his truck. He looked funny—twitchy or something, maybe scared? Or sad, she decided, remembering. "I'm really sorry about your friend," she told him.

"Huh? Oh, yeah, poor old Marv. Is your boyfriend's name Smith?" he asked, coming closer.

"No, it's—"

"*My* name is Smith," came a sleepy voice from the Porsche. "Brendan Kingsley Smith."

"Is that so?" said Snake, peering into the back of the Porsche and then into the front. "Now that's real interesting. Get in the car," he said to Katy.

She shook her head. "We're waiting for Adam. He'll be back in a minute."

"Will he." Snake came around the car and yanked the passenger door open. "In." When she didn't move, he took her by the shoulders and put her bodily into the seat and then closed the door. "And fasten your belt."

She scrambled up out of the seat instead, ready to climb over the low door. "Who do you think you're—"

He took hold of her face in one hand, thumb and fingers sinking into the joints of her jaw as if to crunch the bones there. She couldn't say anything, and she couldn't keep tears from welling in her eyes and rolling down her face.

"You just be quiet now," he said softly. "Unless you want to scare the kid. Put your seat belt on." He squeezed harder, gave her head a shake and released her. By the time she had blinked her eyes clear and reached for the belt, he was in the driver's seat and had started the engine.

"Katy?" Brendan said. "Where are we going?"

"Just . . . for a ride. Hold on to Snoopy so he doesn't blow out."

"Good girl," said Snake, and released the wheel long enough to grip her knee and squeeze it. "Just keep that up."

He didn't worry about scraping or hanging up on the rutted gravel road, just took the car into higher gear and roared ahead. Katy clung to the door through bumps and curves, counted one picnic site and then a second, watched ahead and saw the telephone coming up, just a box on a pole. Saw Adam's blue shirt, and then his startled face looking at them.

Snake braked, geared down, hit the horn, and then yelled something wordless to Adam. Waved his right hand high, middle finger extended. Shifted gears again and took the next curve in a slide that nearly sent them off the road. Katy, looking back, saw Adam as a silhouette in the dust.

The highway was just ahead. He slowed, and she thought: open the door and roll out, maybe you won't get hurt too much. But she saw no other person or car anywhere around; he'd only stop and catch her and punish her with those strong hands.

He slowed barely enough to turn onto the paved road, heading west toward Alturas and Stony Creek. Then he picked up speed again and leaned forward over the steering wheel. She could see his lips moving but caught only an occasional word as the wind of their passage roared in her ears: ". . . damned little prick . . . mess me up I'll show him and his . . ."

The hot wind had dried her face and was making her eyes gritty. "Where are you going?" she asked and then again, louder, "Where are you taking us?"

"Shut up." He hit her without looking at her, a casual back-handed blow across the face that made her head ring. She felt the trickle of blood, found the split in her lip with her tongue, dug in the pocket of her shorts for a tissue.

He was swearing now, softly and steadily. Driving very fast, so any action she could think of to interfere with him, like hitting the brake or snatching the wheel, would probably kill all three of them.

Where was he taking her, and why was he mad at Adam? Why so mad at her? She sneaked a sideways look at him and decided he was maybe not crazy but beyond thinking.

She took a deep breath, and another. Scared, she was really scared but not . . . terrified. *She* could think. Keep breathing right, be ready to move. Clench and unclench hands, relax shoulders, flex feet and calf muscles. Be ready.

The road rose and fell and rose again, and he topped a rise and sailed free for a moment, landing with a jolt and a louder curse. Slowed down just a little. They had long since crossed the summit and left the tall trees behind, moving now through a hot, rolling landscape of scattered cedar trees, Adam had said they were. A car passed in the other direction, going nearly as fast as they were, she thought; no time to signal, and besides, if he hit her again she might be too hurt to move, or to think.

They were nearly out of the mountains now, coming into a hazy valley. She couldn't see the town yet but knew it wasn't far. Would he roar on through? Or slow to avoid notice? How would he keep her quiet?

He hit the brakes, geared down once and then again, turned off onto a dirt road that seemed to lead nowhere. Drove for maybe two minutes, pulled to the edge, and stopped. Yanked on the parking brake and swung his heavy head to look at her.

"You. You're big enough to be trouble, not old enough to be any fun. This is where you get out."

First was a great flush of heat like embarrassment or even anger: He didn't want her. Next came a cool breeze of relief: He was setting her free, she could run away and be safe. Then her mind went into a whirl of thought and it all came together like a jigsaw puzzle: rich Nancy Smith's little kid, the only one she had or would ever have. In the hands of this strong, angry man who didn't even bother to look at you when he hit you.

Katy stayed where she was. "I want Brendan."

"You want shit. I said get out of the fuckin' car!" He reached across to shove her out, but her seat belt was still fastened and the gear console was in the way.

"Goddamn it, get your ass out of there!" He threw his own door open and came around the car at a trot to open her door and take her by the shoulders. "Goddamn belt," he snarled, and punched at it until it came open.

"Out, you stupid little bitch!" Hands under her arms, he lifted her as easily as she had lifted Brendan, pulled her from the car and tossed her aside. Katy rolled and came to her feet spitting dirt and blood and ran around the car. "I want Brendan!"

He brushed her back with another full-armed swing, then

looked at the car and yelled, "Hey, you little shit! You stay where you are!"

Brendan had unfastened his harness and stood up now with Snoopy clutched to his chest. "Katy! I don't like this man!"

With a wordless growl Snake reached for Brendan, taking hold of the little boy's shoulder with one hand and bending to grab the harness with the other. As the big curly head moved past him, Brendan shot his own head forward and buried his teeth in the lobe of Snake's ear.

"Shit goddamn it!" Snake reeled back, clapping a hand to his ear and then staring in white-faced amazement at the bright blood that filled his palm.

In a flash Katy was in the car, its engine still running, and she released the hand brake as she felt around with her feet, finding oops, *there* the clutch, in, now the shift lever which way *that* way. The little car jerked as her other foot found the gas, jerked and coughed she hadn't got the right the lowest gear but then it coughed again and lurched forward *good* little car!

"Hey!"

She knew the clutch now but reverse was . . . too hard never mind, she stayed in second and swung the car as tightly as she could in a turn *there* just missed the ditch and Snake was coming at her from the front and she stepped on the gas.

"Hey!" He jumped not quite fast enough, the right fender or maybe the open door slapping him aside as she pulled out of the curve just barely before the other ditch, *gas* and they surged forward, the door swinging back at her and she caught it. She risked a look over her shoulder, Brendan there and okay and Snake climbing out of the ditch.

In the mirror Snake running and waving his arms getting smaller, and she was straight on the road, pretend she was doing this with Adam sitting beside her, patient Adam ready to help her if she went wrong. Highway now, she slowed and felt the car jerk and nudged the clutch pedal just a little bit and swung *hard*. And came back from the far left side of the road, to her own lane. She drew a long, deep breath and took her eyes off the nice, straight road to look at the diagram on the shift knob, and then she pushed the clutch all the way and got into third gear. Maybe they really would get away.

"Katy?"

"Oh, Brendan!" She braked and nearly killed the engine, recovered and turned her head just enough to look at him. He was dangling forward between the two front seats, grinning.

"Brendan, you're a good boy. A hero. Please put your harness back on."

"Okay. Katy, we forgot to get Adam."

Oh, shit. She flushed hot all over and looked ahead through a blur of tears. She'd completely forgotten Adam, and what if Snake . . . ? No. Snake was miles away from the picnic spot, where his truck must still be, and Adam had the telephone.

"Adam will come later, Brendan."

"So where are we going now?"

"Home! No, I think Alturas." She looked ahead to see the town looming out of the haze, looked at the gearshift and worried. She'd have to be stopping for signs and stuff pretty soon.

She coasted through a stop sign where nobody was coming or watching, saw a big intersection ahead and figured she had to turn left here; she touched the clutch and got through the intersection just as the light turned from yellow to red, hearing a squeal of brakes and a blare of horns.

This would be Main Street, and there was traffic on both sides of her, going both ways. What she needed to do was get over to the edge and stop. As she was looking in her mirror and then over her shoulder to see whether she could do that, a siren shrieked right behind her. She stamped on the brake, the engine died, she put her clutch foot down all the way and let the little car coast to the curb. Then she simply leaned forward and rested her forehead on the steering wheel.

"Hey!" It was a town cop, a big guy she'd never seen

before. He had his hand on the car door, his head bent as he tried to see Katy's face.

"Jesus, kid! You almost caused at least three accidents back there. Who the hell taught you to drive?"

"Nobody!" wailed Katy, and she burst into tears.

· 28 ·

Meg squeezed her daughter's shoulders, dropped a kiss on the damp hair at her temple, released her, and stood up. The young deputy sheriff behind the counter looked up as she approached, and quickly took two steps back.

"Mrs. Halloran—"

Meg didn't remember his name and was too angry to read his badge. "That's who I am. I have done my civic duty, and I have made a statement. My daughter did more than her civic duty and also made a statement. Now I want you to know that in a matter of seconds, two women with strong lungs and loud voices are going to start raising holy hell around here. We want to go home!"

"Uh, yes ma'am. Let me get Sheriff Vukovich for you."

Less than five minutes later they stepped out into late-afternoon sun that hit them like a hammer. Fingers entwined with Katy's in a grip she was reluctant to break, Meg dug with her free hand into her bag for her keys, found them and looked around the parking lot for the Honda, and then groaned as she saw the red Jeep.

"I certainly hope Frances didn't need to go somewhere. I forgot to leave her my keys." She dropped them in her pocket, fished around again in her bag, and came up with Frances's key ring. "Come on, sweetie, let's try to get home before we fall apart or fall asleep."

Katy's immediate response was a yawn so huge it immobilized her for a moment. Then she climbed into the Jeep, buckled the seat belt, and tried to contain another yawn as Meg started the engine and began to maneuver their way out of the parking lot.

"Mom?" she said, and paused to wipe her eyes with the

278

backs of her hands. "It really wasn't Adam's fault, what happened to Brendan and me."

"I know." At their picnic site in the Warners, Adam had recognized the young woman in the red car as one of Emmett Smith's addict patients, had decided she must be following Wilhite, and had assumed—correctly, as it turned out—that Wilhite was the new local drug source. In rushing off to report this to Emmett, he had in his own view personally abandoned Katy and young Brendan to terrible danger.

All this Meg had learned, with some difficulty, when Adam brought his sister to the sheriff's office to claim Brendan; the boy had been so full of guilt and apologies as to be nearly incoherent. "He feels terrible, Katy. You'll have to tell him again tomorrow that nobody blames him."

"Right." Katy let her head fall back and her eyes close. "I think maybe I'll marry Adam and be president," she said. Meg shot a startled glance at her and saw the corner of her mouth quirk, a smile or maybe just the last muscle spasm of a long, hard cry.

"President? Of what, the clinic?"

"Of the United States."

Meg looked at her again, in amusement mixed liberally with respect. Long, dark lashes lay on tear-streaked cheeks that still had a childish roundness, and her mouth was soft and vulnerable. But the jawline was clean and firm, the brow high and straight. Katy had acted today with an awesome combination of raw nerve and swift reflexes; now Meg thought there was, in her relaxed and weary posture, the barest hint of swagger. Go for it, kid.

"That's okay by me," she said aloud, and gave all that remained of her concentration to staying upright, awake, and in control of the vehicle. Oh, good, she thought as she saw the familiar gateposts; she turned in, felt her neck hair prickle, and heard Katy draw a deep breath. Reality check: Not everyone was safe.

"Mom? What's going to happen to Lauren?"

Meg kept her gaze straight ahead as she pulled the Jeep up

beside her Honda. "I think she'll be released soon." From jail, anyway; Meg believed her story, and so, she thought, did Ron Ortmann. Release from the sense of shame and guilt Lauren was carrying around would take some time longer.

"Yeah, okay. But what about—I mean, who killed those guys?"

"Katy, I don't know." Meg turned off the engine and let her shoulders slump. "Lauren thinks it was Sam who shot Chuck. She thought that several hours ago, anyway; but since then . . ." Since then she'd been questioned by the sheriff and presumably had seen Sam. Had had a glimpse of her old, ordinary, daylight world. What did Lauren think, or remember, now?

"I'm really, *really* glad Lauren's back. But Mom, I'm just going to hate it if Sam turns out to be a murderer. I mean, I don't even want to think about it."

"I agree. Let's not, not think about anything at all." Except about the tattooed man, Dwayne Wilhite, presently the object of a manhunt by the sheriff's department and other agencies. As she climbed wearily out of the Jeep, Meg thought about Wilhite for a long moment and pictured herself dismembering the son of a bitch as bloodily and painfully as possible.

"Mom? The door's locked."

The house seemed oddly blank to Meg as she moved across the gravel to the front porch where Katy waited: shades drawn, windows closed tight, no sound or sense of movement. Then, as she fumbled with the door key, she thought she heard someone crying.

"Frances?" she called as they stepped inside. "Sara?"

Not crying, howling in great hoarse bursts of sound: Johnny, and he'd been at it a while. Katy set off up the stairs at a run and nearly tripped over Sara coming down; Sara was crying, too, but softly.

"Sweetie, what's wrong?" Meg scooped the little girl up and followed after Katy.

"I was supposed to stay in the house," she sobbed, and

pushed her wet face into Meg's neck. "And be nice to Johnny. But he's all mad, and he hurts my ears."

Johnny sat scarlet-faced and furious in a crib with its sides up and a covering like a fishing net pulled tight over the top and fastened to all four legs. As Katy untied this, Sara sniffed and said, "That was mine, when I was a baby, because I got out. But he doesn't, he's too fat."

"Sara, where is your Aunt Frances?" Meg put Sara on her feet and crouched to talk to her.

"She went away."

"How did she go? Did somebody come for her?"

"I don't know. I had to stay inside and be good."

"When—" No point to that approach. Johnny had been put to bed shortly after one o'clock, and once asleep, he usually slept for at least two hours. "Sara, was Johnny still asleep when she left?"

Sara put a finger in her mouth and shook her head. "He was just starting to wake up."

So, sometime after three. And it was now four-thirty. Meg got to her feet, saw that Katy was tending to Johnny, and hurried to the stairs.

In Frances's room the French doors were latched, but the bed was rumpled and the closet door ajar. The black handbag still hung there; how strange. No note on the uncluttered desktop, just a notepad and a jar of pencils and the portable phone. Meg turned on the telephone and punched the redial button and got a busy signal.

Something missing from the closet . . . she pulled the door wider and found that Frances's boots were not in their usual place. She bent and pushed clothes aside to look futher; no boots anywhere on the floor in there, but there were two lidded glass jars. Plain, ordinary jars, one of them almost full of what proved to be brandy, the second only a quarter full.

Back through the hall and into the kitchen, where the door was locked as well. Meg went outside, scanned the area, saw Max's impatient head poking over the corral rail. He was there alone, she found; Daisy was missing. Probably a saddle was missing, too; she didn't know how many belonged on the racks in the tack room. She didn't know how many guns in the gun cabinet, either, but it stood open, key in the lock.

Facts tumbled wildly in Meg's mind and began to line up there. One person, presumably Frances, had taken a horse. If she had saddled up and ridden off today, she could have done that before, say on Tuesday night when Marv Jakel was shot and killed. The brandy in the closet was probably not a reserve supply but the liquor she had been assumed to be drinking herself insensible with every night.

"Mom?" Katy, with the baby on her hip and Sara at her side, stood on the back porch.

And Frances or someone had opened the gun closet. Where would Frances be going with a gun?

"Mom, what's happening?"

"Katy, stay there," Meg called, and moved forward at a trot. "Go inside and call the Jakel number, it's in the phone book. Tell whoever answers not to let anyone in the house. Then call Earl Douglas and tell him I think Frances Macrae may be headed there and is probably armed. Tell him I said to come, quietly."

"To the Jakels' house?"

"Right." Keys in her pocket, Honda keys.

"Mom, what are you going to do?"

Good question. Try to stop something? Or at least find something out. Meg slowed her pace, turned, and walked backward for several steps. "Katy, I'll be careful. You do as I told you. Right now."

Probably no need for panic, she thought as she peered through her dusty windshield. Those women wouldn't let Frances Macrae get within a hundred yards of them.

But maybe Marv had. And it wasn't just the women who might somehow be fooled and then hurt; there was also that skinny, sad boy. If the incredible proved true, if Frances Macrae had undertaken a systematic campaign to wipe out the . . . the *clan* she'd hated so long, would she count that child as one of them? Probably, Meg thought, and swallowed bile as she slowed to turn into the Jakel driveway.

She changed her mind and drove past instead, pulling to the edge of the road. Better to leave the car here and approach quietly on foot.

Unlike the Macrae house, the Jakel place stood squarely at the end of a straight driveway. To avoid being seen from the house, she'd have to stay off to one side, behind the screen of bushes and tall weeds.

She moved carefully, trying to make no more noise in the underbrush than a small, ordinary animal might produce in passing. As she got closer, she saw that the old truck still sat in the packed-dirt yard, with no other vehicle in sight. No horse, either; how long would it have taken Frances to get here, across the fairly rough landscape and through the fence? On pokey but sturdy Daisy?

The house was set in a grove of tall, dusty trees and untrimmed shrubbery. Meg stopped some fifty feet away to look, and to listen hard. The scene before her was still except for the movement of those trees under the push of a sporadic breeze, silent except for the rustle of leaves and the creak of branches.

She moved slowly forward while staying in the brush that was turning into another line of trees, perhaps meant as a break against a north wind. In Levi's and a blue chambray shirt, she would not be particularly eye-catching. Scanning like a searchlight, she stopped for a moment as she thought she heard or maybe saw something in the jumble of small outbuildings and sheds behind the house.

She watched, caught movement behind a wire fence, and exhaled as she realized it was a small animal, or several. Rabbits, chickens, something. Closer to the house now, she was tempted to call out but bit her lip against the impulse. With luck she could get close enough to look in a window.

The sound that nearly stopped her heart was a whicker from the mare whose dun-colored coat was almost the same hue as the dusty shrubbery in which she stood. Frances Macrae stood close against Daisy's left side.

"Margaret, what are you doing here?" Frances asked in a low voice. The older woman's head was steady, her eyes clear. She looked to Meg not crazy but inhumanly intent. Not younger, simply like an old woman who had managed for the moment to put age aside and hone herself for her purpose.

"I . . . was worried about you. I forgot to leave you my car keys, and Sara said you'd gone off on a horse, and—"

"Be quiet." Still low, the words had a snap. "And if you were worried about me, why were you creeping up like a burglar?" She stepped away from the horse, and as she moved she pulled a long gun from a scabbard beneath the stirrup leather.

The gun was a shotgun with twin dark barrels and a plain, wooden stock: businesslike. Facing Frances from a distance of some five feet, her arms loose at her sides and her hands carefully in view, Meg wondered why she was not completely terrified and decided it was because Frances seemed to be regarding her as an irrelevancy. Nothing to bother about unless she attempted serious interference. If she was right in this judgment, she'd use the fact later to soothe Vince; if she was wrong, she'd no doubt discover her error painfully and too late.

"Ruth and Verna are expecting me," said Frances. "I was waiting for the boy; he went out to the sheds just after I got here. But probably we shouldn't waste time." She tucked the shotgun under her right elbow, muzzle pointing at the ground, and touched her left hand lightly to the sagging pocket of her jacket. Extra shells, probably, in case those in the gun weren't sufficient for the job. Meg suddenly remembered Earl Douglas's description of Marv Jakel's end, and she clenched her teeth for fear they might chatter. Be quick, Douglas. I don't think there's much I can do here except cause a little delay. Very little, probably.

"Now. I want you to walk about two feet ahead of me, to

the porch and up the steps, and then rap on the door. I hope you won't try to warn anyone."

"No. I won't," Meg assured her, and turned at the gesture of Frances's head to start slowly for the house. "Frances," she began, and closed her mouth as something hard nudged her leg.

Over the packed dirt, up the steps, across the sagging wooden porch floor, Meg in front and Frances behind her left shoulder. The inner door was open, and through the screen came a canned-sounding conversation, probably the television. Meg rapped on the metal frame of the screen door, and Frances said, "Ruth? Verna? It's Frances Macrae."

The figure approaching from the dimness of the room had a halo of almost-white hair: Ruthie. She unlatched the door and pushed it toward them, then backed away. Meg stepped inside and stumbled forward as Frances gave her a solid shove. Ruthie made a sharp noise, something between a squeal and a shriek. Meg, catching her balance, heard the front door slam shut and then heard the click of an engaging lock. Terrific; one access point blocked to any surprise entry by Douglas.

"Go sit with your mother!" snapped Frances to Ruthie, who stood open-mouthed in the middle of the room. Verna, also open-mouthed, lay on the couch as she had on Meg's earlier visit, pillows behind her and the single floor lamp drawing sparks from her red hair and casting channels of shadow along her lined and sagging face. The rest of the room dwindled into shadowy edges and lumps of furniture, but Meg's quick scan found no person in those shadows.

"Hey, fuck off!" Ruthie stood where she was, then began to edge to her left, away from her mother's couch. "You can't—"

"Ruth Ann Jakel! You get over here!" Verna's voice was shrill with terror. "Come here to me right now!"

Frances tipped the gun up and swung its long barrels toward Ruthie, who froze. Meg froze, too, and bit back a yelp. A blast aimed at Ruthie might not kill her, Meg, but it would certainly do her grievous damage. "Frances, please be careful," she said, in a voice that sounded strange to her own ears.

"You invited yourself along on this trip," said Frances in even tones; she held the gun steady, braced against her hip. "Move," she ordered Ruthie, who hesitated only a moment and then obeyed. "Just sit on the couch, by Verna's feet," added Frances. "That's nice. And you," she said, turning her head only slightly in Meg's direction, "close the sliding door, the one to the dining room."

Meg pulled the heavy door shut and stayed right there, at the far end of the room from Verna's couch and, she thought, out of the line of fire.

"And the back door," said Frances, and then paused. "No. I can't see that from here. Just close the hall door, and pull one of those big chairs across it."

This door was at the the juncture where the far wall met the back wall. "And you can sit down there," Frances said when Meg had done as she was told. "And keep your feet flat on the floor and your hands in your lap."

"You told us you were willing to take care of us, to finally make things right," said Ruthie. "You told us—" She stopped on a sharp indrawn breath as the import of her own words struck her.

"Oh my, yes," Frances said, and nodded. "It's time. Things have to be finished, debts collected. Somebody has to pay for Robert John Macrae's life, and for my ten years of pain."

"Please, Frances. Please, I got just a little time left, don't take it from me. I'm begging you, please." Verna, tears running down her face, reached with a shaking hand for the tall beer can on the table beside her and spilled a stream of foaming liquid on her blouse before getting the can to her mouth.

"I never hurt Bobby! Nobody did, he's not even *dead*, you dried-up old bitch!" Ruthie moved as if to rise, then subsided as Frances lifted the gun. "He's out there calling up and leaving messages. And killing people!"

Meg was startled by this, from Ruthie who had earlier declared her belief that Bobby was dead. But Frances just gave a spine-shivering little chuckle.

"You had some ghost messages too? Ridiculous," Frances told her. "Ghosts fill your head and freeze your heart, but they don't use telephones. No, there was only one real message, from Bobby through me. It was meant for you, but your brother got it. Or maybe you did hear it?"

"Next day," whispered Ruthie. "He didn't erase it."

"Frances, please be quiet," said Meg. "If you don't say anything more, if you put the gun down and walk out of here, you can eventually go home to Lauren, and Johnny." And you'll go to hell for such lies, she told herself.

"Are you crazy?" Ruthie wailed. "She shot two people! If he didn't, she did!"

"And two to go," said Frances. "I thought three, but maybe two will make the balance. Bring an end to the pain."

The half of Meg that was there in the room watched Frances and knew her pain was real, whatever the reality of its cause. Saw the flutter of the curtain at the screened front window and was grateful for the movement of air in this stale room. Knew that she was almost surely going to be a witness to murder but not necessarily then a victim: Frances didn't seem personally interested in Meg or in her own future, either. Shifted her position slightly, silently, to her own left, more directly behind Frances's back and out of her peripheral vision.

And the other half, thoughts and senses tuned to the outside, wondered when Douglas would come. Thought he'd read the scene and be cautious: her car just off the road, the tethered horse and the hunter's saddle. Believed he, like Vince, would know the possible consequences of a misstep. Offered in the back of her mind earnest apology to Vince, whom she loved, with promises not to be so foolhardy again. Listened listened listened.

Meg-in-the-room now slid a little further to the left, pulled her feet closer to the chair, and calculated the distance to

Frances Macrae's braced figure in relation to her own position, her own long body and long arms. Have to be one leap or she'd be killed, and bring her near enough to wrap her arms around and down, or the others would die at once. Did Frances believe that the Jakels as a family had conspired to kill Bobby?

"Frances, I didn't hurt that boy of yours. I loved him like one of my own," insisted Verna, wiping her eyes with her bare fingers. As Ruthie once again moved to get up, Verna reached out and grabbed her arm, pulling her back down. "You stay here! Don't you leave me!"

Ruthie slapped at her mother's hand, but Verna shifted her grip to her daughter's loose shirt and hung on. "And Frances, we didn't kill him—if he's dead. I swear as God is my witness I didn't, Ruth Ann here didn't. Chuck didn't, I know that. And I don't believe Marv did, either. We didn't none of us kill anybody. You gonna sit there and let her shoot us in cold blood?" she shrieked suddenly at Meg.

Meg froze as Frances slid a not-very-interested look in her direction and appeared to see nothing amiss. Frances turned back; Meg eyed the distances again and thought she would have so small a chance that her body might well disobey a command to leap.

"The Jakels destroyed Robert Macrae. You taught him to defy authority and morality, to despise his own family. You kept at him until he was just human trash like the lot of you." Frances widened her stance slightly, lifted the heavy weapon, and brought her left hand across her body to support the barrels.

"No. We didn't. Chuck didn't," Verna added.

"*He* was beginning the whole pattern all over again with poor Lauren."

"Bullshit," muttered Ruthie, quickly adding, "Sorry!" as the gun's line shifted slightly in her direction. Watching the players before her, Meg listened and thought she heard a sound outside. Not on the porch. Maybe simply tree limbs rubbing in the quickening wind that again fluttered the curtain at the front window and another on the far side of the room.

"You turned him into a monster, a boy who would kill his own parents. A young man who would assault and impregnate his own sister. Who would threaten and beat an old woman."

Some part of Meg's mind separate from heat or smells or fear did a quick assembly of what she knew or had learned and came up with a silent Wait! He didn't kill his parents, Douglas said that. He didn't rape Lauren. He probably didn't burn down the math teacher's house—Katy had come home with that story—any more than he had shot Lauren's dog. "He lied." She hadn't meant to say that aloud.

"Shut up." Frances didn't turn to look at Meg, but her voice had a quaver.

Which was more dangerous, to speak or to remain silent? "Frances, Bobby was simply a dreadful, fearsome liar. He made *himself* into a monster to terrify people."

Frances took several steps backward toward the door, so that she could see Meg as well as the two women on the couch. "That's not true."

Meg thought the gun was swinging in her direction and was fairly sure Ruthie wouldn't leap to *her* defense. "Frances, wait. Let me—"

The sound definitely came from the side of the house; Meg heard it again and saw the window screen there bulge at the bottom as something pushed against it.

No! She clamped both hands over her own mouth to keep the warning from escaping.

Frances caught the direction of Meg's glance or perhaps heard the rotten screen rip, looked up as a gun barrel broke through, shifted her feet and moved with old-woman's slowness to her left. Her body jerked, and she clutched her right shoulder with fingers already staining red as the rifle blast and women's screams clashed and reverberated in raucous din.

Frances stumbled back, tilted, and crumpled, letting the

shotgun slide from her grip. Half aware of loud male voices outside, Meg made her belated leap, hit the floor rolling, and got there just before Ruthie Jakel. "Get away!" she yelled as she scrabbled backward herself on knees and elbows; then she came upright on her knees and shifted her grip on the heavy gun, ready to aim. "Get back and leave her alone!"

Ruthie backed off, turned jerkily as pounding began on the front door. She unlocked it and pulled it open to admit Earl Douglas, a young man who appeared to be a paramedic, and her own son.

Douglas stopped in midstride to survey the scene as the other man dropped to his knees beside Frances. Ruthie Jakel grabbed Bobby, spun him around, and propelled him from the room. Douglas, eyebrows high, said, "You through with that?" to Meg and reached out for the shotgun, which she yielded.

On her couch, Verna Jakel sat upright, smoothed her beer-stained blouse, and fluffed her hair. "Ha!" she said. "Looks like I'm gonna outlive that old bitch after all."

· 29 ·

Frances, her face gray, was unconscious or nearly so, groaning as the paramedic examined her but not opening her eyes. "Bullet still in there," he said, as if to himself. "Can't tell yet how much damage, but her signs are good." He taped a thick pad of gauze below her right collarbone; then he pulled the bloody shirt gently, decently back into place. He and Douglas lifted her carefully onto a stretcher and carried her to the small ambulance.

Meg followed closely and watched them load and secure the burdened stretcher. "I'm going to ride with her," she said when they'd finished.

Douglas glanced at the other man, who said, "Sure, good idea. I had to come out alone on this one. Sandy Griffith," he said by way of introduction, gesturing at the name badge on his shirt pocket.

"Margaret Halloran," she told him. Sandy helped her into the back of the ambulance, secured the doors, and trotted around to the front; Meg crouched on a jump seat beside the stretcher and took Frances's hand. Griffith was as careful as he could be in guiding the vehicle down the rutted drive, but Frances groaned at every bump or lurch.

"Oh, it hurts. It's so hard," whispered Frances, and Meg bent closer to speak to her.

"We haven't far to go, Frances. You'll feel better once they get the bullet out." Dumb remark—talking just for noise, and she didn't even know that it was true. The bullet was a .22, fired by Bobby Jakel just before Douglas got to him.

"It's so hard. You wouldn't think a skinny boy would be that heavy."

Meg kept her hold on Frances's hand, wondering if she'd seen the boy through the window.

"So ugly, and messy. So heavy to lift onto such a tall horse. I didn't think I could do it. And then trying to get to the meadow in the rain. And find a deep enough cave. I didn't think I could do it."

"Shh, Frances." Meg wiped sweat from the old woman's face with a handful of gauze.

"There's that silly thing people say to children. This will hurt me more than it does you."

"Right. They do say that, and it is silly."

"But it's true. I think it hurt me more. And longer. But he'd been hitting me. So embarrassing, walk around with bruises, people to see." Frances's words were coming in shorter bursts now, as if she were terribly tired.

"Shh," said Meg again. "Try to rest."

The old woman frowned and fluttered her free hand in a quelling gesture that had a hint of her old imperiousness. "Bobby was in the barn that morning. Said . . . come along, ride together, old times. So sweet." Her eyes filled, and she blinked hard. "But not. Hit again. Told . . . terrible things. You said were lies," she finished in an accusing whisper.

"I'm sorry." Meg leaned forward and lifted the edge of the bloodstained shirt to see whether the bleeding might have increased, but the gauze pad didn't look saturated. She wiped her own sweaty forehead on the sleeve of her shirt and looked out the window to find that they were on the outskirts of Alturas. "Almost there, Frances."

"He got the shotgun. From my truck. Said he'd kill. I believed." Frances tightened her grip on Meg's hand and closed her eyes. "He'll be in hell. And so will I."

Douglas had reached the hospital ahead of them and was waiting with an attendant and a gurney. Leaning against his solidness and glad for the weight of his arm across her shoulders, Meg watched the other men wheel Frances away.

As the hospital doors swished shut, Douglas gave her shoulders a squeeze and then released her. "You want to go have a cup of coffee and tell me all about this?"

"Oh—I have to call Katy."

He grinned. "I did that, first thing. Told her you looked fine to me—no blood, no broken bones, on your knees with a shotgun in your hands when I got there."

"I need to see her, Douglas."

"Meg, she's fine. She's got the kids in hand, she's gonna call Vince just in case he might pick up something about all this without knowing the outcome. I'm a deputy at the moment, sworn by telephone, which probably ain't quite legal but means you can give me your statement and then I'll take you home."

"Since this is all quasi-legal anyway, could we do the statement thing in a nice, quiet bar? Like the hotel bar, which as I recall is very close?"

"Worst thing, I could get fired again. Give me your keys, I'll arrange to have somebody collect your little car and take it to the ranch. You wait right here in the truck."

The hotel bar was dark, and cool, and normal, with a television droning from a high perch and the lady bartender chatting cheerfully with the beginnings of her evening crowd. Meg found she didn't want a beer after all, probably just make her fall on her face. A Coke would be fine, she told Douglas.

By the time he had brought her Coke, his beer, and a bag of salt-and-vinegar potato chips to their table in the corner, she had worked out pretty much what she would tell him.

But he had something to say to her first. "I got to apologize for being shit-slow today," he said, looking at the tabletop where he was making a pattern of interlocking circles with the wet bottom of his beer bottle.

"You were in time."

He shook his head. "We knew you were both in there, saw

your car and the mare. Figured the Jakels were there, too. Had to assume Miss Macrae had a shotgun. So we didn't dare yell or announce ourselves. Telephone line had been cut, so we couldn't create a distraction with that.

"So me and Sandy, who isn't even a cop, we're creeping up real careful trying to decide how to handle things, and it wasn't until we got close that we saw the kid. He'd pulled a wooden crate over to the window and was standing there with that big old .22 propped on the sill. Before we could get near enough to grab him or talk to him quietly, he just pushed the barrel through the screen and let fly.

"Scared the shit out of me," he added softly.

"I let it happen," Meg told him. "I saw the gun. But if I'd yelled, she'd have killed somebody—me, the boy, or Ruthie and her mother. I'd been trying to work out how to stop her and was fairly sure I couldn't, not and survive myself. So for everybody but Frances, and maybe even for her, what happened was the best we could hope for."

"Probably you're right. But just letting things happen sorta grates on me. On you too, I believe."

"True. Maybe we both had a useful lesson today."

"Maybe," he said doubtfully. "So, your turn. I'll settle for just the facts, ma'am," he said as he leaned back in his chair. Meg looked up quickly and reminded herself that this good ol' boy was very sharp indeed, and she was more transparent than she liked to believe.

"Yes," she said, and told him what she and Katy had found at the ranch when they returned there after leaving the sheriff's office. "Clearly she'd fooled me," said Meg. "She was strong enough to ride, she wasn't drinking heavily. And the timing was ideal; she could finish off her enemies without further implicating either Sam or Lauren, both of whom were safely in custody."

"And she could have killed Chuck and Marv," he said in a tone that was only half questioning.

"Chuck she virtually admitted to, today. Lauren was sure it was Sam who came after her and shot Chuck, because she looked out and saw his gray Jeep. And she was feeling guilty about being there, and Sam's action would have made a nasty sort of sense to her.

"But in nothing but a little moonlight," she went on after a swallow of Coke, "Frances's red Jeep would have been colorless. And Katy and I, sleeping soundly, wouldn't have heard Frances leave or return in her Jeep so long as she didn't spin her wheels in the gravel or something. As for Marv . . ."

She told him Sara's tale of her Aunt Frances's going out to ride in the night, told him how its facts had mingled with obvious fancy in such a way that she hadn't paid enough attention. "Maybe that's why I felt such a need to go after her today."

"Or maybe you and your daughter both have more nerve than is real healthy for you."

"I certainly expect that to be Vince's view," she said.

"So, Frances tell you why she turned to murder in her old age? Just general dislike of trashy neighbors? Shit, I'm sorry," he added quickly. "It is definitely not funny, but it is real strange."

"She believes the Jakels, Verna and Marv and Ruthie, completely corrupted Bobby, morally and sexually and every other way. She really does believe that, Douglas."

"And Chuck?"

"She said he was starting the whole pattern again, corrupting 'poor Lauren.' "

"Jesus. Not a big believer in free will, is she?"

She couldn't afford to be, Meg thought, and said merely, "Apparently not."

"Did she believe one of the Jakels, or two or three or all of them together, killed Bobby Macrae?"

"She didn't say that. 'Destroyed' was the word she actually used."

Douglas sat up straighter and looked at her. She returned his look squarely, and after a moment he looked away and picked up his beer. "Well, if she survives the gunshot wound, and chances for that are pretty good, Vuke will talk to her."

"Right," Meg said. "Earl, would you please call the sheriff for me and find out what's happening with Lauren?"

He agreed to do that, left, and was back fairly quickly. "Lauren Cavalier is being released. She's having a shower there at the jail; soon as she finishes, they're going to take her over to the hospital to be with her aunt."

"Is Frances . . . alive?" That was the only word Meg could manage. "Doing well," "better," or "surviving" all seemed inappropriate.

"Yes ma'am. They got the bullet out; it did some damage but nothing that won't—or wouldn't—mend. But it turns out the lady has some other serious problems, had a coronary bypass some time back and is in fairly bad shape. It's not real clear she'll be around for long."

"Ah. That doesn't surprise me. Earl, here's what I'd like to do. I'd like to go by the hospital and leave a note for Lauren. Then I'd like to go home to my daughter."

"Sounds good to me. Do you care about Cavalier?"

"Cav . . . ? Oh, Sam. Not much."

"I figured. Anyway, they're holding on to him until they have a confession from Frances Macrae, and I think Vuke would like to charge him with obstructing justice, or creating a nuisance, or something. They may manage to keep him locked up until tomorrow."

"Lovely," said Meg, and meant it.

"And you know what the little shit did then?" Katy said to Adam the next day. "He *bit* her!" Shaking her wet head in disbelief, Katy stretched out further in the low chair and reached for her lemonade. "I mean, that baby had practically stopped eating because his mama wasn't there, he was really like this *depressed* two-year-old person. And his mother comes home this morning all glad to see him and picks him up out of his high chair for a big hug, and chomp!"

"He was angry with her for having left him," said Adam.

"But she couldn't help it."

"Doesn't matter," said Adam, his face sad. Katy, remembering suddenly that his mother had abandoned her family when Adam was eight or nine, was suddenly very sorry for him, sorry she'd raised the topic. Thought she might cry, something she'd been doing off and on all day. Very strange.

Well, she was pretty sad about Frances, too—although she certainly didn't understand the old woman's behavior at all; even Adam didn't. And she had every now and then this thought she didn't tell anybody, that she was more willing to have Frances be a killer than Lauren, or Sam.

Never mind! She got up from the chair, trotted to the pool, and scrambled up the ladder to the top of the diving tower. The water was a long way down there, and her legs were threatening to shake, but she wouldn't let them; she just gathered herself together and aimed her mind and then her body and dived.

Dived *well*, she told herself as she surfaced. And she hadn't done too bad a job with the Porsche earlier that afternoon, either. Adam had insisted on giving her a driving lesson she really did not want, and after several dumb mistakes and some stupid tears, she'd started to feel it go right. She could hardly wait to show Vince.

She settled back into her chair with a deep sigh and wondered where that had come from. She was perfectly safe and happy, and so was her mother. Vince was here, and they would go home tomorrow. She'd have all this incredible stuff to tell Kimmie.

". . . decided to go back to school in September," Adam was saying. "So I'll be pretty busy all year. But maybe next summer I could come to see you in Port Silva?"

This startled her; she hadn't thought of Adam as being anywhere but here, in this odd place she'd dropped into almost by accident.

She rolled her head against the chair's back to look at him, at his round face and pink skin and the hair that stood up in about six different directions. His body that looked as if it had been left out in the sun and melted just a little bit.

He blinked at her, and she grinned. Sam was beautiful and Snake was fairly good-looking, which maybe proved something but more probably didn't. Adam was never going to be either of those things; he'd have to get by on being smart and kind. But if he went back to college, now that he was a normal age for doing that, she bet he'd find himself getting along. Some, anyway. As much as he wanted to.

"Sure, you can come and visit me," she said. "But I'll still be too young for boyfriends. I mean, I'll be almost fifteen, and I'll have real boobs and all that by then, I guess, but I decided I'm going to stay a virgin until I'm at least sixteen. Maybe even eighteen."

"Katy!" He was so shocked that even his ears turned red. "I just wanted to come to visit you as a friend."

"I'm sorry," she said, and thought she might be getting weepy again. "Look, I'll save my money, and maybe next summer we could take a trip to Minnesota, to the International Wolf Center. I'd really like to see that place."

"Sure, if your mother will let you."

Katy shrugged: future problems, future solutions. "The other thing, we could go into the mountains here and join the wolf patrol."

"Katy, I'm not absolutely sure it was a wolf I heard."

"I bet they're there. And I bet Sam Cavalier will be doing something about it." She frowned, remembering a negative she'd seen while helping Sam: a wolf, in what looked like a small cage. Odd thing for Sam to have, and maybe she wouldn't talk about it even to Adam. Yet.

"Adam, what do you think Mrs. Swenson is making for dinner?" Nancy and Emmett had asked Katy to have dinner with them and Brendan and Adam tonight, her last night in Modoc County.

"I don't know, but it will be wonderful. I told her you'll eat anything but liver or brussels sprouts."

"Good. I'm going to be really hungry."

"Do you suppose it's the faint hint of the improper that makes daytime lovemaking so satisfying?" Stretched out in the king-sized bed with only a sheet covering her, Meg dropped a kiss on her husband's bare shoulder and then sat up just enough to reach for her glass. "Of course, I suppose champagne in bed is not quite decent, either."

"It doesn't need to be improper to be satisfying," replied Gutierrez. He dropped his own kiss, on the breast that was uncovered as Meg's reach caused the sheet to slip. "So far as I'm concerned, anytime at all is just fine, and anyplace, too—for love or champagne. Good champagne, anyway," he added complacently. "Bad champagne is probably indecent." The bottle in the ice bucket was not strictly a champagne—just a fine sparkling wine made in California by a fine French firm, Roederer.

If the company was perfect and the wine elegant, the premises were mundane: a cramped motel room with a low, cottage-cheese ceiling strewn with glitter presumably meant to suggest stars, a clown print on the wall, a bathroom that definitely did not encourage communal bathing. But it was spotlessly clean, the bed was good, the price was right. And it was private: no teenagers, no scowling babies.

Meg pushed her pillows into a comfortable backrest against the headboard and rested her champagne glass on her sheet-covered belly, which she noted was decently flat in this position at least. "Okay if I tell you a few things now, Gutierrez?"

"Intermissions are for talking. Are you going to tell me things that will scare me? Because I have to tell *you*, I'm getting too old for heroics, mine or particularly yours."

"It wasn't heroic. Mostly dumb, and sad." She took a deep breath. "Gutierrez, Frances Macrae killed her own nephew ten years ago."

"Jesus, Meg." He pushed himself higher against the headboard and stared at her. "Are you sure?"

"Oh yeah. From what she said at the Jakels' place, and

then what she told me in the ambulance, I'm sure. The night he was supposed to have disappeared, he actually went home and spent the night in the barn. Then early the next morning, when Frances was setting off for a pack trip to the mountains, he buttered her up and said he'd like to come along . . . like old times, I think she said."

"And?"

"And once they were out there, he beat her up, as he'd been doing off and on. And told her some nasty lies. And got the shotgun from the truck and said he was going to kill her."

"So she killed him in self-defense."

"That's a legalistic concept that hasn't carried much weight with Frances over the past ten years, I think. Besides, after she shot him, she packed his body up into the mountains and buried it."

"Meg, the woman had to be, what, sixty years old?"

"About that. But she'd been a working ranch woman for a good part of her life."

"Jesus. What was it the kid wanted from her? The ranch?"

"That's what he said, anyway. Vince, Bobby was just rotten. A truly awful person. From the time he was very young he made a habit of telling vulnerable people, in believable ways, that he'd done terrible things, things that horrified them and kept them frightened of him. Things that he had not actually done." She recited a list of Bobby Macrae's lies.

"So what he in fact did was dig his own grave. Other people's too, I know. But ultimately the little bastard killed himself out of his own mouth. Which should be poetic justice, but it's not. It's just horrid and vile." Her teeth rattled against the glass as she drank the last of her champagne.

"Meg, we don't have to talk about this now."

"Just a minute. Frances couldn't tell anyone about it, of course—not with her stiff-necked sense of family. So she just got older and sadder and sick. Then people started talking about 'tenth anniversary.' And Lauren—I bet Frances had been watching poor Lauren like a hawk—set the family on the road to hell once again. And Frances decided to take care of the enemy once and for all.'"

Meg gave a long sigh and settled back against her pillows. "There. That's the worst of it, I think," she said, and held out her empty glass. "More, please?"

"More what?"

"Oh, whatever there is, lover. When it's ready."

"You're a cruel woman," Vince said as he sat up to reach for the bottle on his lamp table. Meg sighed and bent her attention to the silky gleam of his brown skin and the play of muscles along his arm and across his chest.

Refilled glass in hand, she watched the bubbles for a moment and then took a slow sip. "Um—Vince, I didn't tell the police. Not even good old Earl Douglas, who is a pretty nice guy and fairly sexy, too."

He turned his head to look directly at her, and for a moment she saw his hunting-hawk's face. He'd give away inches in height, a good fifty pounds in weight, but if it came to life and death, she'd want him on her side instead of big, hairy Douglas. Any day.

"So I'm glad you came."

"Me too. Believe it." He blinked and looked once again like a weary, no-longer-young man. "Did you tell Lauren? About Frances and Bobby, I mean." Vince had met Lauren Cavalier and liked her.

"Yes, I felt she was entitled to know. But I made clear that nobody but me had heard the whole thing, and I didn't intend to reveal my conclusions to anyone else. Well, to you, of course, she understood that. But *you* need to understand that I'm talking here to the naked guy I'm married to, not the guy in a uniform with a badge."

"Understood. What about Cavalier?" Vince had met Sam too. Watching as the two grunted "Gutierrez" and "Cavalier" and accomplished a gingerly touching of right hands, Meg had had a sense of raised neck-fur, stiff hind legs, muzzles wrinkled back over gleaming teeth. Men are truly strange, she thought now, unaware that she was echoing her daughter's recent thoughts.

"You mean, will she tell him? Yes. He's her husband and she loves him. From the way they were behaving today, it's clear they've forgiven each other their various sins. I'd bet they're tucked up somewhere right now just like us, occupied in much the same fashion. Although probably without the champagne—I think Sam's a beer drinker."

Gutierrez said, "Humph," or something like it. "Did Cavalier ever say where he'd been or what he'd been doing the past few weeks?"

"I'm sure he's told Lauren; she keeps giving him these loving, conspiratorial looks. What I think is that he's got something illegal going on about wolves."

"A litter of pups on the back forty?" said Gutierrez, in echo of her remark of many days ago.

"No, I don't think so. But something. Sam . . . acts as if the wilderness were his personal kingdom and only he and God have the right to run it. And he'd be more than willing to second-guess God."

"Well, maybe he'll walk off a mountain someplace, someday, and that nice young woman can find somebody better."

"Gutierrez, there are people who would say the same thing about you—that you could find somebody better. Easier to get along with."

"But not better. Meg, you are not in any way a female equivalent of Sam Cavalier."

"I know. But I'm not easy in my mind about us. We're not doing things quite right."

"Meg . . ."

She took a sip of wine and didn't look at him. "I have been feeling miserable and inadequate, and I don't believe it's all my fault. Here's how bad it got: I have actually been thinking about having another baby."

"Another *what*?" His abrupt movement spilled wine on his bare chest. "Was I going to have any say in this? Was I even going to be *involved* in this?"

"Well, I thought so. Your mother thinks you should have heirs or something."

"My mother is old and sick."

"True. But I'm not all that young anymore, and I'm feeling fragile. Anyway, I was thinking along those lines until just a day or so ago."

"And what happened?"

She gave a mock shudder. "I suddenly realized that I might not produce another Katy with brown eyes. I might have a boy. At my age. A boy like Johnny Cavalier.

"Johnny's a fine boy, and I think we owe him a lot." He reached for her hand, and they twined their fingers together in the trough between their two stretched-out bodies. "So what could I do, other than father a child, to keep you happy for the next forty years?"

"I think we need to realize that a second marriage is not just the same thing again as the first one, except you've already got the dishes. It's something farther along."

"Okay. I think I can understand that. Maybe my problem is that I didn't have much of a first marriage."

"So we're out of step there, *I* can understand that. But Vince, however much I love you, and I do, I don't feel like your mother's daughter or your sister's sister."

"Okay."

"I'd thought maybe we should boot the renters out of my house and sell it, and sell your house. Then we could find another one, one that would belong to both of us from the beginning."

"We could do that," he said, wincing only slightly.

"Yes, but Katy would hate me for it. She likes her life the way it is."

"I hope you know that Katy is as important to me as she is to you—or nearly."

"I do know."

"So what do you think, can we make it? If we try?"

"Oh, God, Gutierrez, I hope so. Sure we can."

June, one year later—in the Modoc

Wolves they clearly were, no doubt about it now. Gone were the generic baby animals that had first peeped from the birth den, with snub faces and round fuzzy heads and sweetly folded little ears. The four animals tumbling about in thin high-country sunshine had long, inquisitive snouts; big, upright ears; wide eyes looking for action or trouble. The largest, a male probably weighing twenty-five pounds, was mostly black with a gray underbody; two smaller males were tawny and brown, and the smallest of all, the only female, was almost white.

Grown too big and energetic for a den but not yet strong enough to hunt with their parents, the pups had been brought just the night before to this resting spot, the first of many they would occupy during the summer. Their new play-ground was a patch of grassy meadow bordered by sugar pines and Douglas fir, a boggy area once a beaver pond, and a rocky upthrust of the mountains that dominated the area. From a level spot halfway up the hillside, a silver-gray female wolf with black ears and mask kept a watchful eye on her brood. Curiosity and exuberance could quickly take a two-month-old pup beyond safe limits, and the wolves shared this wilderness area with badgers and brown bears as well as the occasional mountain lion.

As the three male pups yipped and snarled and snapped in

a battle the black male would win, the little female, eyes narrowed to slits, munched on an unlucky ground squirrel. Soon one of the tawny pups fled and the other rolled onto his back, belly exposed in submission. The black pup gave it a perfunctory "I am the boss" lick, then relaxed his stiff-legged stance to look around for more games. He had just spotted his sister when a whine from the mother wolf brought all heads up. A big, black-and-brown male wolf appeared from the trees and trotted across the meadow, the bloody haunch of some medium-sized animal in his mouth.

The pups tumbled and scrambled toward their father in a yelping pack. He dropped the chunk of meat in front of his mate, then lifted his head and howled; the mother wolf joined in, and then, raggedly, so did the pups. That was it, just the six of them; in this place no other wolves ever answered their howls.

Greetings over, the pups began to leap at the big male, to sniff and nudge and whine, to lick his face and bite at his muzzle. Tail waving slowly, he lowered his massive head, opened his mouth, and disgorged a steaming heap of half-digested meat. When the pups had demolished this heap and a second one, as well as the remains of their mother's chunk of meat, they stretched out, round-bellied and panting, near the opening of a denlike cleft in the rock wall, and the adult pair set off in the gathering dark for their night's hunt.